Night at the Belvedere

by Stephen Michael Berberich

Dedicated to Diane.
And to Dad, who loved East Baltimore.

> "These books were a way of escaping
> from the unhappiness of my life,"

from *David Copperfield* by Charles Dickens

Chapter 1: The Unexpected One

Families bound tightly together by deep-rooted customs and manners, like the Espositos of East Baltimore, expect their children to adapt firmly to their ways.

The newest family member, Niccola Augusta "Nicky" Esposito, always wanted to be sociably outgoing and act the right way in his tightly knit Italian-American family. To be accepted as a true Esposito.

But shy Nicky had a problem socially. He sometimes withdrew from the present to visit the past, as if in a trance.

As a very young child, one of Nicky's first lifelike 'visits' planted doubts in his mind that he could ever be like his fun-loving, gregarious family after all.

It started in a drousy, semi-conscious dream. Nicky's dreams were always pleasant. At first, this one made him feel good and accepted. In the dream, he drifted into a family of settlers of the early American colony of Jamestown. He felt worthy and contented as he helped them harvest the colonial family's tobacco crop and load it to a drying barn, just as he'd read in a history book on Colonial America several times.

As he woke, Nicky was troubled about the dream. He thought his hands smelled of tobacco. He could still see faint images of the tobacco field despite being awake. He was afraid. Maybe the vivid dream was a foretelling of things to come, he thought. And being a highly astute and intelligent child, he believed that his fear was well worth bearing in mind.

Nicky was indeed destined to spent parts of his life 'visiting' the past, and not just in dreams. As he grew and matured, he would grow accustomed to sometimes seeing, feeling and being in previous events in the most authentic and believable way. Nicky was truly the unexpected Esposito.

He was born in 1954 and raised just outside the city. As a small boy, Nicky seemed to fit the family mold just fine. He was seen as playful, sociable, extraordinarily bright and studious in elementary school. Little Nicky was surely going to be a typical outgoing, answerable member of the Esposito family.

And then, folks began to see signs, slight at first, then dramatically, of an odd change in Nicky's teen years. This was behavior unlike what the Espositos would have expected in an adolescent in their family. It was a change of life peculiar to Nicky and quite different from the natural vicissitudes of puberty in other kids. The Espositos watched their happy, playful little Nicky slip steadily into the quiet, brooding human being he would remain, the family enigma.

The family saw him display less and less of the expected, reassuringly expansive Esposito persona. Instead of engaging in a conversation, he would end it with strange statements. "I am watching how the British war ships encircled," he once said to his father on a family trip to Fort McHenry when he was only seven. "See? Oh, yea, over there," he said with conviction.

When he was ten on a school field trip to historic Annapolis, Md., he pointed out a pier at the dock and said to his fourth-grade teacher. "Slaves are going to be auctioned. They are already in shackles, Mr. Pinkney. It's terrible." There were no slaves there, not even a reenactment. The auction platform was not there. The teacher Mr. Pinkney had had enough. He wasted no time calling Nicky's home. He told his mother the boy may need counselling by a professional. His mother listened to the teacher without a word, but with considerable trepidation.

Mr. Pinkney told her Nicky was continually holding up the tour by staring into space with a blank look, "They are a distraction, his moods I mean, Mrs. Esposito. We don't know what he is seeing or thinking he sees half the time. Can you come get him, please?" She simply said she would come, without another comment or question for the teacher.

10

Due to that experience with his class, Nicky became more inhibited in school and in public in general.

Nicky was a mysterious youngster, difficult to figure out. He seemed to be cut from a different bolt of Esposito cloth.

Some of his relatives suspected that Nicky possessed a weak and dubious character. Such judgments were unfortunate, even cruel and certainly a judgment, which could not have been farther from Nick's true nature.

And, kindly Nicky Esposito lacked the social capacity to dispel such harsh indictments. He was frightened of his inability to understanding cruelty because he was often not in complete control of himself—what he saw, what he heard, and what he felt—well enough to fully express himself, as all the other Espositos could fluently.

Often, Nicky was compelled to cover his social limitations with phrases such as, "I'm sorry, I wasn't listening." What?" Or, "I don't feel well; got to go. Thank you."

Indeed, Nicky was always polite, tried to be pleasant, though he seemed distant most of the time to almost every other human being. Almost, but not everyone.

"My Nicky is a good boy, just a little shy," his grandfather and best protector Stephen 'Pop' Esposito would protest to anyone ever questioning the boy's odd ways.

Pop was the elder of the family. His people were sanguine, confident and sociable, both at home and at work. They played hard and worked hard, always enjoying the company of others. Birthdays, wedding receptions, graduations were all celebrated in larger-than-life, festive family gatherings.

But such outgoings were not to be Nicky's liking. He rarely ventured out of his room as an adolescent.

"Why is it so bad to read books," he once told his father Carlo, who prayed for his only son to be more outgoing. Carlo kept his disappointment to himself for the most part because in school his moody Nicky pulled down straight A's in every class all the time. Nicky was always the "smartest" kid in his class at every grade level.

11

The family sometimes saw glimmers of hope that the boy would grow out of his social difficulties because of rare moments when Nicky would seem to pop out of his introverted cocoon with boundless energy for a brief and open display of compassion for others.

These rare outpourings were manifested in a show of extreme kindness and generosity for people he thought to be in desperate straits. This momentary, energetic side of Nick appeared to be a natural and normal Esposito impulse to apply his superior intelligence and compassion to a good cause.

In the eighth grade, for example, Nicky surprised his mother by spending his entire $106 savings on a gift certificate at Robert Hall Discount Clothing Store for two pitifully impoverished twin girls who sat together in the back of his classroom. He didn't even know them but had watched them each day and felt their pain. He decided to help them since he remembered his mother saying, 'your money is yours to spend as you wish,' as she had prodded him to get out of the house to cut lawns for neighbors, a solitary chore he enjoyed.

When Miriam, his mother, learned of his gift, she told him he'd foolishly wasted the money on people he admitted to not even knowing.

"I just want to give the gift certificate to those poor O'Connell twins. They huddle every day by themselves at the back of my class, that's all. They are so sad and kids pick on them," he said to his mother.

"But, why? You said you've never spoken to those girls," she asked. It had been weeks of pushing him out the door that spring to at least be with people in a sort of disengaged, easy on the nerves way—cutting their grass, she thought.

"Because Pop said that's what an Esposito would do, Mother."

Nicky said he'd been watching the homely O'Connell twin sisters for weeks in his classroom. He told his mother that Pop had agreed that Nick should help them. He revealed to his mother that he had told Pop about the bullies in the school

12

constantly picking on the twins and calling them fat and ugly names nearly every day.

Nick and his mother were very close. But he still preferred to share his thoughts with his grandfather more than anyone else, even his mother. He had told Pop he was sure that the girls were good people but very, very unhappy.

"Nicky, you should have told me too, instead of always relying on Pop for advice," she said with her usual stern resolve. Her demeanor then softened as she saw his sad eyes pleading for acceptance. She showed a loving smile and tenderly hugged the slender, rapidly growing teenage son around his chest. "You soft-hearted, sweet kid. You are becoming a man more than just in height. It is a good thing to do, Nicky."

"Thanks mother. These girls wore the same threadbare dresses every day and are pale and scrawny. Pop said he grew up with immigrant kids like that and so we talked, okay?" Nick felt guilty by slighting his mom.

The rest of the story he didn't dare tell his mother, however, the 'visit' that he shared with only Pop. He didn't want to worry his mother about the visit, so to speak, a vision of seeing such girls in another place and time.

Nicky worried his grandfather by telling him that he "saw" the twins in an earlier time in American history. "Pop, I don't know, but it is like a trance, I flashbacked to the past I think, hearing and seeing things others don't see. I don't always remember these visits, but in this case, I do. I vividly saw, not imagined, but *saw* the O'Connell twins as two scraggily children caught up in the American Wake of Poverty."

His Pop nodded in agreement, "Eighteen hunnerts when all those Irish immigrants came in, fresh off the boat from Europe."

"I know all about that, Pop, from my books.

"On my way home, I saw the twins as those Early American orphans living in an Almshouse near the docks of Baltimore, begging for coins along Fort St. to buy a stale biscuit. But Pop, I know the twins live in our town like I do. Am I crazy?"

13

"No. You are what people call perceptive."

He told Pop he sometimes would pity the girls he saw as struggling immigrants as he would follow far behind them. They appeared as immigrant kids dragging along on the dockside streets in patched-up, handmade long dresses, leggings and old high-top shoes.

He never spoke of that 'visit' to anyone else. To Nicky, it was real. Then one day, he resolved to help the twins, yet to still stay anonymous, remain the introverted nerd they saw in school, but never spoke to. He watched their habits in class and came up with a plan.

One of the O'Connell twins always left her lunch pail on her desk during the regular morning recess. Before she returned, Nick slipped the Robert Hall clothing store gift certificates into her lunch box. When he opened the dented and faded Minnie Mouse lunch box, he saw only Saltine crackers, an apple and a slice of American cheese. He knew he was doing the right thing.

He left no note. He never told anyone.

When they arrived at school in nice new dresses, Nick hid the joy in his heart, covering his face in his hands at his desk. He never again 'visited' the begging Irish immigrant kids, nor did he care to.

Emily and Maggie soon adjusted better to school as respected classmates with uplifted spirits. Yes, they had names. Classmates then knew them properly.

Maggie told her sister it could have been that quiet boy, Nicky Esposito. Yet, they would only react with pleasant hellos and smiles to the strange boy Nicky from that day on.

He loved it and telephoned Pop to tell him what he did for them. Nicky was especially proud to have used such cunning, he told Pop, that the girls never knew and thus made no fuss over him.

"Why not tell them what you did, Nicky," Pop said. "Be proud. Stand out and be counted." That kind of advice never worked for Nicky, who would remain reclusive most of the time.

* * *

Nicky's rare, heartfelt expressions of empathy for the down and out might have stemmed from his passion for history books. As a child, Nicky read lots of books, each with great intensity, mostly about early American history. He soaked up every detail of historic events--every descriptive sight, sound, smell or touch of historic figures including any factual expression and voice tones. He imagined himself inside fascinating stories he read and systematically filed them away in his mind.

He wondered if his reading made him sometimes throw a sort of mental switch to help himself briefly visit past events. His visits were usually veiled and shadowy, but sometimes quite vivid, such as the O'Connell twins begging on the docks of Locust Point, even though he knew fully well they did not dwell at Locust Point at all and wore modern tattered dresses not 19th century clothes.

At first, Nicky was thrilled with his unique ability. It was very cool. It gave him a kind of an identity, he thought, for the first time. He wanted to talk about it. That would please the family at least, he guessed. He guessed wrong. "I can see things," he told some friends who then called him "screwy" and laughed at the boy. "Really. It's like little bits or peeks moments in past events, vague but people and things are there. I see them."

He learned quickly to stop telling anyone. And then he worried about flaunting that ability and his new-found identity, an identity at last, one he was thrilled to discover. He said to himself, "Keep this up and I'll be the town fool, not just the family misfit if I talk about visiting into the past."

His parents admired their child's imagination and knowledge. It would pass, they thought at first. He was an Esposito after all.

For nearly his entire life, Nick Esposito's trips into the past would mostly remain exclusively part of his private world. For Nick, his 'visits' were fun, free-ranging moments when he let himself trip into a time and place more to his liking than the unforgiving world where he struggled mightily socially.

* * *

Nick's "dreaming," his family believed, was to be expected, because of the influence of his German mother.

Young Miriam married into the Esposito family after falling in love with the handsome and charming U.S. Army Lt. Carlo Esposito in Germany several years after the European war.

Miriam Esposito was eager to be accepted in the Esposito family especially for one particular Esposito tradition. They believed that raising a good child in this country required home teaching your child American values and customs before he or she would enter formal school. Miriam was all in. Her children would be American through and through. This German-American mom was a neat, fastidious homemaker who prided herself in being well organized. And, that included a thorough and exacting Esposito-compelled tutoring of her baby Nicky.

When Nicky was just a toddler, Miriam began a regimen of reading bedtime stories to him every night. He probably didn't understand the meanings of the words or stories and she didn't understand all the English words herself. She kept it up religiously. She loved the Espositos. And she thoroughly enjoyed reading to her lovely baby boy.

All the stories she selected or that friends recommended were set in historical times in America, such as Laura Ingalls Wilder's "Little House" (On the Prairie) series, "Children of the Wigwam" by Anne Chase, and Walt Disney's "Davy Crockett King of the Wild Frontier" and dozens of others.

Long before his school years, then, Nick's bedroom shelves held many children story books of early American fiction and non-fiction. Miriam's stories she read to him were real to Nicky. He believed she was there at the Boston Tea Party, she was sailing uncharted Chesapeake Bay with Capt. John Smith, and riding the trains on Carnegie's railroads.

By the time he was barely five years old, Nicky was reading the books by himself, as well as illustrated books of U.S. history from libraries. His dreams were filled with tall sailing ships, frontier muskets and coonskin caps, covered wagons, Mississippi River paddle boats and barefoot boys on fishing rafts, soldiers in blue and gray uniforms, Fulton's Folly and Eli's cotton gin, Gehrig and Ruth, Red Grange and Jesse Owens, Chesapeake Bay watermen and other images and heroes who came to life in his books. He found a section on Maryland's Baltimore history in the library on Ritchie Highway near home and soaked up every word. He was always mindful of learning local history to please his Pop, who loved to spin colorful tales from his favorite digs in Baltimore.

* * *

Perhaps, it was the imprecise nature of adult-child relations why people didn't much notice, nor make the connection, that Nicky's mundane reading of history books—his primary childhood fun—would form the very bedrock of his development as an adult. No one saw that coming.

The adventures of earlier American heroes were nothing short of magical and transcendental for Nick. He preferred to inhabit their lives rather than his own—to associate with their worlds and their social encounters instead of forcing himself to face people and events happening around him—so odd for a child of the fun-loving Esposito family.

His heroes were men and women like Thomas Jefferson and Harriet Tubman, whose dreams and ideals raised the hopes and spirits of many.

He would feel and touch the lives of individuals with extraordinary gifts, such as baseball player Jackie Robinson, whose profession had been previously limited by racial prejudice, or medical prodigy Walter Reed, who was limited early in his career by his youth. Yet, both rose to greatness when destiny called.

And, Nick especially loved to identify with heroes who rode into American history with daring and risky feats like Amelia Earhart and Paul Revere.

This was life forming and character building stuff for a boy named Nick Esposito, far more influential than boring classroom lessons, family TV time, grass cutting, or stuffy services in his mother's preferred St. Paul's Lutheran church.

17

The boy's grandfather Stephen "Pop" Esposito was first to suspect that "my Nicky boy is getting more pleasure studying history than from finding fun in his own real life." Pop at first shared some concern with his son Carlo, Nick's father, but never talked with Miriam about Nick's odd development. Pop adored sweet, beautiful Miriam but dared not hurt her feelings or interfere with raising him. Nick was a delicate topic to his mother.

It was apparent to the family and to Miriam, though, that Pop loved and trusted Nicky steadfastly throughout Nicky's personality change during adolescence.

Pop became his idol. Nick was devoted to the old man; whose persona was polar opposite of Nick's. Pop was a beloved, happy-go-lucky man, perhaps the most popular man in all of Baltimore.

Lacking the self-esteem, which Pop exuded, gnawed at Nick's nerves whenever he'd be around the old man in a social setting. It left him impulsive and at times desperate to stand out in some way of his own.

Pop didn't know it made Nicky feel inadequate, that is, the contrasting socializing ability.

It was Nick's own fault, he felt. In fact, he felt different, less important in his family, though they loved him no less than his sister Katrina or other children in the clan.

Also, it was never important to the Espositos that Nick was not Roman Catholic like Pop and Grandma Minnie Esposito. His parents raised him Lutheran instead due to his overly protective German mother, Miriam. Nick's "unexpected" behavior was not his upbringing, not a hereditary flaw, and not from growing up in the suburbs instead of the city with all the other Espositos. Pop insisted that Nicky's odd personality was not either due to his unusual physical features for an Esposito male. Nicky was tall and lanky. He had sandy blonde hair and a fair complexion like his German-born mother. He looked nothing like any of the dark olive skin, shorter Esposito men with thick, curly jet-black hair.

No, Nick's off personality was not from any of that stuff, Pop determined. Pop would consider the bright light emitting from Nicky's expressive blue eyes and know there was indeed more to Nick's introversion than anyone else yet realized. And that was fine with Pop if that was to be. For Nicky was a good boy—an Esposito after all and he just knew this special boy had quite a future ahead of him.

* * *

Stephen J. "Pop" Esposito was born on March 25, 1903. He was the youngest of four sons of Michael Esposito, a famous, crime-busting Baltimore cop and an immigrant from Milano, Italy. Stephen grew up mostly in his father's house in East Baltimore's Little Italy during the first two decades of the twentieth century.

Perhaps being the son of a high-profile figure in town, young Stephen began early to connect well with people with a keen sense of understanding and relating to each one as an individual. Despite having little formal education, Stephen became successful in business, athletics, romance, and had easily befriended each successive generation of leadership in the city and state of Maryland.

For nearly his entire adult life, Pop owned the popular little Pop's Tavern on the corner of Ellwood Avenue and an alley, near spacious, tranquil Patterson Park. He was very handsome with thick black hair, a solid build and a strong, confident face—giving him a much more commanding presence than his five-foot, nine-inch frame might otherwise offer.

He took after the qualities of his father Michael, whom he and everyone knew as a warm and friendly cop in public, yet with a tough inquisitive manner at work solving crimes. He was a grateful immigrant to be in America. Michael, like many first-generation immigrants, was serious about his citizenship. He was a no-nonsense cop, which may have propelled him at age 28 to the position of Chief Criminal Investigator for the Baltimore Police Department.

Pop always said that Inspector Mike set the tone and the character of the traditionalist Esposito family as extroverted, sociable people. The Esposito men were to a man very successful in business, from owning small shops in Little Italy to executive careers in the food and entertainment fields.

After Michael's retirement from the police force in the 1940's, Pop stood alone as patriarch of a rambunctious, respectably uninhibited and strictly law-biding Italian-American family, which was, as mentioned, not altogether prepared for the arrival of Miriam and Carlo's second child, the unexpectedly pensive Nicky boy.

* * *

Most of the Esposito family noticed the change in Nick in his teens.

Pop sensed it earlier. He feared it was some unknown force kidnapping the boy's mind to somewhere sinister and evil from time to time. Sure, he knew Nicky was studious. But Pop astutely understood that it was more than natural childhood curiosity that made Nicky have visions and fantasies from all the history books he was reading. He was the first person in the family to heard Nicky claim to "visit" things and places in the past. Something was very abnormal about his grandson.

Pop worried that one day the introverted boy would be exposed to a tough world, which he was not going to be socially prepared for. Pop then, as family elder took on the challenge. He vowed to his wife Minnie, "Whatever it takes and as long as it takes, I will find any way to understand our Nicky boy and help protect him as long as I live."

Chapter 2: Nicky Boy's Big Day

Pop's Tavern, Baltimore – early morning of March 28, 1968
Stephen 'Pop' Esposito always got up before Minnie at their home above the tavern on Ellwood Avenue. Pop liked to start his day looking out to the neighborhood from his big red leather Laz-e-boy chair in the front room. He waited for his devoted wife Minnie to brew the coffee just the way he liked it.

He soon heard her carrying up a silver tray and coffee pot with two cups. "Thought I'd use the silver, Stephen, and we can talk about Nicky," she said sweetly.

He got up to take the tray. "Min, you want I should hire La Scala Ristoranti Italiano for Nicky's party? My nephews practically run the joint now. They can take good care of everything."

"No, indeed," she quickly replied before sitting.

Pop recoiled, "What do you mean no? Nicky's Confirmation comes up next Sunday the seventh, I think." Pop grasped the handle of the coffee pot to help his loving wife.

"I've got it all covered, Stephen," said Minnie. They sat together facing the front window. "All you have to do is just invite the family and friends from the neighborhood, as you said. Me and my girlfriends Gerty and Roselia will enjoy our own party in the kitchen on Saturday before the party. We'll cook all day and night if need be. It'll be fun for us girls to get together." Without waiting for his reply or even looking at him, she added, "Yes, that's what we will do."

His firm, rugged face scowled, but soon revealed a little sly smile. "You and your 'girls,' Lordy be. Okay, fine. For my part, I'm done, according to you. I invited everybody for 3 o'clock on Nicky's big day." He tilted his head to one side and laughed, full of pride.

Coffee in the front room upstairs over the tavern, normally their "sitting room" for reading and radio listening, was a treat that day. This was the favorite place in the house/tavern for

21

the 65-year old Stephen and Minnie who was a few years younger—no one knew for sure.

The cozy room showed solid oak plank floors decades old off the edges of a garish green, blue, and orange Oriental rug, which did no favors to the room décor. The rug was a gift from their other son Alberto, two years older than Carlo, and then an attorney for movie stars in Hollywood. Few people could afford such an expensive floor covering in the early 60's. Pop cherished it. Minnie secretly disliked the gaudy thing.

Between Minnie and Pop were a glass and bronze coffee table and an antique Italian silver gilt floor lamp with hand-crafted imagery of Bernini sculptures along the stem.

"Okay, you wanted to talk? Here we are," Minnie said. "What we do know about celebrating Nicky with a party. It is a party for sure that he will not want it. Stephen, don't look that way. Nicky will not want to be mixing about with all those people. You must know that. Stephen? He is shy. I think this idea of yours may be a mistake."

He stared out the window until Minnie finished the lecture. "He'll be fine. Our party will be our gift to Carlo, and the kids, Nicky and his sister little Katrina. It is the best thing we can give, 'cause we have the tavern and all," Pop said.

"Kat's not so little anymore and we didn't give her a party for confirmation."

"That was different."

"Because she's a girl. Shame on you."

"Of course not. We love Nicky and his sister Kat just the same. You know that. It is different because she wouldn't want a party here. Katrina likes to stay around all her friends, remember? They all came to Miriam and Carlo's church down there and it was great. Kat loved it. And we drove down. She loved that too. But Nicky loves to come here. He told me he doesn't have friends like Kat does. I'm afraid the boy is a loner and it will be good for him to be here with family, my brothers and their children especially."

"Okay, she had a good party too. But, you better tell them soon. Remember? Nicky didn't come to Kat's confirmation party at the Lutheran church. He stayed home with Miriam? [no response] Remember, Stephen? And, by the way, you just said this will be our gift to Carlo. What about Miriam?"

"Oh my, my, yes indeed. She will be the hard part. I will win her over, Minnie. Don't you worry about that!"

He was holding back. In his typical manner, Pop secretly wanted nothing less than a huge surprise party to celebrate his Nicky's Christian rite of passage into church membership, regardless of which church, his or Miriam's. For months, he planned to have the party at Pop's Tavern. Where else? He and Minnie would shower the boy with love in the family tradition.

"I know our shy Nicky will like his grand pop's party if it was to be done right," he said, "and this celebration will be our best."

Lucky for Pop, Minnie missed his implication of "big party," and was instead staring at two large framed photographs on the opposite wall. Pictured were their two sons Carlo and Alberto in their teens, each captured on their confirmation day two years apart at St. Peter's Roman Catholic Church. Between the young men's images was the family's best crucifix, the one they once bought at a fund-raising St. Peter's bazaar for the mission in the Congo and which impressed Nicky very much.

Minnie asked, "Does Carlo know what you are doing? The boy's parents need to know, Stephen," she asked. She searched Pop's face for the truth or if he was lying. Usually only Minnie would know for sure. But, Pop had turned back to look over Ellwood Avenue to think and enjoy his coffee.

"Coffee is outstanding Min ... I'll tell 'em when the time is right. Let's get busy with what we need to do. Could you get a pencil and pad from down behind the bar, please?" he said. He kept his face to the window to avoid her predictably annoying frown.

* * *

By the following Friday, Nicky's doting grandparents and their best friends had decorated the entire tavern gaily in red, green and white crepe paper garland and hanging balls and banners of the Italian Flag. On each of a dozen small tables was a red and white checkered table cloth and a bunch of cut roses in empty Pastore's of Pasadena tomato cans.

Minnie, Gerty and Roselia--all three especially plump and looking contented--got together Saturday morning to prep food for Nicky's confirmation party on Sunday. Each of Minnie's 'girls' was a great cook for her own extended family, just city blocks away.

The three marched into the kitchen at Pop's like Olympic cooking athletes entering opening ceremonies, all in clean white aprons and their hair up in nets. Instead of these Olympians carrying their national flag, they were proudly carrying extra pots, extra aprons over the shoulder and big smiles. By noon, they were elbows deep in cooking multiple dishes, and appetizers, with food stains on their clothes.

Minnie loved hosting pre-party cooking marathons with her girlfriends. "We should open a restaurant together because we do so good together, girls," she said with a needling smile. The three had 'played' together in their respective kitchens for so many gatherings of their families that they knew instinctively the moves and timing of each other.

Gerty and Roselia looked up just long enough to share a laugh when Minnie added, "Oh yeah, I forgot. We already have a restaurant. "Maybe we will leave our men and open a better one, eh?"

All day and night on Saturday they prepared scrumptious cuisine, including Bruschetta toasted Italian bread, Mozzarella Caprese in balsamic glaze with fresh basil; antipasto salad; Baltimore's best Crab Italiano penne pasta in spicy marinara, Chicken Parmigiana, Penne Capricciosa of artichoke hearts, red peppers, olives and mushrooms; and of course, a basket of garlic bread and a small saucer boat of olive oil for each table.

The ladies wanted and expected all to be perfect for Nicky.

They had sent Pop out early for more supplies to get rid of his annoying suggestions and comments. When he returned and saw the converted party tavern, Pop was more convinced than ever that his surprise party was the best thing he could possibly do for his grandson Nicky boy. He hoped it would be well received by Miriam, since it was pretty much all he could do, considering that Miriam's church was in the suburbs 15 miles south of East Baltimore. He was hoping he'd get extra points with his daughter-in-law because Nicky was to be confirmed as a Protestant in the county and not at the Esposito's familiar St. Peter's Roman Catholic Church in the city, as Miriam knew Pop had always hoped. This he would not mention however. Regardless, Pop was driven to do his part for the boy he loved. Religious preference was not at all an issue with Pop, just unspoken guilty points maybe.

Pop and his entire clan respected the choices and the wishes of Nicky's mother Miriam Gunther Esposito, the beautiful blond German immigrant who always dressed with impeccably good taste and manners to match. "Carlo had made a wonderful choice for a bride," Pop told everyone who ever met her.

All preparations were set. But, herein was Pop's only potential problem: He still had not told Carlo and Miriam about the big bash. Pop didn't think it was necessary. He knew from experience that a surprise was always better for the Espositos. It is almost expected.

Early on confirmation Sunday Pop and Minnie left last-minute preparations to trusted friends at Pop's Tavern and drove down to St. Paul's Lutheran Church in suburban Glen Burnie, where Carlo's family lived.

The grandparents were glowing with pride and joy for 14-year-old Nicky.

They arrived early. Pop was habitually early for everything. They parked in their teal-blue, Cadillac Eldorado behind the church, watching eagerly for Carlo's maroon Buick

Regal sedan. Just minutes before the service, the Buick pulled into the church lot slowly, deliberately. Pop was fraught with anxiety, but confident. He still needed to spring the party on Nicky's overly protective mother.

Wearing a wide pin-striped, double breasted dark blue suit and cream-white tie, Pop nearly sprinted to the Buick to greet Miriam, Carlo, Nicky and his older sister Katrina.

Pop opened the passenger side door for Miriam, while he was flashing a broad, loving smile.

His unusual expression seemed to raise her apprehension as she curled up one side of her mouth and frowned briefly and ever so slightly that Pop missed seeing her unfortunate reaction. She glanced quickly behind her for any reaction from her husband at the wheel, and then returned to look directly at Pop. She smiled warmly. Pop had never greeted Miriam before he greeted the grandchildren. She seemed to notice the special treatment and rose slowly from the car.

"Mimsy, you look wonderful as always" Pop said. Miriam hated the nickname but never said so out of respect for her domineering father-in-law.

She wore a smart pink skirt suit highlighted by Carlo's corsage of red carnations in the lapel. Her normally wavy, shoulder-length blonde locks were set in a bouffant under a neat pillbox hat, the kind First Lady Jackie Kennedy made popular a few years earlier.

"Minnie and me would love you all to join us for dinner after Nicky is confirmed," Pop continued. "We have a special treat for you at our place." He hugged her awkwardly. While still holding her shoulders in his muscular hands, Pop added. "I want to do this for our boy. Please." Pop's normally irresistible charm was a bit shaky for once. He was pressing.

Miriam was not swayed. She spoke nearly in a whisper, "We are going to the St. Paul confirmation reception after the ceremony so Nick can meet the church elders and his classmates' families. You should come too, Pop."

"We didn't know about that, Mimsy. Minnie thought for sure you'd come for her meal. She's got everything ready except the pasta and … [His eyes finally met Nicky with a wink and a knowing smile, as his grandson and granddaughter emerged from the back seat in their Sunday best clothes.] … Nicky, you know Minnie's pasta, don't ya?"

The glum face Nicky wore all the way to the church, suddenly lit up. He stood and said, "Let's go to Pop's mother. Please?"

"No Nicky," she said, reaching up to stroke and straighten the 14-year-old's unruly mop of light brown hair. She turned to his grandpop, "Pop, can we take a rain check? This is really important for Carlo and me."

"I could pass on the reception, hon," offered Carlo, locking the car door.

Miriam shot him a cross look.

Their daughter Katrina, 16, wearing a summer dress of bright floral print, chimed in with, "Come on, Mom. We'll waste all this dressing up in the stuffy church basement when we can show off our Sunday best in the city. Besides, going to Pops for Grandma's food is way better than the church food. [She turned to Nicky.] Guess what you'll be eating down there in the damp church cellar? Cold cuts and that yucky potato salad from Eddie's Supermarket. Yuk."

"That's enough Kat," snapped their mother, "And thanks for the grand endorsement Carl!"

Carlo persisted cautiously, "It is apparently very special to Pop, hon. Let's go up to the tavern."

Miriam hated the tavern atmosphere when it was open for business, especially the half drunken weekend crowd always overly excited by sports on the TV. A scowl crossed her face in a flash. She looked over at Nicky leaning against the car fender. He beamed with a rare bright smile of anticipation. She knew he loved Pop's tavern—the retro décor, dark atmosphere, and dozens of mementos of Pop's adventurous life in East Baltimore from the 1920's to the 1960's.

Pop said, "We closed it today, Mimsy girl. Come on, bring the kids up for a nice quiet dinner at our place," Pop said with a convincing expression. That seemed to change Miriam as it reminded her of the love she felt from Pop and the Esposito family, a family of traditions much unlike hers.

Pop pressed his luck, "Nicky boy is going to be a very special man because of you, my lovely girl," Pop said, sugar-coating his plea.

Miriam hesitated before committing. She looked for Minnie. Grandma was still sitting at a considerable distance away in the Cadillac.

Minnie waved. Her face brightened with a maternal, expressive smile because her precious daughter-in-law had finally seen her. Minnie actually hadn't heard a word of the discussion.

"Okay, if that is what Minnie wants," said Miriam, mistaking Minnie's gesture. "You can stop laying it on so thick Pop. What time?"

* * *

The five sat together all morning and then offered well wishes to the other families and the church elders. Yet still, Pop didn't tell his son Carlo that he'd invited half the Italian community in the city, the mayor, and several high-ranking city cops—all personal friends. Most of Pop's guests owed him favors and were delighted with the invitation. Pop had even hired friends' sons and daughters to serve and bartend.

His fun-loving nature was usually infectious. But not for Miriam at that time. She remained seriously worried over Nicky in public, because she knew so little about his wandering mind.

On the strength of his popularity, though, Pop thought he would win the day. He went all out; even asked a four-piece band of Italian brethren to practice some German Oompah-pah music and dress in Bavarian outfits at the party as a special touch for his daughter in-law. That would surely please her.

After the church service, they all exchanged pleasantries with the Pastor, while Pop took Carlo aside, "Just park in my spot in the alley behind our place and come in the side door of the tavern quietly. We will share a wonderful quiet dinner as a family. Wunderbar, eh?"

With that and that alone, he got Carlo to laugh with him.

* * *

Pop's Tavern on Ellwood Avenue was long and narrow. Zoned as a business/residence, it was slightly wider than the 30 other row red-brick houses on the block, which were strictly zoned residential. The block was built in 1920 during a housing boom in the city. The end units, like Pop's Tavern, had been commercially zoned. German bakeries, Polish markets, taverns and other small shops filled the end units in the 1960's.

On the street side, Pop's Tavern had a wrap-around showcase window, which extended an extra foot over the sidewalk to give customers a view into the tavern over a platform of standup cardboard advertisements for beer and snacks. A small front entrance was set back from the corner of the building over a triangle threshold paved with one-inch square black and white tiles surrounding a large 'S.E.' of red and green tiles.

Pop kept the front and two alley-side doors opened in warm weather so sounds of friendly tavern patrons could be heard on the street and alley. It didn't matter where he was in the building, a flap of one of the screen doors meant a new customer had entered and he'd be there with a greeting.

On any normal day, there were just five small tables inside, each surrounded with four stick-backed, round wooden chairs lining the wall on the alley side of the tavern opposite the long bar. An aisle ran between the line of tables and the bar, past tiny restrooms, and on to Grandma Minnie's kitchen. The bar ran most of the length of the tavern, starting from under the front window—always filled with dreamy beer advertisements of splashing, sunny summer scenes.

On the Sunday of Nicky's confirmation party, the tavern looked and sounded quite different.

When Nicky, Katrina and their parents approached the side door of the tavern in the early afternoon, they were puzzled to hear people inside. The tavern was NOT closed as Pop had promised Miriam at the church.

Nick dragged behind as usual in the alley. He was fascinated by remnants of a few 19th century cobblestones in the passageway among paving bricks. More and more cobble stones appeared before him. He let himself drift. His mind's eye pictured a horse-drawn farm wagon of fresh produce at the end of a cobblestone alley. The driver wore overalls and a weathered green poor-boy Irish cap as he chatted with two policemen in dark blue and 1890's styled bell-shaped helmets. They gestured together. Nicky thought they might be talking about traffic on Decker Avenue. Nick saw just past them to the traffic, but it was not automobiles but all horse-drawn carriages and lorries.

Nick walked past his parents on his way to get closer to the men, maybe hear them talk.

Instead, he heard a muffled, "Come on Nicky," his mother said, "you need to go in to the tavern first to see your grandpop."

"Oh, yes. Of course, mother. Sorry." The boy ran up to the door facing the alley. He turned back to Decker Avenue. The old-fashioned cops, the horse and wagon were gone. He did as his mother commanded.

As he pushed in the door, all seemed quiet inside. And then, the silent crowd of Pop's friends and Esposito family relatives inside all yelled out "surprise" together. Nicky stepped back frightened and fell on the alley of brick and odd cobblestones. Panicked, he looked to his mom and saw a horrible scowl on her face as she pulled him up into her arms.

Carlo reacted with a booming, "What in heavens?" Carlo was aghast. He looked at his wife and too saw her unhappiness. "Miriam, I had no idea that Pop was ..."

Too late. Miriam was incensed by Pop's outrageous trick and the panic by her hyper-sensitive son.

Nicky sensed something was terribly wrong. His parents were angry and he tried to gain his composure to aid them.

Miriam pulled Carlo back into the alley after slamming the door shut again. "You and Pop conspired against my wishes,

Carlo. This is scaring Nicky. I hope you are happy. Such a trick when we could have exposed young Nicky to the best parishioners in the state at the St. Paul's reception in Glen Burnie, instead of a bunch of drunken associates at St. Pop's church of debauchery!"

Carlo was overwhelmed by her unusually harsh words and tried to clear himself, "I didn't know. I swear I ..."

Nicky said, "Ah, please Mother, Dad, don't fight. What's going on?" He was confused. His parents argued vehemently in the alley while just inside a loud festive party had broken out with lively, cheerful music. His body stiffened and his lips were quivering. He felt sick, but equally concerned for his parents. The unsettling crowd at the church in the morning was one thing. He'd gotten through that because it was expected of him. But this? ... He was thinking, *Why were mother and dad angry? Where's Pop?* Nicky's muscles began to stiffen and he briefly fainted. That time, Carlo caught Nicky and the boy revived quickly with the touch of his father's hands.

After a moment, they decided to enter the tavern guardedly for the sake of keeping peace with the family.

Pop immediately hugged the boy. He must have felt the tension in Nicky's body, because Pop's smiling face tightened, showing sudden concern. He stared into Nicky's eyes, probing for an answer, but got only a blank stare from the teenage boy.

Carlo swallowed hard. He thanked his father, "This is nice Pop, honoring Nicky's big day this way." Carlo tried to induce a similar pleasantry from wife Miriam, but she dashed red-faced to the kitchen ignoring her father-in-law. "Don't mind her, Pop. She doesn't like being tricked. Hey Pop, please tell her I didn't know, because, damn it, I didn't, okay?" Carlo asked.

"Don't swear, son. There are children here," Pop said. "Don't worry. Some tricks are good for people. He firmly nudged his Carlo and Nicky toward a table of smiling, dark-haired women and girls, just as he had planned. "Let's show off our new man to the ladies," Pop said in his special voice, one full of the harmless devilment, the signature characteristic expected by his friends as the true Pop Esposito.

Nicky dragged behind with no intention of cooperating. His thoughts were nil, his mind mush.

Pretty Italian-American teens around the table had been waiting eagerly for the guest of honor.

Nicky was fear struck and wanted to flee at the sight of them.

The prettiest girl with a smile that could light up all of Little Italy extended her hand. When Nicky didn't take her hand and just nodded reluctantly, she pouted and said, "I'm pleased to meet you at last Niccola. I'm Angela. You sure don't look like the boy I expected."

Still no response from Nicky.

She tried again, and again with a dubious compliment, "I must say you have the most beautiful blue eyes for an Italian, don't you think, Mama?" she said, turning to a plump lady holding the girl's hand.

Nick misunderstood her kindness for ridicule. He drifted away from them without a word.

He gazed around the tavern and it saddened him. He didn't like seeing all the people cluttered about Pop's slender tavern at the little round tables. He always loved the décor as it was—a simple, romantic throwback to early life in Baltimore. He peered over the heads of the ladies to the wall behind the bar, afraid that Pop's mementoes that Nick loved were gone too. They were all there as he scanned the walls anxiously.

He looked around and was surrounded by mostly strangers, a few aunts and uncles sprinkled in, all staring at him. One of them hollered, "Hey Nicky, come here young man. Let's see you." And, "He's so tall now, huh?"

Nick's head was throbbing with a dull pain. Most of his consciousness was hovering outside of himself, as if he was peering through an old film camera capturing a low budget movie set with bad acting and scratchy audio.

This was possibly the worst thing that could have happened to Nicky. At 14, he already felt like the world's greatest oddball in such a fun-loving family. He was embarrassed. He withdrew further. The more Pop tried to brag on his grandson to pretty females, the more embarrassed Nicky felt by their surprise that he just didn't look and act like an Esposito. He heard a few ladies say he resembled his mother and liked that, but to Nick the comments seemed insincere.

He was of course mistaken in thinking the females were patronizing and making fun of him. They wanted to like Pop's grandson; told Pop that Nick was handsome like him.

Nick felt the kind of stage fright a novice actor feels when the curtain suddenly opens and he is dumbfounded with no lines, just fear of the faces all looking at him, and expecting to speak and yet he couldn't. Everyone seemed close. Too close. Too loud.

After Nicky endured about 20 agonizing minutes, Carlo was still struggling to get Nicky to be friendly. But, he became impatient with Nicky's lack of social aptitude. Looking around to be as discreet as possible, Carlo leaned over to Nicky (already as tall as his dad) and whispered, "Just be quiet. You seem to be good at that, or go into the kitchen to help your mother cut celery sticks."

Nicky realized that his dad seemed more concerned with his own embarrassment than his son's feelings. As Nick moped into the back, Carlo said to Pop, "great little party and the aromas are wonderful, Pop. Is La Scala catering?" Carlo failed to fully grasp the hurt he had inflicted on his son by his dismissive attitude.

But Pop saw it on Nicky's demeanor and sensed correctly this could lead to an emotional break between Nick and his father. "No, Minnie's girlfriends are helping," Pop snapped. "Carlo, you better tend to yer boy," Pop was quick to add, placing a hand on his son's shoulder.

"He'll be okay, Pop. I'll get Miriam to bring him out later. Sorry about that, really I am," Carlo said.

Despite all the wonderful choices of his favorite Italian food at hand, Nick declined to eat, even in the kitchen, where it was all simmering and gurgling in pots and pans. He passed up every invitation by the cooks to sample the food. Furthermore, he would not re-emerge on his own from Minnie's kitchen despite his mother's prodding to rejoin the party.

He slipped instead into the small cement yard behind the tavern and sat on a cement block by himself.

Miriam could see him for a while from a little window in the back door. But she was too busy fixing food with Minnie to realize that her son's entire body had locked up. His muscles were so stiff with fear that he could not get up again. He was depressed. He was at that moment convinced that he was an absolute failure to his family. When Minnie asked for Miriam to help take more bread from the oven, Miriam lost sight of Nick.

He was gone from the tiny cement yard.

"It's okay," Minnie said. "When he is here with us, he sometimes walks up the alley and back, is all. Didn't you know that?"

* * *

Nicky walked up the alley across Decker to Linwood Avenue, where he had seen the horse drawn fruit wagon. He liked to walk around Pop's neighborhood when he visited and got bored with the dull conversations by the adults at the tavern.

This walk would be different, however. This walk would be special and unforgettable … to everyone. His muscles relaxed as he approached the end of Pop's alley at Linwood. He began to see flashes of the 19th century horse and buggy traffic again. The closer he got to the avenue more the scenery became old time Baltimore and dim images cleared. He was delighted. He let himself watch his fantasy. His dream or vision. Or, to be precise, his visit.

A block south on Linwood, he decided to cross over Baltimore St. to expansive Patterson Park. What Nicky was seeing, no one around him saw. He was lucky that automobiles and heavy trucks on the busy avenue didn't run him over. He stopped mid-avenue to see the cars briefly, and then rushed to the far curb, frightened by their horns and screams of 'hey, look out, you,' and the cursing.

* * *

"Where did you go," Miriam said, hugging Nicky at the tavern's kitchen door. He had gone missing for an hour.

"I needed some fresh air, mother. Walked to the park; that's all. Where's Pop?"

"Fresh air in the city. That's a good one. I hope you looked both ways crossing Patterson Avenue," his mother said. "Pop was in here a few minutes ago, looking for you. Come on. We'll find him together. I'm sorry I was upset with him. He didn't tell us he was planning this big party. I guess he just loves you very much like we do."

"I'm sorry too mother. Pop meant well."

She took him by the hand. They wove themselves through teens including Katrina dancing to the little band's barely recognizable rendition of the Beatle's *I Saw Her Standing There.* The party had picked up considerably in volume. People were laughing, singing and drinking in great spirits. "Hey, there's my boy," Pop said, reaching up to tussle Nicky's hair. "You okay Miriam? I didn't mean to upset ..."

She replied quickly with a gracious smile, "Forget it Pop. My fault. This was a nice gesture by you and Grandma Minnie. I'll leave him with you, okay?" She started walking briskly back to the kitchen and then came back to say, "Make him eat." She paused for an answer and listened as Nicky began to speak to Pop.

Nicky said, "Pop, do you know that baseball field at Patterson Park?

"Yeah, sure. I played there a long time ago. I told you."

"They had a game today. The scoreboard said the Baltimore Boh Sox won 6 to 0. At the top is that sign that says, 'National Brewing Company. We'll be back, folks.' What does that mean?"

Miriam drifted closer as she could see Pop was stunned by Nicky's words.

35

Pop's attention was focused intently on the innocent wonder in Nicky's eyes. Pop's face showed new tension, concern because the Baltimore Boh Sox were a team he pitched for in an amateur adult league in the 1920's and 30's and the scoreboard with the brewery slogan that referred to the Prohibition of alcohol at the time. It had been torn down long ago.

Pop turned his head away from Miriam's staring. He looked around at the tavern walls trying to remember if any of the framed photographs in the place had captured the Patterson Field scoreboard, which Nicky might have remembered. No, there were none.

Miriam was frozen with worry. Pop saw her concern and diverted the boy, "That's something, isn't it, Nicky boy? You want some of your Grandma's specialty, crab Italiano penne pasta? Sit here with me and my friend Chuck Estrada and his wife Georgiana. Mr. Estrada is a pitcher for the Orioles."

Miriam said, "I'll get it for you." She walked slowly back to the kitchen for a plate of food for Nicky, shaking her stylish bouffant do, perhaps a hint of denial whether her son was not well.

Chapter 3: Miriam's Promise

She hadn't filled Nicky's plate with food before Pop brought him back into the kitchen.

"He'll eat, but only in here," Pop said, sitting Nicky down at the kitchen table away from the party in the tavern.

Miriam sat down with him, "What's the matter, son?"

"I'm sorry, mother, but I don't understand what people are doing and talking about out there."

Carlo overheard; sat down with them, "I told you, hon. You've sheltered the boy way too much. Look. He is all shook up, just by people having fun."

Nicky kept his face into a plate of Grandma Minnie's tasty offerings and kept eating, never looking up, not explaining his shyness while he sat still, among the ladies in the kitchen and his parents.

* * *

Nicky's parents took the hint and stopped talking over him at Pop's.

Later that evening at home, he was alone, reading at a little desk in his room.

"Nicky, may I disturb you? What is that your reading?" his mother asked. She sat on the edge of his bed next to his desk.

"John Paul Jones, Father of the United States Navy. I think it is a little overstated. There were many other captains. Though he was the greatest. Maybe he had the best public relations, huh? [laugh] No, it was his courage. I wish I had his… I'm sorry about today, mother. Did I disappoint Pop?"

"You can do no wrong with him, believe you me. Sit here with me," she said. "Let's talk about that courage."

"This book was disturbing anyway," he said, taking a seat next to his loving mom. "What about courage?"

She took a deep breath and waited for him to initiate the conversation on his own, but she was used to him holding back.

She treaded softly with, "When I saw that party, all that loud yelling and people all looking at us at the side door there at Pop's today, you know what?"

"What?"

"I was frightened out of my mind, Nicky."

"I'm not sure why YOU would be scared, mother."

"Did that frighten you?"

"Not exactly."

"You seemed to faint with fright."

"Not exactly."

"Okay. How did you feel being surprised by the party and Pop shoving you in front of young girls?"

"Fine."

"Nicky, what I want to find out is that … well, you are 14 now, almost a young man. Oh heavens. That is hard for me. Sorry. What I mean is that your father and I are worried about your shyness with people. It is okay, but …"

"But what, mother? I didn't ask for being around all those people. The Esposito relatives, I love them all. I wish I was like them. But who were all the others. I didn't understand. I never understand. I'm not an Esposito, mother. I'm a freak."

She stood and held both of his shoulders, shaking firmly. Lost was her gentleness. She said almost in anger, "You get that out of your head. Who says you are a freak? You are a normal boy. Do you hear me?" She paced the room. "Nicky, we never see you with friends. You don't mention any from school. People say you are getting more and more introverted. Yes, that is unlike your family, but why so withdrawn lately?"

"Don't know." He sulked.

"There! See, you are withdrawing even from me."

"Sorry."

"Son, I want to understand you and you know you are my best friend in this world. Don't tell Kat. She is my best friend too, I guess."

"Don't tell Kat what?"

"Never mind." She sat next to him again, fluffing his thick moppy hair. "Say, Pop said he walked you over to the park after you ate your lunch."

"I guess you are going to ask me if we saw the old ball field like I saw by myself. I shouldn't have told you what I saw. Well, no, we didn't see it."

"I'm not going to ask you if you saw the field because you think you did. We have talked about your visions before. But, I wonder one thing. Do you remember walking back to Pop's Tavern after the vision?"

"No, actually."

"Don't be upset with me, but maybe you didn't actually go to the park. We didn't see you in the alley. Maybe you sat someplace. Maybe went to sleep or something somewhere."

Nicky shook his head. He was despondent.

Miriam pressed on, "Look at me and tell me exactly how you feel just before and during your visions."

"Mother I think I'm crazy."

Frustrated, she implored, "Tell me, please."

"Okay." He paused and looked into her eyes.

She wondered if he indeed trusted her as much as she wished. She added a twist, "Let's make this a game."

"I'm not a child, mother."

"I don't mean a kid's game. An adult game. A game of trust. I'll go first: trust me that I will not tell a soul what you feel in your visions. Now you."

"What do you want me to say?"

It was Miriam's turn to stall and wait for understanding.

Nicky said, "I want you to trust me that visiting the past is the most enjoyable experience in my life, without a doubt. Now you. Are you sure you will not even tell Dad or Pop? Kat doesn't know anything about this either. Don't please don't …"

"This is about trust. Trust me that I will not tell," she said with a pleasing maternal smile. She seemed to be making progress.

39

And then, he told her all. "Mother, I hate the fact that I cannot read people. I cannot understand people. I cannot judge character, motives, intentions or trends by talking with people. I am so ashamed for Pop who is completely at ease with people and ahead of every conversation, encounter and relationship.

"And every year it gets worse. I cannot understand things people do and say. I hear them perfectly. I am sort of play acting when I interact with people. And inside my head, there is a firestorm of thoughts. No, bits of thoughts racing and streaking through my mind as I try to fathom where I am and what I am doing sometimes."

"This firestorm. Is it just in conversations?"

"Yes. But that is just the trigger to my visits, I do believe. I get out of the conversation and I need to see and be someone else, be somewhere else. I need to feel better quickly because I am so tense."

"What happens next, Nicky?"

"Nothing most of the time. I figure, these people shouldn't bother me. So, I calm down."

"But not all the time? she asked. "Let's get back to today. Did you get that firestorm in your head? And when?"

"I didn't think about that, mother. Yes, I did feel it and wanted to escape. Oh, I think it began immediately, even before we stepped into the tavern with all those crazy people."

"They were not crazy. Crazy for making you happy, yes. Don't get off track. Nicky, I want to know if the shock played a part."

"What do you mean?"

"I admitted to being frightened and you were not sure you were. But something must have started you on the way to your 'visit,' as you call your visions."

"I see." He allowed himself to fall back on the bed and held his head in his hands.

She watched his face carefully for direction. He was lost in thought. She whispered, "Take your time."

He sat back up and told his mother, "It is the excitement. I need to escape from myself and there I am in another time and place. It is not difficult, mother. It is just a chance to be free from people and enjoy myself. My mind goes blank and there I am, somewhere else."

Miriam hugged her son and told him to always confide in her and he nodded that he would. She then asked, "Is that all? Do you feel any sensation? Is that the proper word?"

He then trusted that his mother could maybe feel or understand what he felt and he answered, "The confusion around people makes me feel chilly. And then I feel warm when I visit. Not just warm but a soothing, comfort all over. Afterwards, I sometimes sort of wake from the visit and I am chilly again and in another location from where I started."

"Again Nicky, I want you to tell me about these visits when you have them. I can talk you through any trouble you are having. Understand?"

"Yes, mother. I will." He thought again and said, "Mother, I'm no longer a child. I can handle these things."

"I know you will do your best. I understand completely. You can lean on me, Nicky. Always."

* * *

"It is caused by excitement," she told husband Carlo when she returned to their bedroom.

Half asleep, he asked, "What is?"

"Nicky's visions, or he calls them his trips. No, that's wrong, visits, he calls them his visits. Before you start moaning and groaning, remember that there is something very special about our boy. He is brighter than any child I've ever met. And, yet your family's lively nature didn't rub off on him, no matter how you try. If anything, it depresses Nicky because he loves you and can't find a way to join the party, you might say."

Carlo listened carefully and yet said, "I'm disappointed you didn't do anything with him."

"It is you who is disappointing, Carlo. You can't make him into something he is not. Please don't push him. Kat is the

41

outgoing one. I want Nicky to have a quiet life so he doesn't take one of those trips or visits, whatever, and not come back. Don't you love him that much?"

"Of course."

Chapter 4: History Calls

As Nick's body grew in height, his mind grew in scholarship.

Because he was accelerated in middle school, Nick reached his senior year in high school at age 16.

His favorite teacher taught history and the history teacher's favorite student was Nick Esposito. His memory for detail and eagerness to learn dazzled Miss Brown.

Before Spring break, he turned in a brilliant 100-page essay on the post-Civil War shipping and commerce boom in Baltimore. Miss Brown's class assignment had been for a ten-page essay.

His paper covered all aspects of the evolution of the city from a modest port into a major trade center. His reason for all the detail, all the pages? "I had doubts about the truth in each historian's version of the events, Miss Brown. I had to dig deep."

His scholarship had evolved to an insatiable thirst for the actual happenings, not just as written by "the winners," as he told Miss Brown. "Those who recorded their history, are sometimes just the winners. Am I right, Miss Brown?"

He was forming his own vivid composite histories of the expansion of the railroads, for example, or electrification of streets and factories, the perspectives of both labor and management on booming the prosperous and corrupted manufacturing sector—from tomato canneries to clothing mills, from Southern cotton clothiers to umbrella making plants, which in Baltimore were the best in the country. He put all the various histories on the period into his essay for high school class without biases and with meticulous foot notes and bibliography. *Let that tell the truth,* he thought.

Carlo was elated with Nick's grade. He showed Nick's A+ paper and his teacher's complimentary comments to Pop.

Miss Brown had written on top of the paper:

Congratulations Nick. You blew the majority of your classmates out of the water with your skillful writing. You did an amazing job on this assignment in every way possible. This is Master Level work. I predict you will not have any problems with your future writing assignments in all your college classes, especially research papers. YOU KNOW YOUR STUFF YOUNG MAN!!!

Pop was thrilled. He showed the paper and teacher comments to a professor friend who frequented Pop's Tavern. Soon, the professor published it in the Johns Hopkins University Press without a second thought.

By the end of the school year, substantial scholarship offers arrived from Harvard Business School, the University of Pennsylvania and others, due in large measure to carefully crafted applications by his father Carlo, who had long hoped Nick would study and learn business management and follow in his footsteps. Carlo was an executive for a national food processing firm, Esskay Meats, based in Baltimore.

Carlo figured his son may continue a succession of productive Esposito men in industry. Perhaps, thought Carlo, Nick would one day own and operate Pop's Tavern after Carlo's parents died, although antisocial Nick would likely have to hire people to run it. Carlo's motivation to help Nicky pick a business college was not altogether selfless. First, he felt that business studies would strengthen his son's world perspective. And he thought it would also prepare Nicky for the family responsibility and one day Nicky would be able to contribute to the tavern business. Carlo wanted no part of Pop's Tavern and his brother Alberto would not want to leave his successful work in California either to take over from Pop one day.

But Carlo's plan was doomed. Another scholarship offer intrigued Nick, one he had submitted himself. It was a less substantial offer from the University of Maryland history department in the College of Liberal Arts.

"History, history. Always history Nick," Carlo pleaded.

44

"That's right," said Nick.

Carlo had bragged that his Nick, since early childhood, was to be a brilliant businessman because of his sharp mind and focus on details.

But when the Maryland offer arrived, Nick argued with his parents for the history offer instead of the more prestigious business school scholarship possibilities. They frowned on his (unintentional) disrespect.

Carlo pressured his son incessantly. As Nicky was leaving for school one morning, his father stood at the door. "Look Nick, I know about these things. You will be better off in life with a business education, believe me. And you will help our family by going to college on a full scholarship."

"I hate business, dad. It is boring," Nick said.

"But there is no future in history."

"Very funny, dad. I get it. You act like this is about you. It is my future, not yours," Nick blurted out. He regretted saying it.

Carlo was shocked by Nicky's harsh tone and in anger said, "Look boy, I will not give you any money, no financial help whatsoever, if you insist on lollygagging along with your history hobby at the University of Maryland."

"If I can't study history, I'm skipping college all together," Nick replied as Miriam came from her breakfast chores in the kitchen to find out what the shouting was about.

But Nicky was out the door and gone.

"Honey," she said to her outraged husband, "such an introverted young man will have little chance to swim with the sharks in the world of industry. You must realize that, don't you?"

Carlo was disgusted with the boy's passivity, just as he did at Pop's party for Nicky's confirmation. "Okay, have it your way," he said and stalked out of the house, got in his car and went to work without another word. The next morning, still angry, Carlo left for another of his frequent business trips out of town that "just came up" he told Miriam. Carlo, feeling ashamed at his anger, called his wife from Baltimore's Friendship Airport to apologize.

As Miriam picked up, Nick answered the phone too, on the extension line. He could only manage to utter, "Okay. So, I'm still doing the history offer, right?"

Nick Esposito, for all intents and purposes, was then locked down tightly into a quiet life of history scholarship, which his parents would never fully comprehend.

Exasperated, and still at the airport, Carlo phoned Pop next, "He is set on history. Do you think something could still come from his odd career choice in the long run? I don't know what else to expect."

"We'll wait and see," said Pop, who was also disappointed in Nicky's choice, but not because of family pride. Pop worried that Nicky's deepening signs of withdraw might eventually steer him into danger. "True, the boy is passive. But he's an Esposito. He'll grow out of it. You'll see, my son."

* * *

After his Nick was safely cloistered into a quiet world of collegiate scholarship, as the family had accepted, Pop thought he could stop worrying about the young man.

Nick was then a quiet young man who stayed to himself for the first year of college. His family expected no trouble and wished him well.

But then, early one Saturday morning in the fall of 1971, Pop picked up his Baltimore Sun newspaper from the tiles on the tavern porch and he was staring at an image of his grandson in college. On the front page above the fold, was a photo of an angry 17-year-old Nick Esposito, identified in the cutline as "Freshman at the University of Maryland."

Pop called Carlo who had already seen the shocking image.

Carlo answered with, "Yes, I know. I've been trying to reach Nick by phone, Pop. This is awful."

The picture captured a climactic moment of a war protest. More than that, it documented the first time that compassionate Nick Esposito was exposed in real time to historic social outrage and injustice as it was unfolding, not in his history books.

On Friday afternoon, he walked from his last class of the week into a large crowd on campus protesting the continuing Vietnam War. A tide of energy welled up inside of him. At first, he watched sympathetically and joined the protesters surrounding the University's administration building. Police in full riot gear with bubble helmets and wielding rifles had confronted the crowd of several hundred students and some junior faculty.

Nick's Pop later surmised that something had brought out the "true Esposito spirit in Nicky," that compelled him to help people out in a tough situation, just like he or Carlo, or especially his great-grandfather, Inspector Mike, might have done.

The newspaper photo captured Nick on the steps of the building. His gaze was fixed, legs wide apart, between the police and protestors. He was captured by the lens shouting through a police megaphone in one hand. He was raising the other hand in a clenched fist. The story led with the arrest of "protest leader Nick Esposito, student, 17, and several other instigators." The story stated that Esposito perhaps prevented a violent confrontation as he pleaded for the crowd to be civil; that they had already made their point. "Do not fight the police, people. Fight for peace," he was quoted as saying repeatedly.

Of course, the newspaper would not have reported Nick's flare up of "true Esposito spirit," but rather that students and police dismissed him as being in a "trance-like state. Later, he only had vague memories of his moment of valiant leadership.

As the crowd began to taunt a line of cops in riot gear, the police took a few steps back. One cop dropped his battery powered megaphone.

In Nick's mind, the scene was Kent State happening all over again. Earlier that year National Guardsman at Kent State University in Ohio fired on students protesting the war, killing four in cold blood, which elevated the anti-Vietnam War movement nationwide to a fever pitch. Nick saw it unfolding again. He felt it in his bones, in his soul. He saw it developing. It could not happen again.

Nick rushed into the breach, picked up the megaphone, and ran past the outstretched hand of the policeman who had dropped the device. Nick's entire body was pulsating with every pounding beat of his heart. Energy-charged blood rushed to his brain and opened his lungs, allowing Nick to passionately address the eclectic gathering of cops, kids, and adults. He was brilliant, some said, though he remembered little. Nick then continued to shout and bond with the people all the way into a paddy wagon.

Alone again, Nick felt his mind numb up and his body muscles tighten in the vehicle.

He spent the entire evening slumped into a cold corner floor of a jail cell staring blankly while unbuttoning and buttoning his new University of Maryland red, yellow, and black wind breaker.

His father came to bail him out. "What on earth were you thinking?" Carlo said with a look of utter amazement. Nick could not say. Carlo recognized the blank look of an amnesic state he'd seen in Nick previously. It meant that Carlo needed to inform Nick what the newspaper reported that he had actually done.

Nick's eyes sharpened, his brow furrowed and, looking at his father as if speaking to a wise elder in a church, said, "You just can't let such chaos ruin America because, and I quote, 'Life is of no value but as it brings gratifications. Among the most valuable of these is rational society. It informs the mind, sweetens the temper, cheers our spirits, and promotes health'."

"What?"

"Thomas Jefferson, 1784, writing to James Madison, Dad."

"Get your jacket Nick. We are going to Pop's for a crab cake and a long talk."

* * *

Yes, any people then knew that young Nick Esposito was a brilliant thinker and also a very kind-hearted man. But, alone and possessed with a gift only he could appreciate, Nick seemed destined for a life of difficulties coping with the harsh realities of the world by himself.

Would there be some joy and personal triumphs along the way? Maybe some, yes, like for anyone. But few.

There was one joyful, perfect triumph in particular: the lucky day later in his life Nick mustered up the courage to meet a beautiful girl named Janet Jeffries. He would call her J.J. and she would love and accept him as himself, and like no one else could. And later they would share another joyful triumph: the birth of their beautiful twin daughters.

Those moments were still to come.

Meanwhile, after college, and long before he met J.J., his soul mate, Nick became the closet alcoholic he'd remain for life. He experimented with drugs in and after college. Still to friends and family, for better or worse times, he would simply be Nicky the dreamer, always grasping for a true identity.

* * *

After college Nick faced a dilemma perhaps unique to him. He needed to enter the working world while he was still socially unprepared to leave the safe haven of campus life.

Instead of venturing very far, Nick returned to campus the following fall after the university's graduate library approved his employment application there. During the four years in college, he probably had spent more time in the campus libraries then in his dormitory. He carried a 4.0 in classroom studies majoring in American history during his final two years despite perusing all the additional history volumes in the undergraduate library.

The graduate student library had a more extensive collection. Nick was content to be employed at minimum wages among thousands of books for the next three years.

His father seethed over his son's lethargy and often gave Nick the cold shoulder when they met. Carlo accepted his own failure to make more of his only son. Pop was also disappointed but gave his Nicky boy nothing but praise.

Nick lied to his few friends and acquaintances about his new job. His story was that he remained at the university to continue his studies "at the graduate level." He said it was to maintain a 1-S college draft deferred status. He was not in graduate school and never had to have college deferment thanks to Pop. At the time the Selective Service Administration was drafting high numbers of young men into the country's Vietnam War effort. When Nick turned 18 and thus became draft eligible after college, or if he dropped out, Pop used his influence with state politicians to get his grandson a medical deferment. Nick was furious when Pop told him what he'd done for him. It was the only time in their relationship that Nick felt any anger at his idol and best friend for life.

Pop had been terrified by the alternative prospect. "Listen my Nicky, you are not to be safe in the military with your visits as you say. You are a wonderful boy who is sensitive and smart. The world will need you. The war would surely kill you, boy. Please forgive me. It is for your own good."

So, it was done. Only Nick knew the truth. The two swore to secrecy. Nick calmed down and it further solidified their bond.

In 1978, Nick got off campus at last. He joined the legions of educators who fight the uphill battle to improve young minds in grade school. His command of the facts made Nick a potentially good instructor--no surprise perhaps, despite the quiet, unassuming bearing he maintained outside of the classroom.

Within a closed-door history classroom, he was adequate, yet insecure and frustrated that he could not be the best for his students. Early in his career he struggled with confidence and fumbled around without a true calling. He drank and often took sick days with hangovers from drinking or dealing with people.

* * *

For most of the next two decades, Nick was fired from three teaching jobs, on and off employment, while he also would work part time for Pop at the tavern and remaining a recluse with his books. His hair was turning gray, his shoulders were slumped permanently it seemed, and he was despondent until J.J. laid down the law.

She taught him method acting and convinced him that teaching young kids history was indeed his true calling. She helped him relax in the confined and sequestered classroom, away from any outside distractions. It was the only place on Earth where Nick acted consistently in the spirit of his generous and outgoing Esposito family.

Because of constant harping by his loving wife, Nick's fourth school teaching job was the charm, starting in 1995. He was by then supremely confident and convinced that his students excelled through Mr. Esposito, their beloved teacher.

Thanks to great coaching on theatrical methods by Janet Jeffries, Nick Esposito expressed himself effectively in a classroom 'stage,' with well-crafted and often dramatic presentations of history lessons he'd composed with J.J.

She was his social rock. And, she was the daughter of a Broadway performing family.

Nick could at last open up behind the closed doors of his own classrooms and find the true identity in the world that he had been seeking.

As a professional man, he was a paradox: shy to the outside world, skilled communicator in class. Mr. Nick Esposito, the high school history teacher, was generous with his time and cared for the students to a fault.

Unfortunately, only his students knew the performing side of Mr. Esposito, the extraordinary educator.

On the last day of his third school year in that fourth job teaching, Nick was having one of his best days in the classroom. He was giving a particularly dramatic lesson on the Civil War, when …

Chapter 5: Mr. Esposito's Final Lesson
Last day of the school year, May 26, 1998, 3:06 p.m.

In a back wing of old Glen Burnie High School, Mr. Esposito readied his American history class for one of his patented 'living history' tests, as he and J.J. called them. His innovative lesson this time was an intellectual battle between the blue hats and the gray hats.

The battle lines were drawn. Students in room 333 sat alert and eager in two parallel lines of desks facing each other on either side of the room. Their desks represented their battle armor, Mr. Esposito told them. The kids loved it. But, they were anxious. This was their final exam for crazy Mr. Esposito's history class, after all.

Mr. Esposito orchestrated special lessons so dramatically, with so much authenticity that students might actually believe for a moment that Mr. Esposito wasn't himself; that he had emerged out of his shelves of well-worn, crumbly old history books like some kind of time traveler. Little did they know.

Glen Burnie High's third-floor history wing was dark and decrepit, a remnant of an earlier time when it was the first schoolhouse in Anne Arundel County, south of Baltimore, in the late nineteenth century. Nick loved teaching in that wing of the building for no better reason than because it was creaky old.

He gave the 'rebel' Confederate students gray hats on one side of the room, provided at the teacher's personal expense, as were the 'Yankee' Union blue hats for the opposite row of students. The rebels sat along the south side of the classroom under the huge Confederate flag, which Nick hung on the window-shade brackets. He had purchased the flag at the Dr. Samuel A. Mudd House Museum in Southern Maryland on a class trip. Yankee students sat in desks along the north side of the classroom with a huge, thirty-five-star U.S. flag, draped on the blackboard behind them as they faced the enemy to the south.

Nick had purchased that flag in a Gettysburg gift shop on another of the maverick teacher's frequent class trips.

When they entered the classroom, the tenth graders each picked a hat at random from an old duffle bag. "No favorites here, ladies and gents," Nick had advised.

Once face to face with their enemy line of desks, the students in battlefield-room 333 watched Mr. Esposito for instruction. He wrote these words on the blackboard: IT'S ACADEMIC, THE CIVIL WAR. Mr. Esposito had been promoting the theatrical final exam "battle" all year. This was the last class of the school year, but no one was happy about that.

Typical of Nick Esposito's approach, the extravagant Civil War battle lesson was nowhere to be found in the Anne Arundel County tenth-grade history curriculum. But who cared? Certainly not the brilliant, compassionate Mr. Esposito. Certainly not his fun-loving students. They loved Mr. Esposito, plus they consistently got high marks in his history classes—in tenth, eleventh, and twelfth grades.

Once the students were settled down for 'battle,' Mr. Esposito held up his hands in a halt signal and said in a whisper, "Everyone quiet now. I know you are ready and eager. First off, you are going to have to wait just a moment, troops. Keep the safety pins locked on those brains for a minute, okay?"

He slipped into an old cloak closet where he stored props and costumes, plus.

Nick was pumped, yet anxious that he left a class full of teenagers alone for even a moment. He cared deeply for their education. He needed a boost of courage to perform the complicated lesson as J.J. scripted, before trying to send them off in an uplifted mood to enjoy their summer. From his vest pocket, he opened a tiny flask and took a long slug of Kentucky bourbon, a tribute to the birthplace of Abraham Lincoln, he rationalized.

Meanwhile, back in the classroom, all eyes were focused on the closet door as the students remained well behaved.

After a long two minutes, the closet door reopened. Out stepped President Abraham Lincoln. Their teacher had changed into a long, mid-nineteenth-century suit jacket with tails, a stovepipe hat, and a black Abraham Lincoln beard tied ear to ear against tufts of Nick's reddish-brown hair. He paced up and down the makeshift aisle between the battle lines of the blue and gray, as he began teaching the lesson.

"Class, on Monday we learned about the escape route of John Wilkes Booth as some of you visited the museum home of Dr. Samuel Mudd. He was the physician who knew Booth. Dr. Mudd set Booth's leg. The assassin had broken his leg leaping onto the stage of the old Ford's Theatre. That was after shooting me in the head. [under his breath] It was an act, I should say, that my real wife has often contemplated."

The students roared with approval, laughing uninhibitedly, as they often did in Mr. Esposito's wonder-about-history class, in great appreciation for the best teacher they ever had and probably ever would.

"And what did Booth yell from the stage, class?"

"Sic semper tyrannis!" the class screamed in unison.

"That's right. 'Thus, always to tyrants,' which is also the official motto of the Commonwealth of Virginia," said Nick. He hoped the class didn't see his gratified half grin from under the mass of whiskers on his face. He was especially proud of this class. And, playing Lincoln made him proud, for once, to be skinny and standing tall, instead of feeling awkward as usual.

"Now class, Lincoln is remembered as a beloved president, maybe the most beloved. But back then, what were the issues that led to my death?" Nick asked. A sandy-haired boy in a blue hat yelled out first. "Many people in the North hated Lincoln for getting them into a war that wasn't necessary and—"

One of a few black girls in the class, who ironically wore a gray hat, cut him off with, "But the South hated him for freeing the slaves and costing them money from losing all that free labor."

Nick held up his two index fingers signaling partial agreement. "Well, yeah, that's just the beginning of the love/hatred of Lincoln by the public," he said, stroking his whiskers slowly. "But you get the gist. There will be questions on that on the exam at the end of class, as well as how Lincoln did manage to get reelected despite the discontent in the country at the time."

Mr. Esposito had invented a version of the Civil War lesson several years earlier at another school as a fitting final exam, reflecting on the most dramatic event in American history, in his estimation. He felt it deeply as a tipping edge that could have led to the nation's destruction.

Each year, Nick would offer a lead a field trip to the Gettysburg battlefield to "really bring the gravity of the crisis home to them," he told J.J. over breakfast that day.

To Glen Burnie High students, the optional trip was legendary. It would always affect Mr. Esposito deeply. Students learned to stay close to him. On the Gettysburg trip, they observed that their teacher felt the pain of the horrible battle field vicariously. He alone could see the smoke and exploding cannon fire; hear wounded men's screams with their last breaths. A rumor circulated around the school that during one of the guided tours with students by a U.S. National Park Ranger at the decisive battle of Pickett's Charge, Mr. Esposito himself collapsed as if shot by a sniper.

It was a true story. On that trip, Nick had felt and thought he had seen the horror of the massacre of half of Confederate Maj. Gen. George Pickett's 12,500 gray soldiers in just a few hours as they tried to breach a low stone wall, still visible on the modern tour, a little wall that poorly shielded many blue clad Union defenders. Mr. Esposito's students watched their teacher cry openly and collapse. When paramedics arrived, he had recovered. He sat on the tailgate of the ambulance and was heard to say, "I often think of that anti-war protest I witnessed in college and I wish someone here on that hillside could have stopped the incredible carnage. Look, see; it's terrible."

For his latest Abe Lincoln presentation for his Glen Burnie High School class, Nick added a twist. He proclaimed in a mock-Lincoln voice that "soldiers' on whichever side of the Civil

War classroom got the most correct answers on the exam would win a crab cake lunch at Pop's Tavern in East Baltimore. They were all familiar with Mr. Esposito's adoration of his grandfather.

Standing tall as President Lincoln, he told them, "That quaint establishment is owned by Mr. Esposito's grandfather, Stephen "Pop" Esposito—a great ball player, a great businessman, a great role model."

As a rule, teacher Nick used any competitive method in his patented wonder-about-history lessons he could devise to divide the class and pit them against each other because it drove up the grades. He hoped this day they would all excel.

With long, thoughtful strides, Nick paced back and forth in the mid-classroom aisle between the Yankee and Rebel soldier-students. He was preparing to fire an opening volley of questions to sharpen their wits. His every thought was to benefit the kids. He didn't care about himself. He was a true Esposito in those moments—generous, compassionate. Indeed, J.J. had given him that identity.

He strode slowly, as Lincoln might have with his long legs, the stride of a man burdened with a heavy heart of a stricken nation. Nick reached the east side of the classroom and stepped up on a small platform behind a podium. He took out a ragged envelope from his right inside coat pocket and read:

Four score and seven years ago, our forefathers brought forth, upon this continent, a new nation, conceived in liberty, and dedicated to the proposition that 'all men are created equal. Now we are engaged in a great civil war . . .

He looked up at that point and with great sensitivity peered into the eyes of his students. He asked, "Class, stop me when I get to the words that changed the meaning of the U.S. Constitution forever. Have you heard those words yet—the completeness of the change?"

The students shouted opinions as he continued reciting the Gettysburg Address. He and his students knew this didn't count on the exam later. It was fun. It was theater in the classroom. They loved it. He loved them loving it. They studied his every move, as if he actually was Abraham Lincoln as he finished reciting the three-minute Gettysburg Address, while never again glancing at the blank envelope in his left hand.

Class ended 35 minutes later. Mr. Esposito sat at his desk as one student after another dropped off their exam sheets and a blue or gray hat on his desk and left the room. He was tired, but a good, satisfying tired.

A few of the girls hugged their caring teacher quickly with some embarrassment and thanked him before running out giggling.

He was grading their tests as they left. He was an efficient instructor. All the grades were stellar. He considered buying both sides that crab cake lunch at Pop's Tavern.

Just after the last student left the classroom and he was alone in a hollow room with his grading, Nick heard a woman's voice shrieking from the school's public-address system, "Mr. Esposito, please report to Principal Palumbo's office immediately."

What does Frank want at this time of day? he wondered.

Thinking he would amuse the usually stern principal Frank Palumbo, Nick clipped on Lincoln's beard again and put on the Lincoln coat and stovepipe hat to make a dramatic entrance into the principal's office to say farewell and good cheer for the summer. After all, Palumbo was a fellow paisano. Feeling good with the school year ending on a high note, Nick was frivolously edging out of his public, shy character. *It will be fun*, Nick thought.

But his visit to the principal's office would be nothing like fun.

* * *

"Come in, Nick, and for God's sake, take off that stupid beard!" barked Principal Palumbo. The high school principal was evidently trying to impress two Anne Arundel County school officials, who were sitting with him along with Vice Principal Bunker.

Palumbo's tie was pulled to one side and loose, his suit jacket wrinkled. They were sitting around an antique American colonial table in the principal's office. Nick had always admired that table as the possible desk of Colonial Maryland Governor Benjamin Tasker.

Nick immediately sensed that something was terribly wrong.

"Nick, I think you know School Superintendent Crabtree and Assistant Super Symanski?"

They all glared menacingly.

Nick took a seat at the table, his chair at a lower level than the others. Nick felt crestfallen because, after his triumphant afternoon, something was indeed dreadfully wrong to be facing both superintendents.

The prune-dried women in their 60's, dressed alike for the most part—grayish dresses with starched white blouses. Nick noticed an absence of any jewelry such as ear rings, necklaces or wedding rings. They wore somber, even mean expressions. They seemed too formal and composed, considering it was a warm late spring day. The end of the school year is usually a day of relief and perhaps joy. There was no joy at the lovely table.

"Mr. Esposito," began Ms. Crabtree, the older of two supers, sitting high, stiffly erect with her gray hair pulled tight into a bun atop her head. She held her arms crossed tightly at her chest resting on each other. "Do I understand that you once again removed students from the school yesterday for an all-day adventure, without proper adult escorts, and returned them to the school at 10:00 p.m.?"

"It was 8:30 and it wasn't an adventure. It was a history lesson to none other than Dr. Samuel Mudd's home in Bryantown. He was the physician who set the broken leg of—"

"Booth!" she shouted; then, calmer: "Booth, for God's sake. I know my history, Mr. Esposito. Explain to me why that class did not obtain permission slips from their parents for that adventure—excuse me, history lesson, as you claim [her face now blood red] from their parents."

"They did."

"No, they did not."

"Yes, they did."

"Don't lie to us, Esposito," interjected Principal Palumbo.

Nick sat silently. His demeanor had already reverted to his quiet and unassuming look he normally carried in public.

Finally, he mumbled, "It was my last lesson for them before their final exam today. They said they did . . ."

"What!" demanded Palumbo? "What did you say to me, Esposito?"

Barely audible, Nick replied, "Have slips ... Oh, I didn't say anything, I guess."

Palumbo turned to the supers. "He told me this morning that the students got permissions. And then this morning, parents called me complaining that he'd kidnapped their children and that they didn't give any such permission for a field trip. I called other parents who lied for their kids and said they did not go on a field trip. Where is the truth, Esposito? I think we need to know."

Nick could muster up one more ounce of energy left. "That's right, Frank. The whole class didn't go. Only nine of them. Those who got permission. And they followed me in their own cars, not a bus."

"Okay, let me see them."

"See what?"

"The slips, damn it. Excuse me, ladies."

"I didn't actually collect the slips, Frank. I forgot to ask for them, I guess. I'm very sorry if I caused a problem. It won't happen again." Nick was too socially inept to realize he'd just given the wicked witches a perfect opening.

"That's right, Mr. Esposito," said Ms. Symanski, the other lady super, in a sugary sweet voice, "It won't happen again, sir, because we are here to witness your dismissal by Mr. Palumbo."

Nick was fixed in fear watching her eyes flaring deep within her wrinkled face hanging diabolically, cheeks like bat wings, and ghostly dull gray Dutch boy hair. The vampire bat super was known to hate male teachers. She paused for her virulence to take effect.

All eyes watched the pathetic history teacher gasp for air and then exhale with a heavy moan. He gazed upward to try to reach for any thoughts to rescue himself. Five minutes ago, he was exhilaratingly happy with the triumphant completion of his American history class. He gave all to 'his kids.' So now, maybe his superior intellect would rescue him? Could he pull together, put his intellectual skills to work and get out of this?

Not this time, not anytime again in his damned profession. Nothing came to mind. Nick sat stunned for an eternal moment. Emotionally numb. To maybe avoid defeat, he offered, "You can't fire me, folks, for just teaching American history. The students; they love it. I love it. Please, don't. I have twins at home, and ..."

Principal Palumbo showed some phony compassion. He lied, "Listen, we know you've got obligations. But, so do we, to these children, Esposito. What we hear is that your students do not like your style of teaching. It makes them nervous. I don't really think they like you at all as a teacher or as a responsible adult. I'm sorry, but you have pulled too many stunts, Esposito. This afternoon I got a call that you were displaying a Confederate flag out your classroom window since yesterday. People driving on B&A Boulevard could clearly see it. You know how African-Americans feel about that symbol. No sir, Esposito. This was definitely your last chance."

Nick realized he indeed didn't have a chance. He'd never considered that staging that flag behind the South side students in his classroom for the Civil War test, although great for theatrical effect inside, could be seen on the other side of the window brackets it was tacked to from the outside. "Oh, my Lord, no," he mumbled.

Slouching horribly, Nick stood and nearly fainted. Exhausted, he only then took off Abe Lincoln's stovepipe hat. "Here, take this," he mumbled to someone he felt near him as he exited. That someone was the vice principal, Walter Bunker, who had known and supported Nick at that school, but hadn't said a word to defend him during the terrible meeting. "Nick, listen to me," he whispered, putting his arm around Nick's shoulders. "You are too damned idealistic. Find another profession."

Chapter 6: No Place to Be

October 1999

Forty-five-year-old Niccola Augusta "Nick" Esposito was bored silly tending bar at Pop's Tavern, as he was every day. He was lonely and despondent, yet stoic about his new status, or lack of it.

The former teacher, married, father of five-year-old twin daughters, with a useless master's degree in American history, was now left with making his living tending bar for his grandfather, Pop, who was in a retirement home at age 96.

Nick could no longer confide much in Pop. The loneliness Nick felt was deep and unforgiving. He used to talk to Pop and others a lot about history, even form companionships by thinking about and conjuring up his heroes from the past. Now, his only real listeners were drunks and delivery men. Nick no longer wanted to talk much at all.

This was a cool, misty Tuesday afternoon. It could have been any Tuesday afternoon at Pop's Tavern on Ellwood Avenue in East Baltimore. There were no customers, unlike the old days when this was a popular watering hole for the east side of town, where people dropped in for a friendly beer or just to hear Pop tell his colorful stories.

Nick didn't have the heart to tell Pop the truth. Business was beyond bad.

Pop some time ago had asked him to "look after things up there, will ya Nicky while I'm in this prison for old folks? Can't trust nobody else; will ya help yer ol' Pop out?" He had to. It was up to Nick.

On this day in October, Nick was busying himself by dusting inside Pop's large glass display case of treasured mementos behind the bar. He was pausing in a trance-like state to reacquaint himself with each precious piece. Nick could conjure up a vivid back story in living color with sound and motion for each one of the treasures. He knew Pop's stories that well: there was that worn-out pitcher's mitt from Stephen Esposito's playing days at Patterson Park, a Baltimore Chamber of Commerce award plaque, a 1978 picture of Pop with Baltimore mayor William Donald Schaefer and actor Al Pacino, some old bottles of foreign liqueurs, an antique pearl-handled pistol, and other items of great value to his grandfather. And, if they were Pop's, of course they were of great value to Nick too.

Nick treasured them because he still treasured his grandpop, his hero. The framed pictures and items that covered the walls of the old tavern, memories, all about Pop, dated as far back as 1931. Nick still admired and respected Pop at his advanced age for his sociability and generosity, as did everyone else.

Someone pushed through the tavern door at last.

"Hey, Mr. Esposito, looks like I didn't need a reservation. How ya doin' today, sir?" It was Jerry Marcus, one of Nick's former history students at Glen Burnie High School a few years earlier.

Nick locked up Pop's display cabinet and pivoted around to greet Jerry. "Well, if it's not my star history student! What brings you by here, Jerry?" Nick was happy to see the young man, but a bit embarrassed. Nick's abrupt firing from Glen Burnie High still stung after more than a year. Seeing Jerry reminded him again that Glen Burnie was the fourth school to fire him in his 20-year, on-and-off-again, teaching career, or maybe just the third, depending on how he looked at it. Who was counting? certainly, not Nick any more. He was through.

"I heard you were here, Mr. Esposito, so I drove up town to find you," said Jerry. "I'm up for a management position at Delta at the airport, and I wondered if you could give me a recommendation. I was a very good student in school and I just got my associate's degree at Anne Arundel Community College last year, in business administration."

"Why me, Jerry? Why me for a recommendation? I don't think my recom—"

"Why not, Mr. Esposito? You were the best teacher in the school. Everybody knows that!"

Except for the principal and county supers, Nick thought of saying. Instead he replied, "I'd be honored, Jerry. Can I send it to you?"

Jerry wrote down his address and started to the door, and then returned. "Oh yeah, this was on the stoop outside, addressed to you, I guess," said Jerry. "Well, see ya and thanks again Mr. Esposito." He handed Nick a square envelope marked 'FOR MR. NICK.'

Well, that was awkward, Nick thought.

He leaned back on the bar and held his head tightly as if it might fall off. He reflected on how he probably did create a bad rep in local school systems that essentially ended his career as a history teacher in public schools. Nick remembered how he'd foolishly became so sure of his work in the classroom using acting tips from his wife to play historic characters, such as Lincoln, Thomas Edison and Andrew Carnegie.

He stood up straight and exhaled, blowing hot air from his mouth like a beached whale.

After weeks and months now at Pop's, he finally realized how his creative mind got lost and was murdered by the structured public education system. It hurt deeply. He was resolved to be a bartender. He gave up even applying for another job teaching.

Who did I think I was fooling? I can't read people, react to them well and stumble if I try. As he looked out onto the street, he was still angry that he wasn't able to say good-bye to his kids at the high school. He loved them all. *What would I have said to them anyway?*

Now many months later, with an eternity of time on his hands babysitting a largely empty Pop's Tavern, Nick often thought about those kids and the satisfaction he had felt by broadening them. He thought about the irony of the kids loving his skits and then him sitting stupidly, unsuspecting, wearing the same silly Abe Lincoln hat the kids loved, but at Principal Palumbo's beautiful antique office table, being humiliated and summarily dismissed.

His failure drove Nick into a full time quiet zone. He was in a sad state of mind, which perhaps only he could mask publicly, faking, engaging his superior intellect whenever it was needed. Faking a happy persona was easy now that he had a family and a loving wife behind him. But while dusting, chatting small talk, wiping down the bar day after day, Nick felt himself as no more than a particle of dust, overtaken by a self-image of insignificance. Now, stationed at the bar of Pop's Tavern day after day, he no longer related to anything to give him meaning during the daytime except counting on rekindling the comforting love of his wife and kids when he would arrive home late at night.

Still feeling a tinge of embarrassment about his former student Jerry Marcus showing up, Nick was pleased that the young man still respected him.

Nick sighed as he watched Jerry exit through the lonesome tavern's front door and zoom off in a brand new, silver Honda Accord. Nick still drove his old black 1981 Toyota.

His hand then brushed against the envelop on the bar that Jerry brought to him from the tavern stoop outside. The hand lettering, 'FOR MR. NICK' was scribbled on it faintly in gray ink or even pencil. Inside was a folded brochure. It was an advertisement for a party to be held on December 31, 1999, to celebrate the new millennium at the grand old Belvedere Hotel.

Nick flashed on images of the plush and ornate, Beaux Arts style building full of elaborate late 19th century decorated ballrooms. Set high in a fashionable uptown neighborhood, the Belvedere was once a must showplace for Baltimore's elite.

With this mind still adrift, contemplating the period, one of his favorite periods in history, he looked again at the lettering and worried.

"What the …? Who? Why is my name on this?" he muttered.

He heard another noise at the front door.

Before Jerry's car was out of sight, Nick's new cleaning lady, Clare, filled the frame of the tavern's narrow entry door. Short and plump, Clare ambled in with her perpetually happy smile and south Baltimore accent. "Afternoon, Nick. Sorry I couldn't get here this mornin', hon, but ma auwtharitic knee was actin' up again. I couldn't get up. Can I do a little now; an I'll come back tamorra?"

"Of course. As you can see, Clare, we're, I mean, I'm not busy yet . . . ever," Nick finished the sentence under his breath. He noticed Clare's face droop from cheery to concerned, mouth slightly open, furrowed brow. He regretted the slip, knowing he had let his cynicism unfairly greet this simple, genuinely nice lady from up the block. He mumbled as he led her back to the old kitchen. He said to himself quietly, "Idleness is the Dead Sea that swallows all virtues."

Clare tugged at his sleeve from behind, "What? Whose dead?"

He chuckled and put his hand on her shoulder, "Ben Franklin. Ben Franklin's dead. Come on to the kitchen, Clare. Let's find you some cleansers, mops and things, okay?" he said. Nick was glad to see her; wanted to make up for not showing it. Nick was well aware he wore a glum face, but was also aware of the need to remove it in public, especially at Pop's. He said pleasantly, "It is always nice to have you come in the door with such a positive attitude. You brighten people up; should run for mayor."

"Oh, go on Nick," Clare said. She blushed and got busy organizing her cleaning chores. Nick's mind was already adrift and didn't hear her comment.

Nick's eyes surveyed Grandma Minnie's old kitchen at the back of the small tavern. Sentiments aside, he had allowed that space, which he'd held sacred as a little boy, to become messy and cluttered like an unkempt restaurant storage room that it now was.

Ignoring his earnest cleaning lady still chattering, Nick walked slowly back to the bar.

* * *

Nick, with his loneliness, his career in shatters, and clearly a social misfit with his drifting mind, lack of initiatives

66

and let's not forget his 'visits,' was stuck. He was the man in charge at Pop's by no fault of his own.

Pop was gone and so were his parents who had by then had passed away.

As Pop relinquished his Tavern to sit in "that old people's rest home," as he called it, Nick's rich Uncle Alberto assured Pop he would tend to the tavern business somehow, despite his law practice in New York City and on the West Coast. Before moving his parents, Pop and Minnie, to Quiet Oaks, Uncle Al had convened a family council meeting at the tavern. The consensus was to try to continue the legacy of Pop's Tavern even though revenues were very poor by 1990.

To prove the family's intent to Pop, Al fronted the majority of the funds needed to purchase for Pop a dilapidated old tavern on Pratt Street in early 1991 as a fixer upper. It would replace the dying business at Pop's Tavern. They would sell the old tavern when the new one was renovated and opened. That put Pop in to the Quiet Oaks deal and he agreed.

Soon thereafter, however, Alberto, by then a leading attorney for celebrities, moved all of his work to Hollywood and was not able to help in person with the family businesses, even part time.

Also, Nick's sister, the bright and stylish Katrina, was by then married to a brigadier general commanding Anderson Air Force Base on Guam. They were not available either to help with Pop's on Ellwood Avenue.

No one ever expected that anti-social Nick to be heir to the beer taps. As things turned out, there was no one left in the family willing to attend to Pop's Tavern but reclusive Nick. When he lost his final teaching job, he was it. When Pop finally agreed with Minnie that he was too old to manage the place himself, he needed Nick. Years earlier, Pop fully expected the tavern to fall to another family member, probably his youngest son Carlo because he lived in the area. It seemed a foregone conclusion. Carlo would hire, fire, manage, while still maintaining his professional job based in Baltimore.

But tragically, it was not to be so.

* * *

As a youth, Nicky boy used to love Grandma Minnie's magical kitchen with its delightful aromas of her famous crab soup, fresh-baked Italian bread, and her Baltimore's best spaghetti sauce simmering. Pop and Minnie Esposito had lived there together from 1935 to 1997—kitchen in the back, bedroom and front "sitting room" on the second floor over the tavern. There they had raised their two sons, Nick's father Carlo, the food executive in Baltimore, and his brother Alberto, the lawyer in California.

Nick longed to relive the romance and intrigue of Pop's Tavern in its day. But now he was tortured instead by hating and resenting being stuck there tending bar almost every day. It had been more than a year since Pop's offer, which Nick he could not refuse, to take over managing the dying business. It was a miserable job, but truly his only occupation. Desperation employment. But with the twins at home, well …. he certainly didn't choose to be there.

* * *

Later, on that cool Tuesday October afternoon in 1999, Clare was still the only other person in the tavern besides bartender Nick.

People walking by on the sidewalk would see his long, thin frame in his usual stance—standing, or rather slouching, idly behind the tavern bar, white apron too small for his height, in some faded dress shirt and pleated wool-blend slacks—his well-worn workday school outfits—leaning on one elbow, his apron nestled on the bartender side of the highly polished bar top. He'd always be reading a book or daydreaming. He could be mistaken for a statue or mannequin—the man seen through the tavern window always in the same position on one elbow reading a book.

He read history books or historic novels at the bar—last remnants of a lost life presenting dramatic, exciting, and intriguing stories of past heroes and heroines in American history to his wide-eyed students. Now, he could only imagine how he'd script new lessons from his reading.

One consolation for his dilemma was the nostalgia he felt at the tavern. He was fond of gazing over to the far end of the tavern's bar where it flared out into a round server deck closer to the back of the tavern and Minnie's kitchen. When Clare walked toward him with a dust rag, Nick instead saw his little Grandma Minnie walking out of her culinary heaven, carrying huge trays of the best crab cakes in the city, or at other times a tray of hot, jumbo steamed crabs.

Minnie, always with a good-natured smile and a nod to anyone on the end barstool, would leave uncooked crab cakes at that end of the bar for a quick fry up for customers. Nick and his big sister Katrina as children used to love watching Grandma make the crab cakes, mixing all the ingredients, patting them into cakes, and putting them on the white enamel trays to be fried when customers bought them, and not before. Nick could still hear her say to customers, "You pick your raw crab cake and I fry it for you just right, okay?"

Clare began mopping near the bar. "How you getting along, Nick? Bin here most ever day now a couple months, I hear?"

"Huh? Oh, more than a year, Clare. There's nobody left now who can do this for Pop, I guess." Nick tried to sound responsible and hide his despondency.

"How's your J.J. and those little darlings, hon? They been up here lately?" she asked about his wife and their five-year old daughters.

"J.J. won't let the twins come here now. They are old enough to remember things they see; bad influences, she says. Too many drunks, she says. You know J.J.'s parents were alcoholics. They were entertainers in New York. J.J. is very serious about this. She's seen enough of the dark side of places like this, I guess."

69

"My Joe says your J.J. is the most beautiful woman he ever seen. Long, wavy auburn hair, slim and statuesque, and all." Clare acted out the shape and look of J.J. with her hands. "Her face is like a cover girl, Nick. He seen her at St. Peter's, yer granddad's church sometimes, maybe couple times. And, she sings beautiful in church too, I hear. You ain't never with her in church, my Joe says."

Ignoring the religion setup, Nick said instead, "I cover the bar when Pop invites us up to his church and, yes, she sings well. J.J. beautiful? Well, yeah, a lot of men notice J.J., unfortunately I guess." As soon as he let those words go, Nick was sorry he said them.

"Unfortunately? Are you crazy, Nick? You should be proud. She's—"

"I am, Clare. Very proud. How I managed to marry such a stunningly pretty woman is beyond my comprehension. Most people wonder why she didn't become a movie star; she was a fine actress in college, 'til she met me and I ruined that, I guess.

"Oh, you asked about the twins. Well, they are in kindergarten now and J.J. is getting back to part-time work as a day nurse at the Johns Hopkins AIDS clinic."

"Bet that comes in handy, hon," Clare said, already shuffling back behind the bar to wet mop the floor, not waiting for Nick's response.

Handy? Yeah, I'll say. And at what cost? Who's eyeing her at the hospital now? He thought.

Adding to Nick insecurity over losing his career was an escalating jealousy. He was beginning to think he was losing his precious J.J. to another man and he was helpless to prevent it, being stuck tending bar every day, not knowing what she was doing.

Nick barely heard Clare's voice fading as she moved to the back of the tavern, "Hey Nick, you see Belvedere Hotel cards left on your stoop? Wouldn't go near that creepy old thing, would ya, hon?"

* * *

Still, as a middle-aged man, Nick was considered the family oddball. Old Pop would brush off any such notion, straightening out anyone being critical of Nick. He told people that Nick was quiet because he was like his mother, who was a pensive daughter of German immigrants. "Lutherans, you know?" he would say with a laugh to the old folks at the home. Secretly he was disappointed because, since the day the baby was born, Pop had "adopted" his firstborn grandson as the family's heir apparent to the tavern business.

It was supremely important to him. The tavern had always been the hub of his empire, his Taj Mahal, his place of all his gratifications and accommodations, where things happened. Pop built it on solid friendships and favors for decades.

When little Nicky was born, Pop had felt it well within his right as head of the family to press hard at Carlo to convince Miriam to name the baby boy Michael after Pop's father, the famous police inspector originally from Milano. Miriam prevailed, although she did concede to the Italian name Niccola instead of the more Germanic Nicklaus.

With his two sons, Carlo and Alberto, climbing executive career ladders to national responsibilities far beyond East Baltimore, Pop's hope always was that Nick could become like him, the hometown "Balmer" favorite in the neighborhood.

Again, it wasn't to be. He was the unexpected Esposito.

But who could match Pop? Not Nick. Not anyone, actually. Stephen Esposito was one of a kind, even among the Espositos. And, any young boy would be hard pressed to match Pop's gregarious life. Adult Nick continued to envy Pop's lifestyle, but also always understood that Stephen "Pop" Esposito had been well prepared to be socially contented long before Nick was born.

As a young man, Pop was a star athlete. At first, the tavern atmosphere was about young Stephen's athletic reputation and his charisma. And then with wife Minnie, they became popular and devoted members of St. Peter's Catholic Church. It had previously been her family's church. But, due to his people

71

power, Stephen brought half the congregation to the tavern on a regular basis. His winning personality made him a popular figure across the city.

With such positive expectations throughout Pop's life and thriving business, it was quite understandable to Nick that Pop, as a very old man, remained in concrete denial that the neighborhood had become rife with crime and drug dealers. Therefore, Pop surely had no second thoughts about putting Nick in charge when Carlo died and Nick lost his teaching career.

* * *

The lowest point of despondency Nick felt that October in 1999 had come gradually during the 18 months after his departure from Glen Burnie High School.

Idle Nick fought his bartending fate at first. He wouldn't let his imagination die. He'd still keep a sort of third eye open in his mind when he felt the need to transform the printed word or paintings of historic sites and events into occasional visits into the past. He took time to drive around before or even after bartending sometimes.

At the Edgar Allen Poe House on North Amity Street in West Baltimore, the poet's Baltimore home, Nick's mind's eye pictured the writer animated at his desk over paper and pen while whizzing and coughing with tuberculosis. During the visit, Nick became solemn and distant.

Also, more than once in the summer of 1998 he drove past empty Memorial Stadium on 33rd Street, former home field of the Orioles and feel the old excitement of those great teams that played there during his childhood years. And then he would continue to another fantasy stop at nearby 25th and Barclay Streets. Near that corner there were still stones that once supported walls of the old Union Park where the old National League Orioles played from 1892 to 1899, led by the legendary dirty player, third baseman John McGraw. The longer Nick stared at the wall remnant more and more of the old baseball park would appear to him alone. He saw the iconic sign, "Baltimore Baseball and Exhibition Grounds." He saw fans line up for tickets next to a horse hitching post. And walking down 25th to Barclay, Nick would see the back of the old left field bleacher stands.

Also, after closing the tavern, he'd sometimes spend a few minutes on the docks off Boston Street. If he was lucky, Nick would be able to 'visit' with tall ships of a bygone era sailing to-and-fro in the Baltimore Harbor. He knew a thousand true stories of the tall ships. Images would appear to him and he'd be happy for a moment or two.

There was little joy in his visits then. He felt his mind deteriorating. Would Pop have still trusted Nick to run the tavern if he knew how his grandson's mind was teetering on insanity? Not likely.

Nick chose the docks off Boston Street to see the tall ships after his first choice frightened him terribly. It was a Friday in July when the dead spoke to him for the first time.

He closed early because it had been raining hard all day. Not even the town drunks came in to the tavern.

He drove his usual route home through Little Italy—not the quickest route but the most nostalgic—when Nick got the idea of capturing a few moments 'visiting' with the tall ships at the harbor. He planned to stop first at Vaccario's Bakery to purchase their famous Napoleons, J.J.'s favorite pastry. The famous shop was only a few blocks from the Baltimore Harbor where he might see the long-gone tall ships. It was an excuse to arrive late at home.

At Vaccario's, they all knew Nick of course. "How's Pop doing? We miss him," an old lady asked Nick. When Nick assured her that his grandparents were safe and of sound health, she gave him two free loaves of Italian bread. "Give him our love, darlin'."

The rain let up some. He left the car parked and walked with his umbrella three blocks west to the outlet of Jones Falls, where the huge Jones Falls watershed slices through Baltimore's mid-section and empties into the harbor. As he stood next to the outlet and tried to imagine seeing the tall ships somehow only a few blocks out. No particular historic moment or event came to mind. He simply hoped for a glimpse.

If he had been in better spirits that Friday, Nick might have remembered that it was the anniversary of the great Jones Falls Flood of July 28, 1868. Instead, he squinted through the raindrops toward the harbor. *Would those magnificent ships have sailed in the rain?* He asked himself. *Of course not, dummy.*

All of Nick's visits into the past up until that day had been one way—Nick seeing, hearing people and things in the past. There had been no feedback, no messages or talk back to him.

That was about to change.

As he peered south, munching the last bite of his pastry, he heard a roar behind him. He turned around to see a wave of debris and white water rushing downstream from the north. He was soon covered with mud as the water rose quickly. The outlet's sides collapsed. Garbage, lumber, pieces of fences were floating by, then entire sheds, carriages, clothing, and horses.

Nick only then realized he was visiting Baltimore's "Black Friday Flood" of 1868, which claimed 50 lives and damaged some 2,000 homes.

[Jones Falls had flooded several times since 1800, but never so badly. People that day took it lightly that the waterway was overflowing some. It had happened often. But late in the day, a south wind blew a high tide in from the harbor, joining the waters of the Jones Falls. Much of downtown was flooded in the disaster.]

Nick ran back to a higher level. He watched telegraph poles falling, and houses dislodging and falling into the rushing waters. He heard a crack of wood splitting. The wooden bridge at Charles Street upstream gave away and took iron fragments away like they were feathers. People were knocked into the rush.

Nick was horrified.

He spotted a woman floating downstream toward him. She would be within his reach if he could get back to the outlet's edge. Her head was bobbing up and down under the surface and her long garments were preventing her from swimming. Nick saw more bodies upstream coming down toward him, some moving, some maybe not.

The woman cried, "Mister, mister. Please help me!" She appeared to be shouting at Nick. He saw her look directly at him. He was indeed witnessing the great Jones Fall flood beginning. *My God, the flood would nearly destroy the down town*, he remembered. He had to get out fast, but first he came to the crying woman in the water and said, "Grab my arm, lady. I'll save you." She gazed past him. Trees crumbled into the mighty river and pulled her away."

As he watched the water take her down for the last time near the harbor, Nick heard another voice, muffled, yet sharp and demanding. That voice broke his spell, ending the visit. "Are you alright, mister?" It was a present-day policeman, who had pulled his patrol car up to the end of the street to investigate a suspicious man running, yelling and waving his arms about.

Nick was still stunned. He did manage to speak as the cop climbed out of the cruiser. Nick apologized to the cop, and added, "I'm in the Center Stage performance of King Lear, sir. Just going over some moves, practicing lines. Thank you for your concern."

"That so? Maybe we need to go to the precinct for a chat. Got identification, your highness?"

"I'm Nick Esposito. See?" he held up his driver's license card. "I am just in town to cover Pop's Tavern for my family this afternoon."

"Hmmm, Esposito, huh? Is Pop your granddad? Okay. No problem. Just be careful around the water, Nick."

The cop drove off leaving Nick sitting with wet pants down to his shoes on a piling. He hadn't actually gotten to the edge of Jones Falls. He thought, puzzled, *I hope my pants dry out on my way to the car and before J.J. asks about the missing Napoleon pastry.*

After that frightening visit, Nick watched for the tall ships further east along the Patapsco River off the Boston Street docks.

* * *

Previously, Nick had felt good fantasizing about historical events and during his occasional visits to the past, unlike the fear he felt during the flood visit. He truly believed he was seeing things as they had at pivotal moments of history, but even as an adult he didn't know why he could do it.

People close to Nick had their theories about his mind drifting. But, no one considered the obvious influence of his unassuming Lutheran mother Miriam and that the very careful and super-organized German/American mother was the architect of her boy's personality and lifestyle as a bookworm.

And this was not just his childhood life. Nick would always live in his history books. At each of his successive teaching jobs, he worked tirelessly building lessons from his reading, and then, freewheeling his students through magnificent history stories, while unconsciously working just as hard to run circles around the mandatory curriculum requirements that he hated. He strived to build far better, more dramatic lessons, which still technically touched most points of the curricula. His mind was just too creative to conform.

In college, he had quickly become bored with the slow intellectual pace of his education and turned to a Bavarian life as a dope-smoking, pot-peddling hippie on campus, while still excelling in scholarship. After college, while planted in the stacks of the graduate library, he wrote a dozen unpolished monograms on historic events in Maryland, but was never happy enough with them to send to Pop's professor friend at Johns Hopkins University Press. He also used to write fiction. By age 30 he'd nearly completed three historical novels, but was never motivated to get them published. He had difficulties helping himself, preferring to worry about others.

All of the frustration, piled up during his introverted past, somehow made it easy for Nick Esposito to resign himself to his new life, posing as that nice, quiet bartender people knew over at Pop's Tavern in East Baltimore. He was through. All his literary ambitions seemed like someone else's life.

* * *

He was not likely to sink any lower emotionally or go insane. Nick's saving grace was being anchored to good family, including outstanding male lineage. He was known by friends and family as the reserved, moody, and, yes, sometimes impulsive son of the gregarious Carlo Esposito, a successful food industry executive for Esskay Meats, Inc. Everyone knew Nick's lineage as the grandson of legendary Patterson Park sports hero and likable tavern proprietor Stephen "Pop" Esposito. And three generations back, Nick's great-grandfather, and Pop's immigrant father, was a famous Baltimore police inspector Michael Esposito. Everyone knew that too and Nick was naturally respected by family ties.

But, there was no such legendary career in store for him. However, in one way, Nick was like those elders: he always wanted to help people.

For a while, teaching worked for him. Now, the few people whose lives he touched while tending bar did benefit from his kindness and generosity. He didn't see it, but customers appreciated the kind, gentle Nick Esposito behind the bar tapping beer, mixing drinks.

Being at the tavern, Nick thought every day about his inadequacy next to dynamic Pop pictured in photographs all around him. He felt deeply that he'd failed and secretly wished over and over that he was more like his famous and fun-loving, tavern-owning grandfather in East Baltimore.

Pop still craved attention. Nick craved solitude, but he still clung to one deep and lasting link to the Esposito clan: his passion for Baltimore history, rooted in his childhood by the romantic and fabulous stories Pop told Nicky and his sister Kat.

Chapter 7: Janet Jeffries

Nick married Janet after his graduate school.

From then on Janet, known to friends as J.J., would be the steady hand on Nick Esposito's emotional keel. All she needed usually to steer Nick to reality was a reminder, "Nick, we need you, me and the twins. Don't drink and don't worry too much over your episodes. We are fine, if you take care of yourself, okay?"

She grew up in a dysfunctional family of painters, singers, musicians, and actors—three generations on her mother's side.

For little Janet Jeffries, life in childhood was fine at first. No, more than fine; life was magical, being part of her parents' musical careers—the parties, the travel, the money. She was their beautiful child prodigy, with the perfectly symmetric features of a young Elizabeth Taylor. Her parents groomed her to be a star.

That didn't have a chance of happening.

By age four, Janet was living in a house of turmoil.

By her adolescent years, she had lost the drive and resilient temperament that would have enabled her to follow her mother's performing talents into show business, despite Janet's own considerable singing, dancing, and acting skills. By the time her parents divorced, the once glowing spirits of Janet and her younger sisters were fogged over by despair and discontent.

As an adult, Janet would naturally then fear show business life, especially the drinking that ruined her family.

Lorraine Star, her mother, at one time had been a bright, rising singing star off Broadway and in nightclubs in New York. Lorraine gained initial fame singing in her hometown, Kansas City. There, she met trumpet man Paul Jeffries on tour. He was a regular in the New York's 52nd Street jazz clubs, 3 Deuces and Club Downbeat. Paul was a talented but temperamental musician from Glen Burnie, Md.

Lorraine's attraction to Paul was a blinding passion at first glance. But within only a few short years, the passion turned to bitter disillusionment for both of them.

The daughters endured their parents' endless screaming and arguments in their tiny apartment in Brooklyn as the couple turned more and more to drink. Their musical gigs diminished, and then dried up by 1965. Their inability to tolerate living together turned them both into alcoholic has-beens.

When Janet was five, Paul finally left Lorraine during the tumultuous summer of 1968. The U.S. economy suffered from a worldwide economic crisis in the spring and was followed by race riots and anti-war protests in dozens of major cities including New York. The clubs lost money and Paul had trouble supporting himself and his family. He and Lorraine tried to patch up a few times, but with little success. Being together turned their drinking troubles into resentment and blame of each other.

He finally fled back to his native Glen Burnie in a few years and moved back into the house he had been renting out while riding high on his musical career in New York. Reluctantly, Lorraine sent 8-year-old Janet to live with him, as his struggles threatened to curtail child support payments.

Young Janet kept house and cooked for her dad at the Glen Burnie house, until she left for college at Catholic University of America in Washington, D.C. in 1981.

In college, she at first deliberately sidestepped the school's outstanding drama department to major in pre-med. With plenty of care-giving practice with her father, she decided to become a nurse. Why not put the experience to use? she thought.

She could never forget, however, that during her childhood years, friends, relatives, and theatrical agents encouraged Lorraine and Paul to get the child with the beautiful face and powerful singing voice into entertainment.

It was only when Janet dated Nick Esposito—"the oddest-looking Italian I ever met," she'd always say—with his gangling body and reddish-brown hair, yet loving touch, did she take a chance on performing again. Nick's love was the ticket to allow her talents to finally grace the stage in the university's plays and concerts. She drew strength from Nick's kind and loving heart and his happy, stable family, the Espositos of East Baltimore. Nick was a gentleman, intelligent, and well on his way to becoming a fine educator, she thought. Her only doubt was his strange behavior of staring about and withdrawing sometimes among other people.

Chapter 8: J.J.'s Distraction

Again, that cool, misty Tuesday afternoon in October 1999.

At the same time when Nick's former student Jerry Marcus was visiting him at the tavern, J.J. was desperately making a telephone call to best friend Betsy Bowen from J.J.'s nursing job at Johns Hopkins Hospital. She told Betsy that Dr. Stuart Wellborne, a young handsome physician at Hopkins, would not be giving J.J. another ride home that afternoon.

Betsy agreed to come over at 5:00 p.m. to pick up J.J. at the hospital.

It was a quick drive for Betsy across the Orleans Street Bridge from her job. She was a social worker at St. Joseph's Community Services at Saratoga and St. Paul Streets.

The two women shared everything, especially gossip.

At the drive-up roundabout at the hospital entrance, J.J. was pleased to see Betsy's lovely smile of bright white teeth beaming against her dark-brown African-American face. J.J. climbed in her friend's black BMW sedan, careful not to scratch or scrape the impeccable gray leather interior.

"Hey Bet. Whew, feels good to sit down."

"Hey J.J., where's Dr. Dreamboat?" Betsy asked. She put the Beemer into drive and zipped away south from the hospital on Caroline Street.

"You mean Dr. Wellborne? He had to cover the ICU tonight," J.J. lied. "But it was nice of him to give me a lift yesterday. Couldn't take me home today again." Another lie. "Thanks."

"You're spending a lot of time with him, J.J., letting him drive you in and home again. Lots of time to get to know each other pretty well, I'd say. He doesn't even live in your neighborhood," Betsy probed.

"He lives in Severna Park, just down Ritchie Highway from us in Glen Burnie. He doesn't mind picking me up sometimes."

"Mind? Girl, I've seen how he looks at you. And it is more than sometimes."

"Don't be silly, Bet. Nick's schedule and mine are too difficult right now. I work three days from 9:00 to 5:00 at Hopkins, Nick works six days at Pop's, sometimes from 11:00 a.m. to 1:00 a.m. My mom brings the kids over if I can't pick them up in the afternoon from her house. As you know, we have one, old dumpy car, not like this luxury coach of yours and Nate's, and we need the extra money for the twins now. So, let's cool it on my new commuting partner, Stu, okay?" J.J. said. She clicked her tongue against the roof of her mouth and sighed audibly.

"Oh, Stu is it? The handsome and very available young doctor Stuart Wellborne? My word." Betsy teased. She smiled and glanced at her best friend.

Betsy considered asking how the commuting arrangement started but thought better of the idea, especially with Nick going through a difficult time. The women often talked about Nick's mental state since his teaching career vanished.

J.J. saw a troubled expression on Betsy's face. She closed the inquest successfully with, "By the way, Nick's doing well."

They arrived at J.J.'s mother's house and picked up her precocious, yet adorable five-year-old identical twins, Heather and Hilary. The little twin girls immediately began chattering in the back seat of the BMW about finger paintings they brought home from kindergarten. They asked their mommy if daddy could judge whose was the best.

"Your daddy will look at them and pick the winner tomorrow morning," said J.J. "This is his late day at Pop's, girls. He won't be home until you are fast asleep in bed tonight. Remember, I told you that." She spoke carefully, not wanting any questions about daddy and the bar.

Betsy then drove the three blocks to J.J. and Nick's small two-bedroom Cape Cod–style white house with black roof and shutters. Their home was lovely but marred by an overgrown, weedy lawn and untrimmed shrubbery. The house was at the far end of a cul-de-sac in a post-World War II community built expressly for returning G.I.'s and had belonged to J.J.'s father before he died of complications from alcoholism.

"Sorry things look so badly. I thought Nick said he was going to cut the grass. He used to like doing that for some weird reason I can't fathom," J.J. said with discomfort.

Betsy started to dismiss J.J.'s shame, but was interrupted by one of the girls in a demanding tone.

"You said Daddy wasn't going to work at Grandpop's for much longer, Mommy," Hilary barked. "Why can't he play with us at night no more?"

"Anymore."

"What?"

"I said 'anymore,' Hil. Don't say 'no more.' It's anymore." J.J. shook her head. "Not even in school yet and they are learning bad habits, Bet."

Heather said sharply, "Well? Can he play with us or not?"

J.J. seemed embarrassed by the spoiled twins.

"Stay with it J.J. Their parents speak well. The kids will end up talking like you and Nick all the time," Betsy offered.

Betsy joined J.J. for coffee at the kitchen table while J.J. started dinner and the kids went to their room. As Betsy seemed to sense, J.J. needed to talk again about Nick's despondency. "I'm worried about him more lately, Bet. He is so quiet about the situation. I'd rather he be fussing and fuming about being stuck at Pop's. We both think it was totally unfair each time he got fired. Stupid schools, three or four of them now; my God, I've lost count. And the students loved him so much. I met many of them.

"So, you said," Betsy said.

"Didn't you see the videos your husband Nate took in Nick's classroom that time? ... well, my Nick is a genius, I tell you. Now he's bartending to barely pay the bills. It's unfair."

"Seems so."

"Seems so? Is that all you can say? He is so bright, Bet! Last year he fussed all the time about his job at Pop's; about the way people treated him; about bills and other stuff. I could deal with that.

"But now that he's given into Pop and took over full time, I'm worried. He hasn't filled idle time well at Pop's or here at home. It's not like him. No writing. No new hobbies, just reads about history all the time and sulks. As the days are getting shorter, his mood is getting darker and darker. He's changed. He's morose, moody, Bet."

"Take it easy. He's always been moody. Hey, it must be that you hardly see him now, J.J.," offered Betsy. She looked crossways at J.J. "Tell me straight, girl, does Dr. Handsome factor in? The man is single, gorgeous and they say he owns a six-bedroom estate at Point Arthur, a thirty-two-foot sailboat, and pool house on the Magothy River, not far from your house in Glen Burnie."

J.J. slammed down a can of coffee grounds on the counter top causing some grounds to spill onto the floor.

Betsy continued, "Hey, I'm just curious, J.J. Have you seen Wellborne's big spread or just heard about it?" She looked right through J.J.

J.J. snapped, "No way."

"Oh, sorry."

"Look, Betsy. I guess I see Nick enough. We've got Sundays and days when he gets bartending help. I won't let him open by himself on Sundays despite the better business opportunity with the football games on the tube. He gets that cousin of Gus Triandos's, the old Oriole catcher—what's his name?—to bartend." She felt Betsy's stare. "Why do you keep up about Wellborne, Bet? I hardly . . . oh, stop. Whatever's stirring around in that curly cute noggin of yours, stop it."

"Oh, nothing," Betsy said as she looked down at her hands. "You know, Nick has always, as long as I've known you two, been kinda peculiar. This is probably more of the same." She paused while J.J. thought about it, and then risked saying, "J.J., you're a nurse. What's wrong with him, then? Is he manic, bipolar, schizoid, or just plain nuts?"

J.J. said, "His mom—God Bless her soul—knew him best, even better than me. And, she assured me often that Nick was fine. I think he still is. Okay?" J.J. walked away toward the bedroom as she unbuttoned her nurse's blouse, "Betsy, could you please pour the coffee for us and set it up on the kitchen table. I need to check to see if the twins are washing up like I told them. I hear the television. They never listen anymore; Nick lets them do whatever they want."

Betsy sighed, "I'm sorry J.J. if I said something wrong. I'll fix your coffee the way you like it, okay?"

J.J. soon returned in a loose casual shirt and slacks. She sat close to her best bud. The two had a pleasant chat, unwinding from their long work days, without another word about Nick. Or, about Wellborne.

* * *

There had been several times previously when Betsy, as a perceptive social worker, had tried and failed to open up J.J. about her oddball husband. Surely, J.J. had diagnosed him as some kind of mental deviant. Betsy feared for J.J. if Nick would ever go completely over the edge.

J.J. refused to discuss her husband's ways.

The only thing J.J. ever shared with anyone about Nick's state of mind was that perhaps his strange moods were outward signs of the chemical makeup in body due to stress. Any bipolar behavior, if he was bipolar, seemed mild, she would say.

Nick had, as long as she has known him, been able to handle his moods well, that is, until lately with his bartending dead end.

It was Nick's odd behavior that first attracted her to him in the first place. It was a sexy trait, she'd thought, when they dated. Once used to his strange ways, she loved nurturing "crazy Nick," whom she surmised correctly would, in turn, provide her with protection, what she most needed. She was comfortable being his soul mate.

Discussing his state of mind had previously been off limits for J.J. But more recently, J.J. was forced to suppress thinking about her earlier prognosis, because he was changing, apparently for the worse. She lived in denial of her own assessment of Nick's latest turn. What might happen to Nick if she didn't handle him gingerly, go along with his moods, and keep her family stable?

Chapter 9: Old Pop's Still the Man

Back in 1997, Nick and J.J. felt relief when Uncle Al and family managed to put Pop and Grandma Minnie into a senior "rest home" despite protests from Pop. Quiet Oaks Village was in Linthicum, not far from Nick and J.J.'s house in Glen Burnie.

The old folks would be taken care of, Nick thought. Pop could finally take it easy at age 94 and leave the tavern business to hired help. Little did Nick know at the time that he would be that help full time soon when he would lose his income from teaching at Glen Burnie High School.

J.J. volunteered to manage the Pop's Tavern books and Nicky boy "volunteered" to run Pop's beloved tavern. However, Pop as always, was not content. And he was still too clever for them.

The fly in the ointment of the family's rest-home plan was that Baltimore's public, light rail service built one of its rail stations next to the senior home. Uncle Al saw that as an advantage to friends and family to keep tabs on his parents. Easy for him being out of town to not consider the reverse possibility.

Until a mild stroke set Pop back late in 1998, the tough old guy took full advantage of the convenience of the rail line at Quiet Oaks to keep tabs on Nick and J.J. He'd slip fifty dollars to a pretty nurse's assistant. She would gladly accompany him on the light rail to Baltimore, her break from demands of dozens of needy seniors.

Pop would get an enormous thrill out of light-railing it to the city with a pretty, young nurse companion in tow and delight Nick by showing up unexpectedly at the tavern.

Nick felt differently about Pop's dropping in. After he took over the tavern, Nick hated Pop's surprise visits. He feared for Pop's health. He also dislike lying to Pop about how great the tavern was doing. He'd put on a good face, however, for his loving grandfather.

Pop would make his outing a multistep trip to his city.

87

First, Pop and his "date," he'd say, (Let the old man dream, Minnie joked.) would get off at the Camden Yards station just inside the city near the Pratt Street tavern Alberto bought for Pop. A quick cab ride three blocks later and Pop could check on renovations at the project he hoped to complete in his lifetime. The run down, converted row house had been a cheap purchase six years earlier when Alberto speculated on it for their father's investment. He studied legal notices and zoning ordinances. He could then figure correctly that the dumpy old tavern's economically limited neighborhood on Pratt Street, next to the University of Maryland Medical Center hospital would soon improve with the expected addition of a major-league ballpark nearby, the new Oriole Park at Camden Yards.

Later, every time Pop visited the new tavern on Pratt Street, Pop was frustrated with slow renovations for the restaurant side of the prospective new venture. He'd arrive with good intentions and greet the workers well, but seeing little progress, say "you bunch of lazy bums. I'm getting a new contractor. You're wasting my life savings." He never considered dying and not seeing it completed to his satisfaction.

Pop Esposito and his nurse's assistant would then be off to Pop's Tavern on Ellwood Avenue in a taxi, still without notifying Nick. Pop would be in an impatient huff. He'd always say, "Let's go surprise my boy Nicky at a real tavern." He'd say "the boy" loved his drop-in visits.

Arriving on Ellwood Avenue, Pop would burst through the tavern door, like an actor on a triumphant curtain call, and announce his arrival with gusto, even in the face of Nick's sour look.

Nick never complained. And he always loved Pop's stories he brought with him to tell anyone sitting at the bar or few tables, even if Nick had heard them a hundred times already.

* * *

By 1999, Pop was too week to ride the light rail into town. Still, he'd yearn to escape "captivity."

The staff at Quiet Oaks Village knew to watch him carefully for any escape in the works. But on Saturday mornings there were only the cooks and a skeleton staff on duty.

A second cup of coffee at breakfast at Quiet Oaks with the melancholy "blue-hair girls," as he called them, trading tales of dead husbands, didn't quite cut it for Pop. His old leg muscles still held some life.

Pop let everyone know he simply hated Quiet Oaks. "It's full of old people." After his stroke, Pop knew he was too unsteady to climb aboard the light rail train. Instead, he paid an orderly at Quiet Oaks to park his Cadillac hidden behind the Village garage for "when I want to see my boy Nicky."

Unlike his bumbling, shy-natured grandson, Pop made his own good luck during his entire life. No matter what he tried to do, he always succeeded. And if he didn't know the right path, someone among his throng of good friends would, even at Quiet Oaks. With no formal education past the fifth grade, his luck brought him fame and devotion from his city and a good living to boot. It showed. He still got his way with folks.

The irony didn't drift far from Nick's mind: he had a master's degree in American history and worked for the old scrappy man.

One Saturday in late October, after a late breakfast, Pop shuffled off from the common dining room to find his trusted orderly, his buddy Nurse Sam. He found Sam sitting on a stainless-steel prep table and flirting with young girls, who were busy cleaning up the breakfast dishes.

Affable Sam was not a real nurse. The residents called the nice Nigerian man Nurse Sam because he was so caring and smart. He had a civil engineering degree from the University of Ibadan and was in a career transition in America, he'd say.

Sam said, "Hey Pop, you're not supposed to be back here," said Sam, surprised to see the spry old geezer, his favorite resident.

"Who the hell says? And you're probably not supposed to be sittin' up there, boy. As for me, I can go anywhere I please, thank you," snapped Pop. Sam and the girls laughed. "Right now, I need you to take me to my tavern in East Balmer. I need to give my grandson a hand. He can't handle the weekend crowd. Come on, boy, get off there." He palmed two twenty-dollar bills and a ten spot into a handshake with Sam.

Once they were buckled into Pop's Cadillac Eldorado, Pop explained to his chauffeur du jour that his grandson Nick really didn't need help "back home," as Pop said, at the tavern, but just loved to have Pop visit him. "Perks the boy up, Sam," Pop said confidently. "Let me tell you something, young man. You got to be lucky as well as good at what you do."

Pop started telling Sam the same story he'd told many times to everyone at Quiet Oaks who helped bathe, clean, or smuggle food and beer to the that nice Esposito couple in apartment 101. "I was great at sports . . . and fighting too. But, that's another story."

Sam already knew both stories, but gave Pop an affectionate smile and nodded.

"When I was a young man, they gave me my tavern free of charge. You see, this brew master at National Brewing Company in East Balmer did that. They make National Bohemian Beer. It was during what they now call the Great Depression, though we knew it as the No Work years. I got lucky, see? Yeah, they gave me the tavern."

(The story held some truth. In the early 1930's, several investors of the National Brewing Company, which officially shut down during Prohibition, became great fans of local football and baseball on the expansive ball fields of Patterson Park in East Baltimore. Amateur ball was immensely popular at the time. Baltimore had no major-league baseball or football teams. At the park, there was a certain player in both the baseball and football leagues who was a conspicuous star with tremendous talents as a pitcher and batter, as well as a quarterback. Stephen Esposito, then in his late 20's and a veteran player, was far and away the favorite player in both sports with the fans.)

"Ya see, Sam, these men from the shut-down brewery, they still had lots a 'vestments. They had dough. So, they sponsored my team, see? They watched me play ball. In fact, people came from all over to see me play because God give me the talent. As a kid, I played my way right out of reform school just three years after my papa, Inspector Mike, put me there, causin' he was so grievin' when Mama died so young. I was always in trouble and Mike, he was my father, see, he had to put me in that place. But I soon played myself right out."

(The truth was that Stephen, though a gifted young athlete didn't play himself out of reform school at all. The police chief at the time convinced his young inspector Mike to remove the eleven-year-old boy to save him from the deadly "fever" that was sweeping through the school. Chief Police Inspector Michael Esposito was indeed grief stricken after his wife, Stephen's mother, died of the fever. Inspector Mike denied his pain by pouring himself into fighting crime and protecting the neighborhoods, wanting to help his community of southern Italian and other immigrants get a measure of justice against cruel and harsh prejudices in Baltimore. Consequently, he neglected young Stephen, who became the worst juvenile delinquent in the Little Italy neighborhood in East Baltimore.)

Sam asked, "So, if I understand right, Mr. Pop, you're saying that no matter how bad you behave, you can get away with it because you can play baseball?"

"No, damn it. I learnt. I learnt to stay out a trouble causa baseball . . . football too, 'cause I got so much attention, see? And before I was even a man I was playing on amateur baseball and football teams sponsored by National Brewery, which at one point shut down during Prohibition but kept the sponsor's name. We was called the Boh Sox.

"I was the hero in our tournaments. Boy, you think you can get girls flirtin' with 'em types dryin' dishes? No. Girls hung out to watch me in those games, tough and quick quarterback in the winter, star pitcher 'n homerun king in the summer. Yes sir."

(Pop neglected to add that the investors knew Stephen was the son of Michael J. Esposito, the savvy city police inspector with a magnificent crime-busting reputation. With Prohibition ended in 1933, the brewery re-opened and needed to generate business. One afternoon, the brewery managers watched Stephen Esposito pitch a one-hit shutout to win the city championship for the Patterson Boh Sox and get mobbed by fans as if he'd won the National League pennant. Sitting with Inspector Mike, the brewery officials cheered along with the crowd as the boy made an extremely rare unassisted triple play with runners stealing off first and second base; sprinting back behind the pitcher's mound to catch a looping batted ball, stepping on second for a second out, and tagging the runner coming in from first for the third out. "That's your boy?" they asked the famous cop, who just nodded. They asked Inspector Michael to tell Stephen they wanted him to try his skills in business. His father just smiled and said Stephen was his own man. "He's a bin that away since he was just a boy of ten, mister," was how he put it, in a strong Italian accent, "You ask him. You ask him yer selfs.")

Pop continued telling Sam, "At that time, I already had a job, but didn't like it too much. Papa had me working at the police headquarters doing odd jobs, cleaning up, learning to be a good citizen. Then, lucky for me National Brewery owned a bunch of new houses on Ellwood for puttin' in employees for the brewery. The end one of them new brick row houses turned it into a restaurant and commercial tavern. The first month I took over it doubled in business. They said I could have it."

"Wow, just for winning the city championship? I need to play some baseball, Pop!" Sam laughed heartily.

"Yep. My grandson Nick was a history teacher, loves the stuff. I tell him book learnin' is one thing, but now real history—them Patterson Park days and this here taverna, as ol' Mike, my papa, would say—is a better thing entirely, see?"

(In telling the story to Sam, Pop left out, or maybe had just forgotten, that there were some strings attached to Pop's deal with the beer investors, who took the majority of the profits. The deal

92

they made with him also turned out to be a great deal for the investor's share of the National Brewing Company, which opened after the liquor flowed again after Congress repelled Prohibition. As it turned out, Stephen was a natural genius in business, mainly because of his beaming personality. He made good dough for the brewery and for his cut. Years later, he bought them out.)

Pop continued, "Things went real good at my new job, the tavern. I loved it. People came in who knew me, some just to meet me. I had all my teammates helpin' out, too; some tended bar, some haulin' in stuff, some cleanin' up. The Natty Boh boys took care of thems, too. Then, once my two sons were born, people called me Pop because I always had our boys Carlo and Alfredo helping out, running errands and sweeping up. They called me Pop since theys babies.

"Turn left here, Sam. Here it is, Pop's Tavern. Now turn left to the alley to my parkin' space in back. We'll surprise the boy."

Chapter 10: He Just Left with Them!

Pop could hardly wait to see Nick. As soon as he eased out of his Caddy, Pop, all bent over and huffing, was pushing Sam to get to the tavern's back door to see his Nicky boy.

They came through the kitchen and into the barroom.

Pop was booming with delight, "Hello! It's me. Me and Sammy. Hey, who are you? Where's Nicky?" With no one else in the tavern, Pop's eyes came to rest on Clare. The cleaning lady wore a bright orange-and-black Gunther beer apron behind the bar, by herself.

"Nick's gone. He told me to watch the place for a few minutes. He's been gone since 'bout 2:00, though. Don't know why he ain't been back here."

Sam checked his watch.

4:15 p.m.

Pop and Sam were at a loss for words.

Clare spoke first, "Mister, do you know Nick? 'Cause I gotta get on home soon 'cause my grandchile, she's outa school, and 'cause I—"

Pop got his wits about him. "Wait, wait, stop yappin' a minute, lady. I own this place and Nick's my grandson. Where exactly is he?"

"Oh, you're Pop. Oh, my heavens, sir!" She came rushing from behind the bar. "Lemme give you a hug fer my family, hon. They just love you, Mr. Pop."

"Don't want no hug . . . well, okay . . . nice to meet you too, Miss . . .?"

"Just call me Clare, though most folks round here call me Late Clare, 'cause um always late, you know. I'm late now 'cause of yer grandson said he'd be right back."

"People'll think yer dead with a nickname like that, Miss Clare. Now, tell me slowly. Where . . . is . . . my . . . Nick . . . gone . . . to?"

"All I know is this blue and white school bus pulled up outside while I was cleanin' the winders."

"Wait, you aren't the bartender?" Pop asked.

"No hon, just Nick's cleaning lady. I says I'd watch the place, but then when he dinent come back, well . . . people wanted their beers, and I just . . ."

"Oh, I know the rest. God help me," said Pop. "Okay, and Nick got on a school bus? Where'd they go?" He back into a straight back chair to catch his breath as Late Clare explained.

"Well no, not right off. He dinent. This lady come in and she asked Nick if he knew where the Pagoda is, you know, the one at the park, I guess. He said he did. He knew her. She said they were from Perryville in Cecil County and brought the kids to see Baltimore, the sights, ya know."

"What kids?"

"The Girl Scouts. It was a whole busload of Girl Scouts from out there in Perryville, hon. That's what she said. Nick brought them all in for a Coke and sat right down there talking with this lady for a while. Then they all got on the bus and left . . . with him, too."

"That was when?"

"About two hours ago now. Hey, can you take over, Mr. Pop? There's men comin' in here for drinking. I got to go now, okay?"

Pop dismissed her, gratefully, "Fine, bye, Miss Late.

"Sam, you know how to tap a beer?" He acknowledged three youngish men in sport coats and ties now bellying up to the bar. "These fellers look thirsty. Hey, you fellers need refreshin'?"

Sam and an emotionally deflated Pop managed to serve the few customers who wandered in until 9:00 p.m., and then an exhausted Pop closed the tavern early and laid down upstairs in the living quarters, which. though a bit dusty, he and Minnie wanted still kept clean and available.

At 10:00 p.m. the phone rang. It was J.J. She was surprised but relieved that Pop answered. "Pop. It's J.J. Nick's been arrested by the port authority with a Girl Scout troop."

"Arrested?"

"Yes. And do you know Quiet Oaks has been looking for you since noon? You didn't tell them where you were going?"

"Nawh. Why should I?"

"Nate, you know Nate? Nick's friend? Well, he posted bail, Pop. They'll be back here soon, I hope. I can't believe Nick! He marched twenty Girl Scouts and their troop leaders from out in Cecil County right into a cruise ship from South America just as a drug bust or something was happening. Then Nick pushed a policeman into the harbor, Nate told me."

Pop was astonished. "What? Police caught my Nicky buying drugs for Girl Scouts going to South America? When? What? No, no, my girl, no—not Ni—" Pop was confused. He'd been asleep.

Sam ran upstairs and took the phone.

J.J. pleaded, "Oh, thank God. Sam, tell Pop he got it all wrong. Nick's not on drugs or buying them for Girl Scouts."

Chapter 11: Instant Classroom

Earlier that afternoon

Girl Scout Troop Leader Deb Schroeder knew exactly where she and her husband Delbert were taking the girl scouts. A little before 1 p.m. that Saturday afternoon, she turned to Delbert, who was driving the blue and white St. Mark's Church bus, and reminded him to stop at Pop's Tavern on Ellwood Avenue.

Mrs. Schroeder knew the place from her days teaching English at Glen Burnie High in the room next to Mr. Nick Esposito's history classroom. Before he was fired, Nick would often (much too generously, foolishly perhaps) host any teachers willing to come up to Baltimore at Pop's on Friday evenings after school. The practice added to rumors at the school that Mr. Esposito was a drunk.

Deb was now teaching in rural Cecil County and ran a church Sunday school in Perryville. She assured her little scouts that learning about the famous Shot Tower where they made producing shot balls for muskets in "Baltimore's wars," would earn a merit badge for history. She added that no one knew history better than her friend Mr. Esposito.

Pop's Tavern was on the way to the Tower; she took a chance he'd be there.

And he was there, leaning on the bar, reading.

Their arrival took Nick by surprise, but not for long. Those little girls were just the tonic he needed. When he recognized Deb, he said, "You've got to bring them in. It's clammy and warm outside today, Deb. I'll treat them all to sodas, anything they want."

Once they were inside, Nick asked the girls to rearrange the chairs in the bar for a little classroom, bigger girls at the bar, tiny girls cross-legged on the floor. Then he was off jabbering and delighting with the history of Baltimore, telling them exciting stories about the Shot Tower and Baltimore's role in three wars up to 1895.

97

"History badges?" he exclaimed. "Did you say history badges, Deb? Well, we've certainly got some history for them," Nick said. He felt the shackles broken from his bartending doldrums. He was once again Mr. Esposito, school teacher, and so he got off on Baltimore history for 25 minutes until Deb insisted they had to see the city sites before evening.

When the troop exited the tavern, Nick felt quite at ease hopping on the bus with them—for just a few minutes, at least, he told himself.

After the children took their seats on the bus, Nick told them the Shot Tower was next to Little Italy, where his grandpop grew up. "If I show you where Pop was born, I'd have to get back here quickly, though. It is just a few minutes from here. Is that okay with you girls?"

They cheered with delight.

He was pumped.

He directed Delbert Schroeder to drive to the old docks at Fells Point.

The tavern was immediately forgotten; he didn't mention it again.

Nick's mind found a hidden power source, all of a sudden, making him feel connected to life again. He got very excited. "This is the first port of the city, Baltimore's best-preserved historic district that began three hundred years ago," Nick announced to the scouts. "And this house on Shakespeare Street is where my great-grandparents Michael and Marie had a child named Stephen, my grandfather, Pop, on March 25, 1903."

He spoke nonstop. Before Deb could thank Nick and asked to take him back to Pop's, Nick lit another spark under the kids, "Hey, everybody off the bus!" Nick ordered. He bought each kid a sausage on a bun at the famous Polock Johnny's stand.

Deb kept saying he was being too kind, hinting that he had done enough.

No sir, Nick was just getting started.

She asked if he'd left the tavern unattended.

He half thought his fill-in bartender, was covering. "No, it's okay, Deb ... really." Nick had forgotten that part-timer Mr. Triandos was off that day.

Nick never gave it another thought. He was teaching history lessons again and loving every second of it. Nick was consumed with the eager faces of the children. He felt he needed to help the girls buck for their transportation merit badges also while they were there.

Deb stopped him just after he described Baltimore's pivotal position in the Civil War. "That's enough, Nick. We can find the Shot Tower." She was showing some concern for her friend, who was in a frantic state suddenly.

His eyes were glazed over and he was hyperactive like she had never seen Nick at school. Her words deflated him. Just as quickly as he had peak with excitement, Nick appeared to be tired and he slumped down to sit on the bus entry step, with his back to the kids.

Concerned, Deb didn't want to disappoint her friend who had been so kind. She turned to the girls. "Okay, then. Scouts, you want Mr. Esposito to stay for just a little while longer, to show you the famous landmark Shot Tower?" she shouted on the bus.

They cheered wildly.

Nick revived instantly.

He jumped up and faced the kids, ecstatic and soon was rambling on again with animated stories from the front of the bus, once even falling into the lap of Deb's husband Delbert as he drove the church bus.

After the Shot Tower, they swung all the way around the Inner Harbor, down Key Highway almost to Fort McHenry. Nick intended to take them to the Fort, where Francis Scott Key composed "The Star-Spangled Banner" poem from a British ship off shore during the fierce sea battle. It would be their next stop, he thought, immediately after showing and telling them about the historic immigration docks at Locust Point.

But unfortunately for Nick, they never got all the way to Fort McHenry at the end of the Point. He told them that after the

Civil War, the most historic import-export docks in the city's history were on the Locust Point peninsula across from the Inner Harbor. "This is where Baltimore built up its commercial and industrial muscles in the nineteenth century. Hey kids, see the tracks in the road?" No one else saw the tracks in the road.

Before anyone could question the invisible tracks, he explained, "In 1910 the Baltimore & Ohio had the largest railroad terminal on the Atlantic coast here, even bigger than any in New York. See the rows of tiny brick houses? Boarding houses for tens of thousands of immigrants each year in the late 1800's?

He knew the story well. His guests didn't know that Nick was actually beginning to see images of ragtag immigrants in the upper windows of the little houses and on the stoops. He was visiting the 1800's Locust Point.

"This is the envy of shipping magnates of the North because of the lower taxes on importing and exporting," he said waving and gesturing.

Each time Nick ended a dramatic and excited phrase, the Girl Scouts and Mr. and Mrs. Schroeder punctuated his performance with "Wow" or applause and cheers, interspersed with constant giggling from the delighted girls. Nick loved every minute of it and got more and more excited and immersed in a spell of his own making, seeing the long-past events as real, as he described them as a world bigger than the girls could ever have imagined seeing only the ordinary rows of small houses and paved streets.

"This railroad and shipping point covers more than a mile of waterfront. See there? burly, smelly longshoremen, they called them—oh, I can see them now—handling millions of tons of freight every year. See them girls, see them? There, see? This place is ... is always buzzing with trains, boats, and lorries—those are horse-drawn trucks. See 'em?"

"Nick, maybe we should get you back," said Deb. She shot a look at Delbert, who also noticed that Mr. Esposito was getting overly excited.

Nick was on a roll and didn't seem to know he had shifted into the present tense to describe what he saw, heard and smelled in the past. "And ships are bringing in in thousands of immigrants all the time—Germans, Hungarians, Italians, Dutch, Prussians—you name them, many in rags and carrying little more than the coats and shoes they came in with. Those from the south of Italy, including the Espositos, were poor and suffered horrible ethnic prejudice."

"Oh, Nick? Mr. Esposito?" Deb could not stop him.

Nick was glued to the bus windows, glancing back in a flash from time to time to engage the girls. Nick was not himself. As was his tendency when in such a state, he clearly had lost his center and was unable to know when he should be reverting to a more polite, interactive conversation. But just as quickly, something cued reality for him again. He said, "The Italian community here, Fells Point and in Little Italy where Mike raised my granddad Pop—that was his tavern where you had a Coke—was full of crime and protection rackets. Mike became a policeman to help clean up and protect his community from infiltration by a mafia in New York mostly called the Black Hand. His police detectives patrolled the docks here."

Deb Schroeder managed a word, "Nick, there is a pleasure cruise ship at the end of Hull Street. Hey kids see how big it …"

"Yes, Deb, that's a big thing now. Let's take a look, kids, shall we?" he was, for the moment, back with them.

When the bus pulled up to the gangplank of the Santa Monica Fiesta, Nick jumped off the bus and, with his back to the bus, slipped a twenty-dollar bill in a handshake to a young Latino man in an orange-and-green, sort of porter's suit. Nick had seen Pop do the money palming trick many times.

Nick swiveled on his heel and yelled back to the group, "Come on everyone, off the bus!" He hurried up close to Deb and whispered to the concerned scout leader, "That man is the captain of the immigrants' ship, and … and, he said we can go up and take a look," with a funny laugh, then he was sprinting back to the bus waving the little girls off and up the gangplank.

101

The girls were already shrieking in delight and running off the bus. They ran in one line up the red-carpeted six-foot-wide gangplank, a magnificent sight to eight- to twelve-year-olds from the country, though the railings were at certain points only flimsy hemp-like ropes tied to posts at every ten feet.

Deb chased after them. "Nick, oh Mr. Esposito, I don't think this is a very good ..."

Nick also failed to notice a gaggle of policemen looking down at him from the ship, aghast that dozens of little girls were running up toward them. Nick looked for the little man in the porter suit to practice his best muchas gracias, but he had disappeared as soon as he got the cash.

Nick could not have known that the police were accompanied by federal narcotics agents and a full search was in progress on board for drugs.

At the top of the plank, the girls went silent, dazed, and then were hiding, frightened, behind six or seven very angry cops.

And then when Nick reached the top, one cop, who was likely the highest ranking, wearing a blue shirt decorated with colorful badges, grabbed Nick and threw him into the arms of the others. He fell.

They pulled him up roughly.

Stupidly, Nick began fighting back because he was embarrassed in front of his guests, and not because he was altogether belligerent.

Deb was crying. "Delbert, I don't think he knew what he was doing or seeing here," she cried. "Get the girls, quickly. Del. Go go."

But Delbert stopped any thoughts of rescuing the girls.

He and Deb stood by their church bus watching in horror as the cops started forcing Nick back down the gangplank after the girl scouts ran back down first.

Nick was confused. All he kept hearing behind him was, "Just shut up and keep moving, mister," as they poked him with night sticks.

"You don't have to do that," Nick shouted when he reached halfway down the gangplank and looked around to face a cop poking him. Nick grabbed the nightstick to keep it from hurting his ribs any more. He and the cop tugged back and forth quickly on the stick, increasing strength with each pull.

Nick glanced down and saw the distressed Girl Scouts still watching him from the base of the gangplank. Embarrassed, he impulsively let go of the stick, sending the policeman holding on the other end backward violently. The big cop's body broke right through the flimsy roping. He fell into the drink some twenty feet below with a gigantic splash.

"Okay, cuff him!" Nick heard as he gasped, seeing the cop swimming below. Nick was pleased to see that the cop was okay. He thought of little else. Nick was shutting down like a wind-up doll and shivering cold. He was surfacing out of his 'visit' in Locust Point history.

The girl scouts were mum. They filed onto the bus. The bus drove off without another word from Delbert and Deb, or the kids, and before they would see Nick carted off in a police patrol car.

* * *

Later, 1:00 A.M.

She was good and steamed. J.J. sat Nick and Nate at her Formica table while she paced around her immaculate kitchen.

Slumping and disheartened, Nick looked at both of them helplessly. He was at a desperate end of his futile attempt to explain the unexplainable. He didn't remember everything about the wild afternoon. "I didn't mean to hurt the cop, J.J., I keep telling you! I don't even remember much about getting onto the ship. It was a cruise ship, they said," pleaded Nick. "Hey Nate, tell her what the officers said. Was it an accident or what?"

"Yeah, I think so, J.J. That is what the police told me at the jail," Nate said sheepishly, on the verge of laughing. He cared too much for Nick and J.J. to make fun of the ludicrous mess his best buddy got himself into.

"Jail, hmmph" She rattled some dishes and arranged some pots on the stove.

Nate offered, "Nick was just being Nicky boy, the history teacher. Can't blame him, can you? Those Girl Scouts came to see him. They came to see Mr. Esposito, the legendary history teacher. For a little while, he was back in the classroom, kind of a mobile classroom, doing what Nicky does best. That's what he loves."

Nick chuckled and quickly covered up his face with his hand. "Nice try Nate. That was almost as embarrassing as tossing a policeman into the harbor. But, forget it; she'll never buy it."

"You were drinking, weren't you Nick? Were you?" J.J. said, ignoring Nate's plea. Her mind was on another issue: Her greatest fear was living with an alcoholic, raising kids in a chaotic, unpredictable atmosphere as her own parents had created for Janet (J.J.) and her sisters when they were children. Although her mother later in life became a born-again Christian and teetotaler, J.J.'s tragic days stayed with her as her mom, just a few blocks away, was again entwined helping J.J. with the twins.

"No, of course not," Nick answered. "Not around these little kids. You know me better than that J.J.; I always put the kids, the students, first. I haven't changed, and I wasn't drinking today," he said.

Nick stared at J.J. as he wondered, *I've not changed; but she has.*

He did need to change the topic before he said something he'd regret. But then he said something he would regret, "I do remember seeing lots of poor folks with satchels, new immigrants, I guess. We parked our bus past all those people walking from a boat, so we could see the cruise shh … Oh, doesn't make sense, does it?"

J.J. detested Nick's fantasy episodes. She was reduced to whispering, "No, people in rags don't immigrate at Locust Point anymore, of course. My God, man, get off it; you must have been drunk. Immigrants. Oh, my God help us."

Nick read her eyes correctly. J.J. was sending a clear signal between them that Nate would not be privy to: 'you're lying and we both know it.' It was that look Nick recognized whenever he was in emotional free fall and would try saying anything to worm away from her accusing look.

As he stared back, Nick became doubly worried because J.J. was uncharacteristically restrained this time. *Yes, she is the one who has changed*, he thought. J.J. was not lashing out at him furiously as usual when angry about his dangerous and irresponsible fantasies. *I think she's done with me,* he feared.

J.J. turned to Nate and said calmly and firmly, "Nate, I think you should go. I'll call Betsy to tell her you are on your way. You've been a great friend as always, but Nick and I need to deal with this . . . this . . . whatever went on. We just need to talk. Goodnight."

She walked Nate out the front door and the two strolled across the lawn toward Nate's car.

She asked Nate, "What's wrong with him? This was nuts! Is he crazy now, too, on top of being a closet alcoholic? What am I going to do? I can't watch over him all the time. We've got kids now. I'm scared."

Nate was no longer in a mood to take Nick's episode lightly. He had tried that and failed. He was respectfully attentive to J.J., listening carefully.

He then admitted, "I'm a bit afraid for both Nick and you. In recent months, he has lost a lot, J.J. Why don't you do all you can to rally the kids around him before he gets himself too deeply into a rut? He may be there already and, by gosh, he seems so small and gaunt even though he is tall. Maybe he feels utterly insignificant."

"He's very significant," said J.J. "We love him. Everybody does who knows the real Nick."

Nate continued, "Yes, those of us who know him, but do we really know what's inside him now? From what you say, even you don't anymore. I've always thought as long as my strange and lovable friend Nick struggles to keep his independence as an individual of worth, he's fine. But I bet, if I know Nick, he thinks he's lost his place in the world. He might be caught in a tormenting conflict that he is just too proud to share, even with you."

"What can I do, Nate?"

"Do what Jesus would do, what Gandhi or Muhammad might do. Make him stop reducing his own worth, his separation from his old self as a unique and meaningful individual. Count on me and Betsy to help you. She sees a lot of depression as a social worker, that is, people showing anger, or vulnerability, or weak or dark spirit. But what's surprising to me is that she said she does not see that in Nick. He's a puzzle, says my Betsy."

He stopped walking and looked directly at J.J. in the dim moonlight. Nate then said, "We can help save him from conflict. Yeah,"—Nate scratched his head of loose African coilly-curled hair—"he might be feeling totally small, and might do crazy things, like the Girl Scout tour, out of desperation. We must help Nick. We're with you, girl."

"Oh my God, Nate. You should have followed your preacher dad to the pulpit, man. That was wonderful. Thank you so much!" J.J. gave Nate a quick hug.

"Hold on, sister. He might be watchin' us carryin' on out here in the dark." Nate let out a huge laugh, releasing some tension in both of them.

She turned, laughing too, and went inside without another word, determined to take their friend's good counseling to heart.

J.J. walked slowly into the house and was perhaps at a loss for the right words to say immediately to her Nicky.

Nick was still at the kitchen table. He worried that the blowout tirade, which Nick had expected from an angry J.J, never did happen. Instead, his good-natured wife just let him chill at the kitchen table. She patted him on the head and said good night.

Perhaps she recognized the pale, drained look on Nick, the scary, lost look he showed after one of his "moods." She also needed time to think. Any further lecturing could wait until the morning. She walked slowly into the bedroom and he followed, ashamed.

Nick fell asleep convinced she had given up on him. She'd be gone soon, like all else in his life, he believed. He was sure of that now.

First Interlude

Are everyone's dreams made of the same kind of stuff? Are they what we can accept as truth? Or just fragments of unfinished thoughts bouncing around the little gray cells at random? Nick Esposito's fragments were more vivid than those of other people. That night he dreamed . . .

There's that man. Familiar face and easy smile. He watches with great admiration at people coming down off that ship. Look at them.

Hundreds of ragged immigrant Germans amble down the ramp of the vessel. He sees their faces relax, eyes widen. First footsteps onto America.

He's mumbling, "Here I am at the docks at Locust Point, Baltimore, more than six thousand coming in just in this month of May 1889."

"Hey, Officer Mike! I thought you'd be here, checkin' in 'em Germans. Not enough crime over with the Italians?" It's a boy tugging at the policeman's uniform pants.

"Yes, helping to check them in and still they come," says the cop. "These are a good class of people, too, a welcomed group for the most part, like us Italianos. There is room for all, work for all, as long as the mills need hands, fields need tilling. But many of these will be tricked, boy, to stay in these boarding houses too long, lied to, and fleeced."

"How come you are over here and not in the Italian neighborhood?" says the boy.

"I have to check their funds, their money, give them an honest rail schedule to the city, to the factories in the West and farms in the South before these here landlords trick them with those phony

schedules and delay them way too long. These people are mostly helpless here in America, believe anything."

Gun shots shatter the morning stillness. The shots come from the nearest row of the immigrant boarding houses surrounding the docks.

He hands his clipboard to the boy. "Take their names, the Germans, please." But the astonished boy instead runs after the big cop who is already closing in on the house of the gun shots.

Now in court, Judge Hargrove asks the policeman, "Is this the weapon you found on the accused, Mr. Martin Houck, harness maker in the employ of Day, Smith & Company?"

"Yes, your honor, he is Houck, age twenty-nine, immigrant from Germany eight months ago."

Houck, sits quietly, remorsefully.

The policeman says, "He is accused of shooting his wife of just one month, the former Maggie Jones, after climbing into her boarding house window while she folded clothes, as witnesses said. He'd seen her former boyfriend, a musician, leaving.

Now on the stand, Houck says, "I asked if she would move to the boarding room with me now, take my name now. I don't know why I shot her. I love her. I love her, I love her. I do, I do, I do, I . . ."

Chapter 12: She's Changed

Nick was growling and squabbling into his pillow. "I do, I do . . ."

J.J. shook him. "Nick, Nick—wake up, Nick! Nick, you had a bad dream. You're sweating and out of breath. Where were you?"

"Ah . . . I don't know." He panted. "I might have been at Locust Point. It was different, though, sort of black-and-white and out of focus sort of, and it wasn't like yesterday at all. It was like an old movie and . . . you were there. She looked like you . . . her name was Maggie Jones."

"Oh, you've been in my family photo album again. Great-Aunt Margaret. They were all drunks or crazy, just like you, mister dream-head. I'm going to make you a Tension Tamer tea. Just rest there, I'll be right back." J.J., the dutiful nurse-wife, left the room in a sprint.

He thought, *How'd I ever get such a gorgeous and kind woman?*

Nick slept quietly until 7:30, when J.J., dressed for work, checked on him. "Nick, you didn't touch the tea. It will calm your nerves. Want it on ice, with honey?"

"I'm sorry about that Girl Scout bus thing, J.J. I ..."

"Never mind that. I've got to go. Dr. Wellborne is out front in his car. I set the alarm again for 9:30 for you, okay?"

But Nick couldn't go back to sleep. *J.J.'s not acting right*, he thought.

There was a time not long ago when she would never let an argument or issue go so easily. She'd lay down the law for his own protection, he always felt. She'd give him a tongue-lashing for days over his drinking, or for taking spectacularly risky history field trips with his students, or for losing himself in a cockamamie stunt completely out of his character, a welling up of the Esposito zeal for life so suppressed in Nick. J.J. would be quick to remind him not to try foolishly channeling his entertaining grandfather, the one and only Stephen "Pop" Esposito.

Lately though, Nick thought J.J.'s attitude toward him was changing. Of course, he was right. But her change was not about Wellborne, as he feared. It was Janet Jeffries' bitter experience as a youth that was at the root of a "change" Nick saw, especially following his Girl Scout fiasco.

She was more careful with him lately, for fear of the worst--that he would become a full-blown drunk. She watched for any signs similar to her parent's downfall in Nick's newly despondent state of not having a career of his own. She remembered that when her parents lost work, their drinking, fighting and despondence ruled them. J.J. was still very much in love with Nick though. Her "change," if any, was the continence of a sentry dog keenly surveying the landscape for threats. She had daughters now, about the age she was when her parents, Lorraine and Paul, were on top of the world in New York.

The morning after the girl scout fiasco, J.J. rode in to work with Wellborne in silence. Before checking into her nurses' station at Hopkins, she made a telephone call to resident's room 125 at Quiet Oaks. She was relieved that Pop himself answered and not Grandma Minnie or a staff assistant.

Pop tried to calm down his loving daughter-in-law, "I know what happened because that boy Nate Bowen called me first thing this mornin', Janet."

"They didn't get back home until midnight Pop. I didn't want to call you that late."

"Coulda. Always somebody needs something from me, any day, any time. It's okay."

"Nate said Nick is losing his identity, Pop. He is too smart to teach in public schools, too antisocial to work anywhere but at the tavern. Can you get him some help, so he can have some time to look for another job, please?"

Pop didn't speak.

J.J. asked, "Are you there, Pop?"

"Thinking, that's all," he said. "I'll make some calls to folks who owe me somethin'. Nicky is happy with the job; never said nothin' bad to me about takin' over there for us. Antisocial you say?" Pop said to lighten J.J.'s load.

"Well, you know. He's quiet. Okay, so he does like people. Pop, I just don't know what to do. I needed to call to say he is not hurt in anyway except his ego, I guess, after yesterday. That's all."

"Now Janet, you know there was more to tell Pop, don't you?" Pop said. "Tell me."

"He's too moody, seems distant. You know him best Pop. What's wrong?"

"Listen honey, I love you both very much. I hoped I never had to explain Nick to you. Hoped he'd change into a true Esposito, mix good with folks, you know. But it is too late for that and it is okay by me. And if it is okay by me, it better be for everyone else."

"I'm listening," J.J. said.

Pop paused as if surprised to be interrupted, but taking her anxiety into account, "I have come to believe that our Nicky is really two men. One of them lives in the real world. His world is quiet and he is not someone to be social, as you said. He can be distant, seem to be cold. But he isn't really."

"I know that."

"Then there is the other Nick we only see glimpses of, like what happened yesterday. There is a Nick who creates worlds all by himself. That is why he is a good story teller like me, and loves to live through the tales of history. His mother, God bless her soul, got him into loving history and I guess I told him a lot of tales too. Well anyway, it sounds to me that the two Nicks are a little out of balance right now, Janet. The creative Nick is bound up. I know. I think that is the one he likes the best, to travel back and see things only he can see. I don't really understand it, but I am sure Nick does."

"You mean he really believes he visits? I mean, oh, that is what he calls it when his guard is down. Visits ... to see things that have already happened in the past."

"We need to keep him happy, Janet. If not, he might spend more time visiting, as he calls his little trips. Okay, we can just say that it is all nonsense. Just a way of understanding. But, to Nicky, it is real.

"Now, back to our problem. I'll get him some bartending help so you and Nick can have some fun, let that Esposito side of Nick out sometimes, okay?"

J.J. said, "Thanks. I am so worried, Pop. You are right. He sees things, he says. I don't want to encourage that."

"Yes. He is really smart. What he says about those visits can be awfully accurate. I do know that, but we shouldn't encourage him that way. No, I meant, help him be creative with the family, not the past. Don't get too distant, spend time. Got it?"

"Well, okay, if you say so. Thanks Pop. I have to get upstairs. I'm at work now. See you soon." J.J. didn't want to buy into Pop's version of his grandson being two men in one. She needed time to think it over.

Pop probably figured that's why she got off the phone.

As she rode the elevator to the AIDS ward, she wondered how Betsy would react after hearing from Nate last night. She made a mental note to call Betsy on her lunch break.

* * *

Nate had woken Betsy as soon as he got home from talking with J.J. on her front lawn. He shared his worst fears about Nick, that Nick was now a danger to himself.

Betsy agreed with Nate's decision to remain abstract in consoling J.J. after the Girl Scout fiasco.

Betsy also agreed that Nick was in trouble mentally. "Before now, Nate, I didn't want to alarm you, but Nick to me has seemed to be truly lost for months. He may be going insane."

They vowed to help J.J. and Nick through the crisis.

* * *

The next day Betsy asked J.J. if she could give her a ride home—not to get around Dr. Wellborne's advances--but to get J.J. to talk about her and Nick.

Betsy, thinking more like the social worker, believed that Nick's occasional episodes were a severe personality flaw and that her best friend J.J. was in serious denial. She was prepared to say so. Their marriage had survived fifteen years of Nick's wackiness. Yet, as far as Betsy knew, J.J. had always refused to diagnose a sickness.

Over coffee again in J.J.'s kitchen, Betsy raised the issue of Nick's erratic behavior.

J.J. repeated what she always said, "Nick is just being Nick."

"But is he depressed? Is that what you think?"

"I don't know if it is depression, Bet, just resignation. I think he's given up on himself," J.J. admitted. "What do you think?"

"You two need to talk it out."

"I know."

Chapter 13: Nick's Special "Moods"

Indeed. J.J. and Betsy vowed to work on helping Nick. Since she first met Nick and especially after their marriage, J.J. was aware that Nick had some kind of infrequent visions, distant moods that were unpredictable, sometimes shocking, sometimes just entertaining, he'd say, but not so dangerous as the Girl Scouts and the cruise ship on a drug bust.

But, before the two women knew Nick, he had been on visits just as dangerous as the Girl Scout episode.

In one instance, it was on a cold December day when 19-year-old Nick was shivering with his dad at old Memorial Stadium in North Baltimore. Their beloved Baltimore Colts were taking on the Green Bay Packers, the best rivalry in the National Football League at the time. They sat close to the field in the lower-deck forty-yard-line seats reserved for Carlo Esposito by his employer, Esskay Meats, Inc. for "entertaining" buyers.

Taking Nick along with his dad was Miriam's idea, to help bring her two men closer together again. Despite the bitterly cold wind cutting into their faces and snow flurries, Nick was content with drinking beer and being with his father Carlo in the great 'company' seats.

The stadium was jumping. There was a capacity crowd and the Colts were crushing the visiting Packers.

Carlo spent more time talking with friends along from Esskay on his left. Nick on his right was quietly getting drunk.

Like all the Espositos, he tried to be as much an avid sports fan just like his Pop. The Espositos were especially fans of football and worshiped the likes of defensive all-pro Gino "The Giant" Marchetti and the greatest quarterback of all time, Johnny Unitas.

That Sunday afternoon with the sun dipping behind the bleachers by the third quarter, Nick was also watching two pretty, flirtatious teenage girls sitting quietly to the right of him through the first half.

They took a liking to him.

He considered them out of his league.

But the girls flirted and encouraged the shy young man to open up. He lost his normal inhibitions with women in his inebriated state and bragged about the game, his grandpop's rep in Baltimore Sports and the genesis of professional football in the United States. They were delighted and Nick got playful.

When his dad went to the restroom, Nick made a bet with the girls. With the Colts comfortably in the lead. Nick said, "Hey there, if Colts quarterback Johnny Unitas--that's him down there on the bench wai ...waeey ... ah, waiting to go in to play--so, here's the deal: He throws one more touchdown, I'll shake Johnny's hand."

Carlo returned and was pleased to see his introverted son acting like he was picking up girls. He pretended not to notice, but this was something new about his son. He tried not to laugh when he heard normally shy Nicky say, "Oh yeah, we are old friends, Johnny and me. I've seen him at my grandfathers' establishment downtown."

That was true.

They egged him on more when they saw Carlo approve. Carlo smiled proudly back at them and returned to chatting with his Esskay friends.

But Nick was already in a trance. He didn't acknowledge his father returning to his seat.

With the Colts' offense back on the field, their fullback Alan Ameche, another Esposito favorite, caught a swing pass from Unitas and plowed into the end zone for a score. Carlo leaped to his feet and began pounding on the backs and arms of the friends on his left.

Carlo didn't see Nick on his right. He was gone.

Nick left his seat entirely and ran down toward the field. In his mind and heart, Nick was feeling and living a pro-football life. He was one with the other players. He ran onto the field as

116

the crowd cheered into a frenzy. The great Unitas had thrown what proved to be his last touchdown pass for the Colts. Nick never reached Unitas. Instead, Gino the Giant himself left the bench and tackled Nick hard, knocking him cold. He was taken directly to the hospital with a concussion and broken ribs.

When Carlo asked later, "What the hell did you think you were doing, boy? These games are gifts from my company." Nick replied, "I don't remember doing that. I guess they waved me in off the bench. Seriously, Dad, I did all that?"

Carlo didn't like the little joke and gave the boy a weird look as if he wasn't sure Nick was kidding.

Through Nicky's adolescence and early adult life, Pop prayed often that the boy would not get injured when Nick lost himself, like his war protest in college or at the Colts game.

But Pop's prayers couldn't prevent Nick from embarrassing the family. He considered Nick's worst personality digression was when Nick surprised everyone by announcing he would plan his own party after his college graduation. Other boys had done it. Classmates had egged and dared the shy Nick into trying too.

Privately with no assistance, he went all out, as he expected anyone in the family would. Nick spent all his available cash to rent a party room at Valencia's Restaurant, one of the biggest and best rooms in Little Italy. No one could believe Nick booked a party. He refused to take offers to help. He asked his parents to invite everyone in the extended family and friends. They did, nearly two hundred family members and friends responded, mostly because of Pop's personal phone calls. The mayor was there. Three Baltimore Colt players were there. Even Father Brandini from St. Peter's.

The day arrived and Nick got cold feet. He didn't show up at his own party.

The next morning, he called his mother to apologize despite his nearly blinding hangover. He'd spent the night getting drunk by himself at the Tiki Bar Grill by the pool at the Princess Royal Hotel on the beach in Ocean City. Incoming ocean tide

117

woke him at 4 a.m. on the beach, where he was fully clothed soaking wet and cold due to the low ocean temperatures in June.

He spent the next month apologizing and trying to explain himself, especially to his proud and suddenly very angry grandfather, Pop, who had really believed this project of his Nicky boy was to be the boy's chance to show his true Esposito nature.

But later, Pop said to his wife Minnie, "We Espositos enjoy people, parties, eating, and dancing. Our poor Nicky is so different. But I do see his businesslike daddy in him sometimes, don't you? So, nothing to worry about Nicky boy," he replied to Minnie's ambiguous nodding. He added, "He's just not like us; don't know why in heaven; gotta love the boy, though."

"Yes, Stephen, yes," Minnie answered rather indifferently.

* * *

In his years with J.J., Nick's 'episode moments,' as she called them, had been very rare and certainly not as prolonged or quick to develop as what he did with the Girl Scouts.

She was convinced that the episode was sort of an escape from his captivity as Pop's barkeep during his dreadful 1999. She was tentative and gingerly with him. He showed no further signs of a breakdown nor did he stop displaying his bighearted smile and generosity around customers and friends. It was an act of course.

No one noticed, not even J.J. that the real Nick was slowly shrinking farther and farther back into being the introvert he had been in his teen and college years.

Chapter 14: We Need to Talk
Three days after the Girl Scout trip.

J.J. asked Nick to get a bartender to cover Pop's Tavern. The reason she invented was that she needed him to help her at home "with some things."

She sent the kids to school with Betsy and took the day off herself. She made breakfast for two and a full pot of fresh coffee before Nick woke up.

She sat at the kitchen table facing the bedroom. "Nick, we need to talk," she said as soon as sleepy Nick shuffled in wearing his robe and slippers.

"What about? Where are the kids? Oh, I knew it. You want a divorce, right?"

"Don't be silly. This is not about me. It is about you. People are worried; I'm worried about you lately, Nick. Pop says we need to spend more time together. Nate and Betty say you seem lost. And I can't afford to have you flipping out or destroying yourself, wandering off on history tours with buses of kids."

"You didn't answer my question, J.J."

"Betsy picked up the kids and took them to school for me. Sit down Nick. We love you." She got up and poured him a cup of coffee and put a plate of bacon and eggs with toast across the table from her where he finally decided to sit down, adopting a compliant but uneasy look.

"You think I was drinking," he said.

"With the Girl Scout thing? I don't care about that now," she said. "Since you stopped teaching you've crawled into yourself. I can live with your normal mood swings, your thoughtful concern for people you don't even know. But the twins and I can't take a chance on a guy acting like a ghost, a non-person we don't even know anymore. What is your problem?"

119

"I'm fine. Coffee's good, thanks. I just don't know how to feel about being stupid enough to lose my career, especially when my family needs me so. I'm bored silly. Just bored silly and disappointed with myself."

"That's good to say, but before now you didn't even want to share your thoughts with me. Am I not trustworthy?"

"It is not that. I don't want to burden you with my troubles. I'll be fine."

"No, you will not be fine. Listen to me, Nick. You cannot think you will be fine, like you were at Glen Burnie High School if, at any time, you are capable of flying off on your visits to la la history land."

She paused for emphasis, and then continued, "I remember you telling me that you stopped seeing things and people from the past. Nobody knows about this but me and Pop. But, it is dangerous to be that way with others. Don't you know—of course, you do; what am I saying—that people may think you crazy?"

"I don't tell anyone about that, except you. Haven't in many years. Well, maybe Pop a couple of times. ... You are right. People can't accept my gift."

"Gift? Well, okay; again, I can't have you doing that. Betsy says you seem to be getting too weird. Are you angry still about Glen Burnie High?"

"Never was. It was my fault. Maybe I was angry with myself for not seeing it coming; that's all, and just for a while. I'm over it."

"Do you feel lost and alone? Betsy says ..."

Nick perked up, "Forget what Betsy says. She has never appreciated me, accept as her best friend's husband. I'm not one of her social work cases."

"Do you feel vulnerable? You know, fighting off demons and bad thoughts about yourself?"

"More Betsy, right? No, I'm fine, I tell you. Just disappointed in myself. I should do better for you and the kids."

"So, you are telling me that your spirits are down, that's all?"

Nick nodded reluctantly.

J.J. tried probing for a solution, "Nick, I think your problem is that bar. Get out of there and find another teaching job, hon."

"I can't let down Pop."

"Call your Uncle Al and get him to agree to sell Pop's Tavern. Use the money to fix up the Pratt Street tavern. My God. The new Oriole Park has been open down there for several years and the new tavern's restaurant side has never been finished and opened to all those fans walking to the games right by the tavern."

"We don't have the money. Besides, Pop wouldn't let the Ellwood Avenue tavern go just like that?"

"Ask your uncle to work on him. Then teach again, please. You are driving me nuts with the silent treatment, Nick."

"There is no treatment. I'm not doing anything to you. And, I cannot teach anymore. I know now I don't fit into public schools."

J.J. stood up, exasperated and walked over to a little Sony television and VCR player she kept in the corner of her kitchen.

Nick asked, "What are you doing?"

"I dug out those videos you let Nate make of you teaching three years ago, in your classroom. I want you to see yourself at your best. Remember when you shared your secret with me, Nick, that you once had diagnosed yourself at an early age as perilously antisocial? And then you self-prescribed yourself teaching as the perfect self-therapy? Your form of biofeedback. I helped you develop that approach with acting methods. I'm part of this too, you know."

"I thought I got rid of those tapes."

"I made copies. You know something? I never forgot you telling me about your secret of seeing into history, a secret you never shared with anyone else. We were still dating. I believed in you and it worked. Teaching worked for you, bartending does not."

Nick objected, "You don't need to play those tapes for me. I'm an unexpected oddball in my family. That is what they say. You've heard it. I don't fit. So, I tried teaching. I don't fit there either. I don't need another reminder."

"You are a genius in the classroom."

"Yeah, only because of you. You taught me how to act as long as I had a captured audience in my students behind closed doors, and no one else around to judge and criticize me. I was grateful to you. But, again, the school system hated me. A lesson learned. I'm over it."

She changed her tact, "Nick these are like audition tapes, hon. They can get you another job."

"No. I'm not opening myself up to that again. My classroom was my foolish tonic to get as close to a normal life as I could get. That's all. Besides, the tapes were Nate's idea. He sat in the back corner of my classroom with a camera after he won that stupid bet with me."

"You didn't tell me about any bet. I thought it was a tool for your resume. If that was so, it was brilliant."

Nick elaborated, "I had Jeopardy on the tavern TV one day. Nate came by... Hmm, probably to see if I was doing myself in, as you say."

"Stop it."

"The category was famous black women in history and I bet him I knew more about it than he did. Nate trapped me. He said that if he won, I'd let him tape me in the classroom. He told me I might need some professional help to become a better public speaker because I am so shy in public. He was bullshitting me and I didn't buy that.

"What he really wanted was for me to be his guinea pig for a class he teaches in public speaking at Morgan State University, which is okay by me, of course. In that class, he uses video analysis student-by-student in his own classroom. Surely, I could benefit from the same method, he said. I agreed because I thought he would never win on history facts. 'Come on, Nate, bring it on,' I said. But he won. It must have been a rerun he already saw. Darn if he didn't get every single answer correct."

J.J. laughed and said, "So he taped for two days in your classroom and instead of seeing a pathetic shy nervous Nellie. Nate saw a Nick Esposito on the video he never knew about you, right Nick? A polished pro, thanks to our training, right?" She was delighted for the extra incentive, giggled a bit, then popped in a tape.

They watched.

Mr. Esposito of the video gave stimulating lessons on the feud between two of the richest Americans of all time: railroad tycoon Andrew Carnegie and Oil baron John D. Rockefeller, between 1870 and 1900, Nick's favorite period of American history.

One day Mr. Esposito dressed the part of Carnegie in a graying fake beard, black suit and bow tie, which Nick tied himself. He taught the kids about the greed and insensitivity of Carnegie during the great steel workers strike. He described his folly in helping to form the South Fork Fishing and Hunting Club retreat for the wealthy upriver and behind the dam that eventually collapsed, flooding Johnstown, Pennsylvania on Memorial Day 1889 and killing thousands of people.

The following day Mr. Esposito played a ruthless Rockefeller in a double-breasted dark brown suit and neck tie, while wearing the arrogant smirk characteristic of the billionaire. Nick told the kids how he founded America's first oil company, Standard Oil, providing oil to light homes. He gave details of Rockefeller's predatory pricing, collusion with railroads, and wide-scale bribery of government officials.

In both lessons, Mr. Esposito sat down close to the students to wrap up with a perspective that the two men essentially helped create the foundations for modern industrial America and, following passage of anti-trust legislation in the Teddy Roosevelt administration, formed philanthropic foundations that still exist.

When she finished playing the second video J.J. pointed at her husband, whose posture was repulsive to her—his hands folded on his head, leaning back and looking rather sickly. "Hey Nick, come off the sour looks. You were great. And, that feud, you know, between Rockefeller and Carnegie? I never heard of that when I was in school."

Nick replied, "Yeah. Well, those lessons were not in the public-school curriculum that way. And bingo! You hit right on it. You made my point for me. That is why I'm not teaching anymore."

She cherished the videos, yet at the time Nate taped them, Nick made her promise not to share them.

The video performances reminded J.J. of the first time they met. "Nick, you never act that way that you do in the classroom, except when the first time we talked." She cherished the memory. It was the day when young Janet Jeffries (J.J.) caused young Nick Esposito to come out of his shell. Nick's intense, excitable awakening that day 15 years earlier, would pay big dividends for J.J. and Nick, and the entire Esposito family, because of the couple's lasting relationship.

"Yea, that was a special day for me too," Nick smiled remembering meeting the girl of his dreams.

That most rewarding, rare and bold episode happened to Nick, completely out of the blue for the mild-mannered, reserved graduate student. That day, he found strength to miraculously charm and capture the heart of the most beautiful girl to ever cross his path: Janet Jeffries.

Nick began to daydream about that day. J.J. said abruptly, "Okay, you got my point, right? I hope you can teach again. It would be good for everybody. That's enough talking. Get yourself dressed and I'll drive you up to Pop's. Just don't forget what I said."

He already had forgotten. Nick spread out across their bed again and relived the best day of his life.

* * *

Nick remembered it as an otherwise ordinary evening at Ledo's Pizza Restaurant.

He was in the midst of his first career change. After several less than fulfilling years of teaching English literature and grammar, Nick applied for an opening in history education in the Baltimore County Public School System. When he was not hired, Nick returned to the University of Maryland campus at College Park for a master's degree in American history to increase his value.

Meanwhile, Janet Jeffries was settling into a second semester, freshman year at Catholic University of America, on Michigan Avenue in Washington, D.C. Socially awkward Nick Esposito and pretty Janet would meet by chance, or perhaps fate, or a blessing, at Ledo's halfway between his apartment at the College Park campus, and her dormitory at Catholic.

Janet had never been to Ledo's.

Nick only knew the place for carry-out during his undergraduate days, but had never dined there. He happened to be there that day because he was dragged to Ledo's by old acquaintances. When Nick pushed open a classroom door earlier that day, he heard someone yell from down the hall, "Hey, there's ol' Nick." It was Willie Chilcote, a huge Baltimore Colt fan who had known Nick all through grade school. He didn't know Nick well but he was a classmate and Willie said Nick was a sight for sore eyes, just to be sociable. Football had been the only thing Willie ever got Nick to talk about. Willie was wiry and hyper and already balding at 31. "Hey, man, how about getting together with me and a few friends after class at Ledo's."

"I don't think …."

"Come on, let's catch up on the Colts."

Nick politely declined again. Chilcote had always made him nervous. After class, Willie buttonholed Nick again and insisted they talk about rumors of the team being sold to another city. That annoyed Nick, but he figured Willie knew what the team was up to. Nick agreed to meet Willie at Ledo's in the evening. He considered not showing up.

125

The original Ledo's was a favorite getaway for college kids. Ledo's had great pizza, a great variety of beers, and was a restaurant, which later franchised across the region into separate pizza parlors that never had the ambience of the original spot. On one side of Ledo's was a long bar, which reminded Nick of Pop's Tavern. When he was an undergrad, he'd pick up carry out food from that side and imagine Grandma Minnie coming out of the kitchen with a tray of steamed Chesapeake Bay crabs.

That evening Nick felt guilty about not going, so he changed his mind and arrived later than the others. Nick and Willie with two of Willie's friends settled into a table at the back of the restaurant side where Nick had never been. Still, the aroma of beer and food was reminiscent of Pop's. Nick felt somewhat comfortable.

At Catholic University, Janet had just begun studying human services before committing to nursing studies. The day she met Nick, Janet and four college girlfriends came waltzing and giggling into Ledo's together. It was early on a Friday evening and the restaurant was packed and loud, with mostly young customers.

After just finishing his first National Boh, Nick was already feeling good when he spotted Janet, a breathtaking, brown-eyed beauty with auburn hair to the shoulders, coming into the restaurant with her friends. He had previously, from the carryout window many times, spotted attractive female students coming to Ledo's. But this girl was special, spellbinding. She caught him looking, and he kept right on looking and was not shy about letting this girl see him staring. She came closer and closer to the table. His heart was racing. His head, perhaps his soul, was calmed by her gaze back at him. He had never felt such an effect from a female.

Owner John Beale, in a tomato-stained white apron, seated the girls at the only open table, which was right next to a table with Nick and his three unlikely drinking buddies. As the girls were seated, Nick noticed the man in the apron lingered at their table. He seemed to want to retain the attention of the

126

attractive young women. He offered them menus and handed them out very slowly and deliberately, keeping their attention longer than perhaps necessary.

Seizing a chance, Nick gave a signal and a discreet wink to Willie, to go to the bar for another round of beer, even though a new round of beer had just recently arrived for them. They both understood that Mr. Beale was not about to notice their needs for a while.

Nick was surprisingly determined. The second Willie left his chair, Nick faked standing in a courtesy gesture to the girls settling in at the next table, and then switched himself quickly to Willie's seat. That put Nick near the beautiful brunette. The switch was made before Janet or the other girls were finished ordering. They didn't notice the two young men maneuvering.

Completely out of his nature, Nick spoke immediately to the girls, mostly addressing the two across the table from Janet, so as not to intimidate her and maybe she'd see or hear something she would like about him. A long shot, but she was worth the try, he thought. For once, he was not at all nervous.

He was more determined each time he caught a glance and soon he simply felt her near him in spirit.

He offered to buy the girls a round of beer. They thanked him for offering but declined with polite half-smiles.

As the four girls began chatting among themselves, only Janet turned to Nick and said, "Thank you so much. You are so kind." She spoke and looked only at Nick, not the other girls nor at Nick's buddies.

Nick's heart melted. He loved the new found feeling.

She seemed to see something in him, Nick thought ... and hoped.

Janet had the sweetest voice he had ever heard. And no, he was not intimidated, shy, or lacking the words he needed to keep her engaged. Nick dominated the conversation, something he never did, for two hours and kept Janet laughing.

He later remembered little of the conversation, but felt sincerely he had made the right move, brazen perhaps, bold sure, but the best 'move' of his weird life.

When he asked for her telephone number she declined, but she offered to take his number, saying she didn't like to give her number to "boys" she didn't know. Nick tried not to laugh, and found her logic charming.

Nick spent many hours that night sorting and mulling through feelings he'd never quite experienced. Why did this girl move him so? His take on girls had been rather flat and matter of fact. Either there was eye-catching beauty and little else or an occasional strong sexual attraction such as a needy school librarian he dated while teaching in Baltimore County or a studious but handsome girl with a fine figure who had tracked him down in the college directory following Nick's daring act seizing the moment when he prevented violence at the Vietnam War protest.

His reaction to Janet was unique. She set his heart on fire, not his libido nor his empathy for another person. He was astonished by himself, how free and relaxed he felt. It was as if this girl opened an entirely new and bright chamber in Nick's haunted mind, pushing aside cluttering history stories and images to open previously unknown abilities he perhaps inherited as an Esposito. Maybe Nick Esposito wasn't so dull after all.

But he had failed to secure her telephone number or even her last name. He went to bed thinking it was all for naught.

She called him at 7:00 a.m. the next morning from her dormitory, Spellman Hall at the Catholic University campus.

For the remainder of his life, despite anything else he ever did, Nick was mostly proud of himself for that encounter, making it happen, how he had asserted himself and found his soul mate, his J.J. Nick would always feel completed with his J.J.

* * *

Nick's bold play for J.J. led to several years of dating without him making a marriage proposal.

He wanted to go on forever dating his girl. He lacked the same boldness it took when it came to the subject of marriage, or even a wedding engagement he could still run from if need be. They dated on weekends for the four years she attended Catholic University. In her final year, he would also take her to her nursing rotations at Children's Hospital, which was a short ride close to her campus. Also, anxious Nick would often show up at the hospital for coffee or lunches, not bearing to be without her a full day. They also dated for a year after she graduated.

Nick got a master's in American history and nailed down a teaching job at a high school in Bowie, Maryland, in Prince George's County the same county as his College Park apartment was in and near his love.

She continued working at Children's Hospital for a year after she got her bachelor of science degree in nursing at Catholic, and all that time, Nick never asked her to marry him. He was afraid she'd say no.

J.J. was not so patient.

He felt blindsided when J.J. told Nick one day that she was going to interview for a better position at Holy Cross Hospital in Chicago. One of her former Catholic University professors, who had also dated her a few times, was then at the Chicago hospital and promised J.J. that he could get her established. She told Nick it was right for her.

Nick was desperate. He didn't want to lose her. But still, he believed he didn't deserve her. He'd ruin her because she already knew that he was a head case. He argued for her to stay and keep things the same—selfish yes, but it was consistent with Nick's lifelong social incompetence and low self-esteem.

But Nick was also bright. He put all his conscious hours into trying to convince her that holding just a bachelor's degree would not help her much in a new hospital system. "Plus, working on the south side of Chicago is not the place to go right now, J.J. It is not you at all."

He didn't see the selfishness in his arguments. Nick knew because he was not socially at ease like other men in the Esposito

129

family were, he had simply gotten very lucky to have a woman like J.J. drop into his lap. He wasn't about to lose her to "an old friend," as she called the former professor, nor to Chicago.

I need her here. She just can't leave, he thought over and over at night.

He set his mind on minimizing the jealousy killing him inside. He finally convinced his girlfriend that her best bet for advancing in her career would be to return to college for graduate school to get a master's degree in pediatric nursing. She loved helping children. Nick was manipulating their love life and felt regret.

She agreed.

He thought incorrectly that she bought into his rationale for the best opportunity in her future. In reality, after all the talk, the deciding factor was their desperately strong physical attraction for each other. Her passionate attraction to Nick Esposito was perhaps too intense to shut down.

J.J., in her heart, couldn't bear to lose Nick, either. She needed his devotion, his solid family, and his love. She stayed and earned a master's degree in nursing and moved into Nick's apartment.

Six months later, Nick was fired from Bowie High because of far too many late mornings and absent days, according to school officials. But it was mostly due to his drinking.

For the first time J.J., now stuck with him, got the full taste of his cavalier attitude over his drinking and losing his job. She took it as a sign of an alcoholic. J.J. then had serious doubts about their future and announced she would move out it he didn't quit.

"Look, I'm not worried, why should you," he told her without thinking. Seeing the hurt on her face, he realized he was revealing his selfishness. "I'll get another job teaching; believe me J.J. I will, I swear."

He knew he had potential to be a good teacher, but outside the classroom he didn't talk about his teaching. She wondered why. No one saw his abilities, not even J.J., who was turned off by his lack of commitment to any goals and direction, not to mention his fondness of drinking.

J.J. resisted thinking about a marriage that might end like her drunken parent's split.

Nick didn't share his teaching days with her because he paid a heavy price at Bowie High. In the eyes of the school leadership, Mr. Esposito showed little ambition. Of course, he was unaware of their probing into his behavior at school. Nick's insatiable intellect wasn't satisfied by the confinements of the high school history curriculum. Mostly he hated the public-school system for its lack of a safety net for the needy child, lack of flexibility to support adolescents who would fall behind in studies because of emotional or family problems.

He frequently did the decent thing, in his judgment, by tutoring the slower students, meeting their parents if they had parents, and even bringing one or two of those kids home sometimes for some of J.J.'s superb home cooking and some well appreciated TLC.

Again though, what did him in from the Prince George's County school system's perspective, though, besides disapproving of his methods, that is, his close personal relations with the kids, was that the school officials suspected Nick was a drunk. Nick had built more barriers of denial than a lustful Caesar feasting as the barbarians reached the gates of Rome. Nick thought he had hid his still modest drinking habit well.

A decision on Mr. Esposito's employment came down to the principal giving Nick three warnings about calling in sick far too often—thirty-four times in the past year. The principal finally recommended to the county school superintendent to allow the principal to dismiss Nick.

While at Bowie High, Nick feared that his principal, who was African American, was determined to replace him with a "brother," Nick thought. For once, unfortunately, he read people correctly. The new history teacher who replaced Nick was not only an African-American, but also was a former Howard University classmate of the principal.

As Nick was clearing out his locker in the teachers' lounge two days after his dismissal, the new teacher showed up with confidence to resume his acquaintance with Nick's history classes. He had already substituted for Mr. Esposito ten times. Nick felt no resentment and wished his replacement well. He knew he had done himself in.

The root cause of his lackadaisical attitude was difficult for him to explain to J.J. Whether intimidated by the system, trying to live up to expectations of his famous grandfather Pop or his successful business executive father, or just wallowing in discontentment, Nick was shrinking within himself for the first time again since meeting J.J. And he was not aware that others could possibly see him as irresponsible. As he later experienced at Glen Burnie High and other schools, it was a social dragnet that snagged him when he least suspected.

Chapter 15: Tempted

Late November 1999

Several weeks had passed since J.J. conducted her anxious kitchen talk with Nick and highlighted her effort with Nate's videos. She saw no change in the remorseful Nick, however.

In fact, her stern advice seemed to have had the opposite effect that J.J. had planned with Betsy, with the video tapes, with her consoling of Nate and Pop, or after all the worrying.

The impressions of her tone, her anxiety stuck with Nick. Instead of giving him resolve to feel better about his life, her words, over and over in his mind, fueled his paranoia of losing J.J. He carried with him an open soar in his paranoid mind that festered into a private stage of complete, no-turning-back delusion. The mental take over was so dominant that he had no visions, no visits into the past, no fantasies as he read leaning on the bar at Pop's Tavern. He could hardly drive his car or tap a beer without drifting into a pit of suspicion.

At home, he imagined her attitude change badly toward him—from the good, obedient wife to the firm and determined watchdog. It was profoundly worrisome. He was still embarrassed and ashamed over the Girl Scout incident and, to make matters seem worse, J.J. resumed commuting with young Dr. Wellborne.

Nick began seeing disturbing tendencies in J.J.'s approach to their relationship.

She had been distant in church Sunday, and then scurried off shopping, supposedly with Betsy, for the entire afternoon. She served leftovers on Sunday night, not her habit at all. She was resisting his affections, and was showing rude impatience with his lethargic moods. "Nick, please get with it and find better employment. You can still teach!" Her usual pleasant voice seemed sharp and embittered.

Those days, Nick drove their only car, which was a black 1981 Toyota Tercel, from their house to Pop's Tavern. And, three days a week, J.J. left the house earlier to ride in ordinarily with Betsy or Wellborne to her job at Hopkins. All too often lately in Nick's mind at least, she was riding into the hospital with "that Wellborne fella," as Nick called the handsome physician ten years his junior.

He could not forget that on the same Monday morning after the Girl Scout fiasco, she had flown out the front door for Hopkins, leaving him still pathetically apologetic in bed. She was surely unhappy with him. He had gotten up in time to see her laughing as she jumped into Dr. Wellborne's silver BMW convertible sedan with tinted windows for a ride, hopefully straight to Hopkins. But, maybe not.

But, Nick misread his companion.

Far from wanting to leave Nick, J.J. was forever grateful for his kind heart and deep-rooted values and morals that he carried from the fun-loving, gregarious Esposito family. They were great for her little daughters. And she was grateful for that also.

* * *

As the autumn days grew shorter and darker in 1999, Nick let his worries build as he waited for customers at the tavern. He'd get uptight, anxious, and then panicky. He was going to lose his once-loving wife, or soon lose his mind, whichever came first, he thought.

Nick was often tempted to drink. He was drifting close to an alcoholic relapse. It would break a pact he made with himself to never drink while bartending. It was an obligation he felt to Pop to stay sober minding "the prison" in which he was both an inmate and the warden.

But late one of those short autumn days, with no customers for the past hour, temptation was eating him up. He could surely sneak just a little nip at the tavern when no one was looking. But he was torn. Liqueur on his breath could mean J.J. would throw him out without visitation with his kids. She'd leave him for Wellborne.

Nick held back until late in that afternoon.

He opened Pop's display case with 20 antique liqueur bottles Pop had collected as mementos through the years. He stared at Pop's prized, hundred-year-old Dutch absinthe in an ornate bottle decorated with tulips and pigtailed blonde maidens. That particular bottle represented the ultimate taboo for breaking his pact not to drink while running Pop's Tavern.

The absinthe was sealed for eternity, or "Maybe one day until an auctioneer will stumble on in here and see how valuable it is, Nicky," Pop had once reasoned.

Pop's policeman father Michael Esposito had given the absinthe bottle to young Stephen to keep after federal agents, added by the inspector, raided a speakeasy in downtown Baltimore during Prohibition.

The antique bottle had always fascinated Nick. He could imagine seeing Inspector Mike demanding the doorman to open the speakeasy before he perhaps ordered cops to bust down the door. Nick could see images of that splintered door, hear women scream and whiff the scent of liquor and thick tobacco smoke in the place. Nick still had his visiting capacity if he bothered to feel it. He desperately needed some excitement in his life.

All he saw was the absinthe splashing inside the dark glass bottle. Yet, he could faintly taste its anise flavor in his mouth already. Nick stood frozen, staring at the old bottle that had been sealed tight for many decades. He reached for it. He was thinking, *Oh, hell's bells, Pop's too old to ever know now.*

Nick was familiar with the black licorice taste and powerful kick of absinthe from his graduate school days at College Park and the pseudo-hallucinated drunken state it could deliver. His imagination actually created a far more dangerous high than a drink of absinthe might deliver.

He had the old bottle in his hand when college boys from Loyola University burst into Pop's and demanded beer to celebrate their rare lacrosse victory over Hopkins. They were already lit pretty well. Nick just smiled appreciatively and said, "Thank you God."

"Hey, Mr. Nick. So, glad to see us, huh?" said one boy. Another said, laughing, "No need to bring God into it, my man. He has been with us all day. Here's to Loyola."

Nick gave them a free round for the toast. He asked the college boys to tell him the entire story of the game, as he quietly closed and locked the display case, with the antique liqueurs still sealed tight, for the time being.

They stayed for an hour and left the tavern empty again.

Nick needed a hug. He closed early and as he drove home to J.J. in Glen Burnie, he felt extremely proud of his willpower.

He embraced her tightly before taking off his jacket.

"What's this? It's not my birthday," she said a bit too sternly for Nick's taste.

"I nearly had a bad accident, and I was thinking of you, you and the kids, and I'm just glad I made it home safely. And I . . ." He rambled on as if he'd been drinking. He couldn't understand why her face then turned from delight to disgust.

Nick vowed again to himself never to be tempted at the tavern.

Chapter 16: A Party for J.J.

A few days later, the ever-present Nick Esposito was a fixture tending bar for no one again, leaning one elbow down, reading something. No surprise there. But on this day, he was reading only a piece of paper.

A few minutes earlier, he found another brochure from the Belvedere Hotel in the men's restroom. It was again advertising for parties there. The brochure was not the same as the one left on the stoop weeks ago marked, FOR MR. NICK. Nick remembered tossing the first one away. And Clara the cleaning lady always emptied all the trash regularly, including the men's room. He couldn't figure how the second Belvedere ad got into the restroom waste basket.

It was different, but also marked. In the same handwriting, also faint and indistinct were the words, PLEASE COME, YOU MUST.

The men's room had not been occupied.

Nick mumbled, "No one's gone in there yet. How did this get in?"

He had been denying that his mental state was deteriorating bit by bit every day. He was clever enough, however, to conceal his despair on the job by talking to the few customers each day, his special brand of self-therapy.

After all his troubles, Nick still believed he was a natural philosopher, an intellectual, an amateur historian only to become overwhelmed by the consequences of his own mistakes and some bad breaks. But this thing was something else entirely: Reading the Belvedere Hotel brochure was troubling in its obscurity.

He talked to his image in the bar mirror, "I'm nuts or cursed or something? Who is doing this to me? These Belvedere ads. I've never been there. This is not normal. Who am I anyway?"

He put the paper down and felt like crying, but could not be seen in such a state. He thought, *I can't fit anywhere in this damned world. I wish Pop was still around to help me now.* He then thought of his dear mother, then J.J. *Who's doing this? J.J. won't accept another tall tale. She'll leave me for Wellborne. Could this be him doing this to me?*

He wished he could go back in time on a visit permanently. He still had a rich and fulfilling imagination and perhaps, he thought, *I need to just take my mind back somewhere to be comfortable.* At his age, flipping into a visit was not easy, such urges tempered with obeying J.J.'s wishes to stay in touch with reality. He could sometimes look at a building or a street and see visions of life there in earlier times, the people in old-time clothes, and the events of those days. But lately resisted thinking about those images.

He spoke louder to himself in the mirror, "Yeah, living in the here-and-now is too sad. Whenever I take a risk, I fail. Jobs blow up in my face without warning. People think I'm a freak. Maybe I am. No, someone doesn't think so. J.J., oh J.J., don't leave me now."

He fingered the Belvedere brochure. "Somebody is messing with me. Wellborne!" he cried out loud. "If Wellborne tries to steal my J.J., maybe I'll kill him. At least that would be something meaningful," he kidded himself, as he leaned again on the bar exasperated. Of course, he could do no such thing.

He'd reached crisis stage. Something had to be done to throw off the boredom before it smothered him. "I'll read some of Durant's account of the Age of Reason. Damn. I can't. I forgot to bring it. Durant got most of it wrong anyway." Nick had forgotten to bring any book to read.

He fidgeted around on the bar. His eyes landed again and again on the colorful Belvedere Hotel party brochure in front of him on the bar. Nick picked it up to throw it away but he couldn't release it from his hands.

He gave in. He straightened it out and looked closely. The hotel was offering several New Year's Eve parties.

It's a big place, old. I think thirteen stories, Nick remembered reading. He sensed a revelation coming of some kind.

"Yeah, New Year's might help us. My God, yes, it's the millennium coming up in a month." The thought frightened him a little, though.

No way, he thought.

Nick tossed the brochure into the trash under the bar and walked the nearly empty can into the alley. He heard the garbage truck approaching from Fairmount Avenue.

Returning to the bar, he began tidying, but he could think of nothing but the crumpled-up brochure in the trash can and the New Year's parties it promoted.

What were the five parties again? he thought.

Nick ran back outside to look for the brochure. He rifled through a trash can in the alley, coffee grounds and food waste on paper plates and plastic utensils sticking to his hands and wrists, and finally found the wet and slippery brochure, and brought it into the bar to wipe if off and study it.

The ad announced five New Year's Eve parties at the old Belvedere Hotel on Chase Street. He unfolded the six-panel brochure. He didn't remember it having folds at all before.

Hmm, a hundred years old this year too. Back then, this was at the northern top of the city. Tons of famous people stayed there back in the day. I didn't think it was still open.

"Maybe J.J. and I could go there for the millennium," he said to the mirror again out loud. He wondered why he'd never visited the intriguing relic of Baltimore's hay day. In fact, his family never mentioned the Belvedere Hotel. "That's odd. People know I love the gilded age of the city."

Nick's curiosity aroused, he slipped into his state of desperation, *Maybe some act of romance would warm her up again. Maybe this is it,* he thought, forgetting for a second that he hated parties. To Nick, parties were about as appealing as being sold at charity slave auction.

He reached under the bar for the telephone and called Nate Bowen at his office at Morgan State University. Nate was a professor of urban development. "Nate, hey bro, it's Nick. How'd you and Betsy like to go out with us on New Year's? There's a funky party at the historic Belvedere Hotel."

Nate reacted roughly, protective of his friend. "Nick, the girls won't buy into New Year's this year. This is not you anyway, buddy."

"You don't understand. This is different," Nick pleaded.

"I already tried Betsy going to the Hyatt, or the New York trip, or just the Inner Harbor fireworks for New Year's," Nate said. "No go, man. You know that J.J. and Betsy won't go for a party that night at that old hotel or anywhere else. They're afraid of this stupid Y2K thing. You know Year two thousand? They buy into the media fears that the world's computers will stop everything at midnight because their clocks don't program a change to 2000."

"I know. I know. That's just stupid, Nate. But they will get over it, my friend. Help me here, please. We have just got to get out of the house and have some fun. She's acting funny. I think she is smitten with young Wellborne."

Nate laughed a bit. "Talk about stupid. I know she loves only you, Nick. Look, just be yourself. Bring her chocolates and flowers for no reason. Works every time. Hey, I bring Betsy chocolate turtles. Always shuts her up, so I don't hear about buying a better house and stuff for at least a day!" Nate laughed heartily. "Or, until the turtles are gone."

"Look, Nate, if I can talk you and Betsy into going to a party at the Belvedere, I know J.J. will go. That old dinosaur hotel is one hundred years old, from another era, another style. She loves that old Victorian stuff. Besides, this is the millennium. Get it? It's perfect. There's this brochure I have here all about the parties there, see?" Nick was channeling his hero Pop. "New Year's is special, man! We need to celebrate the millennium by going out." It was Pop talking, and Nate knew it.

"Nick, this is not you, my friend. Maybe I'm talking to your grandfather now. This is about J.J., isn't it? You just want to warm up things with the woman. I get it. But maybe a quiet dinner with the four of us that night might be—"

"No, Nate. You are dead wrong. If we do that, we will regret spending the millennium without doing something special. It's in the cards as I see it. An historic event!"

"Nick, you are scaring us lately. You need to stop shrinking into yourself. You turn yourself into mister taciturn, a distant and moody person we don't recognize. We get nothing out of you for weeks and suddenly you are promoting a big bash party in Baltimore. Yeah, okay maybe get out and party. But just not that night, Nicky boy."

"Nate, this brochure on the Belvedere party, well, they've got several going on that night. It will be a blast, a stone soul blast." Nick was trying too hard to sound hip.

"And where did you get this brochure, then? Did you go there? Check it out? It's probably a dump. I don't think I want to—"

"I found it in the bathroom."

"At the Belvedere?"

"No. Here. I don't know how it got here. And a while ago someone left another Belvedere ad on the stoop with my name on it, reading for Mr. Nick."

"You are REALLY scaring me now. You mean reading material is that scarce at Pop's these days? Are you sure it wasn't in there for some drunk's TP last night? That's it, right? You ran out of toilet paper. Or, you were that desperate for reading material, right?"

"Very funny. Well, I did clean up in there last night and emptied the trash too. Hmm, maybe it was Clare's. The cleaning lady. No, she wasn't here today."

Nate insisted, "Sorry. I just think this is not going to happen. But I'll talk with Betsy, only after we've had a look at this place. What ya doin' Saturday?"

141

"What do you think? What am I doing every Saturday until eternity?"

"Oh yeah. Can't you get your Triandos's friend?" Nate asked.

"He works Friday night; doesn't work two days in a row, he says. Lucky stiff. Listen, I'll run up there sometime soon. Talk at ya, Jack," Nick said, still trying to sound hip.

"Solid, bro. Later." Nate laughed at the exchange.

They always signed on and off in some old '70s street lingo. The routine had begun years ago, when Nick first got to know African-American friend Nate and tried some hip black lingo with him at first. It sounded so lame that Nate made it a regular joke during their phone conversations.

* * *

"I think he is serious," Nate told his wife Betsy that night about Nick's wacky idea to visit the Belvedere Hotel on New Year's Eve. "We vowed to help J.J. manage his moods and we've done nothing. I think the time has come."

"Yeah maybe so. The old Belvedere, eh? A crazy idea. Why, folks in the shelters I council in the city say there are ghosts all through that place," Betsy added.

"Don't be silly, Betsy. Just tell J.J. to say no." I think it would be risky to parachute Nick into such a scene," he advised.

Chapter 17: Nate and Nick

Nick and his best friend Nate Bowen were cut from different cloths. But they were as tight as friends could be—like-minded intellectually, and they shared a love of history, sports history and a romantic naïveté about the recorded past.

Nate was always fascinated by Nick's mood extremes, being brooding and melancholy most of the time, but occasionally dangerously freewheeling and impulsive; as Nate would say, he was imitating Pop unconsciously. Nate had figured it out right after meeting Pop. Why would Nick occasionally built up courage to perform generous and bold acts? He'd have to channel his grandpop, an observation exclusive to Nate and one Nick didn't resent Nate from considering.

Nate once agreed to help Nick deposit a free case of National Bohemian beer on doorsteps in his entire Ellwood Avenue neighborhood on Christmas Eve, even for people he didn't know.

Another time, Nate met Nick at Patterson Park to walk and talk through the decision being organized by Uncle Alberto to get Pop and Grandma Minnie into a retirement home. But suddenly, Nick stopped the conversation to explain the proper rules of soccer to a group of children kicking around the correct kind of black and white ball, but incorrectly at random, it seemed to Nick.

Nate tried but couldn't stop Nick from soon joining right into the kids' pickup game, towering over the kids until he scored the winning goal and bought them all ice cream at a vender cart nearby. The delighted children swarmed the vender.

Some mothers from a park bench had witnessed the bizarre scene of a grown man playing as one of the children and objected mildly. Nick bought ice cream for the ladies too, sat them all down and told them the history and origins of European football, as they sat on park benches enthralled by the 'professor' pacing about lecturing.

Nate loved it and chose pistachio. Nate was amazed that a little history teaching would make his awkward friend so charming with the ladies, even though it was not Nick's intent or desire. Nick never tried to get to know people any further.

Nick also considered his friendship with Nate to be very special. He shared everything with Nate, things he told no one else, not even his Pop.

He once opened up to Nate over lunch at the tavern that as a teen and young adult, Nick became a borderline, then a full-blown, alcoholic and pothead as he felt isolated in society and withdrew into his books and movies. Nate was horrified to hear Nick admit that in and after college, he smoked weed every day except when fear of failure forced him to knuckle down and study. He told Nate he was still ashamed that he could still ace a test with ease when stoned.

From then on, Nate knew this was a very special relationship because his very odd friend really trusted him. Nate grew to love Nick and would worry over him. He did whatever he could to protect him, especially with Pop reaching an advanced age and no longer actively advising and protecting Nicky boy.

At first, Nate was puzzled why such an intelligent man like Nick Esposito was brooding and doubting himself constantly. He never knew Nick's parents before they died, but Nate surmised from Pop that Nick was the unexpected Esposito.

Pop told Nate that Nick would probably never shake the "ridiculous notion that the boy was some kinna oddball. Too much has happened. But we all love Nick for who he is, Nate, my boy. And, ya know what? I preciate your friendship to my boy Nicky."

It was apparent to Nate that all the other men in the family were indeed extroverted and gregarious men who depended upon and enjoyed being with one another. Nate thought it a shame that Nick wanted to depend on no one, because he was always slow to understand the feelings, desires, and intentions of most other people. What Nate liked in particular about his friend Nick was how he depended on his own wits and cunning, unlike himself.

Nate was socially well connected in his profession and church for needed support.

Nick's take on Nate was that he was an honest, non-judgmental human being, much like many of his heroes in the history books.

When Nick met Nate Bowen, he was delighted to learn that Nate was a genuine people person who was very concerned with others, just like his Pop. Nick let Nate into his trust to the extent that eventually he approved wholeheartedly that Nate would share an emotional interest in the old man's last challenge, the rundown tavern in South Baltimore near the site of the future baseball stadium.

And, a mutual baseball passion may have sealed the friendship. Nick was overjoyed that Nate was a great baseball fan like he was, though most men in Nate's circles seemed to like to follow basketball and football. Nick knew the entire history of the pure American game dating back to the Civil War including all the stars of the Negro Leagues that preceded Jackie Robinson of the Brooklyn Dodgers breaking into the major leagues in 1947 as the first African-American player.

Nate was never bored listening to Nick's baseball stories.

By the late 1990's the Pratt Street tavern project slowed because of the decreasing income from the Ellwood Avenue tavern to apply to the new tavern. There was a chance, a good one, that Pop would die before it was finished. Although Nate was a teetotaler, he considered Pop's project a brilliant urban development move, as it is within four blocks of the new Oriole baseball park.

* * *

Years earlier, Nick Esposito and Nate Bowen and their wives, J.J. and Betsy, met by a lucky coincidence. Both couples were signing up for guided tours of historic Annapolis, Maryland—although for different tours.

Tours began at the Annapolis Museum and Gift Shop at the downtown piers that float high-end pleasure boat slips.

Nick chose the standard history tour of Annapolis. Historically, the small Maryland city was an important port in colonial America and the first peacetime capital of the United States temporarily in 1783, and currently the state capital.

Nate and Betsy chose the African-American tour, owing to their heritage as descendants of Virginia slaves. Their ancestors likely were sold at auction just steps away from the gift shop. The African-American tour began with a bronze sculpture of Kunta Kinte, the African slave who was sold at on the Annapolis city dock in 1767, according to author Alex Haley's historic novel, "Roots."

J.J. didn't care which tour Nick bought. She and spent a few minutes chatting about gifts with a nice woman about her age. Betsy enjoyed the girl talk after putting up with Nate's black history chatter on their half hour drive to Annapolis.

The four each rented Sony Walkman players that played tapes to guide their respective walking tours.

To begin their separate tours, Nick and J.J., and Betsy and Nate, left the museum at exactly 9:04 on a Saturday morning from different angles in the shop. The four literally bumped into each other getting out of the door, in a Three Stooges-like exit scene that made them notice each other's friendly apologetic manners.

They all had a good laugh and were on their way, Nick and J.J. up Main Street toward the Maryland State House and the governor's mansion, while Nate and Betsy walked to the dock and the bronze statues to Alex Haley and Kunta Kinte.

By coincidence, they all returned to the city's museum at the very same time, 11:17 a.m. after finishing their walking tours.

Delighted to meet again, they decided to have lunch together at Pusser's Café on the dockside. The two couples clicked. They built lasting bonds starting with Nick and Nate's interests in history and J.J. and Betsy's careers in the social services in Baltimore.

Nick was fascinated that Nate was the son of Nathaniel X. Brown, a fiery Baptist Minister from Washington, D.C., who proudly sent his son Nathaniel X. Brown Jr. to seminary school in Virginia. It was not far from where his great-grandfather had tended crops as a slave on a plantation.

Nick told Nate stories he'd never heard before about slavery in Virginia.

(Although Nate Jr. remained deeply spiritual in his life, he lacked his father's passionate calling to the ministry and has soon transferred to the University of Virginia in Charlottesville, where he met his future wife working in a local dress shop.)

Nick admired Nate's steady and methodical approach to life and was secretly envious. And, he was delighted to learn that Nate was a new ethics professor at Morgan State University in Baltimore, with a Ph.D. in the social issues of urban development and was especially intrigued that Nate knew the history of many Baltimore neighborhoods.

J.J. and Betsy discovered they worked close by each other, on either end of the Orleans Street Bridge between downtown and the Johns Hopkins Medical Center (hospital) in East Baltimore.

They discussed their similar career fantasies about how they would "reinvent" health care to be more socially responsible to low-income folks.

Betsy told Nate later she was surprised to learn that J.J. was knowledgeable about social and spiritual life in West Africa, but that J.J. never explained why she knew so much about such a culture so far away.

Chapter 18: This Belvedere Thing

November 29, 1999.

The Monday after Thanksgiving was one of the slowest business days of the year at Pop's Tavern.

Nick was kicking himself for forgetting to bring a novel or a history book to work. However, that bookless day would be different than other bookless times when he'd resort to a newspaper or watch the TV at the bar. This day, Nick's mind was firmly fixed on the millennium party idea that Nate thought was so stupid.

So, what would the Belvedere party be like? he was thinking. Nick wanted more than anything to take J.J. to a fabulous millennium party. It would be a sensational opportunity, a gift. It would give them a time of togetherness again, like it used to be, he imagined. True to Nick's nature, he let the idea build up quickly into a desperate need. Unrealistic, yes, but he was putting all his hopes to save his marriage into one solitary thought, a party for J.J.

The Belvedere party brochure came to represent more than just an idea, a whim. It became a device for relieving himself of his misery. *What else can I do? I'm trapped*, he thought. Nick could no longer put off the chance to do something about his big idea. But he was stuck as usual at the tavern.

This sucks. When can I possibly check it out? he thought.

He gazed toward the tavern's kitchen; considered making a ham sandwich. Instead he again imagined his grandmother's warm smile when he was a child, as she would come out with her crab cakes. His image of her was directly under the old television on a high platform that was flickering silently. He blinked and she was gone. He sighed.

On the TV screen Nick saw actress Susan Lucci's face in the latest episode of All My Children. *Poor dear, she must be crying over something. Bet it was very personal*, he thought.

148

The TV's sound was broken since a drunk threw a beer bottle that broke the volume control instead of hitting the baseball umpire he was aiming for. The ump had made a bad call that cost the Baltimore Orioles the game one late summer night.

Nick hadn't gotten the television fixed yet and was losing the Saturday college football crowd for the past few weeks. He didn't care. Pop wasn't around to lecture him on how to run the business.

He was also missing many of Pop's loyal Friday night customers, though Minnie wasn't putting out the crab cakes anymore. It had always been always on Friday and Saturday nights when they'd chose from the pile of steamed crabs while catching prize fights or college football.

Nick meant to get a new TV. He strained to see the muted program. A close-up fixed on Lucci's classic Italian features. Nick studied her face. He greatly admired the Italian-American soap opera star. That day he thought she looked prettier than ever, even in her sad moment. He began seriously wondering what was worrying her. He tried reading her lips. He saw her come to life, standing nearby him in fact in the tavern. He worried about her. *Wish I could hear what's troubling her. Maybe I could help.*

He was about to say something to her. Then he got a grip, talking out loud, "What have I come to?" he reflected. "I'm reduced to little more than gee what's wrong with Susan Lucci, queen of the soaps?"

Nick turned away from the TV and the bar. "My God," he muttered. "I can't stand much more of this!"

He gazed into a mirrored background of a Budweiser promotion propped up on a shelf behind the bar. "Damn it, Nick, this day will be different. Maybe it will," he muttered again out loud to himself.

If he could only find a way to close the miserable tavern early, he'd drive over to the Belvedere and buy New Year's Eve party tickets for him and J.J.

He leaned back against the bar again and pondered once more how he managed to get stuck there. His mind drifted back to his childhood.

Chapter 19: Pop's Tavern

Nick's memories of Pop's Tavern back in the day were vivid and still in Technicolor. The corner row house with a downstairs tavern where Stephen "Pop" Esposito, and Grandma Minerva raised their two sons, was on the same side of Baltimore as Little Italy, where Stephen's immigrant Italian father Michael raised his children.

Nick didn't care if Pop's Tavern was not in the traditional Italian neighborhood as he perhaps should. Once an adult Nick felt little kinship with his roots. He was only half Italian.

He'd say to Pop, "It doesn't matter if you are not in Little Italy; it's where you are you that make you what you are."

Nick would remind his proud Italian-American grandfather that he was a full-blooded American, not Italian. Pop just laughed, as he managed a crooked smile and shook his head gazing downward to hide his affectionate laughter and slight disappointment.

Nick reminisced with vivid memories while leaning back on the bar that lonely Monday in November. He recalled that he and his older sister Katrina in the '50s and 60's thought Pop's Tavern was pure magic. Carlo and Miriam sometimes took them to visit Pop and Minnie at "the bar," as the family called the charming little home of Carlo's parents.

Pop would invite Carlo and the kids that included Mimsy (Miriam) to visit on Sundays right after Mass, still early enough before the dregs and drunks populated the alley, plopping around and stumbling in and out of the tavern's side door. A vision Miriam expected on each visit but rarely was apparent.

Nick, still leaning on one elbow, smiled and remembered that when the kids visited, they would immediately dash into Pop's Tavern and race down to the basement. They looked for coins. Knowing the grandchildren were coming, Pop "accidentally" kicked some change from the cash register down a small crack in the floor behind the bar onto the basement floor.

Nick remembered when he ran errands for Pop. He would send the boy out for "those little fruit pies, you know Nicky boy, the ones with jelly inside" from Mrs. Wall's German bakery on Decker Avenue. And often, Nick would run for fresh tomatoes to Johnny Long's produce stand on Fairmount Avenue.

On the boy's return from those errands, Pop would say, "Hey Nicky, you know what your name Niccola means, don't you?" He'd give the boy an extra dime and a little pie after Nick would answer, "Champion of the people, Pop!" and make his grandpop laugh. Such things planted unreasonable expectations as an Italian into Nick's mind at an early age.

But in 1999, it was tough for Nick to remember how clean and safe the neighborhood was when he was little Niccola. Those days of innocence at Pop's Tavern were long gone.

The bar room now smelled its age—stale beer and smoke odors soaked into cheap interior paneling Pop had installed twenty years ago, as a favor to help an old pal's failing home improvement trade during the 1979 recession. In hot and muggy days that fall, Nick would expect any breeze to waft in odors of rotten garbage through the side door of the tavern.

On that Monday afternoon following Thanksgiving, Nick put his head on the bar and felt terribly sad. It was getting warm and wet outside. Nick again contemplated closing early. The damp, foggy, miserable weather was close and still. It seemed to Nick that everyone in the neighborhood was burning rubbish. Nick walked, slumping, to the side door and heard Arraber Jesse Abdul Ricky Jones call from his fruit wagon pulled by his nag, Ol' Blue, "Wateemelon, can'loop, wateemelon . . ." down an alley on Fairmount near Johnny's.

Nick smiled hearing the kind, old man hawking his produce. Old black Jesse, who'd lost a leg in WWII, was one of the last of the traditional Arrabers in East Baltimore, who sold fresh produce from horse-drawn carts.

Nick closed the side door. But the heavy, smoky odor remained as he resumed his station, one elbow on the bar, then with one cheek of his rump on his secret stool hidden by the bar itself. *My God, maybe I'll get lucky and the whole place will burn down . . . put the insurance money into a new tavern . . . yeah, I'll tell Pop it was an accident. . . be a good idea . . . nah . . .*

The smoke still drifted into the bar through cracks in the window frames and ceiling tiles.

Second Interlude

Even in broad daylight, vivid images of the past could drift up and out through Nick's psyche as he napped with his elbows holding down the bar. That same Monday in November there came …

A policeman on the gray horse shouts, "Men, look—the flames are heading east across Gay Street, hurry it up, men. Hurry!"

Ten cops, stunned and wary, nod affirmative. While breathing smoke through dirty handkerchiefs, they stop onlookers from getting near a massive inferno.

Oh, it must be. Yes, it's Sunday evening, February 7, 1904.

Soot covers the police dark-blue uniforms, and many of them are shirtless now, few still wearing their high-dome, blue helmets to fight off flying cinders.

"I'll be back," shouts the one on horseback. He races east on his mare down Pratt Street and across the little bridge over Jones Falls creek. He sees his immigrant wife Marie holding their infant Stephen at curbside in the Italian section.

She's terrified, watching the smoke and flames some two hundred feet high above Baltimore.

"Come on!" he says, dismounting. He lifts her up with their precious bundle.

Mother and child ride along on the mare to safety on Patterson Street.

Nick's eyes opened a crack as he murmurs, "What's that? Yes, that's right. She had relatives up there they say. She will stay with her aunt." He drifted back into the dream…

The policeman on the horse rides back into downtown engulfed in flames. It's Lombard Street. Must be well past midnight, then.

He's dismounted and inspecting those few buildings untouched by fire so far. He lashes reins to a post. Oh, that policeman is great granddad, Chief Inspector Michael Esposito directing firemen. What's that? He's been rocked nearly to his knees. A tremendous explosion on Pratt Street; up there, a block away.

He's running. He can see it now.

"Oh no, not the new Edison plant!" he cries out.

The gigantic powerhouse, the largest, most expensive electricity-generating plant in the United States, is reduced to ruins in minutes.

He cries out to anyone near him, "That's going to spark the fire across Jones Falls Creek into East Baltimore!"

A small army of firemen surround him now, men from New York, Philadelphia, Wilmington, and Washington, D.C. were there. Yes.

He hears the hissing and then roaring, then sees whitish snakes of water spray from hoses on naval militia boats in the harbor arching over to the angry flames. The water is reduced to steam by the deadly red-orange and yellow flames, which roar higher as if to scold the boats and their spraying.

Images blur.

Daylight. It must be next evening, Monday evening. Must be that. The city smolders; no more open flames.

With his left hand, Inspector Esposito rubs his tired eyes that have had no rest in two days probably. His right hand holds the reins of a horse-drawn, flatbed police patrol wagon. He steers it around the remnants and rubble where stood the fine architecture of the city's banks, law firms, and stores—all now a befuddling mass of wreckage, massive piles of smoky black debris.

His hands work the reins to guide the workhorse around the harbor basin to the Negro neighborhood east of Federal Hill. Their section of modest row houses and shanties are untouched by the fire.

A little black boy looks up to the big policeman holding the reins. "I ain't seen ya much down here 'specter Mike. Is it true, the fire was the work of the Lord?"

"Don't know, Jesse. How are you folks down here?"

Boldly the boy inches closer, talks quieter. "Reverend said it's a visit by God's anger over dem Jim Crow law dey passin' now at us Negroes." Jesse stops talking abruptly when he sees an adult approaching quickly, and says, "Oh, I sorry, Reverend."

Reverend Dr. P. Sanford is a statuesque figure in a gray monk's robe, lighter skinned than most Baltimore blacks and with reddish, matted hair. He crosses the street opposite Jesse's side, where he remained standing, as if waiting for some authority, anyone, to finally make an appearance for his people after the Great Fire.

"Hello Officer. The boy is right. I heard the voices of thousands who believe it so. It's punishment. It is surely to thems who crush us po' folk to get richer theyselves."

Inspector Esposito appears uncomfortable with the Reverend's words, but says calmly, "Oh, I don't know, Reverend. I think it started on German Street in a store, they say. Somebody just—"

The reverend interrupts, "I believe that's what people saying who watched them flames and what they decided burned to the ground, mercy me. It was God's order not to touch the anointed houses, spare the poor, burn the rich. They say the Negro needs whites to give him back some love. But I do say this, Officer—or is it Inspector?"

"It's Chief Inspector. But Reverend, please call me Michael. We go back some years."

"Michael, and you know this truth, 'cause you work for 'em. Taken the vote from the Negro was cruel. It was a cruel thing for the Democrats. With them, we folks have no bridge to cross to the promise land, as we shoulda with the Republicans."

"Well, Reverend, lots of black folks are gonna lose their jobs to the fire. Why would God do that?"

"Those were jobs workin' for rich whites downtown, butlers and waiters over there and such."

The two men and the boy peer out at the harbor to survey the disaster across the water once more. A promising city is in ruins. The reverend breaks down crying; walks away shaking his head down, tears falling on broken cobblestones.

"Come on, Jesse, you can be of some help." Inspector Michael Esposito gets down and lifts the young boy onto the wagon bench next to him and proceeds to renewing his rounds, back around the harbor basin and into the charred remnants of Baltimore's downtown

They are checking with each detective stationed at each iron safe left bare in piles of brick and stone, each half-fallen jewelry shop, each pile of rubble that used to be a law firm, a bank, or a newspaper building.

"It was eighty city blocks, Jesse, from Liberty Street to Jonestown, Fayette to Pratt, and down along the harbor across from you folks living down there on Hughes Quay. The fire stopped right at my house across Jones Falls." He knew that?

"Nothing we could do until it burned itself out at the docks. This is not punishment, Jesse, just an accident, a colossal accident of fate. We'll rebuild better. And you folks will overcome that Jim Crow business, I promise you . . ."

Chapter 20: The Last Customer

Later that Monday after Thanksgiving, 1999.

A lone customer wandered in.

"Hey, wake up, man. Hey barkeep. Nick, can I get a beer in this joint? Or are you runnin' a flop house now? Hey Nick. Nick, wake up. It's me, Buddy. As you always tell me, I'm 'like clockwork,' it's Buddy, here for my 2:00 buzz-on. Hey, you okay Nick? You were sleeping, right there, head on the bar. Wake up and tap me one, please."

"Oh yeah, Mr. Buddy. How ya doin', sir? Guess I dozed off," Nick said to his first customer of the afternoon, Buddy, whose face appeared sideways from Nick's perspective. He remembers the dream, rekindling moments in Baltimore history. But such a dream had never happened so vividly at the tavern. He was dazed and momentarily worried about losing reality entirely.

So, there he was. On that slow Monday afternoon after the long Thanksgiving weekend, his mind drifting once again; no reading material. Robot-like, he served up yet another National Boh draft to yet another lonely neighborhood drunk.

"Buddy," he said, "have you heard of the great Baltimore fire?"

"Can't say that I have. Where's that beer?"

"Oh, here. Yeah, just thinking about the big fire."

"What?"

"The fire."

"Fire!? Where?"

"It burned the entire downtown to a crisp."

"Nick, my God. I gotta stop drinking. Is it in the news?"

"It happened in 1904."

"Is this Natty Boh, Nick? Don't taste right."

"Here, try this one." Nick tapped beer into another tall Pilsner glass from the same keg as the first one.

"Ah, that's better. Hey, what's wrong with you, boy? You look like you lost your wife or som'in."

Buddy didn't wait for Nick to answer. He propped himself in a heap on the end stool of the bar to admire the soap opera stars on the silent TV, forgetting his question.

Buddy Burkhart was his name, truly a lonely guy, out of work since a layoff at the Bethlehem Steel mill on Sparrow's Point by the Bay in '91.

Nick wondered if Buddy was happier with his life than he was with his own miserable existence. *Buddy seems contented with who he is*, he thought.

True to his afternoon custom, Buddy had drifted in about 2:00 p.m.

Good ol' Buddy, last customer left this afternoon . . . I hope, Nick thought.

Yep, just one guy left, he repeated in his numb head every ten minutes.

Nick imagined himself as Buddy the drunk. *If not for Pop's business, I guess I'd be Buddy. This damn place keeps me sober, at least. Well, not really. I've got to think of the kids. Got to think of the kids. Got . . .* He fought off drowsiness again; not wanting his sour mood to compromise his public behavior.

The afternoon slipped away. Susan Lucci and other beautiful faces in the soap operas came and went. General Hospital came on, Buddy's favorite. So, he got drunk while Nick got a sinus headache.

No one else came in that afternoon.

If he could just get rid of Buddy, Nick figured, he could close up with some lame excuse, jump into Pop's Cadillac parked in the alley that long weekend, and cruise uptown to find New Year's Eve party tickets someplace around the harbor. *Maybe Nate was right that the Belvedere Hotel would be too creepy for the wives, especially Betsy*, he reasoned. *Maybe, the hotel to her and Nate would still be a reminder a cruel time place for the rich and powerful white society early in the century. Nah, they are not into that shit*, he dismissed.

Buddy slurred unintelligible comments to Nick, to make sure he was getting his money's worth paying his favorite barkeep for his company. Nick was kind that way.

But Nick turned away and mumbled to his reflection in a mirror-surfaced beer poster behind the bar, "It sure would be nice to take the Caddy for a spin before heading back home to Glen Burnie, wouldn't it ol' Nicky boy."

Nick was always mumbling those days. And the habit was getting worse.

He formed a plan: Buddy couldn't last very long and the timing for Nick's planned getaway in the Caddy couldn't have been better.

Pop and Minnie were in Annapolis for Thanksgiving at Uncle George and Aunt Mamie Esposito's. Nick's aunt and uncle had picked up Nick's grandparents at Quiet Oaks for the entire Thanksgiving weekend. They wouldn't be ready for Nick to bring them back until at least Tuesday. *Ha, of course, Pop will want to come back in the Caddy*, Nick mused. *He'll make me wear that chauffeur's cap Pop keeps for me in the car he thinks is so funny.*

Nick watched the rear of the barroom and listened for a flush from the men's room.

Fully saturated with his afternoon booze bath, Buddy had shuffled into the restroom one last time and didn't make a sound for a long time. Nick wondered if he was passed out. *Maybe Buddy was dead. Who would I notify? Does he have family still?*

Nick heard the drone of a small plane going east. He looked out the front window and "saw" Charles Lindbergh at the controls of the custom-built Spirit of St. Louis—drowsy, alone, determined. Nick moved his hands, Lindbergh's hands, on the throttle, then tap, tap, tap on faulty gauges. *Never make it to Paris with these darn gauges*, he was thinking when …

Whoosh. Finally, the toilet flushed. "Buddy must not be dead," Nick almost shouted.

Nick chuckled and thought, *Last Bud for Bud?—nope, last Boh for my bar room, Bo. God, I hope so.*

He watched Buddy wobble out of the restroom. The lingering, drawn-out last customer stumbled, righted himself, and gave a sloppy military salute to Nick, then made his way to the side alley door, slurring an indistinguishable farewell to his beloved barkeep, Nick Esposito, who had eased Buddy's pain for another day. Buddy bumped into the door frame and stumbled out into the alley, sloshing his feet through dirty puddles on the ugly patchwork of brick pavers.

Buddy was pathetic and harmless when drunk, which was all the time: a vision of Nick's later life if not for his loving J.J., the twins, and that everlasting Pop, with his constant tall tales from his life in Baltimore's heyday.

"Good God, he's finally gone! Buddy's out the door. And so am I, Brother Boh!" Nick said at the top of his lungs to the empty tavern.

As fast as he could, he propped up a CLOSED FOR REPAIRS sign in the front door window. He'd been doodling the sign on the back of a cardboard National Boh ad for the previous three hours of nothing but soap operas and boredom.

Nick rushed to turn off the muted TV. He locked down the side and back windows to the alleys and locked the double doors and three dead-bolt locks to the tavern's entrance, while making sure the little green porch light was on and the POP'S IS OPEN neon-lettered sign was definitely out. He ran back into the kitchen to unplug all appliances where he had grilled some sandwiches in the morning. He quickly checked the back door.

In his head, Nick was already cruising in the Caddy across town to score primo party tickets for the New Year's millennium night. It was coming up fast on the calendar, much too fast.

"Much too fast," he muttered. And he worried that the afternoon he had counted on was slipping away.

Chapter 21: To Go, or Not to Go

When Nick got to the alley and before getting into the car, he reached into his pocket for the thing he needed to make his ride in Pop's Caddy more pleasant. He turned on the ignition and paused.

Before driving off, he carefully unfolded yet another glossy flyer for the Belvedere Hotel from his pocket and spread it on the opposite seat. It was from the Sunday *Baltimore Sun* weekend section. Off and on that day, he had been gazing at the brochure. He wanted to deny himself the temptation to commit to it. But he could not.

That thing he needed now, that brochure, seemed to have a mind of its own, perhaps somehow connecting to Nick's bias toward the historic.

Still, it bothered Nick that Clare said she did not get the brochure in *her* Sunday Sun.

The four-color ad invited Baltimoreans to join in a gala masquerade ball for New Year's Eve at the old Belvedere. Before starting the Caddy, he read the words again:

ONCE-IN-A-LIFETIME CHANCE
BE HERE
CELEBRATE THE PAST 100 YEARS
PASS THROUGH TO THE NEW MILLENNIUM
RIGHT *HERE*!!!
HISTORIC BELVEDERE HOTEL

"Intriguing little message," Nick muttered. He put it back into his pocket as he spun his mind back through Baltimore history since 1900 when construction of the Belvedere, north of the then-downtown, was being talked and read about in the papers.

He closed his eyes and saw the city east of the famous hotel. Instead of the modern streets and rows of homes, he saw fields and forest trees, which he knew covered East Baltimore back then. They appeared faint where there were backyards, fences and alleyways.

He opened his eyes and the trees were gone, giving him pause. *Well . . . the historic Belvedere is intriguing, but maybe not quite the right party. I might be caught up in it. Maybe something more upbeat,* he thought. He was reminded that no one in his family had ever said they had been there before. He hadn't either.

No, no, I'm checkin' it out. Maybe not tonight, but soon. He reached to turn off the engine. Maybe he'd leave the big Caddy and just get into his old Toyota and go home early.

He looked around again and saw a harsh reality—the paint-chipped, mildew-covered back walls of row homes on the alley with trashy yards of garbage cans and half-dead climbing vines, typical of a low-income section of East Baltimore in the dim light of a late fall afternoon. No people were around.

The only 'person' around was Eloise Johnson's mangy old pit bull. The dog was her last possession from her womanizing ex, long gone. The mangy dog stared at Nick in the Caddy, as if he knew Mr. Esposito was cheating, too, that is, sneaking away without leaving him a scrap of meat as was Nick's kindly habit for the mutt.

Nick felt physically sick—it had been another halfhearted day managing Pop's business. But it wasn't just his work that bothered him. It was the old neighborhood that he once loved that had gone south, too.

He re-started the car. He sat with the Caddy engine idling, until a firm direction would come to mind.

The little corner tavern and indeed all of East Baltimore had declined tremendously since he had run errands for Pop during Sunday family visits. That magical neighborhood of Nick's childhood was gone and replaced by crime and tension between whites and blacks, young and old, and welfare families and Latinos and Koreans, who ran small corner stores. Young

164

punks in hooded faces and baggy pants now sold drugs at night in shadows near street corners, right in the alley where Nick sat with the Caddy, waiting, puzzled once again by his loss of control of his own mind and lack of conviction.

It wasn't that Nick would be sentimental about the changes. Like his grandfather, he liked everybody he came across, even in the current state of the neighborhood. But it held no magic for him now, just vivid memories of better days.

He looked at the gleaming controls on the Caddy and thought no, his domineering grandfather couldn't possibly know Nick was borrowing his prized sedan. Nick eyed the neighbor's pit bull again. This time, there was instead a much younger, muscular dog baring his teeth and about to jump the small fence toward his open window in the Caddy. Nick blinked and there was the old mutt again, drawing sadness from watery eyes. *God, I'm going nuts. Time to go.*

Nick tried to relax as he eased out of the alley going onto Fairmount instead of Ellwood Avenue so folks wouldn't see him sneaking off. He slipped south to Lombard Street to avoid some of Pop's best friends along Orleans Street. And then, up Charles Street into the light, post-holiday rush-hour traffic.

To lift his spirits, Nick decided he'd blast Led Zeppelin from the Caddy's twelve Bose speakers. Maybe people would think he was hip. It didn't occur to Nick that his "hip" music was out of date by twenty years. Anyway, it helped him feel free.

The top-of-the-line sound system he had installed in Pop's car provided no benefit at all to the old man. Pop always told his driver du jour to "turn that noise off."

Nick dared not disturb dust on the face of the audio unit that could be evidence of his 'crime.' "Thank you very much," he muttered.

Nick reminded himself not to leave the Best of the Hair Groups CD in the car and to make sure to insert Frank Sinatra's My Way CD back in the player when he got back to the tavern.

Meanwhile, cruising along the streets of downtown, tapping his feet to the old rock 'n roll, Nick covered twenty blocks up and across town toward the inevitable, the old Belvedere Hotel. The can't-miss-it structure was a rather mystical stone and steel monument to the 19th century. It dominated the highest point of formerly rolling farmland. As he got close to the old building, he grew tired of the too-familiar oldies and turned off the CD with some disgust at himself for being so juvenile.

His thoughts turned to his wife. He missed her. He figured she was home with the twins by now. J.J. would be asking them about their day. She's turned out to be an excellent mom, he thought, feeling a little left out. He worried she'd be calling the tavern for him to bring home milk or something she needed to prepare dinner. He was sure she would make that call, track him down, investigate what he was doing, wondering if he was okay because of what happened in the morning.

* * *

That morning argument had not been pretty. Before leaving for work at the tavern, Nick had broached the subject of New Year's with J.J. again at the breakfast table, but gotten nowhere fast.

He had almost finished his rehearsed lines, pitching the Belvedere party brochure, when J.J. abruptly said, "Nick, you know it's probably too late to get tickets to any good party, anyway. Let's just stay home as a family. If I go out on New Year's, I want to be around people like me."

"You always seemed to squeeze me into a dilemma; you are so complex," he said with too much anger. He headed for the door as he shouted back to her, "Darn it, there are no people like you J.J., not in a long shot."

Another frustrating rut. He shouldn't have said that. He'd been trying to stay away from anger. He knew what she really meant was "classy people like me," or something more modest along those lines—to be around classy people or educated ones with stuff in common with them perhaps.

J.J. was not insulted though. She said, "You know what I mean, people we can be comfortable with, like Nate and Betsy, or

Katrina or my mom. Not total strangers on Y2K night. Suppose something happens?"

Nick plopped into a chair, frustrated, "Like what, dare I ask?" It was a topic to avoid at that moment, he realized too late.

She said, "Do you know if computer clocks really falter when they don't recognize the change from 1999 to 2000? Nick, what if the power outages from the giant cyber crash then trigger widespread crime and looting? And we are stranded in the city? We won't get away before the missile silos open and start nuclear war."

He tuned her out for being too dramatic.

"Well, will it, Nick? . . . Are you listening, Nick?"

"All that Y2K hype is a hoax," he answered. "There is a world full of newly empowered cyber geeks today who see a chance to gain more power. They smelled a bonanza, a perfect scheme to make money—lots of it. They're selling fear. This is just like the gas shortage scam when you were in college. It turned out to be the U.S. oil companies masterminding the so-called great gas shortage. My God, J.J., they had people lining up their cars at gas stations like dopes, hoping to get their share of fuel before the station ran out for the day. Well, it was a setup, just like this Y2K scam. Don't you see that?"

She turned her back and walked into the kids' bedroom.

He yelled, "Whatever. I'm out of here before I get in deeper! I've got to go open the stupid bar. This is going nowhere fast." The Y2K thing bugged him to know end. He couldn't believe that J.J. actually feared each and every wacko, doomsday idea on the news that fall, plus all the talk shows about the calendar turning to year 2000. *This from an educated woman, too,* he thought.

He slammed the door, and the twins started crying.

His rare fit of anger added one more important element to, or rather subtracted from, a miserable day ahead because in his anger he again forgot to take a book to read at the tavern.

* * *

In the Caddy on North Charles Street, Nick was feeling badly about how the morning went and took his eyes off the street. He nearly hit a police woman ticketing a parked car. But it wasn't the woman he thought of first. *Whew, it would surely get back to Pop.* He was no longer thinking straight nor with his usual compassion as he closed in on the Belvedere Hotel.

But, back to reviewing his plan: *Get tickets and surprise J.J. She'd buy into a romantic night out on New Year's Eve. Money spent. No refunds. Yeah, I'll tell her that. It will be okay, yeah sure.*

But a little more up Charles Street again he doubted himself. *Would she like the idea?* Then he said out loud, "Hmmm, dunno." And then, just as quickly, he shrugged off doubts. It was a gamble the impulsive, unpredictable side of Nick's mind was desperate to take. He figured she would consider it because his wife loved anything from the Victorian period, especially nineteenth-century BBC America mysteries, like the Sherlock Holmes and Agatha Christie cases. *We'll dress up. A costume ball at the Belvedere will erase her worries and fears of Y2K. If she is not excited maybe she doesn't care about me anymore. Test of her love ... no, Nick, don't go there.*

Chapter 22: Tough Party Tickets

Nick drove on. He tried to focus again, to overcome his doubts and J.J.'s fears. But it was impossible.

Soon, he wasn't focused at all on what he really wanted to do. Against his will, Nick's options were getting mixed up in his mind.

At first, Nick Esposito thoroughly enjoyed his afternoon drive, temporary freedom from his troubles, especially behind the wheel of Pop's Caddy. Yes, it was good to get away from the stale-beer smell of the tiny corner bar.

But paranoia filled his mind when he neared Baltimore's famous Belvedere Hotel. He started to get upset. Had he waited too long to close the bar and get on his way? Maybe the hotel business offices will be closed. *I'll miss a chance to buy our party tickets after all,* he thought. *This is stupid, like Nate said.*

The rooftop of the ostentatious and antiquated Belvedere architecture came into view just after he drove up the hill to Mount Vernon and Baltimore's monument to George Washington. The sight put Nick's imagination into overdrive. Excited again, he imagined talking with the Italian stonemasons who finished the Belvedere facades, decorative edging and cornering a century ago. "Anyone here know the Esposito family in east Milano?" Nick rehearsed his line and laughed.

For history crazed Nick, the Belvedere was not only old, it was symbolic. Just as Baltimore was built along the eastern fall line, dividing the hilly western Piedmont land and the sandy Atlantic coastal land, the Belvedere too was at Baltimore's social midpoint on that Piedmont line. It was halfway between where the old country mansions once ruled the rolling, fertile pastures of the rich and privileged on the northern side of Baltimore, and the gritty south side of the city, where the working classes sweated and toiled.

Nick knew Baltimore's history well but wanted to know more about the Belvedere. Once again, he tried and failed to remember anyone in his family ever mentioning or talking about going there. *How odd,* he thought. It was like a black hole in the family's Baltimore lore. "Mmm, maybe there's a reason they never mentioned the old gal," he said to himself just as he got his first close look at the top floors of the fourteen-floor monolithic hotel on Chase Street.

From what he'd recently read, though, Nick considered the Belvedere the perfect setting for his millennium party, and for trippin' into the next thousand years of Baltimore history. *Wow, what will that be like?* he thought, focusing again on his mission, for a minute, at least.

He looked for the full hulking structure over other roof lines as he inched north. *But, oh God am I going to be too late to get tickets?* he thought.

Finally driving through slow afternoon traffic, Nick arrived at the hotel and caught a break. There was just one, huge open parking space right across from the hotel entrance. He carefully eased the Caddy into the space. He thought, *God, please don't let me scratch it.*

Nick fumbled for quarters to feed a parking meter He didn't find any.

But by then, he was standing, mesmerized, gazing at the big old structure across the street. Such a trance-like state was not unusual for Nick in the presence of historic sites, of course. He pictured the people and events from the past unfolding in his mind; great private party fun in better times.

Nick was not himself and felt light headed. Was another one of his dangerous visits into the past coming on? Perhaps he'd return another time. *Screw it, I'm going in,* he thought, forgetting all about the parking meter. He'd not actually seen a meter because he had parked next to a fire hydrant and didn't notice it.

He scanned the hotel facade, letting his eyes enjoy the dramatic architecture of a long-gone era.

Next, he took in the brassy, covered entrance, added in later years. Tacky, too tacky, he thought. Then he slowly lifted his gaze to take in the impressive front side of the Belvedere, each one of its 14 stories at a time.

The French Beaux Arts, neoclassical style of the Belvedere stood apart from any of the modern, squared-up buildings nearby, though Nick knew it was typical of an architectural trend of prominent Baltimore structures in the late 1800s.

Its walls were warm brownish-pink brickwork with brawny cornerstones, giving the building an indestructible appearance. The front wall was framed by a thick masonry cornice over the third floor, likely part of the support for a two-story lobby ceiling; and a much heavier cornice just below a steep and tall slate roof. Extremely ornately carved dormer windows jutted under the roof line all across, so the top of the Belvedere seemed to cover the streets around it.

Nick saw roaring lion's heads and grotesque gargoyles high on the corners facing north across the high ground of the city keeping watch over the estates of many of Baltimore's richest residents at one time.

Nick was hooked.

Wow, a hundred years old and perfectly creepy, he thought. *They certainly don't make 'em like this baby any more. How many parties did Pop and Grandma attend in this old relic?* He wondered again why he had never heard his family talk about the place.

For most of its hundred years, the Belvedere had been the premier hotel in Baltimore, especially during the first half of the twentieth century, and a gathering place for many momentous occasions.

He was talking out loud now, "Yeah, just perfect. J.J. will adore this place! Well . . . maybe she will. She may just go for this place and forget why there's a 'two kay at all'!" He laughed out loud at his stupid little joke."

As a son of an old-city family and someone who'd tried hard but was never able to break its shackles, Nick still loved Baltimore's old buildings and the historical secrets they held. He was grateful that this particular old building was too far north in the city to have been touched by the fire that destroyed downtown Baltimore in 1904.

All caught up in the image before him, with his dreamy state of mind, Nick had no notion of the absurdity of why just a party, regardless of how unique and special, could heal a couple's relationship by itself. But that was Nick—introverted, intense, and private, and too out-of-touch sensitive for his own good.

Filled with wonderful images of the Belvedere's unusual, nearly magical exterior, he walked slowly across the street, not looking left or right, and then he bounced up the hotel's four well-worn marble steps as if he owned the place. And maybe for the moment, he did. He was excited, nearly giddy, expecting the spectacular lobby—the marble floor; the huge gold-framed mirror atop tiered levels of ceiling adorned with cream, gold and dark-blue insets of hand-crafted floral trim; the immense crystal chandelier—all splashed liberally across his brochure.

He took a deep breath. Slowly, Nick pushed through the huge, gold-metal revolving door to enter what he expected to be a magically enchanting lobby.

But this lobby did not at all match his expectations. He was dumbstruck. The spacious reception area, under an eight-foot-wide, eight-foot-tall crystal chandelier, was laid out in a style that lacked class. It was in ill repair with gaudy furniture.

He thought *What the hell is this? Late-American tacky?* Expecting Windsor Castle, he walked into something far less elegant, even grotesque, in his opinion, way too dated and rather shabby. The red-velvet stuffed furniture scattered in no special order was too much. Half the lights in the chandelier were out or flickering as if they were gaslights. Flowery wallpaper was peeling along some edges near the high ceiling, which was full of cracked plaster. He couldn't get over the gaudy interior. But parts of it were clean and neat, as it newly renovated—the carpet at his feet, curtains near him and a few sitting nooks with squared off leather couches in purple and black and glass coffee tables. Parts of the big room seemed to change from classy to gaudy and back again. "It's like two lobbies thrown into one," he mumbled. He seemed to be transforming in and out of how the Belvedere lobby appeared in 1999 or some more difficult period in the past.

He shook his head, hoping to change the scene into the picture on the brochure, as he'd shaken away the mean old pit bull dog in Pop's back alley. No luck.

He stood scanning the big room, standing just a few feet inside, when his thoughts were interrupted by a very creaky, old voice, which spoke in kindly and strangely familiar tones.

"Young man? Oh, young man, you'll love it here. Za Belvedere Hotel in Baltimore is one hundred years old, you know."

He didn't see anyone. The voice came from no particular direction. He turned, and then he saw her, slouching right behind him somehow in a navy-blue, ankle-length frock with dime-size white polka dots. How she got behind him shocked Nick. Impossible, he thought.

"I'm Miss Ellen Krantz. I wait for some people. I wait for you," said a very old and tiny wrinkled lady. She was the last sort of person, a shrunken-down, gray-haired lady that Nick or likely anyone else would expect to be initiating a conversation with a total stranger at a hotel. Yet, she greeted him so boldly.

He was sure she hadn't been there when he walked in. And how did she squeeze behind him when he was barely inside the door?

He froze as Miss Krantz walked around to look into his face, appearing there much more rapidly than a typical little old lady should move. She seemed very happy to see him, as if she had been expecting him.

He was too surprised to ask or say anything about why she was there. Yet she told him, with no hesitation, "The tickets to the hotel's five New Year's parties are being sold in the Owl Bar. Come."

She pointed to the back of the lobby and smiled over her shoulder at him as she doddered away as if she'd lost use of her arms and legs.

The Owl Bar was deep inside the lobby to the left. Miss Krantz continued in that direction, not looking back again to see if he followed. She had a deliberate speaking attitude and took on a gimpy gait once she found her leg muscles. He wondered if she was injured perhaps.

Considering all his anxiety in his efforts to decide to be or not to be at the Belvedere for New Year's tickets, he felt he had no choice but to follow her toward a dark, narrow hallway. He reasoned that since he was already disappointed with the look of the place, maybe he was lucky to find her, or maybe lucky that she had found him. Yet again, he had a sense she had been expecting him.

As he slowly followed behind the feeble woman, Nick had a chance to look around.

They entered the poorly lit hallway. Only its walls were brightened with spots hitting dozens of black-and-white photographs hung tight together in an eclectic assortment of frames. Nick realized these were walls of fame, pictures of nostalgia for the old hotel itself—famous people who had stayed at or visited the Belvedere earlier during its 100-year history.

Almost every inch of wall space in the hall, from ceiling to knee height, was covered with memories that management or someone had decided were significant to the old gal—the hotel, not Miss Krantz, although Nick imagined that at her advanced age, she could have witnessed many of those special moments photographed down through the history of the Belvedere.

He glimpsed at posed shots of wealthy and famous guests from previous decades up to about the 1960s, none any later. There was Massachusetts Senator Jack Kennedy from the 1950s with a party of attractive young women. There was a fuzzier image of Douglas Fairbanks, Jr., smiling broadly and next to shots of other early stars of the silver screen: Jean Harlow, Jack Cassidy, and Mickey Rooney as a teen. Nick recognized a formal, signed portrait of former mayor Thomas D'Alesandro, Jr., with his kids, Nancy and Tommy III, from the '50s, decades before they launched their own political careers. Tommy III became mayor himself and Nancy became Congresswoman Pelosi from San Francisco.

There were photos of General Douglas MacArthur, Tyrone Power, Humphrey Bogart, and Gloria Swanson. There was Jack Dempsey, Cab Calloway, and the Nelson Rockefeller family. Nick spotted President Woodrow Wilson, then Will Rogers, then the face of Andrew Carnegie. And then . . . *Yes—could it possibly be?* Nick thought. He spotted a fuzzy shot of Thomas Alva Edison of Menlo Park in a dark photo of several other people in formal attire standing near early electric lamps. Focus was bad and the faces not clear.

Nah, couldn't be. Was Edison in Baltimore sometime? Guess he was everywhere in his day. Nick flashed through his memory to place Edison in Baltimore, but to no avail. He looked back, squinting to try to make out the fuzzy images in the possible Edison photo. Only Edison's face was in focus, others were distorted or washed out. *Yes, looks like the man himself.*

Nick's thoughts were interrupted by the old woman. Perhaps sensing she was losing Nick's attention, she spun back to face him, as if gliding on roller skates. She said, "Remember, I said I wait for you?" Without looking for a response from Nick, she turned away and took up her limping gait toward a tiny wood-carved Owl Bar sign at the end of the hall of fame hallway.

"Ma'am? Excuse me, have we met?" Nick said.

"Of course, at the door, Mr. Nick. I wait for some people. I've always been here." She was almost whispering, but he could hear Miss Krantz's every syllable clearly.

He was stunned. *How'd . . .? Have I told her my name?*

She spoke with an accent, sounded Northern European, Nick thought. Her voice was self-assured and definite in tone. He tried to remember meeting such an old woman previously.

The situation was not what Nick had expected when he stepped through the entrance of the once-stately hotel.

He decided to start anew. "I'm Nick Esposito and I'm wondering about New Year's party tickets, if there are possibly still available—"

"Wait, excuse please, just a minute, Mr. Nick." She turned and motioned impatiently for a waitress to go away, who had also approached out of nowhere. The young, waitress wore an old-fashioned, full-length Bavarian beer garden outfit. Nick saw the pretty girl frown, then pivot on one foot with a light feminine flair he liked. The girl glanced back at him with a slight, inviting smile, and then scampered off without a sound. She seemed pleased to be working there, though she apparently feared Miss Krantz and disliked the old lady's sharp tone.

Nick felt the girl's energy, and his optimism surged again. He felt more welcomed. Could he buy into spending the millennium eve night right here, just like he had been dreaming about for weeks? *Damn right*, he thought.

The Owl Bar, though half empty of customers, was cozy and dark; a socially pleasing room, a contrast to the opulent hotel lobby. Nick and the old lady slipped onto a long row of barstools. The few patrons didn't look at them.

He was feeling freer and happier than he had felt for years, though the feelings didn't make sense.

The room had yellowish lighting, mahogany furnishings, and stained-glass windows that Nick thought depicted court jesters, knights, and dragons, and such, but he wasn't sure. There was no consistent historical period presenting itself.

The few patrons, the happy-hour crowd, were young and a bit too snooty, he thought, to engage in conversation with him. Besides, they were dressed in rather drab clothing, no youthful flair and style at all. And not one person looked at him or even seemed to notice that Nick and Miss Krantz were there at all.

The dark room was punctuated with a maze of dark wood-trimmed alcoves and secretive, isolated corners and booths with seven-foot-tall bench backs that hid tables of patrons from each other. A twenty-foot ceiling belied the intimacy of the room, which was reinforced with ancient, porous brick walls—obviously the original bricks riddled with imperfections—pocks and scars. Nick saw there was no modern brickwork in the walls.

To Nick's astonishment, the ancient woman Miss Krantz seemed to belong there, part of the hotel and part of the din of the Owl Bar. Though she appeared much too old to be an active employee of the establishment, Miss Krantz was firmly in charge of the Owl Bar operation, he gathered.

She told Nick that her job was to "watch over" the bar. She said that was just one of many of her duties at the old hotel.

Her smile was so oddly wry it made him shiver.

"I can do it all now, Mr. Nick," she said.

Now? What does 'now' mean? he wondered. He didn't know quite why, but he was becoming more and more fascinated with watching the old lady talk and move about against the backdrop of the many coves and recesses of the room, the old Bavarian outfits of the waitresses, and, for that matter, the entire late-Victorian setting in the hotel. The tacky first impression was not apparent.

Nick saw light coming through three stained-glass windows over the bar, each with a verse. One read: A WISE OLD OWL SAT ON AN OAK. Then, the second: THE MORE HE SAW, THE LESS HE SPOKE. The third: THE LESS HE SPOKE, THE MORE HE HEARD. *Well, that doesn't even rhyme. There's something screwy about this place,* he thought.

Behind his reflection in large mirrors spanning the length of the wall behind the bar, he couldn't make out the other customers clearly. The mirror glass was wavy, imperfect glass.

He saw things differently in the room's reflection that were not actually in the room itself. The mirrors didn't show the ceiling fans, but they were definitely spinning behind him. They didn't show the TV at the corner ceiling. Nick moved his head around to clarify, to locate the missing objects because the mirror was faded in parts. *Maybe it's the angle. Maybe a fun house effect they put on.*

He began to think he was wasting time. *I definitely want to find a great New Year's party for me and J.J. so maybe things will get better next year. Is this really the best place?*

Again, his thoughts were dashed by Miss Krantz. "I am in charge of this plaez because I always know what to do 'bout these kids, too," said the old one. "They are here for years and years."

He asked how long she had been with the hotel.

"They say maybe forty-five, fifty-some years. But I tink . . . always, maybe one hundred, maybe more." She laughed quietly, with a smile and a quick wink, that might say 'yes, he's the one all right,' as her voice cracked, straining to keep her volume down, but barely audible as Nick stepped in closer to hear her faint words.

He walked with her to the end of the bar, which stretched the back length of the dimly lit room. Her face revealed that his question saddened or maybe disturbed her.

She cracked out stern instructions to two other pretty redheaded waitresses. They dispatched drinks and tended to new customers, all the time following the old lady's instructions. Why they all feared the little old lady was unfathomable to Nick.

As he watched the carefree, relaxed movements of fifteen or so customers in the dark and mysterious room, Nick (as he was prone to) reversed his thinking yet again. He began to doubt that his big idea of partying at the hotel would be worth his time and effort. Nick put his head in his hands to try to think, *What am I dealing with here? It's late November, damn it. Why the hell did I put this off? I'm wasting time. This place is not right and we might miss all the New Year's fun. We could stay home like J.J. wants.*

His confidence was in a dead funk.

He recalled how the day began—all wrong, as he had tried his best, one last time, to convince his J.J. that it would be safe to party somewhere special. Feeling lost and alone, he remembered more of their nasty argument and regretted it.

With his head down at the Owl Bar, he also remembered her saying flatly, "Nick, we have kids now. People don't know what will happen. We need to think of the girls." Then he remembered Nate telling him that it was just natural that J.J. became more careful and more protective, like all women, and was now less willing to take chances."

Sitting in the Owl Bar with his own thoughts for a moment, Nick tried to find more reasons to forget the Belvedere. But he could not. The party idea, the building itself, had a grip on his reasoning powers.

Despite his current state of extreme anxiety, Nick supposed that his wildly fluctuating indecision over the party idea was not all his fault. The hotel and his feelings for J.J. were each tugging for control. He had to drift along to find out who would win.

He wondered, *What is J.J. doing now at home now? Making dinner? How will she take the news of me buying New Year's party tickets without her consent?* He flashed on their argument and her angry face as she expressed her Y2K fears. *She can't really believe all that crap.*

Nick shook his head and smiled, reassured. He dismissed his doubts and his mind at last was set, despite his recalcitrant wife. The Belvedere Hotel had taken hold of Niccola Augusta Esposito, the oddball dreamer of the family. He was bewildered by its grip. He let his love of history take hold. He let himself fall in love with the place. And, it felt good.

He was afraid and thrilled at the same time. Since he entered the Belvedere, he no longer had complete control of his visions, things past, things others didn't see or hear. He was going in and out of control of his own thoughts.

He considered, *I might be caught into a new sort of visit like never before.* He didn't care that Miss Krantz was surreal. She came and went. He didn't know how. And, she was 'expecting' Mr. Nick! The Owl Bar patrons and waitresses wore old fashion clothing. Was that real? The wavy mirror across the bar produced a different room than the one he sat in. Yet, with all

179

the strange things, he could, or was permitted, to revisit thoughts of his family wife and friends as he mulled over the party decision. *Yes, it seems the hotel is helping me decide,* he thought. *So, what?*

Chapter 23: Tormented? Or Enlightened

Indecision aside, then Nick focused on the task at hand to check into the advertised masquerade party at the Belvedere. This had been his designated task before Miss Krantz started messing with his head.

This . . . yeah, this is unique, very cool, Nick thought after he shook off his anxiety and bathed in a blissful feeling he got from the Owl Bar. It was soothing. Even the sinus headache while watching Susan Lucci with Buddy Burkhart was gone.

One of the pretty redheads in a shapely Bavarian outfit put a drink in front of him. He hadn't ordered. Bourbon on the rocks. It smelled wonderful.

Miss Krantz, from somewhere hidden behind him again, said firmly to the redheaded girl, "Thank you, dear; now go get the ticket book for the gentleman. Go. Make it quick."

Nick watched the girl, and sipped the drink. It was a smooth-tasting bourbon with a rich fragrance of fresh peaches and spicy wood grain. Nick loved bourbon. He had never tasted one as good. *What label is this?* he thought.

He noticed that the girl was enjoying seeing Nick react to the smooth taste. He found her irresistibly attractive and then caught himself. He felt guilty and feared losing his sense of purpose. *I'm here for J.J., not to flirt*, he reminded himself.

Irritated, he turned and said, "Look, Miss Krank, whatever your name is, I wonder what this bar has to do with—"

"Miss Krantz is my name, son. As I said, to get tickets, yes, I understand. But I see you want to think. Okay, she will be awhile, needs to go to fifth-floor office for ticket book. Look around if you want. It's okeydokey, huh?"

Perturbed that the old lady might be mocking him, Nick tipped his head back and chugged the drink. Nothing! It gave him not the slightest buzz.

He sensed an opening, a chance to flee from the weird old lady. He got up and walked back into the Belvedere lobby quickly. *I'll find my own tickets. No, I'm getting out of this place, out of the comfy Owl Bar, out of the creepy Belvedere, out to my car on Chase Street, even if there are party tickets available. It's all just too uncertain, too weird,* he thought. But, somehow, he was unable to step toward the hotel doors. He could not leave the hotel.

When he reached the expansive lobby again, there were different fixtures. Fuzzy figures of people milling around in the lobby. In just a moment, Nick's passion for history, desire for his visits, and his present state of mind were one, entwined neatly. He let himself go back, way back ... finding comfort in his false identity.

He looked back to make sure the old gal wasn't following him.

He strolled wide-eyed around the first floor of the old establishment.

In the lobby, the few people coming and going, clear images now, seemed robotic, perhaps a bit intoxicated. *Oh, maybe happy hour is on,* he realized. *In daylight, this place must be a kind of hundred-year-old temple for pretentious alcoholics of Baltimore's old north side,* he thought, imagining what the old lobby had "seen" in years past.

One more time, thoughts of antiquity evaporated and again he changed his mind.

Nick wondered where all the New Year's parties will be. He peeked into an empty, ornate, restaurant off the lobby with its own high ceiling and crystal chandeliers. Powder-blue and white balloons at each table set up for a wedding reception were standard for a party of that sort, he thought. No, not at all—the crepe and balloon decorations clashed with the permanent, overbearing floral trim of gold and royal-blue framing and latticework that seemed to be dripping from the ceiling and walls all around. His attempt for his own tour, search for party rooms was disappointing.

He was more comfortable daydreaming instead. He returned to scanning the expansive lobby. He let himself enjoy fantasizing, *Creepy, yet beautiful, whew! Maybe, maybe . . . J.J. might think it's wonderful, though. She is a sucker for my history stuff. Why else would she have married me, listened to my stories all these years? She might just go for this place and forget 'Y' there is a 'two K'!* He didn't laugh this time at his joke. He was too deep into his fantasies.

Nick looked back to the center of the lobby, took a deep breath, squinted and, *Well then, okay. That's better.* There was Carole Lombard in a cream-white, tight satin dress, floor length. She leaned on the hotel desk tapping her fingers impatiently and standing next to a cloth overnight bag upright on the floor against the registration desk. *Oh, there's Clark Gable with her.* Gable tipped an eager bellboy who smiled widely, and said, "Thank you very much, Mr. Gable." *And well, that's the child actor Alfalfa from The Little Rascals . . .*

Further off there was Ronald Coleman in a well-tailored dark suit smoking a cigar like the Boston aristocrat he played in the 1947 film The Late George Apley. Nick then saw Gloria Swanson pouting at herself in a handheld mirror . . . and . . .so it all appeared to Nick.

The reality was that in 1999, there was no registration desk and the lobby was tastefully welcoming, not run down or tacky at all.

Yet, Nick continue to visit. He thought, *This place is a black-and-white, old-time movie set, only in color.* His vivid imagination had hooked him once again. He considered risking a visit to their period, *just for a while,* he mused, but Nick assessed his recent situation and thought better of visiting. He might have little control, perhaps not return this time, considering the haunting atmosphere he was perceiving in the lobby.

He snapped back and thought he'd return to the Owl Bar, but first he muttered to himself, "Well, I guess that Owl Bar over there is the coolest hotel lounge I've ever seen. Magical, historical! Why couldn't Pop rope me into bartending there? He knows everybody, especially in old Baltimore. Maybe I could talk to him about—nah, forget it."

Nick really didn't want to leave now. Back in the Owl Bar, the old lady might finally give him the real skinny on the masquerade party at the historic hotel. That is, if the old lady ever started to make some sense. As he returned to the bar, he pondered, *Oh yes indeed. One hundred years old!* He pumped his fist feebly and stepped back into the Owl Bar.

Miss Krantz was in exactly the same spot, in the exact same pose as when he'd left her, leaning on the bar and not attentive to anyone, like she had frozen in time until he returned. She appeared to be a stone statue.

He grabbed one of the flyers on the Belvedere's coming events from the maître d's desk. He started to shove it into his pocket, intending to show it to J.J. and to his friends Nate and Betsy Bowen later. An ever so slight frown surfaced on his face as he felt the flyer. The paper didn't feel newly printed, but brittle with a dull finish. He stuffed it away anyhow. He arrived back at the bar without reading the party information on the flyer; he was too close to the old lady to complicate conversation with reading material.

His presence broke Miss Krantz's stone-like trance at the end of the bar. She turned and faced him, but with a sterner demeanor. A curl of a smile appeared on her lips he hadn't seen, a smile lacking the warmth she had shown before.

Miss Krantz seemed part of the ambience, a fixture, not unlike one of the stained-glass floral lampshades or the well-worn barstools scattered about. He thought, *Did this lady just peel off the wall and come to me? Was she born and raised within these walls?*

Aware that she was keen to listen, he muttered, while reading beer slogans on the walls: "National Boh, from the Land of Pleasant Living; Hamm's Beer, made in the Land of Sky Blue Waters; Ballantine is the 'Take the 22' bottle beer." *Wait a minute*, he thought, *when's the last time they changed these ads, anyway—thirty years ago? They don't even make some of those beers now.* He felt insecure and queasy about the place again and drifted into his usual doubts. *It's getting creepy in here again; high time to ask the old gal about the parties again. Maybe the office was closed. But where's that girl with the ticket book, anyway?* He did not see the redhead around. *Doesn't matter, the Krantz lady seems to know everything,* he thought.

Nick opened his mouth to ask the old lady about tickets again, but she was able to stare him down with a tough expression of authority on her face and body posture. She interrupted him with a finger to her lips, for him to be quiet. She looked directly into his eyes with a resolute expression. A more deliberate, knowing smile appeared on Ellen Krantz's lips. She told Nick in a soft, yet commanding voice, "You will soon be sick of hearing yourself mumble and mutter on and on about nonsense, about not getting the good things in life that you once counted on having, Mr. Nick. Already you don't care if you are right or if you are wrong about almost everything."

She paused and stared at him, with a now-that-I've-got-your-attention intensity that froze Nick in his tracks. She continued, "Do you really want to grow old like that, Mr. Nick? No. If so, you will lose any desire for the smallest pleasures you once thought enjoyable. You'll have nothing, my Nicky boy." She paused, kept a stern gaze aimed right through him to his brain.

Nick was motionless, perplexed. But not afraid, nor was he nervous about her lecturing. Her words pierced into his soul harmlessly.

"But Mr. Nick, hear me well: Open yourself up to the faces of old, as well to the new faces you see. Let them turn you around. Close the door on the devil's garden of excuses, worries, and indecision, my boy, before it's too late for you and your family. You will soon ruin yourself if you do not."

Nick gasped, gathered himself as best he could, and swallowed hard. *What?*

For no apparent reason, he turned to the left. Then, he turned to the right. He shook his head. Nick didn't know if this shriveled-up woman—obviously cheating death—wanted to counsel him as someone she mistakenly thought she knew, or was parroting the odd prophet from the Land of Oz or the Matrix, or somewhere unknown. *What is she up to?*

He stepped back, almost fell to the floor.

But instead of delving into what she had said, he tried hard to adjust to his true intellect and came up with a chess move of his own. He asked her in a quivering voice a totally unrelated question, starting with, "Good enough, then. Okay, well . . . let's begin again. Hello lady. Hey, listen, there was this ad about New Year's I picked up at . . ." He fumbled in his pocket for the event flyer he had just grabbed from the maître 'd's desk. But instead he pulled out crumbles of dry-rotted paper.

Miss Krantz laughed kindly. Gone was the stern, lecturing look, replaced by a maternal smile. "Well then, Mr. Nick . . ."

I wish she would stop calling me Mr. Nick, he said in his mind, but not out loud, sensing that she was somehow able to monitor his muttering and would mock him.

She paused, kept a kind of glare trained on him, and then finally explained about the coming New Year's at the old hotel, while Nick, sweating, listened for the only thing he wanted to know about: the blessed tickets!

Miss Krantz, slowly and pleasantly, said, barely moving her thin lips, "There's to be five New Year's parties here at my Belvedere home, Mr. Nick. Which one for you and your wife and friends?" Her wrinkled face now looked slightly bored with pragmatic stuff.

Nick couldn't remember having said anything about a wife and friends. But that certainly added to attending to her every word concerning the now tenuous ticket situation.

She turned from him, and then dropped a harshly burning cigarette with eye-piercing smoke into a dirty-brown cup of water on the bar, a cup already filled with soggy butts.

The cigarette must have been behind the old lady, in her other hand, he thought.

But, he considered it was more than a cigarette. She used it as a kind of old-fashioned transition to another act in a play. End act one, put the cigarette out demonstratively on cue. Nick hadn't actually seen her smoking, though a lot of people in the bar were smoking, despite state laws prohibiting smoking in public establishments.

Nick tried to talk, to show he was aboard for the next act, "The ti . . . tic . . . the tickets! Five parties! Wow. Well, I—"

"There is the ballroom dancing party in the main ballroom on the second floor," she began.

"I don't know if that's what—"

"That's sold out."

Thank God, he thought. *I would hate to deal with that formal crap on New Year's Eve. This party thing is not just for J.J. It's for me, too, after all . . . I think.* Careful not to mutter out loud anymore, Nick's mind raced, thinking, *Okay, what else, you old biddy? Do you ever fully smile nicely or would your face crack and fall off? Youi be nice, Nick. Maybe she's really somebody else under a mask. Maybe she is really Lon Chaney or Vincent Price. No, too short. Mary Pickford, yes. God, did she just hear me then? Guess not, what else?*

She said politely, seemingly only after he finished his thoughts, "There is the masquerade ball in the Betsy Patterson Ballroom on the twelfth floor. That's my favorite." She gave the slightest smile that hinted at tragedy. She looked down and waited for his response.

"Well, yeah, that's what, I mean, my wife would probably . . ."

"That's sold out, too," she said.

Okay, she's going to walk me through five sold-out parties. She enjoying this? Her favorite . . . my eye.

He tried to picture the old gal working a party room but nothing came to mind. It did not work at all for him. Maybe she was the bartender or something—her sad sagging face, not a pleasant image.

187

She continued, "Then, there is the sit-down formal dinner and za big band, Mercer Ellington, Mr. Nick? It's five hundred dollars a couple," she said quickly, teasing, as if she knew he was not a banker, not a high-roller attorney, or a prominent Johns Hopkins surgeon.

Now, he thought she was a teasing temptress and Nick was not amused. Again, not a pleasant image. *Damn it; she is enjoying this!* It was becoming apparent that the lady was deliberately tormenting him. But why? For what purpose? Had she already selected a party for him? She had one more piece of bait.

"There is a jazz party upstairs, too."

"Sold out, right?"

"Don't know. I don't handle that one."

Handle?

"Miss Krantz?" interjected the prettiest of the redheaded waitresses, passing by with a tray of drinks. "We just happen to have four tickets to the jazzy party. I think there may be room there for him and his party," she added, giving Nick a pleasant, penetrating look with warm hazel eyes and a quick, alluring smile that vanished in a flash, perhaps before Miss Krantz could notice.

Geez, there's a real contrast with the old girl. I guess I didn't really see that living angel before. Nick tried to respond with a thank you but was dumbfounded. The pretty girl flitted away.

He muttered under his breath as he watched her with his back to the old lady, "These pretty girls, the way they are coming and going, could be part of this game they are playing on me. But why me? I'm nothing special, am I?" He turned back to face the old woman. "Okay, where's that jazz party, then?"

"Fourteenth floor, Rumba Room. We can learn about tickets in the business office. Walk this way."

No, she did not say that. He observed the stooped posture of the old woman as she began to lead him, in a gimpy yet steady pace, toward the light of the hallway into the main lobby again.

Perfect, this is damn perfect. She's doing Young Frankenstein's Igor now. Whew! I wonder if she can show me the party. This can't be happening.

He told her, "I don't know if I would like the jazz party; my wife is not fond of that kind of music." He somehow felt that the old lady would know that. "Could I see where that party will be? You, you . . . said Rumba Room?"

"No, it's closed now. Won't open until 8:00 p.m. tonight; it's a nightclub on weekends; tonight, it's not nightclub, see, and it's . . ." She turned to face him. He thought she was about to lecture him again.

Instead, she smiled in a flirting manner, creeping him out. He would have preferred another bone-chilling lecture.

"Okay, I give you a quick look," she said, shifting her thoughts with no warning, as if that had been her plan all along. Nick was irritated, thinking that the old lady had been manipulating him to choose the nightclub party for him and "your wife and friends" all along.

He watched her with renewed interest and, for the first time, felt some hope of a good outcome from the bizarre encounter with the old lady.

Miss Krantz seemed to slide across the lobby room, stopping within breathing distance of what passed for an elevator, a very old elevator, with a little split door, painted black. It was the only elevator Nick saw in the lobby that day. He couldn't believe it was operable.

There are fourteen floors to the hotel. Surely this is not IT! The only elevator, he thought.

Once free of the cozy Owl Bar, he felt insecure and lost. Still, he felt drawn by an inexplicably strong compulsion to obey the old lady. No thoughts of J.J. were surfacing in Nick's mind. His mind was overcome by imaginary thoughts; he saw snips of shadowy people conversing and moving among each other in the lobby, as Nick's rational mind was subdued by all the weirdness happening to him at the hotel. He struggled to justify those mini-visits and his commitment to the Belvedere. *I don't know about this anymore,* he thought.

Without observing Miss Krantz so much as push a button or click any kind of switch, the elevator doors slowly open just as the two arrived in front of its dull black doors. A lifting mechanism creaked in high-pitched, metallic tones he had never heard before with an elevator. The doors took about ten seconds to fully open with repeated hesitation.

Once Nick followed little Miss Krantz into the door frame, both sides of the door pinched back toward the center and stopped at about three feet wide, as if to frame its capture before devouring him like a Venus flytrap plant would. He stepped in completely. Nick felt motion under the red-carpeted floor, a motion different than that of the doors clanging. He impulsively looked at the floor.

The doors finished closing much quicker than they had opened and slammed together with finality, as if they sealed a sinister dungeon in the old British Hammer Production horror films. The mechanical box of bygone days, vault of stale air and paint-chipped metal walls, began moving slowly.

Nick didn't see the old lady punch any of little round porcelain buttons marked 1 to 12 and 14, but the elevator began going up anyway. The vertical row of porcelain-like buttons lined up next to each number. An unnecessary sign beside them read SELECT FLOOR. Above the '12' button was a key slot and a label marked BALLROOM STAGE.

"I will take you up, so you see where . . .," serious and earnest, Miss Krantz nodded toward the top of the vertical row of buttons a good foot over her matted gray head that was tied in a loose, ragged bunch in the back. Her voiced just trailed off, as if she went somewhere else briefly. Then, she turned to give Nick another flirty little smile.

It frightened Nick slightly but he figured, *Hell, I've gone this far; need tickets.* He was getting used to her, and that frightened him more.

She seemed energized by his uneasiness. He realized she had skipped telling him about the fifth party. Before he could ask, she spoke.

"Oh . . . that's going to be a private VIP affair. No tickets there. It's been booked for a very long while. Business people, politicians, you know . . . big shots. Going on since we opened. Never mind that. So, Mr. Nick, we go up now."

He told himself silently, *Don't ask who goes to that party, Nick. She wants me to nose in, and then she'll just laugh at me again. No need to know about the private party. Then again, who?* He imagined such a VIP gathering on New Year's Eve when the hotel first opened and how it might have been way back when.

He was curious, but he changed the subject when the elevator jerked with a loud, deep groan and a whir, likely of naked cables and pulleys. He asked cautiously with a playful smile, "The people on the phone said the Belvedere is a hundred years old. Are there any ghosts?"

She surprised him by a swift response, clearly with not a second of hesitation. "Yes, the Belvedere ghosts are well known, of course. I know them personally." She laughed mordantly at her little joke.

Nick pondered: *What! I work in Baltimore every day . . . born here, for God's sake . . . know the whole damn history of the city, . . . and have never heard anyone talk about ghosts at the Belvedere before. You old coot; I don't scare that easily.* "Or do I?" he muttered without thinking.

Miss Krantz turned and gave him the long, deep stare again. This time the stare wasn't followed by personal advice—fortunately for Nick, who was trapped with her in the little box and not mentally set for another soul-searching lecture. He was grateful.

The elevator was truly antique, very slow, obviously torqued very low. Nick figured that above them was clockworks of oversized pulleys and gears like in the old movies, the kind that would leave lots of room for error in the pre-electronics era of the gay 1890s, his favorite period of Baltimore history. The hotel was undoubtedly a big deal in the early twentieth century, he thought—very exclusive and specially designed and equipped with turn-of-the-century technology at the start. *Surely this is electric powered, isn't it?* Nick thought foolishly. He glanced at the unlit porcelain buttons again. He decided that the elevator was probably just a relic that the old lady was using to try to scare him. Surely there were modern elevators in such a famous building, no matter how old she was, the hotel or the lady.

At the fifth floor, the hulking, bulking machine bumped to a stop with a distinct thump and circular shimmy, which left Nick imagining bungee-like elastic cables, over worn and fragile, splitting and tangling. He saw the funny little box in his mind crashing him to his death or at best injuring him for a long hospital stay.

Miss Krantz let the doors open and told Nick to wait. She pointed a bony finger at a purple-velvet couch opposite the elevator. "Just for a second," she said, "while I get the key to the Rumba Room on the fourteenth floor." He noted there was no key slot below the 14 button in the elevator, just between 12 and 14. *Mmm, special entrance to 13? Figures, in this haunt.*

There was no 13 floor button.

Nick lingered inside the elevator to inspect the antique control board of numbered floor buttons again. He cherished a moment to himself. Ordinarily these moments had drifted to thoughts of J.J. and the twins. Not this time.

He was puzzled with the 1 through 12, then 14, buttons and tried to figure it out. He certainly didn't want to ask Miss Krantz any more questions that she could use to twist his mind around. Maybe the hotel's original design did not include a finished thirteenth floor. Could it be a sort of observation area beneath the fourteenth, much like the mysterious and undisclosed windows between the fourth and fifth floors of the prison-like agriculture department building on Independence Avenue in D.C.? he wondered. He and J.J. had spent many weekends in college and after in the museums on the National Mall between

Independence and Constitution Avenues, including exhibits at the agriculture department where they noticed the missing floor.

He stepped out after a minute and let the elevator doors close behind him, quite gently he noticed. He stood in a hallway of lavender-velvet wallpaper to wait for Miss Krantz, who had disappeared much too quickly, defying logic, to the left somewhere. He was puzzled, *She couldn't possibly move that fast.*

The couch looked decrepitly worn out and dirty. He didn't want to sit on it.

"This continues to be a really strange afternoon," he said to himself. "Afternoon? Oh God, what time is it?" He looked at his dad's gold watch he had worn faithfully since his parents' deaths.

4:50 p.m. "Wow, I think time stopped," he muttered. He had only been at the hotel for fifteen minutes. It seemed like hours.

Miss Krantz returned.

The elevator doors opened again without any apparent command.

Leading him aboard again, she said without feeling, "Yes, it is true. There are two tickets for couples left for the jazz party, so you can buy them down at the Owl Bar at the bottom. I don't know what happened with that girl, anyway." She pointed down angrily and shrugged.

Then her feeble left hand reached above the floor buttons and she pushed 14.

Again, with a deliberate and almost painful moan, the machine began to move up, the mechanical clanging noises more pronounced above them, closer to Nick's imaginary clockworks, and getting louder and louder as the weird lifting box rose. *Surely it won't make it to fourteen if it made all that ruckus one to five. I'm going to die,* he thought.

* * *

After another slow ride, the elevator doors this time opened quickly to a cheery, well-lit clubroom, which pleased

Nick instantly. It had large picture windows all around, revealing spectacular views of Baltimore in every direction. Glossy, clean wooden dining tables lined the outer walls on three sides near the windows. On the east side of the room was a spacious bar and a counter Nick took for a food prep area in front of twin swinging doors, propped open to reveal a bright fluorescent-lit kitchen of white wall tiles and extensive stainless-steel equipment.

Nick warmed up right away to the Rumba Room. *If this is indeed the party room, I'm in,* he thought, though not fully convinced it wasn't another trick.

"My God, you can see the whole city all around!" he blurted. "There's the Inner Harbor and Federal Hill behind it, across the harbor to the south. Old Memorial Stadium, where the Colts played and now slated for demolition, is over there to the northeast, see? And to the southeast the smoke stack section of the city of Dundalk, and Essex. Wow. To the southwest there's University Hospital, where my wife wants to get a full-time job when the twins start school the next year."

Nick, who knew the details of how this city was built from colonial days to the dawn of the new millennium, was absolutely thrilled with the visual panorama from the old hotel. This was his city, not College Park, where he had lingered for years to stay close to J.J.; not D.C., where he had hung out at her job at Children's Hospital.

He stared at the Baltimore skyline while he retraced its history in each direction. To the north, he followed the thin green valley of the Jones Falls creek twisting and turning through the neighborhoods. To the east he could see dome of Johns Hopkins Medical Center. To the west, he made out the famous original layout of the new City of Baltimore, the small, squared-off symmetry of the surveyed street plan by surveyor Thomas Poppleton, who was commissioned by city officials before the War of 1812, though the plan wasn't completed until several years later.

Nick walked across the Belvedere's party room to the south windows, where he squinted to find Fort McHenry at a far distance into the wrist of the hand-shaped Patapsco River stretching toward him and into the Baltimore Harbor. Nick's eyes wandered. He saw himself on deck of a British battleship in 1814 as attorney Francis Scott Key, leaning against a cabin door scribbling a draft of "The Star-Spangled Banner" as bombs burst in the air, and gave proof through the night that our flag was still there. The vision made Nick smile broadly, proudly. Seeing the city's history laid out in front of him on a living map was suddenly worth all the craziness of Miss Krantz. He thought, *We've got to see the new millennium in right here!* He began planning where he and J.J. would sit, which table, which barstools. He became delightfully obsessed.

As he continued to admire views of his city and its history, another voice came from behind him. Nick turned to see a short, wide Hispanic man in perfectly white coveralls. The man stepped away from his work with a wash bucket and mop and looked with a frightened face toward Nick.

"Oh, hi there," said Nick, trying to be as friendly as possible. "Who are you?"

"I eim Guad'lupe, maintenance man, please sir."

"So, this is the party room, eh Guadalupe? Sala de fiestas?"

"Sí. How you get here, meester?"

"Why, it was her, there—I came with her. It's okay, Guadalupe. It was her. She . . . brought me up in . . ."

Nick pointed to where he thought Miss Krantz was, only to see the back of her faintly, scurrying past the bar and disappearing into the kitchen.

"She? Who?" said the little man. He didn't seem to see Miss Krantz, perhaps had not noticed her at all.

Nick called to Miss Krantz. She didn't respond, and Guadalupe looked very nervous to be alone with such a tall stranger.

Nick remembered to focus on his quest: for New Year's party tickets. But he couldn't locate Miss Krantz, even after trailing her to the kitchen.

His only hope was to go down to the Owl Bar and see if the girl had left the tickets for him.

After the maintenance man showed Nick back onto the elevator, it opened smartly and carried Nick right down to the lobby floor efficiently. There was no clanking or mechanical moaning this time.

He walked through the lobby, which then seemed modern with tasteful décor, to the Owl Bar.

Maybe here I'll see Miss Krantz or the redheads who might have the tickets. She must have sneaked back down when I was looking around the city. He wasn't sure.

But the good-looking, redheaded young waitresses in their cute Bavarian outfits were no longer around. And no old lady Krantz either. The barroom was brighter and people were dressed fashionably, chatting and laughing. The tobacco smoke was gone.

A burly balding man behind the bar spoke when he saw Nick. "You da guy for da four tickets? Here. Cash or credit?"

"Credit, yes sir. Credit," he said.

Nick thought, Well, at least the young lady, or maybe the old lady, came through. Maybe both. He couldn't remember shaking hands or touching either of the women. But he did see them. He thought, *Yes, I did see them; well, anyway, I'd better get out of here and get on home with the tickets.*

Chapter 24: Making His Case

Nick rushed back to Pop's Tavern. He parked the Caddy in the alley parking space next to a metal parking sign of reflecting orange letters, RESERVED FOR THE BOSS, made specially by Pop's friends in the public relations office of the Baltimore City Police Department, complete with the BCPD logo at the bottom.

Anticipating his dutiful drive to Annapolis the next day to pick up his grandparents, Nick carefully checked everything inside the big car for evidence that might tell Pop he had used it. He removed his Best of the Hair Groups CD and put it in his pocket, and replaced it with the Sinatra CD in the audio system, being careful not to disturb the dust on the CD player. (Pop later knew Nick used the car. He secretly paid the $200 parking ticket sent to the Caddy owner's address, a ticket that blew off the windshield when placed there loosely by a meter maid shortly after Nick had parked by a fire hydrant as he was being swept under the spell of the magnificently ornate hotel.)

Nick jumped into his rusty-old black Toyota and sped home to J.J. in Glen Burnie, with his spirits high and a new confidence. He was certain that he could convince her to go out on New Year's Eve. She would feel his enthusiasm.

With four tickets to the Belvedere party in his pocket, Nick could hardly wait to tell J.J. about his adventure at the Belvedere. He'd emphasize the post-Victorian motif and the wonderful panoramic view of the city. After that he will tell her how much he loves her and that the party will be his gift to her.

* * *

Just inside the front door and after the first words he spoke of a party, Nick faced an angry J.J. She was confronting him with the kind of anger he had not seen in her for a long time.

Apparently willing to suspend all patience with Nick's delicate condition, J.J. shouted, "Millennium party? What?"

"Yeah, after all the talk, I did it. You seemed agreeable. And wow, you should hear where we are going, because you're going to love it!"

"I'm not going anywhere on New Year's, Nick. I thought we agreed. How can you say that I agreed to go out? Nick, I'm very concerned about you now. I don't think you are in touch with reality."

That struck a nerve. *How uncanny,* he thought, considering all the unreal things he saw and heard at the Belvedere not more than an hour earlier.

J.J. was livid. She was holding a special dinner for Nick and the twins—until Daddy got home—because she had felt guilty over their morning argument. His news was thus twice the shock. Without hearing any sensible or persuasive reasoning from Nick, J.J. vented, reminding him of their tight budget, chastising him for spending good money for a party when she'd already told her mother they only wanted a quiet night at home on New Year's.

"But you don't understand." Nick said in a hopeful tone. "This party is up at the old Belvedere uptown!"

That did nothing for J.J. "Nick," she stepped back, put hands on hips, and shook her head, "that crummy old hotel is in a bad neighborhood. Have you lost your freakin' mind? I hope you didn't spend much, because I'm not going."

"It is not crummy, just old. And, the crime there is not bad. J.J., it is a very cool place. There is a dimly lit bar on the first floor behind the lobby with a hallway of framed photos of celebrities . . . I guess they stayed there."

"Nick, I—"

"And in one of the photos I swear there was Thomas Edison of Menlo Park. I didn't think he'd ever been in Baltimore; I don't know when, but when we go there I'll check into the hotel history and . . . I love that guy, as you know . . ."

"Nick, I'm through with your adventures. This is going to be a dangerous time to be out. And in Baltimore City at night, my God, man! Who knows what can happen that night in the city!

198

Did you buy bulletproof vests for us, too? How much did you spend?"

He decided to lie. "Just two hundred dollars, but Nate and Betsy are going, too." He had actually paid the burly bartender at the Owl Bar four hundred dollars, two hundred for each couple.

"And when were you—and Nate, for that matter—planning to tell me?" snapped J.J., building on her outrage over just how much truth she was really hearing. "Does Betsy know about this? She's not one for going out at night, you know."

"I think so," said Nick meekly, further deflated. He thought he had Nate aboard; but when or not Nate told his wife Nick didn't know, nor did he care at this point. J.J. was his prize, not Betsy.

"J.J., this is the millennium. I think we should go and have a good time. It will be good for us. I was there today. I can tell you about it . . . an amazing afternoon I had. But first you have to see my point of view. I think both of us need this to start out the new year right. I love you, J.J., and want to give you a good time. Have your mom watch the kids while we go out."

"I love you too Nick. But, why do we have to risk it?" she said.

What did that mean? He wondered. Nick started to pace. He still had only taken a couple of steps into his house during the argument. Yet, now he was in free fall emotionally. He'd had his heart set on seeing J.J. break out of her funk and getting behind him, at least for the one big party night. Stymied, he wondered where the kids were. He wanted to scream. He was hungry. He was frustrated. Desperate, Nick blurted, "Look, Pop's lending us the Caddy and everything." It was a gamble, and another lie.

"Nick, I don't think it is a good idea. But we can talk about it at the table," she said more in the tone of a nurse to a sick patient.

Nick heard progress in her voice after his Caddy ploy. "J.J., honey, give me just one night at the Belvedere. That's all I'm asking," he said calmly.

No response from J.J., who walked into the kitchen to warm up the meal.

His eye dwelled on her lovely curves evident even in gray sweatpants and T-shirt. "She really is gorgeous and a gem of a woman. How in the world do I keep her?" he mumbled to himself as he shuffled slowly behind.

"Where are the girls, J.J.? How was their school day, anyway? Did you get there early to see them in class?"

No response.

Instead, he yelled down to the basement rec room where he heard the TV. "Hey, where are my girls? Heath, Hil? Are you ready to eat?"

The twins ran in, hugged their daddy, giggling all the way, running on about their day at "school." J.J. had planted them in front of the TV until Daddy got home.

The girls resembled their mom—auburn Dutch boy haircuts, dark eyes, and playful smiles. None of their daddy's moody disposition yet, but they did have the Italian olive skin that had skipped right past Nick.

They all sat down to a cup of homemade tomato basil soup, pasta primavera and salad—Nick's favorite meal, and apple strudel. J.J. had slaved in the kitchen to serve him a great supper, working extra hard to please Nick that day, worrying about them arguing in the morning.

Nick didn't have a clue about J.J.'s all-consuming concern over his despair and moods. She'd also given Nick no hints on her advice on the matter from their friends, the Browens including Nate's front-lawn pep talk.

And J.J., for her part, had no clue how worried Nick was that he was in danger of losing her to a "better" man. She never considered leaving Nick for any reason.

So, true to form, the good wife stopped arguing, stopped upsetting her idealistic husband, and gathered the twins to pray at the dinner table, while Nick swallowed his thoughts of false jealousy.

It was little Heather's turn to say grace. "God be good, God be great, please bless this house and this food, in Jesus's name . . ."

* * *

J.J. wasn't listening. She was praying privately instead, for inspiration. She was delving back into her nurse psychiatry training. She recalled Nick saying he taught school because children would learn from the lessons of history to make a better world. She thought his ideal was an expression of Nick's quiet, private desire for something, which, like all ideals, was not fully achievable. She'd been at his side, then, to see and feel his ideal crushed by an education system that rewarded conformity, not imaginative teaching. She saw that his crushed ideal led to a loss of purpose, a halt to his growth as a happy person. Was Nick's world becoming fiction, full of compulsive and irrational aims?

Still in prayer, J.J. was hoping he had not lost all sense of his own freedom as a person as Nate suggested. She saw him hurting himself inside. She was praying harder than she could ever remember, still not listening to Heather's angelic grace.

* * *

". . . and God bless Mommy and Daddy, and don't let them argue—please, Jesus, please. Amen." Heather looked up and saw her mom's eyes still shut, hands folded, and motionless several seconds after "Amen."

"Mommy, you're crying. Don't cry, Mommy."

Nick said, "Honey, are you okay? Heather meant well." He turned to the child, who was about to cry, too. "That was the best grace ever, kids. Heath, you didn't upset your mom. It's my fault. You were right. We argue too much." He turned to J.J., who was wiping her tears with a paper napkin and said kindly, "Okay, hon, let's eat?"

Nick focused on talking to the kids for the entire meal, thinking he had made progress with J.J. and the party idea. They all enjoyed their family meal as usual, and Nick and J.J. didn't discuss the tickets in front of the twins.

Third Interlude

Do we make our own dreams? Or do they make us?

Nick Esposito's continual ponderings about past events often manifested in his dreams.

He slept well after the pleasant family dinner together. His mind smoothed out the day's dark anxieties and then illuminated bits of past ponderings into a dream scripted for his 'eyes' and 'ears' only:

> *That young boy is looking at the big iron building on the corner of Baltimore and South Streets. The building is glowing yellowish.*
>
> *"Is it on fire?"*
>
> *"No," Mama says. "It's electric lighting. Maybe Mr. Edison is here."*
>
> *"Mama, Mr. Edison must be here today!" the boy shouts.*
>
> *The building has hundreds of slat windows behind five stories of stacked columns, which are all glowing, some dimmer than others, all a slight yellowish white. And no flickering as gas lanterns flicker! the boy notices.*
>
> *"Yes, Mr. Edison's got to be here."*
>
> *"That's right, Nicky. It's a big iron building. We've seen it on the way to market. Now it glows in the night." The woman grasps the boy's hand tight and pulls him, as he still stares at the big, glowing structure.*
>
> *They walk quickly past loud clacking of horse-drawn street cars on cobblestone. She leads him into the corner entrance of the big iron-gray building that glows.*

Inside the lobby, she strains to lift him up. The boy can see six bright white lights.

"Are they safe, Mama?"

"Mr. Edison says they are, Nicky. Remember what teacher said at school? Mr. Edison had a New Year's party with light all around his workshop in New Jersey."

A large crowd gathers around them, all gazing at the glowing lights.

"Will they catch fire, Mama?"

A thin man in wire spectacles stands on a soapbox near Nicky and his mama and brings a large, red megaphone up to his mouth. "Ladies and gentlemen, please come up front so we can get started on your tour of the Baltimore Sun Iron Building, now lighted with Edison Electric Lamps. Yes, every corner of the newspaper operation—the lobby here, the newsroom, the mailing room, the layout room, the basement machinery—are all lit up electric."

The man waits for people to walk in close to him. "My co-presenter is the Sun's Mr. Mencken. My name is M. F. Moore, general manager of the Edison Company."

"Mama, you said Mr. Edison would be here, right?"

"Shush, Nicky—the man talking works for Mr. Edison."

"But it's not him. He's not him. Thomas Edison. I want to see Mr. Edison like his picture in school, Mama."

The man holds a big light bulb in his right hand. He says, "The incandescent lamp is perfectly steady light, not like the arc light our competitors promote. The Edison incandescent is uniform in its intensity and will replace the gas jet in illuminating interiors like you see here. Why, I dare say one of our lamps has burned for more than four hundred hours straight!"

The boy reaches out and tugs at the side of Mr. Moore's baggy wool trousers.

"Oh hello, young man. Do you have a question? What's your name?"

Mama pulls the boy back. "I'm very sorry, sir. I told him Mr. Edison would be here. Nicky is his name and he studied about the electricity in school. Is Thomas Edison himself here, sir?"

"He may be here later, ma'am." He looks up again at the crowd and resumes. "How many folks read about our New Year's celebration in electric lights two years ago at Menlo Park? Well, then you read about the lighting of New York's Broadway last year and streets in Philadelphia earlier this year. And now, where better to demonstrate the wonders of the Edison electric light than at the Baltimore Sun Iron Building?"

"Mama, they'll catch fire. Mr. Edison's not here. I'm scared."

"I don't think so. Mr. Edison says they're safe."

"But he's not here. 'Lectric wires kill people, Mama. I want to go, Mama!"

The boy breaks free. Men in round hats and long coats scramble to catch him.

They all rush the door and knock down one of Edison's electric light fixtures. It breaks on the stone floor and sparks fly. Fire ignites huge piles of newspapers. Drapes burn. The entire ceiling is aflame.

Mama reaches Nicky outside a block away. As they turn back to look, they see people running from the Sun Iron Building on Baltimore and South

Streets. And the building has disappeared. Gone. Just a smoldering mound of hot metal remains.

Chapter 25: Quiet Oaks Calvary

Early morning, the day after Nick's Belvedere visit

Standing next to the bed in blue scrubs, J.J. shook Nick's shoulder, and then tugged on his pajama collar. "Nick, Nick," she said softly. "You've been having one of your dreams, hon. Wake up. It's late. I'm leaving now. Don't forget to call the crab cake man for the bar today, okay?"

Nick opened his eyes. "J.J., oh thank God. Wow, what a dream. I think great-granddad Mike was there, except he had my name and was just a kid, in the old Sun newspaper building in the last century. It burned down, sort of all melted. But the date was all wrong. And, no, Mike was older then."

"Oh, you and your history. Have a nice day, my Nicky whacky." She rushed out the door to her ride to Hopkins with Betsy Bowen.

Outside, in her Beemer, Betsy immediately asked, "Where is Dr. Handsome?"

"Shut up, Bet." J.J. paused. "You may be right about that guy."

* * *

Nick shook the cobwebs out and worried about J.J. He had not heard another word of anger from her that morning, no screaming, no lecturing, no continuation of their argument over the Belvedere party tickets the night before.

Damn, bet she rode in with Wellborne and happy to do so, he thought.

J.J. had already stopped commuting with the handsome young surgeon. Wellborne got frisky and touchy with her, pretending he'd gotten lost driving her home on Anne Arundel County back roads near her Glen Burnie home. He'd stolen a quick kiss before she could push him away. Not the kind of stuff she would tell Nick.

Fully awake after breakfast, Nick figured he'd wasted their money and time buying those party tickets. But, despite his freaky experience with ghostly old lady Krantz at the Belvedere, he was not going to give them up. "I've got to bring in the

206

cavalry," he said to his image in the mirror over the bathroom wash basin. "I need Pop to warm her up."

He contemplated his day. Triandos was scheduled to bartend. Nick then was planning his chore to pick up Pop and Minnie in Annapolis, following their long Thanksgiving weekend there. He'd work on Pop during the drive.

* * *

After the 30-minute drive from Annapolis back to the senior center in the Caddy that afternoon, Nick walked the old couple inside.

"Hey Pop, get some rest at Quiet Oaks today, okay? Because we are all coming over to see you at dinner here tonight," He let Grandma Minnie walk ahead and stopped Pop to say, "I want you to talk with J.J. She is too distant, Pop. I think she's leaving me. Don't say I said so. I just want you to show her some love."

"We all love J.J.," Pop whispered with a disapproving growl. "Don't be so stupid, Nicky boy. You treat her right, hear?"

Nick told Pop he needed to convince J.J. to take a night out on New Year's Eve because it would help their marriage. He kept it vague, but implored him to help him soften her up.

Grandma Minnie, who'd wandered too far ahead for her comfort, came back to them, having heard. "She is not leaving you, my Nicky. But you come anyway. Bring the kids, too. I want to see them."

* * *

Nick loved his twins with all his heart. They were precious gifts. But they were also the keys to the jailhouse door for Nick. He served his time at Pop's Tavern to support them.

When J.J. gave birth to their twins, Nick needed extra cash. He allowed Pop to pressure him into helping at the bar as Pop praised Nicky's mild manners as a bartender and believed in his heart that his grandson would gladly work for the sake of the family. Pop reluctantly agreed to pay him a good salary after saying, "Oh okay, but a grandson should not have to get money to help his poor ol' Pop." The guilt trip stuck with Nick and he obeyed his Pop as always, but with pay now.

J.J.'s pregnancy had been a big surprise. It happened after they had been lovers for many years and married for seven. Nick had not wanted kids for fear of them inheriting his closet insanity.

Then, after she spent her first year working too hard at the Johns Hopkins AIDS clinic, J.J. had a mild stroke. She too lost interest in having children. Her health was bad and she was emotionally drained with constant, great empathy for every AIDS case—especially the children—trying to do the impossible task of offering a bright future when there were no effective treatments at that time. Finally, she collapsed on the brick stairs to the parking garage on Broadway near the hospital.

Her stroke was not evident to the attending physicians while they attended to her head and back injuries. Once they diagnosed a stroke, neurologists told her never to risk having children, which was fine with J.J. The medical bills piled up and Nick could no longer ignore the family business, no matter how unpleasant. He stopped looking for tutoring jobs and went to work at the tavern, reluctantly insisting on that salary from Pop. In effect, Hilary and Heather put Nick under Pop's big thumb for good.

* * *

Quiet Oaks was a two-story brick "home" for seniors. First floor residents live a safe and restful life with the expected health and dementia issues of old folks. On half of the second floor Alzheimer's patients needed their continual care and protection in a locked ward.

Security at Quiet Oaks was tight for the other fifty residents who lived on the first floor. The building was pleasing to old folks. It was designed to look like a large version of J. R.'s Ewing's ranch on the '70s hit TV show Dallas. The staff kept it very clean. They managed precise scheduling of meals, TV time, rec time, and lights out. The old folks moseyed with their walkers, canes, and wheelchairs back to their two-room apartments at

10:30 p.m., just the time of day when Pop always had the most fun in his life.

Again, he hated Quiet Oaks. Minnie tolerated it. It kept Pop safe from himself, she said.

Little Heather spoke up first as the family gathered around the two dining room tables, which Nurse Sam pushed together for his favorite family. Sam sat with them, too, at Pop's insistence.

"Grandma, I love your crab cakes," Heather said after one bite.

J.J. corrected her daughter. "Heather, no, these aren't Granma's, but good, huh?"

"Yes, they are, Mommy."

Pop beamed. "So, you like the crab cakes, girls?"

Heather and Hilary screamed together, "They're Grandma's!"

Sam tried hiding his big Nigerian smile and finally laughed, "Tell 'em Miss Minnie."

"You're right, dearies," Minnie said. "I gave them the recipe." She smiled and shrugged.

Nick was amazed. "It's a family secret. I can't believe you gave it up and—"

"So, what," Pop stopped him. "Nicky boy. It's part of history now. There are no more Minnie Esposito crab cakes sold at Ellwood Avenue, my boy. I know you get them from Gunner's Crab House now, even though we gave you the recipe, right? Did you think I didn't know?" Pop's laughing eyes looked adoringly at his grandson. "I tried one of them from Gunner's, Nicky, that day of the Girl Scouts. Not too bad, but not my Minnie's. You left about fifteen crab cakes at the end of the bar that day too. I brung 'em back here, 'member Minnie? And these here people cookin' these god-awful meals, well, they never tasted good crab cakes."

"I told them we can do even better than anybody's," Grandma Minnie said to the twins.

Pop finished the story, "So we went in there with 'em in that kitchen there and taught 'em. Now we got good ones here."

Minnie added, "I still watch over them and make sure they don't use fillers and plenty of mustard powder, Nicky, like you like."

Nick did know the recipe. He could have been making them for the bar still, but lacked the incentive. Wouldn't have been authentic if Grandma didn't make and present them like in the old days. "Well, I never want to deny a piece of history going into the books," Nicky said. "Do you kids know how Baltimore became the crab cake capital of the United States?"

"Oh God, not that story!" J.J. said. "It's too long." She rolled her eyes and mouthed 'I'm sorry' to Granny Minnie, with a smile of resignation.

Checked by J.J., Nick decided to cut back the story, only tell the family an abridged version of crab cake history. After all, his reason for arranging the family gathering was for the benefit of J.J., to soften her up for a New Year's outing at the Belvedere, not a family history lesson.

"Kids, the colonial people who landed on the shores of the bay and settled Baltimore came up with a whole bunch of crab recipes, including minced crab meat mixed with bread pieces and spices, the first crab cakes . . . except they were not called that at first—and weren't as good as Grandma Minnie's, mind you.

"In my favorite Baltimore period, the late nineteenth century—more than one hundred years ago—when the city grew real fast, so did the popularity of crab paddy or croquette recipes. The name crab cake for a fried patty of crabmeat became the accepted term in the early twentieth century, and at the New York World's Fair they served 'Baltimore crab cakes.' The reputation grew too, along with Grandma's version and . . ."

Nick glanced several times at Pop as he concluded his quick crab cake history lesson, looking for the pre-arranged wink from the old man that it is time to talk about the joy of a New Year's Eve party with your wife.

Nick finished the story with, "As his luck would have it, during World War II, Pop's Tavern was only half a block beyond a two-mile dry zone imposed by the army around its Fort

Holabird. Soldiers and officers found a home away from home coming to Pop's and enjoying themselves.

"As soldiers and sailors shipped out, they took memories of Minnie's crab cakes with them. Those crab cakes became legendary in parts of the world Pop could only dream of seeing where the soldiers told of Grandma Minnie's crab cakes in Baltimore. Pop never left Maryland his whole life. Right, Pop?"

"Right, Nicky. Plenty of fun right in town." He gave Nick the wink Nick wanted.

Pop came through. He began his best New Year's story, "Girls, and that means you too, J.J.," he began, although he focused totally on Hilary and Heather now. "When your Daddy was about your size, I told him lots of history stories, and that's how he became a scholar in the subject. Ain't that right, Nicky?"

"Well . . ." Nick just smiled knowingly, and then checked J.J. in case she suspected the conspiracy.

Pop's old eyes collected J.J.'s watchful mothering gaze, along with that of her wide-eyed twin daughters, who were eager to hear a story from their colorful and jolly great grandpop. He began, "Back in the year 19 and 33, I think it was, end of that year, very end. It was a terrible year; just terrible. My business at the tavern was not hurt a lot, but the whole country was hurtin'. Depression, they called it. Lots of people out a work, see?"

(Of the many colorful stories by Pop that inspire Nick's love of history, Nick's favorite was about the time when Baltimore Police Commissioner Charles D. Gaither gave twenty-six-year-old Stephen Esposito a VIP seat between him and the mayor on a cold New Year's Eve afternoon in 1933. This story forever tied Nick tightly to his grandfather in more ways than one.)

Pop continued, "The occasion was the dedication and cornerstone laying of the new police headquarters at Fallsway and Lexington Streets. Well, do you remember me sayin' that my papa was the great police detective Michael Esposito, who was from Italy?"

211

"Yeah," the twins said in unison, as they stared raptly at Pop.

Nick watched the girls' eyes gazing at the storyteller, soaking up every syllable, every facial expression, all his frequent dramatic hand and head movements.

"Inspector Esposito, that's what they called him. Well, he never wanted to be seen at such public events. He didn't want criminals to recognize him, caus'in he was tryin' ta catch 'em, see? But he was big. He was big in reputation. Nailed all the bad crooks and sent them to prison. A hero, to be sure.

"Mayor Jackson sent Inspector Mike a special invitation to be a VIP—that's Very Important Person—at the ceremony." Pop broke into a laughing smile. "Now, who do you think Inspector Mike, my pops, gave that invitation to?"

"You!" both girls yelled and giggled.

"Sssshh," J.J. instructed them, as twenty or so gray heads in the dining room turned to look at the children. Then J.J. turned to Nick and whispered, "I think I know where this is going and it won't work."

Nick couldn't look at her.

"Like I say, Inspector Mike Esposito, a true hero in town and my papa, was not fond of publicity. The mayor reserved a seat in the front row for him. But Inspector Mike preferred to stay out of the limelight; his job would be better served to stay low profile.

"So instead, my papa asked the mayor if his son, me, from the best little tavern in East Baltimore, the one near the brewery, could take the VIP seat at the much-ballyhooed thing, and to represent him proper, but quiet like, he told me. So, I did, quiet like, if you can believe that."

"Grandpop, what's a ballyhooed thing?" little Hilary asked.

"A swell occasion."

"What's a swell occasion?"

"Okay. Let's just paint the picture for you little cuties. The streets were blocked off with long lines of uniformed policemen.

Dozens of dignitaries and Baltimore's best business leaders sat, gathered around a newly cut granite stone that held a bright copper box to be cemented into the corner of the huge new police building.

"There I was, as a very young man, sittin' in the front row facing a grand podium, that bein' in front of the new shiny cop—I mean, police—station on Lexington Street. On my right was Commissioner Gaither. On my left was Mayor Jackson.

"I wasn't nervous 'cause, see, I just thought I belonged there, too. Why not, huh?"

Nick shook his head slightly in admiration, gave Pop a very Italian gesture to proceed, opening both hands spreading toward him in deference to a wiser man, nodding toward him.

He continued, "They were all these big businessmen in the city sittin' right behind us, and as each one's name was called, one of them business leaders would get up and walk to the mayor at the podium to shake his hand. They'd been told ahead to put their business cards into a copper box for the cornerstone."

"What's a cornerstone?" Hilary asked.

J.J. noticed Nick sighing as he said impatiently, "Hil, it's a traditional box cemented into a new building with things like letters, documents, even business cards that are sealed away for people to open way off in the future when the building is replaced. But Pop didn't have a business card, did you, Pop?"

"Nope. Never needed no business card. Everybody east of Jones Falls knowd me." Pop's face again beamed as he broke into his rusty laughter.

"So, I just sat there in that reserved seat wondering what to do. Didn't want to embarrass my papa, the famous Inspector Michael Esposito, even though he wasn't even there, as far as I knew. Didn't see him, but you know, no one ever saw him until he slapped handcuffs on ya." Pop laughed hard and coughed. "Sorry 'bout that dear," he said to a now frowning J.J.

Nick hadn't heard the date; the suspense was killing him. "Pop, wasn't it New Year's Eve?"

"Oh yeah, of course." An obvious pause as Pop recalled Nick's instructions. "Yeah, that's right. They wanted the dedication to be a happy occasion when people don't mind gettin' out and spending time with other folks, being with family and all, you see. Thought it would help brighten things up for 1934."

J.J. mumbled, "Didn't work." She didn't mean the 1930's.

Pop frowned. "It took a little longer to get back to happier days, yes. About that business card thing . . . er, it didn't matter I didn't have one. I found out at the last minute I'd be right there with them VIPs."

Nick said, "Didn't you bother reading the program?" He was laughing again. Only Nicky could talk back to Pop.

"Thank you so much for that, Nicky," snapped Pop, and then winked at him. "Unbeknowin' to me, the plan didn't call for the mayor, and commissioner, and Inspector Mike to contribute business cards. Why would they? They's VIP's, right up front. Instead, the plan had VIP guests dropping a shiny copper penny into the box instead of a card."

Minnie noticed the twins getting fidgety. They didn't remember what VIP meant. "Stephen, get to the point. We all know by now you were a VIP, if just for one day."

"Well, okay. At that moment, the city treasurer formally presented Baltimore Mayor Jackson and Commissioner Gaither each with a special, shiny penny to drop into the box. In better times, it would have been a silver dollar, something you girls have never seen. But the mayor wanted future generations to never forget the Depression, though the terrible economy of the country was not called the Depression yet, in 1933. That was history, right, Nicky?"

"That's right, Pop."

"The mayor's penny was a 1918 penny in honor of the fighting men who lost their lives in the Great War. He dropped it into the box with a few patriotic words for our brave men in uniform.

"Then, it was Gaither's turn. His was a 1933 penny to commemorate the dedication, the date for the new police

214

headquarters. After the mayor dropped in his penny, followed by polite applause, Gaither approached the podium with his hands in his coat pockets. It was a cold day. Did I say it was New Year's Eve, J.J.?"

She rolled her eyes and nodded.

Nick thought, *Darn it, he's blowing it.*

Pop stood up and supported himself palms down on the table. "Ya know what he did then, kids?"

"I do," said J.J., trying not to sound sarcastic, and to remain pleasant.

Pop: "I know you do, dear." He held up one hand toward J.J. "What happened was a switcheroo. The commissioner managed to switch pennies in his pocket, and then dropped in a replacement. He did that for me and Grandpa Mike!

"Returning to his seat next to me, he shook my hand and palmed the real 1933 penny into my hand. He put his other hand on my shoulder and slightly pushed down, signaling me to remain seated. Then he whispered, 'Here, Steve. This will last longer with you than it will in this damn building.' Sorry ladies. He told me later to hold on to it to recognize the fine work of Inspector Mike, 'cause my father never did want no awards or nothin'.'"

"I love that story, kids," Nick said. "As it turned out, Gaither was right about his penny outlasting the ballyhooed police headquarters. In 1977, the 1933 police headquarters was razed for a new police headquarters, but not before there was one last role for the building to play. It was used as a movie studio and set for the film "... And Justice for All." Pop told me he was on top of the world that day. What'd you do after the police headquarter dedication, Pop?"

"Well, on that night after the 1933 dedication ceremonies, me and my papa, the inspector, threw the best New Year's Eve party in the city. Without me knowin', he arranged for his police friends to close the entire block of Ellwood, from the alley behind the Baltimore Street row houses to Fairmount Avenue. Only locals were allowed to enter; others were directed through the alley to Decker Avenue parallel to Ellwood.

"I kept the tavern open until 2:00 a.m. Inspector Mike had already told all the neighbors, and they opened their parlors for each other's families until well after midnight.

"Even Gaither and the mayor with their wives stopped by the tavern at 11:00 p.m. to wish me and Minnie girl a good new year."

Nick added, "Pop, I believe that evening, more than any other thing, made you a big success in city circles for good. Is that right? Didn't the party turned things around for you, even in the Depression?" He was pumped.

"And that day made your Grandma Minnie very proud," Pop told Nick, while checking to see Minnie nodding in agreement as she kept eating quietly, with a subtle nod in the affirmative. Only the twins detected her smile from their low vantage point, looked at each other, and giggled.

"Them's the kinda things you'll enjoy most in this life, Nicky. This year's special, too. You need to go out and show off your beautiful bride, boy."

* * *

In the Toyota on the way back home with the kids, Nick said, "Hey kids, how'd you like Pop's story?"

But J.J. nipped their reply in the bud. "Yes, Nick, great story, yes. I still do not want to go out on New Year's Eve. But getting together with Betsy and Nate is one part of your scheme I do like, Nick. We can do that."

Nick took her "that" as another step forward.

* * *

After Nick became an adult, remembering Pop's penny story always cheered him. And it made him wish he was more like Pop. He had heard Pop brag many times, "We made that penny switch in the year 19 and 33."

While the twins sat before Nick on the floor watching TV that evening, Nick snoozed on the couch reliving Pop's stories, revisiting what he had pondered about at Quiet Oaks that day. He saw the adolescent friendship Pop shared with Babe Ruth at St. Mary's Industrial School for (bad) Boys. As the story goes, young

216

Stephen taught the Babe to throw a curve. (They were indeed both at the reform school at the same time. But it was of no consequence to Pop's well-worn stories that George Herman "Babe" Ruth would have been five years older. Nick always ignored that little inconsistency and since his college days always passed on the story as Pop told it.)

Nick also dreamed of Pop's frightening tales of Inspector Mike pursuing gangsters such as flamboyant Jack "Legs" Diamond and rival bootlegger Dutch Schultz when known to be visiting Baltimore. According to Baltimore legend, Schultz an awesome scare at the tavern on November 30, 1929. The thug had the audacity to enter the very tavern of Michael Esposito's son with several of his "associates." Pop recognized Schultz who owned a tavern in New York. Pop walked calmly back to the kitchen for his pistol. He told Minnie and their two son's playing cards at the kitchen table, "Legs is out there with his men. I sent someone out to get word to you-know-who."

Minnie and her little children Carlo and Alfredo ran upstairs to their bedroom and hid under the bed shivering for the remainder of the evening. It was Minnie's birthday. She thought it was another bad omen of bad times, a sort of a curse, a fear, which was suddenly running through Baltimore following the stock market crash just one month earlier. Pop had lost a lot of money in the past few weeks through investing in friends' stocks, without her knowledge. (He never told her anything about business.)

Pop closed the bar early that night when the out of town thugs left in a hurry after a few drinks. Gunshots were heard in the alley, as Pop told it, but the tavern was long darkened and locked.

Pop often told his grandchildren that during Prohibition, because he was tight with "the Sheriff," he was never again forced to close the tavern early, even for one day. Nick's parents Carlo and Miriam didn't like Pop telling that story to their kids because he was breaking the law to still sell liquor during the ban. But he told them anyway.

He said that during Prohibition he could keep selling liquor anyway because one of his best 1920s cronies, Baltimore

Police Commissioner Charles D. Gaither, would always warn Pop whenever the feds were in the vicinity. The tip would trigger a mad scramble in the tavern. First, Pop would lock the doors, even with customers still drinking.

The entire tavern of customers would work feverishly to help hide all the liquor under the coal pile in the basement and over false ceilings Pop had installed in closets.

Sometime later, the phone would ring. Pop said he would hear Gaither whisper, "Steve, they're on Eastern Avenue heading up Ellwood now." The tavern lights would go on again, doors would fly open, and customers would find their seats "in a jiffy, sippin' coffee and sodies," Pop said, before the feds marched in smiling and knowingly.

These stories were more than real to Nick. He slept well remembering all the details and dreaming. They were the kind of romance in life that he wanted for himself, but could never grasp or imitate in any way. They were what he admired in written history too; what he admired in his Pop, and why he romanced in reading and learning about the legends of history: legends like, but not equal to, his idol, Stephen Pop Esposito.

He took Pop at his word that it was all true, even some parts of the story he knew weren't.

Chapter 26: The Truth About J.J.

"Hey Nicky, what's happenin' bro," Nate bellowed as he entered the tavern.

Nick replied, "Yo. Talk to me, my brother!"

"Well. That's better; I was worried when you called. You just said you needed me to stop in at Pop's Tavern tonight. Are you okay? On the phone, you didn't talk our stupid jive. Why?" Nate asked. "Are you sick?"

"Oh, I just forgot. Not in the mood for joking around I guess. Thanks for coming, Nate," Nick said, extending his upturned right hand for a high-five handshake.

"What did you want to see me for, Nick? Need help here tonight, relief?"

"No, Nate. Mr. Triandos will tend bar tonight. He's over there stocking the beer cooler. You and I need to talk in the kitchen. You got time?"

"Sure thing."

"Alex, make me an Old Grand-Dad with rocks; make it a double. What are you drinking, Nate?"

"Just a Coke. What's the problem, Nick? Double bourbon, huh? You said you don't drink here."

Nick and Nate walked back to the kitchen table, where Nick had chips and pretzels in bowls and two chairs.

He told his buddy, "Well, guess what? J.J. said she wants to spend New Year's with you and Betsy. She'll be asking Betsy. I'd like you to convince Betsy to go with us to the Belvedere for New Year's."

"No way, Nick. You don't know her like I do. She is not a party animal, especially at some yuppie uptown blowout. It's going to be a mess, Nicky boy. And, I don't even like that scene anyway."

Nick knew this would not be easy, "Look, even if it is a wild scene, which it won't be, it is very classy, believe it or not. I was there in the party room. We will all be together for the millennium. Think of it. We'll always have that, Nate. I need you guys to come with us."

"Us, huh? You got J.J. to buy in?"

"Well . . ."

"So, she's still against it, right?"

"I bought the tickets."

"What?" Nate couldn't believe it. "For us too, Nick? Oh boy, you've got more to say, I bet."

"I'll pay for yours, too," Nick said, as Nate shook his head. "Look, you won't believe this, but a ghostly old lady, must have been a hundred years old, greeted me at the entrance to the Belvedere. She showed me this party room and all. But the weird thing was she knew my name. She knew my damn name, Nate. I think she was not real, man. It is so spooky up there. This place will just be perfect for a party. It is wacky and we'll—"

"Nick."

"What?"

"I called the hotel after you called me the other day about this. I told them to look for you. I was worried. I said you'd be coming there soon. I told them what you look like. Nick, I'll level with you. We think you are losing it, buddy. We, especially me, Nate Bowen your friend, are all very, very worried about you. And J.J. is not leaving you, ever. Why are you so desperate about this party?"

"You don't know the real reason why. I don't want to have to tell you, please."

"Come on. I know you better than that. What's up? This wild idea, tossing yourself into a bunch of strangers in a celebration? This is not you, Nick."

Nick fiddled with a peanut shell. He took on a lost expression and said, "I never told you something."

"What?"

"It's something about us, about me and J.J."

"What could you possibly mean? You've told me your entire wacky life."

220

"This was a secret, Nate. Let me talk." Nick took a slug of his whiskey.

"Okay, shoot."

"You know she took that nursing mission trip to Africa years ago? Well, what I never told you was that it was not a wonderful and fulfilling experience like we said. That is our cover story."

"Is that the hang-up? Is that the tension between you two? Or, better, is that the tension between Nick and Nick?"

"Stop. I'm not bipolar. I wish Betsy would stop saying that. Well, maybe I am a little. I just get excited sometimes. Hear me out."

"Sorry. But Betsy says you've had worse delusions than ever lately. J.J. told her so."

"No, Nate. As I said—I just get excited. I see an opportunity and sometimes, not often, I want to grab it. Most of the time my fun time doesn't work out very well. I get down in the dumps. But I can even handle that now.

"I just know that if you and Betsy go with us to this Belvedere party, this opportunity for a fun time out together will be great. Please."

"I don't know. I just don't."

"Okay, I'll tell you what's at the bottom of our problem; been that way since Africa. I've never told the entire story, okay?

"Sure, I'm listening."

It was a tragic, ill-advised, nursing mission that she took to West Africa, one she never finished. I worry that it's still a problem with us. We don't talk about it but I think we both know it. She resents me for it."

"I doubt that. It couldn't be that bad."

"Let me finish. You know we weren't married then, right?"

Nate nodded.

"I had to learn the hard way, Nate. I could have stopped J.J.'s Africa nursing mission, she told me. She wanted me to propose to her and I was too afraid to lose her. Well, we talked about it, usually after sex, when I was open to talking."

"Hey, stop right there. Don't need to know." Nate smiled, waving, crisscrossing his hands between the two men.

"I'm serious, Nate. I wasn't good enough for her. You see how men look at her. As things turned out, I could have kept her home in America if I'd asked J.J. to marry me after many years of putting it off; I rationalized she would not be happy with my, you know, ... I'm not the most confident human being."

"Oh, please. I've told you before, it's just your imagination, Nick."

Well, okay. That's fine."

Nate leaned closer across the little table, "Just tell me what happened, if you must."

"Back then, she was very open about our relationship, telling me she was wary of tying the knot to a man who has bouts with the bottle. 'I'm not going to repeat my parents' tragedy,' she'd say. You know how she lectures me; always has. I had many opportunities to get her to the altar. Our passion was colossal."

"There you go again. Don't need to know that part, Nick."

"Oh, shut it, would you, and listen? I was hesitant, right? Couldn't commit. That's the point I'm trying to make. I cursed the day I let her nursing friends talk her into signing up for the mission to northern Nigeria."

"Why's that, Nick? She was nursing, helping kids. What's wrong with that?"

"She got malaria, Nate."

"What? Bad?"

"Just short of dying. The worst. It was all my fault."

"I doubt it. What happened? Forget your medicine or something?"

"Let's start at the beginning. There were the long dog days during that summer before she left for Africa when I just hoped for another teaching job to appear magically. I just wanted to be near her so I looked for another job in the D.C. area. She got tired of waiting for me to pop the question. With all her new training in pediatric nursing, she decided to try at last to follow her brain instead of her romantic heart. Her nursing friends told her about the dire needs of children in West Africa. AIDS was already epidemic in some parts. She would have a chance to put that big heart to work helping needy children in a foreign land, instead of staying with me, I guess."

"Bull."

"I know this to be true, Nate. No longer willing to wait forever to get married—for she did love me, she said—I think she lost confidence in me, just a closet alcoholic who couldn't keep a job. So, the rest is history, bad history. In that same summer after earning her master's degree, she signed up to follow her college pal Anita, a social worker, to a health center in Kano, Nigeria for a two-year stint with a Catholic mission. It was designed to provide proper hygiene services and education to the women and children in local villages.

"Not an easy job, by any means; and, as it turned out, far more demanding than any situation J.J. had ever known. But, once licensed as a nurse practitioner, J.J. was free to make more choices for herself and she was less willing anymore to do what I said or wanted. I let her go."

Nate stopped staring at his hands, sighed deeply, and raised his eyes to Nick's. "Damn it, Nick. You are even dumber than I thought. You need a guardian, man. And, I still don't see how a New Year's party will help you with J.J."

"There's more, Nate."

"I don't need to hear more. It is difficult for you to tell this story. I can't take seeing you like this. I take it that this secret story is out-of-bounds for Betsy?"

Nick acted like he didn't hear the question and continued. "J.J. uncharacteristically committed to join that two-year humanitarian mission in Nigeria without consulting with me. Once in Kano, she committed unwittingly to the dusty town of Jos in the eastern highland of the northeast corner of that sub-Sahel region of the country, where Western professionals tried to teach

Christianity while serving health care to children in the Moslem-dominated north. Tough order, huh?"

"She's not particularly religious, is she, Nick?"

"No. But in a letter to me after a couple of weeks there, she wrote that she was moved to tears over undernourished, impoverished children. 'It just shouldn't happen in today's world,' she wrote, not only to me but to her friends and family in a constant stream of words written small on little folded, lightweight blue mailers.

"Meanwhile, in the fall I began preparing for a new job, in D.C. I became desperately lonely while starting my new duties teaching history at Backus Middle School, on South Dakota Avenue, and near Catholic University. There was no longer any need for me to be there with J.J. gone. I just never thought she'd actually leave. But she did. Nate, I never did fit into my family, not my schools, not my jobs. People never related to me; some actually feared or ridiculed me. Except J.J. She was and is the only person on Earth who understands me. With her gone, I finally I knew that I was lost without her. I feel it again now."

Nick looked intently at Nate, who's face then reflected fear of perhaps hearing the worst in Nick's story. Nick continued, "And now she could easily leave me again, Nate, if I don't do something big and dramatic for us, like a romantic millennium party in the old Belvedere. But I digress.

"J.J. had been in Africa for just a month when, after a couple of letter exchanges, I chucked my new job and left for West Africa to be with her."

"Wow. You do have the guts. I'll say that for you."

"Maybe so. But that's how I lost my second teaching job, although the school system had already grown tired of the rumors of my whiskey drinking during school hours. Fellow teachers reported smelling it on my breath first thing in the morning. I can't deny it. I missed my woman.

"I felt better right away when I left for Nigeria. The airport in Lagos was crowded and chaotic. I bribed the officials to okay my passport without proper shots. I took a barn burner to

Jos, some six hundred miles north, and bought an old powder-blue Volkswagen Bug for the short drive to J.J.'s mission center in a dusty region that looked like parts of southeast Colorado. It was hilly and dry, but the people were thin and hungry-looking most of the time."

"You had it bad for her, buddy."

"Of course. I knew by then I'd been stupid. Shoulda married her. Well, J.J. loved seeing me again, but she questioned the wisdom of my compulsive behavior more than ever. 'Why did I want to marry this guy?' she must have been thinking, right?"

"Don't be so hard on yourself."

"We stayed at the mission awhile in one of their cottages of cinder blocks with a tin roof, me helping her and the others as a volunteer, getting her supplies, running errands to Jos. But a few months into her 'once-in-a-lifetime experience,' as she called it, in the African bush, sharing life with naive, pleasant people in a rural village, it was all turning very, very sour. She was already bitterly disillusioned. J.J. hadn't been fully prepared for this kind of missionary work—the constant sadness of being a caregiver in a strange land, dealing with desperately ill women and children with AIDS, many who could not have responded to anti-HIV drugs even if they were readily affordable and available. Of course, back then, the meds were not available anyway. If we bathed more than once a week or ate special American food mailed into us from home, we felt guilty and selfish.

"Her desperate quest for her own brand of heroics as a world saver proved to be insanity, in my opinion. She had hoped to help the world's poor. But instead, I saw firsthand that the male dominance in a conservative Islamic culture in the northern states was wearing her down. Local officials deliberately made simple day-to-day activities far more difficult for women than for men, especially for so-called Western women.

"Yes, I had been caught up on the romance of it, too. Going off to the Dark Continent singing that Toto tune 'Gonna take some time to do the things we never have . . . in Aaafrica,' and to protect my girl, to be with her no matter what. Like in the Toto song.

"My rationale for joining her was that I would write our story there. I began a journal about our experience, a book maybe, a best seller. Oh, right!

"And I tried in vain to help her get some respect in the clinic. She was the brightest worker, but still disrespected. Finally, appealing man to man, I went to J.J.'s supervisor, a spirited, kind, tall Hausa man of twenty-nine, who granted her a much-needed weeklong break from her duties. The health center officials were glad to rid themselves of us with our constant complaints and worries. They also didn't like us anyway, an unmarried couple, staying together, as a bad example to young people.

"I drove J.J. and me in my little blue VW Bug across Nigeria from northeast dry zone to the humid subtropics southwest, weather like Orlando in spring, and crossed the border to the Republic of Benin, a Francophone neighboring country on the treacherous Atlantic coast.

"Soon, like a mirage, we saw the place we sought for vacation, but which had only been a rumor: a fine Sheraton hotel in a very odd place for a luxury hotel. However nice it was, it was outrageous."

"What do you mean, Nick?"

"Outrageously comfortable, a modern oceanfront Sheraton where expatriate Westerners found refuge and relief from the realities of African poverty, pollution, and urban sprawl."

Nate asked, "What's wrong with that?"

"After nearly six months or more in remote villages treating and counseling poor people, this was a very strange retreat for J.J. If not for her need for R&R, I would have considered the luxury hotel a total sellout for us, fledgling 'missionary angels,' idealists from America. The hotel, in fact, was a twelve-story monument to luxury. It was not more than a block from destitute poverty-doomed sections, miles of them, in

226

Benin's largest city, Cotonou. But the clean, modern luxury hotel, even near streets of garbage, was a welcome relief to both of us.

"It was perfect for chilling out. Perfect, that is, until one evening over drinks at the hotel's poolside Tiki Bar, a mosquito turned our lives inside out. I imagine the pest first visited and poked its bloodsucking proboscis into the sweaty arm of a malaria-infected visitor from Zaire, or the jungles of Cameroon. Still hungry, the mosquito then found J.J.'s blood running warm beneath the skin of her soft, exposed belly as she sat in her red two-piece, sipping a gin and tonic.

"She felt fine for a day or two and then she got very sick. To this day, J.J. still doesn't remember anything about the final two days of her Mini-vacation at the luxury hotel in Benin. But I knew all too well what was happening and who was to blame. Not the mosquito, but me. I had taken us out of Jos too hastily and had forgotten to bring our malaria medication.

"She was so sick. I drove my beloved J.J. to a small medical station back inside Nigeria. It was near the heavily congested traffic around the Lagos airport. The drive there was a hot, wearisome stop-and-go trip through a 'go-slow' for the last twenty miles and four hours. J.J. was in and out of consciousness and she once collapsed against the car door. I thought she had died right in the car.

"I headed for that medical station instead of a crowded hospital because it was near flights out of the country. I knew the medical center because when I first came to Nigeria to join J.J., I had to stay there for one night. My unscheduled stay there was out of necessity, following an entire afternoon arguing with airport police until I bribed them with a wad of U.S. dollars to get my passport back from them.

"So, I desperately drove my girlfriend-shoulda-been-wife back into Nigeria where at least I knew the station was a place to rest and hope for medical help. On top of blaming myself for forgetting our malaria medicine and being stuck in a sweaty go-slow, I was greeted by the so-called medical staff with a cavalier neglect. They did not schedule J.J. to see a doctor until the following day.

"I sat that evening by her cot at the station, totally distraught, putting cold towels on her head and keeping her covered."

As Nick sounded more and more desperate telling Nate the story he'd never wanted to tell, he began to sweat, as if he was the one with the malaria, not J.J. in the story.

Nate sat stunned, realizing Nick was sweating profusely in the cool tavern kitchen. Nate put his head in both hands staring at Nick. "My God, Nick."

A tear ran down Nick's cheek. He continued, "At that dingy, so-called medical center, I dreamed in my chair next to J.J.'s cot. I dreamed she died. In my sleep I felt the guilt about ruining her life, about her 'adventure' into acting as a student at Catholic University, for me alone, it seemed. In the dream by her dead body, I remembered her perform on stage in the bright lights of the Hartke Theatre. This is a vision I knew. She had indeed been adventurous and daring on stage. At Catholic University, she minored in drama. She was a standout lead actress in school plays of Henrik Ibsen, William Shakespeare and Arthur Miller. As I dreamed in the hot room in Nigeria, I remembered each of her performances. Yeah, Nate, I had never missed a performance. She was my beautiful superstar. And in the dream, she was gone. I dreamed all of it vividly that very night.

"When I woke, I was sick with the thought of all she had done for me and seeing what I had done to her in return. Then, seeing her lying sick, dying at the crummy, corrupted stopover in Lagos, I couldn't stand the sight of the shining star of my life suffering any more. She lay there unconscious with cold sweats. It was too much to bear. I harkened back to the boldness that possessed me the first time I ever saw J.J. walk into a pizza joint when she was a college girl and I had to know her. Miracle upon miracle, I pursued her and she had always responded."

Nate asked, "What did you do? I mean in Africa that night. Obviously, she survived."

"Luckily, Nate. When I bought the car in Jos, I discovered the only safe place I could keep money and other valuables was inside the vinyl panel of the VW's driver-side door. I left her lying in that cot for a while that long night. Then, after retrieving a screwdriver from the glove box to open the door panel, I pocketed all my money and left J.J. at the medical center temporarily at 2:00 a.m. I drove to the airport, just ten minutes away, and again had to bribe the Lagos police and airport authorities with the remainder of my cash, to get her on the next plane to Paris in a hurry, to get her to the Hopital Saint-Joseph.

"I showed our return tickets from our separate flights to Africa, but just got more hassled, as they expected more cash, I suppose. At one point, I nearly jumped over the counter to beat up the Pan Am ticket agent, who was trying to rip me off with a grossly inflated price to secure two seats together on an early-morning flight that I knew had to be less than half booked."

"Wow. That's not you. Did you punch him out?"

"Didn't have to, thank God. He was enormous. His supervisor came to my rescue. At 5:45 a.m. we were at high altitude, flying to France. But J.J. almost died in the pressurized cabin air of Pan Am flight 540—they called it 'The Debussy'—from West Africa to Paris. My J.J. desperately needed medical treatment. All the flight attendants nursed her the best they could with cold packs and meds, and scolded me for getting her aboard with a high fever.

"Yes, I indeed wanted to join J.J. in Africa, perhaps to write a book about our time there. I was totally committed for once in my life. But in hindsight I should have kept her from such danger in the first place. And then, even writing the book, I was thinking of myself.

"The flight to Paris was a sad ending to an adventure that she could regret for many years to come. If I hadn't shown up, it would probably have worked out for her, Nate. I again screwed up. J.J. was the one getting hurt. I think that unfortunate situation, ending with J.J. nearly dying from a serious bout with the deadliest strain of malaria, is the source of her anxiety now, the negativity, paranoia to protect her family and especially the twins. She still resents me. Since then, I firmly believe that she has no longer trusted me or herself to take adventures of any kind. I have been completely in her hands.

"At the hospital in Paris, she was treated and recovered after a week. But before she was discharged, I was handed a telegram from a nurse at the hospital where I had camped out on a lobby couch for several days. The telegraph was a shocking message from my sister Kat. Our Mom and Dad were dead."

"No! That is when you learned of their passing? They died on the highway, right?"

"Yes. Welcome to my life. Some timing, huh? I think you know this part, Nate. It was an auto accident in the Baltimore Harbor Tunnel. They had finally gotten time away from Dad's demanding executive career at Esskay Foods and the thankless task of managing Pop's old tavern, in addition to supervising the slow renovations of the promising new tavern, getting no help from me at all. We rarely spoke. They took a vacation while he could also attend a food convention in Atlantic City.

"On their way home, a drunk driver swerved through road barriers to drive right into the wrong-way tube of the tunnel and hit my parents' car head on coming out of the tunnel. They had fun in Atlantic City I'm told by my aunt at the beach. They died in the car before they returned. This too was my fault—I should have stayed in Baltimore to help out with the taverns. Maybe my dad wouldn't have come back in such a tired condition from their vacation.

"All this I brought on: taking J.J. for granted, ignoring my family. You do know J.J. had a stroke at Hopkins earlier too." Nick's face was flush of any color and his hand's trembling. He steadied his hands by clasping them together, but his woeful eyes revealed all the turmoil he'd been hiding for the past months. He reluctantly looked up into Nate's eyes for compassion.

Nate's face was now streaming with tears. Nate stood, pushed the little table aside, and embraced his best friend. "Oh, my man . . . I am so sorry." He held on to Nick's shoulders. "I had no idea, Nick. Betsy and I always see you and J.J. as the perfect couple."

Nick continued, "Well, just keep this stuff to yourself, okay? Maybe just Betsy, I don't know. But I'm forever conscious of J.J.'s emotional scars, childhood and the adult scars I gave her. I let her down and my family down."

Nate paused and glanced about the room absently, seeming to reevaluate what he'd just learned about his close friends, the Espositos. His eyes then showed his firm resolute and he bellowed, "Bullshit!" Nate's outburst was so loud that Mr. Triandos at the bar came back to look in. Nate never swore.

Nate said, "Nicky boy, sure the story is tough, but you didn't cause any of the outcome. Forget it. Things happen because of collections of people in an ever-changing matrix of circumstances. Those circumstances just spit and cough up outcomes, which no one human can fully predict. I know that sounds stupid, but that is how I see the world. I am as sure as I stand here today that that is how it is. All people have to do is keep the faith, especially in themselves. Don't go getting sorry for yourself. I mean it, my friend. Or, if you do, I am out of the Belvedere thing."

Nick forced a half smile, "You mean, … you're in?

Nate sat back down and leaned back on the back-chair legs, looked at the greasy kitchen ceiling, and meshed his hands behind his head for support. "Ground rules, my man. Ground rules." He paused for a long moment.

"First, stop feeling guilty over things that you know darn well were not entirely your fault. It is not exactly a charming feature in an otherwise bright, likeable guy like you. Second, at the party let the girls be girls, they tend to support each other, not challenge each other for fun like we do. We guys can hang out together, you and me at the party. Third, forget the nonsense that she doesn't love you anymore. I know she does. Fourth, relax. Leave the jolly times to me. I don't like these kinds of parties. But, in this case? I'm with you all the way." Nate paused and let a hint of a smile emerge on one side of his mouth which grew into a joyful and affectionate wide smile and chuckle.

"Fifth, don't blame me for this." Nate stared at a startled Nick, who showed no response. Nate hugged him again, saying "Just kidding, bro. See? You are too uptight about this."

"Oh."

"So, agreed?"

Nick said, "Agreed."

Nate added, "We're going, Nick. I'll win Betsy over and she, by gosh, will win over J.J. What will you do with the kids that night?"

Chapter 27: Full-Time Barkeep

It all seemed sadly inevitable three days after the death of Carlo and Miriam that Nick would manage the tavern. Pop had even made a little ceremony of it. In a private moment at Meadow Ridge Cemetery, Pop gave his Nicky a special gift, his 1933 penny from the dedication of the new police headquarters that year. Pop took Nick's right hand and slipped the penny into a firm handshake, just as he'd received it from Commissioner Gaither many years earlier.

Just a penny, but there couldn't have been a more valuable gift, as far as Nick was concerned. Nick had it mounted in a special picture frame and hung it in the family room at home, next to an autographed photograph of Pop with Al Pacino, the star of "… And Justice for All." Pop had charmed his way onto the movie set in Baltimore in 1977.

"I need you now," was all Pop had to say. And besides, Nick could not refuse his grandfather and after the Glen Burnie High School incident the inevitable became full time bartending and managing Pop's Tavern.

Years earlier, when a young Carlo Esposito was attending Loyola University in northern Baltimore, he took turns tending bar for Pop. Carlo hired bartenders, a book keeper, suppliers, cleaning people, grocery boys and of course handled the drunks. After college, Carlo supervised others or often ran the bar himself when not working his day job. In typical Esposito manner, Carlo never expected any thanks; it was a family duty. That's all.

Yet, concerning Nick, Carlo never did fully trust his absent-minded, dreamy son to take on any responsibility at Pop's. He would not have wanted Nick to help even if Nick offered to take the load off his dad. He didn't want to risk a chance that Nick might make a fool of himself and the proud family.

After Carlo died, Pop tried out several hired managers. But all the reliable friends in his old network were either dead or retired. He grasped for good people and ended up hiring men who stole, drank too much profit, or didn't show up half the time.

Pop, unlike the late Carlo, felt that his grandson could be trusted, despite the laziness they took for Nick's lackadaisical manner. Pop trusted Nick's loyalty. That was enough. "Well, at least Nicky wouldn't steal from me, Minnie," he said. It might also do him good to get out with people every day, Pop thought. Nick, after losing his teaching career, started weekend bartending, then covered part-time on weekdays, then every day.

Pop's Tavern then became Nick's full-time "duty," as mentioned. He was stuck because he was an Esposito. It was family.

* * *

Nate hated to see Nick suffer quietly at the tavern. His smart and likable friend, a closet alcoholic, was entrapped into the family barroom business, and then suspecting J.J. would abandon him. It was too much for Nate to bear. "She's just moody as a working mom," Nate would plea.

Against his better judgment, he committed himself to helping Nick seal the Belvedere Hotel party deal with J.J. One day Nate came by the empty tavern with him a two-pound box of milk and dark chocolate cashew turtles from famous Rheb's Candy Store on Wilkens Avenue in Baltimore. "Here, take her these, Nick. They're the best." Another day Nate popped into the tavern and said, "Hey Nick, Homestead Gardens is selling gorgeous red miniature rose bushes in crystal bowls. I got you one, too, for your bride because you are too stupid to be romantic. Here."

Nick laughed at his buddy's audacity, "Hah, so you say. What makes you think I'm not romantic, you damn fool you?

"Well, daahh. Yes, I do," his friend said.

Nate also rented chick flicks and shoved them under Nick's nose at the bar: *Breakfast at Tiffany's*, *Elvira Madigan*, and *Love Story*. "Say they were left at the bar . . . Blockbuster said they weren't due for three days or something. You've got to come up with some stuff like this, you big skinny fool," Nate prodded.

As they attended a University of Maryland basketball game in College Park one evening, Nate also suggested that Nick spring for a dress. "No woman is going to back out once she's got the New Year's dress!" Nate roared and slapped Nick on the back. Several women sitting nearby shook their heads and laughed. "You got that right!" one of them said.

Nick bought a four-hundred-dollar gift certificate to Lord & Taylor for J.J. for Christmas for that special dress for the millennium party in the Rumba Room at the century-old Belvedere Hotel.

On the day after Christmas, Nate asked Nick the pivotal question.

"No Nate, she has not yet agreed," Nick admitted.

Chapter 28: Finally! A Good Laugh

By New Year's Eve, J.J. was reluctantly ready to go to the party, just to please Nick, though she told Betsy she still thought it was a dangerous and stupid idea. She'd put away saying whether or not a New Year's Eve night out in the city was a wise thing. "I'm going simply because Nick needed it, but only God knows why he needs it," she supposed.

Nick had also opened his heart to her, laid out his recent insecurities–his boredom at the tavern, his fear of losing touch with reality, even being jealous of handsome Dr. Wellborne—as a way that the party, that particular party, would help both of them. But, being mister clumsy socially, it surprised him that his confession had the effect of frightening her instead of reassuring her.

J.J. told Betsy she was more concerned than ever about Nick's shaky state of mind and his weird reasoning that the Belvedere, "of all places, would help us feel better about things. My God, Bet, she said, "With all the gifts, I was beginning to think Nick was having an affair and wanted to renew his love."

Betsy responded, "Nick's not crazy or having an affair, J.J. He loves you. God only knows what his problem is. In my social work, I've met all kinds, and he takes the cake!"

J.J. laughed, "Well that adds nothing to the equation. But thanks anyway, Bet. Oh well, who knows what Nick thinks half the time, anyway!"

The foursome was set to go. The old charming Belvedere Hotel awaited them.

* * *

Nick and J.J. left their modest home in Glen Burnie the evening of December 31, 1999, and arrived much too early at the big old hotel, about 7:45 p.m. anticipating a late night of dining and dancing.

J.J. looked fabulous in a sultry, strapless black dress of satin, in a style of gorgeous simplicity accented with a cascading black bow on the side and layered black-satin bands spiraling down from waist to knee.

Nick was pumped and treating his wife like a queen.

Still, she didn't have his full attention, as usual, because she still privately worried. She accepted the inevitable because a night like that at a hundred-year-old dinosaur hotel in the historic Mount Vernon neighborhood was perversely appealing to Nick, her amateur scholar of American history. She'd let Nick be Nick.

Since bagging the tickets, he had been studying more Baltimore history as he leaned across the tavern bar every day like a sloth on a forest tree. Even though his passion for history hadn't exactly been his lucky charm, Nick was ready to wow his friends with his knowledge of the Belvedere and the old city. Maybe he'd make new friends for the couple by talking Baltimore history as only he understood it. *No, maybe not. The night was for J.J.'s,* he pondered.

As they drove into the city, he decided that his weird experience of maneuvering around Miss Krantz to secure the tickets was out of bounds to bring up that evening. It would freak out his wife and guests. It was still a mystery to Nick anyway. *But then again, maybe the tickets are fakes,* he thought. *Why was I so caught up with the old lady, and trusting her?*

* * *

For J.J., the night started out on a bad omen. After Nick had promised for weeks to get his Pop's teal-blue Eldorado for the evening, he had to renege. They wouldn't be driving "in style" to town in the big carriage after all.

J.J. thought it had been a lie all along.

It wasn't a lie. Nick did get Pop's okay to use the car because Pop was impressed with Nicky getting out on a big social night in Baltimore to take care of his beautiful wife, even if it was the old hotel. Nick didn't get the Caddy because Pop and Minnie received and accepted a last-minute invitation to attend Mayor Martin O'Malley's "private" gala at the Inner Harbor Hyatt

Hotel. It was supremely important to Pop to be seen arriving in front of the fancy Hyatt in his big Cadillac. No taxi for him and Minnie on New Year's Eve.

Since Pop was no longer driving himself, Pop wanted Nick to drive them to the Hyatt. That compelled Nick to remind his grandfather that he had plans and admit that it was his heartfelt wish to really show J.J. a grand time in a hundred-year-old place, the Belvedere Hotel.

The historic 'significance,' if any, did not impress Pop. He was happy for Nick taking J.J. out, but it would not be with his caddy, not that night, and especially not in that place. Pop's reaction made Nick feel uneasy. "Nicky, I don't like that old tomb, that Belvedere. You didn't tell me you were goin' there, boy. Papa Mike said it was cursed. He never said why, just told me to stay clear. Please be careful. And be careful with Janet up there, you promise, boy? Hey, you promise? This is yer Pop talkin' with ya, now, boy. Here me?"

A driver from the mayor's office was assigned, thanks to Pop's influence in the city's Democratic Party, to chauffeur him and Grandma Minnie in the big showy Caddy to the mayor's high-profile New Year's Eve party. And Pop, always the genius at business networking, asked his general contractor, Edmond Jackson (who was dreadfully behind schedule in renovating Pop's Tavern on Pratt Street) and his wife, Teisha, to escort them to the party as well. Jackson took the guilt bait for the project being behind schedule.

With Pop's entourage intact, the Caddy was a dead issue for Nick.

And that night, J.J.'s royal carriage to the Belvedere on Nick's special night would be their faded-black Toyota Tercel, pock marks, dents, rusty edges and all.

* * *

Even while driving the Tercel into Baltimore from Glen Burnie, even with his great victory of getting J.J. into the car and on their way, Nick kept selling his party idea, using the Belvedere mystique—the once-in-a-lifetime millennium party opportunity. "The damned place is a century old, J.J. It's perfect."

"You are being overly dramatic, Nick. I don't understand why this is so important." His persistent sales job was nothing but annoying. She kept quiet for most of the drive because one thing she understood was that it had become supremely important to Nick to be his own man, for once, for this special night, to make the decisions and not always be led by the nose by his grandfather, she figured.

Nick drove the rusty-old Tercel uptown to the Belvedere, all the while working his one-way conversation hard into the humorous absurdity of driving his girl to the prom in a rust-bucket, dumpy car. Eventually the humor worked.

As they approached the Belvedere entrance, Nick chuckled, and looked over at J.J. with a devilish grin. "Watch this." He drove the little rust bomb, unnoticed, closely behind a huge, shiny black Cadillac limousine, which, in turn, was behind a long, silvery Infiniti and, in front of that, a pink limo, from which apparent VIPs were emerging into a ring of admirers flashing their cameras. He sneaked the little car behind them, as close as possible so not to be seen.

As Nick imagined the scene to be a red carpet opening of a Hollywood film, he fought off the images of Ronald Coleman, Gloria Swanson and the others he "saw" just weeks ago checking into the Belvedere in the lobby. He focused on having fun with J.J. instead. But, she still looked troubled.

When the time came, and the pink limo and Infinity moved out, the Cadillac limo was driven off by a valet, exposing the little rusty Tercel, which might as well have been a trash dumpster on wheels.

An eager valet, who was a handsome teenage boy in his starched, gray Belvedere uniform and hired just for that occasion, sprang off the curb and around the limo. When he spotted the old rust bucket, he took a half step back and retreated to the curb, staring, frowning.

Nick and J.J. stepped out. The boy valet reached out to Nick for the keys, but only with his index finger, the minimum flesh possible. Nick looped the keys to the Tercel on the boy's finger.

The boy reluctantly eased himself slowly onto the badly torn vinyl driver's seat, his weight exposing more and more foam rubber stuffing as he adjusted himself into the spongy seat.

Nick held his laughter. He turned his face away from the boy to see J.J. quietly distancing herself from the car, while giggling. Nick caught her eye and winked. He gestured with his head to the boy, who was not pleased to get the $20 bill Nick handed into the dark car interior. The car's interior light bulb had died many New Years ago, leaving the exposed yellow foam in the torn seats as the only thing visible at night inside the dumpster car.

As the boy steered the little carriage into the hotel garage, J.J. laughed out loud and nearly stumbled onto the hotel steps. Nick saved her and held her close. It was the first time all day he had seen her loosen up. Nick hoped it wouldn't be the last time that evening.

They hopped up the marble steps and pushed through the revolving door of the famous old Baltimore landmark hotel.

Chapter 29: Just Wait, You'll See

The funny valet scene was perfect for Nick. He felt better. J.J. seemed to be more relaxed. The perfect beginning for what he hoped would be an elegant, fun-filled evening for his anxious wife.

They had plenty of time to wait for Betsy and Nate. Nick anticipated a thrill of walking the foursome into the Rumba Room with the city views from the big windows.

He 'waltzed' himself into the big lobby restraining laughter. *What a bizarre place*, he thought, *for J.J. to wait for and greet Betsy, a gaudy reminder of a past era. They'll freak.*

But then he realized he was looking at a different room entirely. This time the big room looked far more appealing, more coordinated in its style, tasteful. It wasn't tacky at all, as he remembered from just weeks ago. He thought, *That Krantz lady messed up my mind.*

He could have sworn there had been a front hotel desk at the back of the lobby. But now there were only catering offices. No peeling walls. No tacky furniture. He dismissed the thought and turned back to J.J. quickly before he would feel funny about it all. But his grandfather's words surfaced: '*Nicky, I don't like that old tomb . . . Papa Mike said it was cursed, cursed, cursed, cursed . . .*' The word reverberated in Nick's head.

He shook off the thought and sat down with J.J. on a little love seat trimmed in teak floral carvings.

"You okay Nick?" J.J. noticed Nick's face took on gravity. He had frowned for the first time all day.

"Of course, I'm okay. Let's watch people arrive."

Guests streamed in the door for the five parties at the hotel, an eclectic crowd if ever there was one. Most were in evening dress, but others were in costumes.

A man and woman dressed as Queen Victoria's Beefeater guards approached J.J., "We've just sent our carriage driver off since we plan to spend the fortnight, my dear," said the woman, who giggled and looked away from Nick shyly as if playing the part of a powerless English woman from the previous century addressing the chivalrous gentleman.

After killing time for thirty-five minutes of chatting with other guests, J.J. turned sour, "I told you Nate and Betsy wouldn't show," she said. "This place is just not Betsy's style; too confusing, maybe scary to her, not to mention the risk of the whole world blowing up around us. I know it won't, I guess. But something could happen."

She paused to look around. "Did anyone hear me? ... Do you think they have those out-of-date computers here? I bet this old hotel's not up on the problems people are talking about, you know (she whispered), Y2K."

Nick, resigned not to argue or make her seem foolish, joked instead, "J.J., this place is so old, the people who work here don't use typewriters yet."

She continued, "Betsy and Nate are country folks at heart, Nick. They're not gonna come to this city and this ho—"

"Oops, there they are!" cried Nick.

"Where? I don't see them."

"There, climbing out of Nate's big black Beemer—see, through the glass in the revolving doors? Nate's not going to spend two bills on a party and not show up. No sir. You know, there was no revolving door a few weeks ago. They made improveme..." he realized his words.

J.J. was shocked, "Two hundred? Oh Nick, that's too m—"

Nick cut her off. "Oh hi, you guys. J.J. was beginning to wonder if you were coming."

Sour no longer, the actress in J.J. beamed with a smile that lit the room when she saw Betsy's magnificent, tight-fitting black-draped dress, floor length, with a sequined, lacy top. J.J. stood silently, taking in her radiant friend Betsy. The dress had an asymmetrical high neckline and elbow-length lacy sleeves. J.J.

seemed stunned to see Betsy looking so sexy and still tastefully modest.

"Wow, you guys look great!" Nick injected on purpose before J.J. could get started into the interminable girl-chat over their attire. "Have you lost weight?" He too was fixated on Betsy's figure in the stunning dress."

Nate spoke sheepishly, "I know we are late J.J. It's my fault. I closed her new dress into the front door at home and it ripped at the waist, see where the lace meets the solid black, here." He pointed to the spot.

"So, just show everybody, why don't you, Nate?" Betsy snapped, then covered her outburst with an awkward laugh that seemed to help her release built up tension. Betsy wore a smile for her friends. Preferring to stay home that night, Betsy had been fussing at good-natured Nate all the way from their suburban home in Severn. She avoided eye contact with Nick. Instead she said, "You look great yourself, J.J."

J.J. ran her hands down both sides of her beautiful dress and wormed from side to side, drawling, "Oh, this ol' thing?"

"And, hey you guys, take a look at Nate, will ya?" Betsy said, perhaps secretly pleased that Nate's tuxedo was much newer and better-tailored to his large frame than the old tux hanging loose on lanky Nick.

Nate, slightly embarrassed, said quietly, "Betsy handled the dress situation admirably. I feel terrible about it. But, she darted back into the house and did a minor repair on the sewing machine. Took no time at all," he said Nick's way. He figured correctly that Nick was itching to get to dinner.

Nick was already tiring of the lobby chatter while the others were still taking it in. He was secretly freaking out over how different the stately, all-marble Belvedere Hotel lobby looked. *I must have been half nuts that day*, he thought. He snapped out of it with, "Would you look at this place!" then said a second later, "Let's go, all. Shall we?" in a mocking, English gentleman's accent, as he stepped away from the love seat.

He pushed his three guests to the far corner of the lobby for what he feared was another anxiety-filled ride up to the fourteenth floor in a rickety elevator.

They stood at the end of a long line of party goers waiting to board the contraption where Miss Krantz had taken him for that strange, bumpy, scary ride.

Nick realized that this, however, was a bigger elevator, in the same location, not so old and decrepit. Nick noticed there was a second set of doors next to it, presumably another elevator, but it appeared to have been out of commission for some time. The doors were mirror gold, not dull black as he remembered them.

The pair of elevators appeared to be the only way up into the hotel. Nick still felt anxiety pangs. He could see that the illuminated 'UP' button was rotated sideways, not up. *That figures. I hope that's not the only thing twisted tonight,* he thought.

J.J. seemed nervous, and Nick slipped off her jacket. "May I carry your cape, my dear? Hey, you will love this party room, J.J." He squeezed her to him tight with his left arm around her bare shoulder.

"Calm down, Nick. It's just a party. I'm getting cold."

Nick wrapped her jacket back over her shoulders and pulled her close again.

As the four friends stood in the slow-moving line to the elevator, Lenny and Cookie Stein approached Nate. The husband-and-wife photography team worked the hotel for the evening. The Steins were loaded down with three single-lens reflex Canon cameras, a variety of different lenses and a flash motor device.

When Nate saw Nick's face turn pale at the sight of the Belvedere elevator, he jumped at the chance to cheer him up, as Nick's designated protector for the night, which they had discussed at Pop's. He said, "Hey folks, I got this. Let's get a portrait of two dopes with the prom queens, shall we? While we're dressed up for the Copa, huh?"

Lenny took twenty shots of them chatting informally and finally in a more formal portrait pose, while Cookie, looking a lot like a smiling, adorably brunette version of Doris Day, moved the flash device around for different shadow effects, never losing her bright smile. They both were irresistibly charming, and Nate gave each a twenty-dollar bill with his business card. "Just bill me and send the proofs to me, folks."

"Nate, no I ..." Nick said weakly.

"Don't listen to this fella. Never seen him before." They all laughed, letting Nate get away with paying.

Nick was irritated, however, that they'd lost their place in line to the elevator and had to go to the end again. When the foursome reached the front of the queue again, Nick noticed a strange face reflected in the gold-mirrored door to the elevator. It was a weird demure hat-check "boy," named Mr. Bojay. He was a very old man, who wore his name on a loose-fitting gray Belvedere shirt, which was so wrinkled the old fellow could have slept in it. He smiled with ugly yellow teeth directly at Nick.

Mr. Bojay told Nick that his job, night after night (God only knew for how many years), was to manage the coats behind a half door in his tiny, stuffy cloakroom. It gave out an odor of mildew and cheap aftershave. He spoke only to Nick in an all-too-familiar manner that confused Nick. The voice riveted Nick's attention to his creepy face and raspy voice with distinct New York City enunciations.

Nick alone nodded hello in return and asked, "Have we met?"

J.J. and the Browens continued to face the elevator door, then very near. "What, Nick?" J.J. asked.

"Nothing." Nick looked to the mirrored elevator door and was startled. He saw Bojay's face in the reflection, as a much larger image than his actual face. It appeared younger, and in a coat and tie. No one in line offered their coats to him, whether they were freaked out by this little Mr. Bojay with a severely pockmarked, ashen face and tiny black mustache, or perhaps they didn't see him at all. One after another, all the people in line moved past his invitation, which he half whispered, to check their coats, always displaying a crooked smile of yellow-green teeth.

Bojay's demeanor reminded Nick of his encounter with the weird old lady. He shivered, then turned away quickly and jumped ahead of J.J. into the elevator. He didn't offer their coats to Bojay. J.J. looked at Betsy, puzzled.

J.J. laughed at Nick and the women both shook their heads. "Oh, go right ahead Nick," Betsy said.

Am I to be the butt of their jokes all night? he thought. Nick let some doubt creep into his thinking about the big evening he'd planned.

He heard the same creaking in the elevator works. "Get a load of this thing," said Nick nervously, recalling every frightening second of his ride up to the fourteenth-floor Rumba Room the Monday after Thanksgiving with old Miss Krantz.

Nick forgot himself and said, "Last time I was in this death trap, I ..." but he quickly realized it would not be wise to start out a party with the other passengers thinking he was an absolute nut, though he wasn't convinced that he wasn't.

After a dozen or so guests crammed into the elevator--including a cowboy, a man in a tall top hat and long, nineteenth-century coattails holding hands politely with a woman who Nick thought could have been Mary Todd Lincoln, and there were the Beefeaters again.

Nick also noticed a man who looked a lot like his hero Thomas Edison. The Edison man was also acting the character in the way he was fixated on the lamps on the elevator's side walls. Nick smiled, thinking, *Part of the act of authenticity. Good show, Mr. Edison.* He believed it was a good omen for the evening.

They took a squeaky ride to the twelfth floor then stopped quickly. The door opened to an incredible ballroom scene. It was the masquerade ball. People in costume from the elevator scurried off wide-eyed and were greeted by a smiling young lady, a ticket collector. The Grand Ballroom, previously called the Betsy Patterson Ballroom, was magnificent: a twenty-five-foot ceiling of ocean blue and cream colors held up by gold framing arches.

Roman columns on the sides were topped with gold floral end pieces against the ceiling. Murals of the old Belvedere country estate of the Howard family, previous landowners, covered the walls.

"Mmm, yes, top of Howard Street, named for the Howards . . . of course," Nick mused. No one responded.

Nate turned to Nick behind him and beamed with joy. "Hey buddy, that looks like a great time, eh?"

"I'll say," Nick replied quickly, grabbing his friend's shoulder to stop him from following the gaily attired folks off the elevator into the masquerade party. "But our party is up in the Rumba Room. Just 150 people. So much more fun and more intimate." Nick glanced at his J.J. with unusual authority and pride.

J.J. and Betsy looked at each other and rolled their eyes up.

Nick vowed to himself not to tell the others that their tickets were likely the only ones left or that a wrinkly old lady might have chosen the party for him. He shivered again, just thinking about it.

"Intimate, Nick?" said J.J., suspicious of his sales pitch. "How intimate can 150 people be? That ballroom party looked awesome, didn't it, Betsy?"

Nate and Betsy nodded as the doors closed on the ballroom. Nate said, "I want to go there, don't you, Betsy? Shoulda gotten tickets to that one, Nick. Is it too late to change?"

"Yeah, can't be better than that," added Betsy sheepishly, sneaking a peak at Nick hoping she had annoyed him. "Sorry, Nick, but that looks like the place to be. Yeah, why didn't you get tickets to that party?"

Give me a damn break, thought Nick, deflated. He again braced for an evening of skepticism from Betsy.

The elevator doors sealed them in again and, with a herky-jerky start, the creakavator resumed its way up. Nick, J.J., Nate, and Betsy were the only passengers left aboard.

After being seduced by just a peek at the fabulous masquerade party, they all noticed that the ride up to the fourteenth-floor took longer than it had been between each of the other twelve floors.

"Where's the thirteenth floor, Nick?" J.J. wondered out loud.

"My guess is there is no thirteenth floor, just extra space to make up for the tall ballroom on the twelfth," he said. He added quietly, anxiously. "Or, maybe people here are superstitious. They keep the ghosts there," Nick added just to bother the complaining women.

The doors opened to the Rumba Room.

J.J. and Betsy jumped from the elevator. They each held their heads cocked to the side sarcastically, expecting the worst. But the scene stunned them. People had already half-filled the center of the room, already celebrating with party hats and drinks in hand. Recorded pop music played moderately.

Finally, there was the party Nick had painted for them: a tastefully decorated New Year's Eve club and dining room, bar, and dance floor—gold and silver balloons strung across the ceiling, white and blue streamers and bunting along every side of the big room between the picture windows, which revealed the city skyline in all directions. It was a room fit for a Hollywood star-studded party. Or better, a room fit for a fun-filled travel into a new millennium.

The two women paused to take in the sophisticated layout of the party room. Both were astonished and delighted. In tandem, they turned toward Nick, maybe feeling guilty that they they'd been so skeptical.

J.J. was about to apologize to Nick, but too late. She opened her mouth, "Oh my Nicky, I ...."

Before J.J. could complete her thought, she and Betsy watched Nick dash off toward the south side windows, with Nate walking quickly behind, laughing at his friend.

The boys' minds were set on something far more important than the skeptical, tired attitudes of their wives. The two sprinted toward their prearranged target, shoving people out of their way if necessary to seize the prize—the dinner table next to large windows, the spot that Nick had picked out six weeks ago. He'd said that table would be the prime spot. They didn't want to miss the midnight, downtown fireworks at the Inner Harbor, which would be seen from the south view, Nick said.

City officials had billed the downtown pyrotechnics as the greatest fireworks its citizens would ever witness. Nick had convinced Nate that they would certainly be spectacular and the climax of the evening.

Chapter 30: Eat, Drink and Bygone Days

Most of the men at the party were younger than Nick and Nate, but only Nick cared enough to notice.

Nate was content anywhere, with anybody to talk to. And, his mind was set on making sure his strange and unpredictable friend enjoyed himself. He'd try to stay close.

Nearly all the men were in black tie, with a few in snappy black tuxedos topped with black or a few red bow ties, while the ladies were all gorgeous in their best evening dresses. Many had arrived with glitter in their hair and glitzy, very visible jewelry.

Nick and Nate grabbed two seats at their chosen dinner table facing the expansive windows to the south, toward the Baltimore's Inner Harbor and the expected pyrotechnics. Their women squeezed their form-fitting dresses into seats tight against the window facing their husbands and close to adjacent tables, all squared off and lining the south windows. Nick bounced up to hold the chairs of both Betsy and J.J.

Betsy couldn't resist one more crack. "What's with your guy tonight?"

"Enjoy, while it lasts," J.J. whispered in her friend's ear. "Just look at all this." They reigned over a wonderfully laid out formal dinner table and a center view of the dance floor, while a band was setting up and a huge bar was all decked out in blue and white lights.

Before sitting back down, Nick put his hands on top the back of his chair, facing the women sitting across from Nate as a professor might begin a lecture. He said, "Drinks, ladies? Nate? I'm buying." He laughed as he swung his left arm to point toward the bar where a few "paying" customers were already bellied up with their drinks. The joke was that the party package included an open bar.

"Well, well, Nick. I shoulda brought my video camera to record your generous offer, sir!" Nate laughed heartily showing everyone how happy he was that Nick was in good spirits.

Nate told Nick quietly that he would wait on a drink, maybe have a beer later. He hated champagne but intended to take a taste for the social occasion. Nate possessed mental discipline to bear anything, even what he thought was the nauseous sweet taste and feel of champagne in his mouth. His plan was to take a sip or two when the time came, just to show support for his buddy.

J.J. was more than willing to drink. After all the arguing and anxiety about the party, she wanted a drink badly, even though she wasn't used to drinking.

Nick was surprised. He didn't know her sorrow lately had led to sneaking an occasional glass of wine to cope with life's mounting complexities of raising twins, going back to work, and dealing with Nick's moods. Since her pregnancy, five years ago, she had not consumed much alcohol, but this night was different. She asked Nick for a dirty martini, that is, with the olives squeezed into the glass, before dinner was served.

Betsy asked Nick, "Can I get something nutritious? I don't know ..." And, after an eternity of indecision, with Nick three steps toward the bar, she said, "Okay, red wine spritzer."

Order complete. Nick headed right to the bar while J.J. and Betsy raved about the classy table setting.

Nate gazed out over the harbor lights, and zeroed into where the fireworks might be at midnight, making a mental note to ask Nick if it wasn't a bit far away from the harbor to enjoy the fireworks. He forgot to bring it up, however.

Gold-edged china--dinner plates and salad dishes, tea and coffee cups and matching flower vases--were arranged symmetrically at each setting on a black, silky table cloth. An appetizer salad was already at each setting.

J.J. and Betsy looked up together with the same thought, to make sure Nick reach the bar. Before he could return to hear the table talk, they had the same funny thought. Both had expected to see paper plates and a plastic table covering instead of an elegant setting. J.J. spoke, "This is not what I expe..." She stopped short.

They shared a loud, private laugh, a good, long one.

Nate sat puzzled and just shook his head, smiling.

Their appetizer was a citrus herb salad sprinkled with back-fin Maryland crab meat, fried capers, and wasabi cream. Tomato quarters framing the salads were so fresh they made Nick ponder about his Anne Arundel County in bygone days.

"I can't believe it is winter and the tomatoes are this good. They might have been summer tomatoes from the fertile fields at the Johns Hopkins family plantation down in the country near our house," Nick said.

"What?" Nate said with a big, happy smile. He poked an elbow into his buddy's side. "What would Johns Hopkins be doing with tomatoes, a new cure for cancer?"

That was all Nick needed. He took the cue to show off his Maryland history. It was his social niche, he thought, a way for an antisocial oddball to fit into the party he so desperately needed for J.J. Filling in conversation with any appropriate Maryland history would be his entre into the party nicely. He put down his fork, straightened up and launched into one of his familiar classroom lectures.

"More than 150 years ago, the Hopkins family farm was in what is now Crofton, south of the city and very close to where we all live, you guys in Severn, us in Glen Burnie, but very nearby."

J.J., Betsy and Nate were disinterested. They were more hungry than ready for history from Nick. They didn't look at him at first.

Nick ignored their sour expressions. "Yeah, THE Johns Hopkins, known for the world-famous medical system that bears his name, was earlier running his family's produce business, and then for financing the B&O Railroad, as well as ships and savings banks in early Baltimore." Ignoring his salad, Nick went on to explain that Johns Hopkins began his career in his uncle's grocery business.

252

His classroom of three managed to give Nick patronizing glances.

"Ah huh, great Nick," said Nate, chomping away.

"Oh yeah, Nick," said J.J., "I believe that our nurses' employment orientation at Hopkins mentioned something about Baltimore's best-known hospital patriarch was actually raised in Anne Arundel County, but I didn't know it was in what is now Crofton," she said, then whispered to Betsy, "Happy to see Nick talking at dinner and not drinking."

She looked up for Nick and said, "That was very interesting, Nick. The salad is divine; you've not touched much of it..."

Nick had skipped off for another bourbon and was on his way back to the table and said when he arrived and plopped down, "What's all the whispering. Betsy tell a dirty joke?" He didn't wait for them to laugh. He was excited now. "As I was saying, Hopkins was living during the pinnacle of Baltimore's commercial growth, you guys. Look at this city out there. This all came out of a quick spurt of business in manufacturing and shipping, leading to a handful of philanthropists, not the least of whom was Johns Hopkins. They created the great institutions of the city."

The frustrated history teacher went on to tell the full Johns Hopkins life history in mid-nineteenth-century Baltimore, and more. While most of the party guests were boozing it up, Nick, the alcoholic in denial, was getting intoxicated with his love of history, showing off his intellect like he had not done since being fired at Glen Burnie High School.

With little help from Nate, the four managed to drain the bottle of champagne iced at the table meant for midnight toasts.

He was also mellowed by excellent bourbon, which he thought tasted like the Owl Bar bourbon, which wowed him in November.

But his real comfort zone at the dinner table was role playing as the educator, Mr. Esposito, who through passionate lectures helped thousands of students memorized and relive history and most likely become better citizens by knowing the great role models of history.

Despite the spirited party going on, he was almost oblivious to J.J.'s growing impatience.

Soon, only Nate was half listening. Betsy glanced up occasionally with a thin smile. J.J. clenched her teeth in exasperation since they were no longer able to engage in conversations, due to Nick's monologue.

"Strategically, the city of Baltimore in the late 1900s was closer geographically to the big Midwest markets than any other eastern seaport and had easy access for southern farming regions as well to get their crops to the nation by ship and rail."

J.J. was politely ignoring him, hoping he would notice her disinterest and stop the lecture.

But Nick felt and imagined only the images of Baltimore of the 1890s vividly as he took glimpses toward the big window. "This town was booming in trade and manufacturing. And to feed its textile mills, seafood and produce canneries, as well as its fertilizer plants and its shipyards, Baltimore was second only to New York City in manufacturing and mercantile jobs for the hordes of immigrants coming in at Locust Point, downriver from what is now the Inner Harbor."

He then related the various food groups on the table to stories of the canneries and processing plants in old Baltimore. He wanted his 'classroom' to fully appreciate the rich significance of his town, at least as it was a century ago. He pushed on as he gulped his double bourbon.

This for Nick was a rare chance to show off, and thus entertain J.J. and friends Betsy and Nate. And, strangers at adjacent tables began listening in.

He latched on to his old teaching style, colorful stories for high schoolers, who used to gaze back silently for whole periods at a time, mesmerized. The same wasn't the case with J.J. and friends.

But Nick didn't notice. Nor did he notice people sitting nearby were then glued to his "local lecture" during the entire dinner hour. He might have stopped and become self-conscious had he noticed all the other people at nearby tables leaning in to hear. But he didn't because he was talking for J.J., who looked up occasionally and smiled.

Other people, though, saw a man having great fun, enlightening them with Baltimore legacy stories. And, they seemed pleased.

Throughout the salad course, he continued with the Hopkins legend—how after the death of Johns Hopkins, it was Dan Gilman, the first president of Johns Hopkins University, who fulfilled Hopkins' wishes by opening the medical school and admitting women on the same terms as men. "That was a bold and smart move on Gilman's part, for that era," he said.

Nick ran on about Gilman, while his 'students' munched away in silence on pan-seared scallops with crispy prosciutto, artichoke hearts with a sprinkling of lemon and olive oil.

He said, "Daniel Coit Gilman—or just 'Dan, my imaginary history friend' . . .oops. . ."

"Nick, that's enough now," J.J. said softly.

He didn't hear her. ". . . along with some wealthy peers in 1897 started the Country School for Boys to help young mom Anne Galbraith Carey get her son Frank into a good private school in the country, on the Johns Hopkins campus, rather than have him attend a stuffy New England boarding school. You've heard of the Gilman Country School for Boys, right?" Nick asked the ladies.

"Well, I've heard of the Gilman School, but that's in Roland Park in northern Baltimore, not at Hopkins," J.J. said tersely. "And I would certainly not say that the Hopkins hospital is in the country, Nick." J.J. was starting to frown, then began stroking her forehead as if anticipating a headache.

Undeterred, Nick responded, "The Hopkins campus was country then, J.J.! So was this hotel site. The Gilman school moved out to Roland Park later to keep it rural." He pushed his chest out like a male peacock in mating season. He felt purpose in his lecture and it was beginning to feel good.

255

However, Nate was becoming concerned. He watched some restlessness on Nick's face and decided to pay more attention; he'd help his buddy before Nick would realize he was getting overly excited over the lecture his wife was ignoring. Nate waited for an opening.

Nick was glancing from person to person as he spoke with both elbows on the table and touching his forehead from time to time, as if straining for details. J.J. held her hand out to his face in a stop gesture. This, Nick noticed and was perturbed slightly.

"I read about the exclusive Gilman boys school when I was pregnant, remember?" J.J. offered. "That was before we knew I was carrying twin girls, and not a boy. Has anyone here sent their son there?" Her question seemed to be aimed more at encouraging someone, anyone, to stop Nick and get the subject changed somehow. She had tolerated a full twenty-five minutes of Nick's lecturing and thought he was just rambling along in his private little land of bourbon-on-the-rocks history trip. He had to be stopped.

Nate and Betsy watched her dour expression as if anticipating an unfortunate argument was ensuing.

Nick kept marching his narrative through Baltimore history as the ladies mmm'ed over mouthwatering pineapple sorbet brought out to clear their palates.

It wasn't ice cream, so Nick figured it wasn't enough to make him stop enjoying himself 'teaching.' He had nibbled through his dinner with little sense of taste. He just kept talking. "You know that Enoch Pratt arrived in Baltimore with 150 dollars and built a fortune in banking, transportation, coal mines, and the iron works in Baltimore's Canton neighborhood?"

"Wow, I drive across Pratt Street every day," managed Nate between licks of sorbet, trying to listen to Nick, and smiling at his buddy.

"Same guy, Nate," said Nick, still ignoring his cup of sorbet.

"Enoch Pratt founded libraries. I do know that!" said Betsy.

"Yeah, that's right, Betsy. Some of those rich guys who walked these streets a hundred years ago or more, like Pratt and Hopkins, had no children, no heirs. Yeah, Pratt gave tons of money to civic improvement in the city, mainly to start the Enoch Pratt Free Library. He wanted a free circulating public library open to anybody regardless of property or color or religious faith. By 1890 it was the largest privately funded, free-circulation library in the whole country," added Nick, finally tasting the delicious sorbet and uttered a sound to match it. "Mmm! My God, what's this again?"

Nick's pause offered a chance for a man at the adjacent table to speak to J.J. and Betsy, but focus on J.J., "Great meal, eh, ladies?" J.J.'s cover-girl looks seemed to have caught the man's attention. Nick's sorbet breather finally gave the man a chance to introduce himself to the stunning woman next to him.

Betsy nodded in agreement with the man, but he still didn't acknowledge pretty Betsy was there at all. Just J.J.

J.J. mumbled "Mmhmm" without looking at the man.

Before they could reply, Nick began talking about entrepreneur and philanthropist George Peabody. Everyone but Nick was digging into the duck confit with fingerling potatoes, pears, and arugula. The scrumptious aromas wafting from the waiter's tray passing by would have distracted most people from continuous talking. But, not Nick. He was still on a roll, speaking faster and faster.

"Peabody, like Hopkins, never married, as I said, and had a bundle to leave behind. Peabody, a New Englander, only spent twenty years in Baltimore and left to live in London well before the Civil War. Yeah, Peabody is the real father of philanthropy, not Carnegie, Pratt, John D. Rockefeller, nor even Johns Hopkins, for that matter."

"Don't tell me. He started the Peabody Institute for music?" Nate asked quickly.

"Music, art, literature—you name it. He was big in these parts, as they would say, though much earlier than Pratt, he started a big library in Massachusetts, too, and a huge Peabody

Education Fund that only grew stronger after he died, plus he was an early financier of education for Negroes."

"You mean blacks, don't you, Nick?" asked Betsy with a guarded little smile and a quick head tilt to the right, leaning back. She was too sweet to make a scene over an inappropriate yet innocent racial remark.

But her husband Nate inserted quickly, "No, dear, he does mean Negroes. We needed all the help we could get back then. Lord knows." Nate gave out an expansive laugh that seemed to fill the room and give the moment some needed levity. The four friends had a good laugh.

Nate also wanted Nick to stop then. The food was running out, too.

J.J. thought maybe, just maybe, the big laugh would end Nick's lecture and get them back to party-hearty time. She whispered to Betsy, "Well, that will do it, I hope."

No, once again. Although Nick slowed down a bit during dessert—apple tart with homemade cinnamon ice cream—he gulped it down before anyone else, and spun his fertile intellect right into black history for his marvelously bright, social-working friend, Betsy.

"There were these three Baltimore black entrepreneurs of the previous century, you see, Bet," he said, suddenly channeling his Pop Esposito for a moment with a bit of Italian accent as he was prone to do rarely when relaxed. "Most woodworkers were Italian. But cabinet and coffin maker Alexander Hemsley and embalmer Samuel Chase teamed with black hearse owner John William Locks to run a thriving funeral business before the Civil War. This is what blacks in this city needed to do then, combine resources to—"

Nate interrupted in a paternal tone. "Nick, save it, my friend. That's great stuff, but we came here to have a party. Funerals, coffins, and hearses? Oh man . . . come on. We don't really want to know where that story is going, do we, girls?"

J.J. and Betsy shook their heads and said in unison, "Nooooo," with dramatic, pained smiles.

Nick was taken aback. "Oh, no interest suddenly in black history, Betsy? What about the black history tour of Annapolis? You guys said that was so great, right? And it is. I've done it too."

Betsy replied, "Well, I prefer to look forward. By the way, when's this party of yours going to pick up, Nick? That piped-in bubble gum music is lame."

But Nick felt hurt. He thought Betsy was dismissive. Unfortunately for J.J. and their friends, who were thoroughly tired of his ramblings, Nick felt obligated to continue—to fix things. "Well, if I were you, I might want to know that African-Americans in this city were far ahead of black communities in other cities even before the Civil War. I find that interesting, and I'm Italian-German–American. Even though slavery was legal in Maryland, free blacks here were critically important not only to the Underground Railroad to get slaves to freedom in the North, but they started many public groups to assist their sisters and brothers from persecution."

Still trying to change the subject, Nate chimed in to support Nick, but just a bit. "I'll bet they had lots . . . of that business, that is," he laughed self-consciously.

Nick answered quickly, "Yes, and actually way back in 1827, they held the African Methodist Episcopal Conference in Baltimore the same year the first private school for African-American girls was founded, along with St. James' Episcopal Church."

Nick thought he was losing their attention fast. So, he talked even faster, to recapture his teaching zone. His mind's eye could see Fredrick Douglass standing before crowds on a soap box. "Betsy, you went to Frederick Douglass High School next to Mondawmin Mall, right? Well, the man himself, Mr. Douglass, worked all over Baltimore and especially in the southern sections and docks where laborers did the city's real work. He actually freed himself by impersonating a sailor and spent his early years in Baltimore."

"Wow, that's great, Nick. Thank you," said Betsy sincerely, but still hoping he would stop.

J.J. looked angry.

Nick continued talking mostly to Betsy, "Then right before this building was constructed, the Belvedere here, the Baltimore Mutual United Brotherhood of Liberty was founded, and this organization used the courts to pursue civil rights for African-Americans in the 1890s. Yeah, the 1890s, guys!

"And, the Baltimore Afro-American was first published here in 1892 and continues today. Nate, bet you could find plaques at Morgan State, saying 'Founded as Centenary Biblical Institute.' It was sometime around the Civil War, I think."

J.J. seemed genuinely pissed off. Nick noticed. She and the Browens all then sat in a glazed-eye state, looking at the table or each other, but not him. Nick had no inkling simple casual chatting would be better to help his guests enjoy such a party, rather than listening to him go on. All he could think of was that he was losing his audience.

Afraid that he had somehow embarrassed, or even worse, insulted his Betsy and Nate by focusing on their African-American roots, Nick slouched and seemed to be finished with his stories. He'd thought of dozens of other good Baltimore history stories, but all of a sudden, he knew he wasn't appreciated.

Nick shrank rapidly into the recluse of a beaten man he'd been for the past weeks. He got on his feet to get another double bourbon. What he also didn't realize is that all along Nate and Betsy had quietly been very impressed that Nick knew so much about all the patron saints of business in the great boom years of Baltimore and especially his knowledge of the city's black history.

With an exchanged glance, however, they decided not to tell him. They too were tired of Nick dominating the conversation and didn't want to further encourage him. They all just sat still and hoped he was done. Nick would get over it. J.J. trusted in her husband's intellectual capacity to overcome his weaknesses. She believed that he always covered well.

But in Nick's mind that night, everything would be exaggerated, due to his intense emotional planning and surreal attraction to the Belvedere during the past few weeks, which Nick himself could not fully explain. Earlier, he was so very intent on telling some stories to help make a great time. The entire episode could have done him a world of good.

But it didn't.

"Nick," said J.J. "Thanks for the stories, honey. You have really impressed me about all great men who walked the Baltimore streets and visited in the front room parlors more than a hundred years ago. But, my dear, now it's party time. Right guys?"

Nate and Betsy overreacted with cheers.

Nick was deeply insulted, however, by J.J.'s patronizing tone, as he misread it, and his friends' tepid, then sudden cheerful reactions. He didn't believe J.J.'s consolation. He unfortunately recoiled from his manic lecturing. He was doing nothing but boring them.

Nick got very quiet. He then excused himself to go the bar where he began drinking heavily.

* * *

As the liqueur soothed his soul at the bar, Nick gazed out the windows to the southeast, reflecting on the 1890s industrialized Baltimore. It was a time when the city had finally outgrown its post–Civil War schizophrenic loyalties and, ironically because of its proximity between the agrarian South and manufacturing North, as he had said to deaf ears. He thought, *Baltimore was peaking in commerce like no other American municipality. Who the hell cares? Not them.*

He saw cars inching through the streets. He thought, *I bet those folks living and working on these same streets never heard or cared to hear what happened before them. They don't give a damn.*

Back at the dinner table, J.J. and friends thought it was apparent that Nick's favorite native son was Johns Hopkins from Anne Arundel farmland.

J.J.'s support for her husband's brilliance won over the others. "Guys, you have to admit we didn't know that Enoch Pratt had turned a fortune in hardware into building the city's free library system. And that George Peabody; art collector Henry Walters, son of William Walters; Gilman; and many others were the giants of the little town that had sprung up on the perfect harbor off the Patapsco River, which branched off the long and protective waters of Chesapeake Bay."

Nate, Betsy and J.J. agreed that Nick's lecture was okay after all.

Unfortunately for Nick, they forgot to tell him.

Instead, adrift in Nick's consciousness was J.J.'s tepid thank you. Not enough. Not appreciated. *I'm a bore,* he thought, while gazing into his drink, one elbow on the Rumba Room bar. His familiar pose.

After two drinks, Nick returned to the table quietly. He was half drunk and instinctively tried to start up again with more history. But his voice was weak and uncertain.

Betsy joined her husband with her rolling eyes and then said to Nick in a kind, constructive tone, "Nick, you can't be for real? Baltimore? With more millionaire philanthropists than any other city in America, you say? Baltimore?" She giggled. "Oh, come on Nick. Baltimore?" She misread him.

Nick did not understand that see she was razing him in good fun.

"Yes, that's what I said, Betsy." He paused quietly and took a breath. "Well, I guess that's enough of all this history stuff, then. I can take a hint. Time for more drinks?" Nick typically hid his feelings.

All who were within earshot of his voice knew, however, that that fellow talking Baltimore history had been in fine form.

He faked a big smile and tried to remember the exact taste of that perfect bourbon drink they served him at the spooky Owl Bar weeks ago. Perhaps he could find that perfect taste again.

Chapter 31: Clever Diversion

J.J. and Betsy exhaled and leaned back to gab while digesting a great, satisfying meal.

Nick popped up and walked off, looking again toward the bar.

Nate watched him. He folded his arms and admired his slightly drunk friend. He was fooled by Nick's act, however. Nate thought Nick was enjoying himself for once, after a long year of torment and brooding in 1999. He stood up and went after him. "Hey, wait up, Nick. Things going well, right?"

"I guess," Nick said, only half facing his friend. He stopped and faced reality, "I don't know why I'm here, Nate. This was stupid. I am so uncomfortable around all these folks. They are all young and enthusiastic and I'm a middle-aged ball of nerves suddenly."

"If you think we didn't appreciate your conversation ...

"You know darn well it was not a conversation. I got carried away once again. It was a monologue, a trip down memory lane, memory lane of my imaginary friends in Baltimore history. I'm sick; a sick man, Nate. Too sick for this party stuff."

"You are not sick, just too anxious. You were fine back there. We know you. We love you, you damn fool. Now straighten up, Nick, before I start drinking."

"Right, that'll be the day." Nick paused and looked at his hands as if to read his fortune. He added, "Honestly Nate, I don't know why I'm here. But, I am here. For several weeks I have been so sure that I am supposed to be here somehow. But why?"

"May I be blunt?" Nate asked, wrapping his arm around Nick's shoulders. Without waiting for permission, he said, "That is dumb, okay? Just dumb. You felt you should be here because you stupidly thought you were losing J.J. Don't be stupid. It is NOT the case."

* * *

Betsy leaned into her best buddy, J.J., to point out someone across the room looking their way, "J.J., isn't that the handsome, Dr. Wellbred over there?"

"His name is Wellborne, Betsy, and I don't think he would be here. He's single and most of these folks seemed to be . . . oh my God, it IS Stuart—I mean, Dr. Wellborne."

"Does he have a daughter?" asked Betsy. She scrunched her face up and pointed to a baby-faced redhead in a tight, glittery green gown on the doctor's arm. "Some young pretty chickee is on his arm, honey."

J.J. said, "Oh, her? She's a pediatric nurse; just hired last week. He must be nuts—half his age," J.J. said. She could not stop her curious eyes.

"He sees you, J.J. He found you here."

"I swear, Bet, I never told him about this . . . I don't think I did, anyway."

"You do work with the man, right?"

"Yeah, often our paths cross in the ER, but . . ."

Dr. Stuart Wellborne smiled at the two ladies looking his way and waved. His puckish redheaded date noticed his attention to a charismatic woman across the room and leaned into him--a cozy sight. Wellborne pointed to J.J. and Betsy with some hand gesturing, never taking his eyes off Mrs. J.J. Esposito, with whom he had enjoyed many hours of commuting to and from Hopkins.

* * *

Nate placing a heavy hand on Nick's shoulder, suggested, "Come along, you old history buff. I thought you said this would be a party! Let's take a walk to the bar together, eh?"

"You? Are you sure about that, Nate? But, I thought . . ."

"Well, I didn't exactly say I wanted a drink. Just let's take a walk and look around at the scenery," said Nate, tipping his head at a group of attractive women chatting nearby.

"Oh yeah, I get it. Well, the scenery up here is pretty spectacular . . . yes, I see," Nick said, enjoying the sight of all the happy, smiling women, looking their best. "Nate, take a gander at the one at the door, the blonde. Looks a little like Deborah Harry, eh?"

"You mean the singer with the old rock group Blondie? Yeah, I guess a little. Too young, though. But you know, Nick, she was screaming at us when we dashed off the elevator. Did you catch that? She was taking tickets," Nate said.

"I was too busy grabbing the window seats."

Nate explained, "That's why she was screaming at us. We ran by, didn't notice her, I guess. She's German or something. She kept yelling 'Halt! Halt!' like she was Gestapo. I think she's well suited for guarding the elevator exit. She came to the table for our tickets when you went to the bar. Betsy didn't like the girl intruding. Thought she was rather nasty. Actually Nick, I was just wondering if we could get the girls and slip past the Blondie-like to get into the masquerade ball for a while. It's not yet close to midnight."

Nick checked his watch and sipped his bourbon. He said to Nate, "It's past 10 o'clock. Isn't that Charlie Dupree, the singer with his sax setting up with the band?"

"The guy checking the microphones, passing out music?" Nate asked Nick. "You sound like you know Charlie."

Nick shrugged, "Looks familiar, but I don't think so."

Nate recognized him, "He's played at Morgan many times with this group. I've talked to him before. He's a fireman during the day. And, his guys are fantastic, R&B stuff, pop, you know. Hey, it's a good idea to make a move to the masquerade ball a floor below now, so Betsy doesn't get me up to dance when Charlie's group starts up."

"Okay, I guess," Nick said, still staring at the band leader. "I don't know Charlie, but now I know why he is familiar. I've seen his picture on the Belvedere flyer for these parties like a thousand times. Looked at it every day at the bar for the past six weeks. Feel like I should know him by now, imprinted on my cranium with a lot of other useless junk. He does look damn familiar." Nick chuckled to himself.

Nate bumped shoulders with Nick and waved toward the elevator. "Come on, let's try."

Feeling inspired by Nate and wanting to just goof off with his friend for a while, Nick thought he'd approach the pretty German girl innocently, with a sort of tipsy attitude of some charming twenty-something Baltimore young man, like Pop might have done back in the day.

"I remember you," he said to the young blonde woman.

Before she responded, Nick was surprised that the girl looked no more than sixteen or seventeen years old, though legally she had to be older to be working there. Regardless of her true age the girl was simply an astonishing beauty, he thought. Her alluring looks were impossible to ignore.

Nick stammered a bit. "When we came up here, you . . . you were the first thing I saw off the elevator. Remember us?"

"First thing, huh? So, I am a thing. Now you are back, are you?" she snapped. "You cannot go to za maskraid ball like zat." She said glanced up and down Nick's old, baggy tuxedo and gave him a first-rate smirk. It was the kind of downward corner-of-the-mouth smirk that a pretty girl might reserve for old men who make foolish advances. "I heard you two talking there, you know. But if you leave party, I will see identification, which to match you on return."

"Oh no, we don't want to go to the ball," Nick said. He was impressed that she even recognized him among 150 guests—the eternal power of a pretty face on the male ego.

"Right. You say dat now. But zae won't let you go to the twelfth floor mit no ticket," she said, replacing the smirk with an icy look of suspicion across her very pale, pretty face.

"Mit nein ticket, eh Fräulein?" said Nick sarcastically, still happy with the attention of such an angelic beauty despite her apparent youth and nasty attitude. Was she goofing on the accent? he wondered. Grasping for his senses again, he regretted his tone and hoped the foreign girl didn't understand the meaning of his snarky remark.

Nate, who had held back, then came by, not at all impressed with the girl's looks nor her nastiness, and offered, "Come on, Nick," pulling him back toward their table. He saw Betsy's eyes set in an unforgiving gaze toward him and Nick, who looked like they were trying to pick up the pretty blonde "child" not twenty-five feet from their wives.

Nate recoiled from Betsy's cold stare. He then said, "Nick, I have a plan. Go ask our wives if they want another drink while I stroll over to the band to talk with Charlie Dupree." He didn't want to deal with Betsy, and he was counting on Charlie remembering Professor Nate Bowen from Morgan State University across town.

After a few minutes of chatting with Dupree, Nate swung by the open bar to get himself a National Boh—the friendliest beer in Baltimore, he figured—as a prop, then rejoined Betsy and his friends at the table.

With his prop held high, he said, "Hey everyone, since the band is still tuning up and won't be playing for a while yet, Nick and I thought you girls would like to crash the masquerade ball to see how that's going before we get close to midnight." Nate smiled and patted Nick on the back as if the whole idea was Nick's, the night's designated leader of their little gang.

J.J. and Betsy thought it was a great idea.

The four walked to the elevator.

"Hey, whatcha do with Blondie?" Nick whispered in Nate's ear. The girl was not at the elevator door.

"Over there, Nick—she's over there with Charlie," said Nate in a hush. "I told him she's Deborah Harry's daughter who is trying to crash the party. I told him she wants to meet the band and tell her mom about them. Charlie, I think, asked her over. He knows she's not really Blondie's kid, eh? He's totally charmed by her, anyway. Wouldn't be surprised if he asks her to sing! He seems smitten." Proud of his little ploy, Nate looked away to hide his laughter from the women.

The four, carrying their drinks, easily slipped into the elevator—Nate holding a Natty Boh low and out of sight, Nick a bourbon on the rocks, J.J. a martini, and Betsy a wine spritzer. Nick punched button number 12 as the others huddled at the back, dark wall of the elevator.

When the doors opened, the four moved quickly into the vast, ornate ballroom to blend in without notice, but obviously sans costumes.

J.J. whispered, "Nick, we shouldn't be here. We aren't in costumes." She kept moving in, though.

"Just say we lost our masks," Nick offered.

They slipped among the masked guests and mysterious characters, which ranged from Sherlock Homes to Buffalo Bill Cody, to a cluster of Franciscan monks in floor-length brown robes. They saw Marie Antoinette, Napoleon Bonaparte, George and Martha Washington, John Smith and Pocahontas, a trolley driver, a policeman, a pirate and, of course, the Beefeater guards and more cowboys, devils, and ghosts.

In no time, Nick also spotted the Thomas Edison look-alike fellow who had ridden the elevator with them. Nick was fascinated. He thought the man was so into character he could be an actor.

"We'll just stay until they realize we don't belong," said Nick. "Or until we see . . . well, I already see. Hey, this is not half the party as upstairs at all. But oh look, J.J., quick look. See that fellow? Who is that guy?"

"Nick, he's just a guy with mussed-up hair and a nice antique rumpled suit. Maybe a lost soul of the past," J.J. said to poke good-natured fun at Nick's history habit.

"No, no, that's Thomas Edison of Menlo Park. Don't you see, he even has the visionary glance about the room as if he is dreaming up inventions?" said Nick.

"Nick, you're deluded. Don't drink anymore."

"Yeah Nick," chimed in Nate, "whatcha been drinkin', buddy?"

"He looks like the real guy, I'm telling you. He is Thomas Edison. My God, look at him!" Nick said excitedly. "I've gotta talk with that guy. Maybe it's the makeup or something. Anyway,

I'm going over, got to talk with him. I bet he really knows a lot about Edison."

"Not more history, Nick, please!" pleaded J.J. "Besides, that guy doesn't look anything like Edison. Everybody knows what he looks like. That's not close."

Nate and Betsy stood surveying the room of odd folks and realized that in the dim light that all the people at this party filled only half the cavernous ballroom. Nate hated the music, recorded oldies pumped in. Nate was the first to get the situation right. "Hey Nick, maybe your Thomas Edison there needs to invent a new party in here. Please man, let's get out of here before they start playing the Monkees' greatest hits, okay?"

"That wouldn't take long." Betsy laughed.

Nate was right. They had walked out of the best party and into a dud.

"Come on, J.J.," said Betsy. "We're missin' a good party upstairs. It is upstairs, isn't it? The floors must be far apart with this high ceiling, huh? Oh, whatever; we're wasting time. Come on."

"You guys go ahead. I'm going to meet Edison," Nick insisted. "Okay, I'm nuts. But I've always wanted to talk with Edison, and he's getting away. He's going behind those loudspeakers by the stage—probably wondering how they work. Look at him, see?"

But the Edison character was all the way on the other side of the ballroom by then.

Betsy and J.J. stood dumbfounded.

"Nick's losing it again," Betsy whispered to J.J. as if to say 'get him, quickly.'

As the man dressed like Edison disappeared, J.J. stepped in front of Nick, "Hey Nick, we can't get separated, we just can't. Don't ruin this night for me."

They took the creakavator 'express' back up to the fourteenth floor, where 'Blondie,' back at her post, immediately stopped Nick before he could take one step into the room, keeping the others so tight to the elevator entrance that Nate's and Betsy's bodies blocked the elevator door from closing.

"Zo, you vent behind my back. Very clever. Maybe I need your IDs or tickets, misters," the girl said, pointing a finger in Nick's face and showing no mercy.

"Zo maybe not, babe!" Nick quipped, still irritated from not meeting the Thomas Edison guy. He pumped his right fist up at the elbow and grabbed J.J.'s arm with his left hand. "Let's go." He led the four quickly to their table as they all tried to muffle their laughter into their hands and chests.

Chapter 32: Serious Party Time

Nick's quick move past the girl may have been uncharacteristic, a little mean and inconsiderate. But, he was lucky. The band started playing that instant, putting the room in motion and freezing Blondie in a guarded stance by the door.

The room was buzzing with excitement--some people dancing near the band, some just clowning around with the silver-and-black noise makers, New Year's 2000 top hats for men, tiaras for women. The party crowd was in full spirit.

The broad, happy face of Charlie Dupree seemed to fill the room. He sang Oingo Boingo's 1990 hit tune, "Dead Man's Party":

> *I was struck by lightning*
> *Walkin' down the street*
> *I was hit by something last night in my sleep*
> *It's a dead man's party*
> *Who could ask for more.*

Nate shouted over the music to Nick, "Hey man, are you listening? They should be playing that song downstairs where the deadbeats are, eh?" He was about to sit back at their table by the window when Betsy grabbed his hand.

"Not so fast, big guy," she said, dragging Nate to the polished hardwood floor in front of Dupree's band.

Nick, feeling a bit insecure again in the midst of the mass of human commotion, celebrated with another drink and listened to the band. He pondered the meaning and composition of the song, learning how they put it together.

Analyzing fine details was one of Nick's fall backs when insecure. He couldn't help but think everything thoroughly through. It was Nick's fate, or curse. He had no idea if he was having a good time, or not, still not knowing why the hell he had

271

to be there at all. He remembered then, *Oh, for J.J. Okay,* and he felt a little better.

He watched J.J., milling about, meeting more interesting people casually than she had encountered in five years at home raising the baby twins. She appeared relaxed, perhaps contented, knowing the girls were in bed by then at mother's house.

Meanwhile from his barstool, Nick struck up a conversation with wry and playful bartender Penny Waite. She was a tomboy of a woman, slim and friendly. Nick was observing people and seemed to get Penny's attention, perhaps because he was ordering a lot of drinks. Everybody else seemed to be super-friendly with everybody else. Nick though ended up talking with the smiling bartender, who had what he wanted, drinks.

She was one of three snappily dressed bartenders at the party that night in their black and silver uniforms and silver "Happy New Year, 2000" top hats.

Penny made an instant connection with Nick that evening because of J.J., not so much Nick. She had spotted the couple the moment they entered the Rumba Room earlier and was captivated by lovely J.J., who kept watching Nick closely each trip to the bar.

Penny misread J.J.'s watch dogging and thought the beautiful woman fancied her. When J.J. eventually noticed the bartender watching her table, she came over to meet Penny hoping for an ally to help her contain Nick. She whispered in Penny's ear, "Be good to Nicky, okay?"

She returned to the table and confided with Betsy, "Nick might stay soberer with a little idle flirting from that bartender Penny. Nice girl. Don't you think since Penny is probably a lesbian, she'd be a perfect set up, safe with Nicky? Might help us out to keep him occupied."

"Good move, girl. Yeah, she's gay alright."

Penny took J.J.'s advice to heart and was too good to Nick. She gave him whatever he wanted to drink and more, an extra shot each time, while occasionally gesturing back to J.J.'s table.

* * *

The band picked up the pace with snappy rock 'n roll tunes.

J.J. waved over to Nick. She persuaded him to join her on the dance floor.

Nick could not help but noticed J.J. was more relaxed as she danced.

Perhaps recruiting Penny had put her mind more at ease about watching Nick's every move.

Soon, as they danced, all eyes seemed to fall on the gorgeous brunette in the strapless tight dress dancing with that odd, hunched-over skinny fellow. Her small feet seemed to float as she showed off delicate movements only a trained performer would have. Her body turned and twisted, coiled then released to the rock 'n roll beat, with her ivory skin on her arms lifting and twirling like dancing ribbons, her lovely, smooth shoulders gyrating, spinning in unison with her breezy hair—pure poetry in motion.

Nick was happy watching her but worried that she was performing too much for an audience. He kissed her on the lips and encouraged her to cool it on the alluring dance moves. "Aren't you showing off a bit too much, honey?"

J.J. nodded yes and took some steps toward their table. Nick offered to get them two drinks from Penny. He split off and told J.J. he would join her back at the table.

Behind Nick's back, Stuart Wellborne made his move, perhaps having seen enough of J.J.'s entrancing dance with her fool husband. Wellborne reached for J.J.'s hand as she walked away from the hard boards. He pulled her softly to him. He said he was cutting in, though in a charming manner. He moved in front of her, held her waist in his right hand, her right hand in his left, and spun her, intending to finish the dance Nick had left for him.

Betsy, dancing nearby with Nate, watched Wellborne's move. After Nate shoved Betsy toward J.J. deliberately, Betsy grabbed her friend's arm, "Come on, honey." She and Nate had already seen enough of Wellborne's bold action.

Betsy, shouted over the music, "Oh J.J., you just have to taste the brandy. Look the waiter put a glass at each place setting. Come on." She tugged her friend from Wellborne's arms and said, turning close to his face, "Back off, doc." She took J.J. to their table.

Nick missed all of it. He was retreating to the bar where Penny kept him occupied. Penny was also wise to the man hitting on J.J. She poured him a double. "Your wife is into the brandy with those ladies. Stay here with me for a while. I'll take good care of you."

As J.J. settled into a gossip session, Nate was a third wheel but soon interjected, "I can see Nick across the bar talking with the bartender, J.J.? I think you are right. He will be okay now with Penny watching over him."

Despite all their conceding and compromising to Nick about his crazy, out-of-character Belvedere party idea; despite the Y2K fear in the heart of a big city; despite landing somehow in a wonderful appropriate celebration on the most festive of festive evenings, Nate and the two women were still very mindful of that at any time Nick's dubious adventure could slide downhill. From time to time that night, each would worry over the state of mind of one Niccola August Esposito.

The joyfulness and levity of the exciting Belvedere party however overruled that potential and no one saw what was happening to their Nick. He was imprinted lifelong with refusing to letting down his walls and having his history 'lessons' ridiculed in his mind at least, Nick did not want to join them at the table. He didn't want to try to trust them again. He had reached a point where he could not possibly "belong" to the party.

Down-hearted, he no longer cared if he got dead drunk. All the people, all the inane talk and joking still bothered him. The room was too ruckus, too unpredictable. Nick began relying more on visions of the delusional kind. A diversion might help, he thought.

While glued to the bar, he wondered again if Edison himself had ever been to the Belvedere in its early days, at the turn of the previous century. *Wow, a complete century ago. It is possible,* Nick mused. His mind drifted while Penny pondered his hypnotic expression. Should she alert J.J.? She didn't. Too many other customers to serve.

He surveyed the party happening and pondered over the shape of the room, the huge windows rising from three-foot ledges to the ten-foot-high ceiling. Strings of cream-colored rope light illuminated just above the bar areas through frosted glass in the ceiling. A swelling of bluish light spilled out into the Rumba Room from a still-busy, noisy kitchen behind the island bar.

He wondered if the room was set up the same way a hundred years ago when the dinosaur hotel was new. *What was all this like in the beginning? Was this room something else? A penthouse for a wealthy industrialist? Or the architect, maybe?*

Love of pre-1900 history surfaced. Nick could see ghostly figures of people dressed for that era and milling about the room and whisking about party balloons and streamers of primary colors, as they went in and out of a foggy vision.

Just as Nick began feeling comfortable with images of the room perhaps 100 years ago, he was jolted back to the present.

A disturbing voice cut right to his heart like a poison dagger. "Nick, Nicky boy, hey man, it's almost time for Y2K. Ready for the end of the world?" It was his old colleague, boss—no, his Judas—Walter Bunker, the vice principal at Glen Burnie High School.

On the day Nick was fired, it was Walter Bunker who was the zombie with a cold stare who had sat silent that day as Nick was being humiliated by Principal Frank Palumbo and the county officials, the warm body who had escorted Nick out of the principal's office and his career forever. It was the voice of the man who allowed them to fire Nick without defending his talented history teacher. Technically, Bunker had nothing to do with the decision, but did nothing to stop it.

Bunker was certainly not a friend of Nick's and the last person Nick would want to see, or should see, at the millennium party to spoil things. He instantly believed that hearing Bunker's voice, of all things possible, certainly meant he was indeed going to lose his big chance to please J.J. at the big millennium party. The night would surely be a flop, just like he was.

"Hey Walter," Nick grunted.

The diminutive sixty-ish Bunker wore the same crooked wire-rim glasses Nick remembered him wearing at the high school. He had on a rumpled black suit with a narrow black necktie, and looking like he hadn't slept since Nick's firing. He looked unhappy and his eyes said it all: deep, dark bags under watery, bloodshot bulbs behind perfectly round black wire specs.

Nick remembered most about Bunker that he was a bureaucratic coward. He stared at Bunker for an eternity in disbelief that this man had joined the party, his party. The man looked like an undertaker, Nick thought, his.

Finally, Bunker cleared his throat—maybe sensing Nick's tension—and said pleasantly, "Hey man, where the hell are you teaching now? Must be doing quite well, Nick. I didn't expect to see you here in these exclusive digs," said Bunker, thinly sarcastically. "Some dump, eh?"

Bunker seemed to be very insecure, Nick detected, but he tried to be nice as always. Nick replied, "How have you been, Walter? Enjoying yourself?" Nick was downright dejected and still hiding it. He thought, *What a drag to see Bunker when things still could have turned out okay. I hope J.J. doesn't see this jerk.*

"It's wonderful to see you, Walter. It really is," Nick lied. "But hey, it's ten minutes to midnight and I promised to get some friends drinks before the fireworks start. So, I've got to get back. Again, good to see you."

Nick slipped quickly to the other side of the bar island and downed a double Old Grand-Dad straight, which Penny already had waiting and then he ordered another double from Penny "for the road, dear" and another martini for J.J.

Penny accommodated him and sent a thumbs-up sign across the room to J.J. Penny ladled the liquor generously for him—treating him good, as J.J. had instructed. Penny was eyeing J.J. as she poured.

Charlie Dupree's band kicked into the funky tune "U Got the Look" by Prince. "Perfect, where is she?" Nick said to himself.

He found J.J. and they danced a few steps in place, and then moved toward their table again where Betsy was enjoining her husband to get up and get a groove on with the enticing Prince beat.

Nick looked back toward the bar, surveyed the room, wanting at all costs to avoid Bunker, who just might put the fear of Y2K right back into his party girl. *She's doing so fine so far,* he thought.

Nick still had not seen Stuart Wellborne lurking in the shadows.

* * *

No one else on the dance floor could know that J.J. and Nick, dancing together, would each remember far different accounts of what happened during the exciting final moments before midnight.

Chapter 33: J.J.'s Midnight Thoughts

J.J. smiled when Nick pointed at her because at 11:53 P.M. the band segued from Prince's bouncy tune "U Got the Look" to his funky hit "1999."

Well, that's predictable, but I love it, she thought. She grabbed Nick and tugged him onto the dance floor.

Everyone sprang to their feet except Nate. But, he couldn't hide. Betsy jumped up and yelled to her soul mate, "Wow, perfect. Let's go, Natty Boh boy!"

J.J. thought, *Wow. Bet never said stuff like that.*

All at once, everyone at the party started dancing, jumping, and clapping.

J.J. watched the band as she danced. She kept Betsy and Nate in sight too. *This party was far better than Bet would ever expected, she thought.*

Still the loving wife, the sensible, cautious J.J. was concerned, *Why had Nick been so possessed by this place? Weird, even for Nick.*

She looked around. *I don't see Stuart. Maybe he left. That could have been terrible if Nick saw Stuart grab on to me.* At least she was now protected by the surrounding dancers.

She looked at Nick within arms-length and saw trouble on his face. She wondered again about the Y2K disaster scenario people feared. That dreaded moment of midnight was closing in too fast.

What a great party, J.J. thought to clear her head again. She shouted over the loud music, "Nicky, this is way better than I expected. Thank you!"

But she couldn't get away from worrying still, *Perhaps Nick was right; it's okay to be here. But, then again, it isn't yet midnight, not Y2K yet.*

She reconsidered. *Don't let Nick see me worrying.*

She was happy with the moment however, though a bit guilty about drinking too much. She shouted, "This is my time, Nick. Looks like a 1979 disco!"

It was more important, especially for Nick's sake, for her to put away any thoughts of a national computer shutdown at midnight, or any fears at all. She let herself spin and glide gracefully, yet a bit self-conscious. Male eyes, all around, were focused on her.

Darn it, this is the New Year of New Year's, she thought. *I'm going to enjoy it.*

Band leader Charlie Dupree sang the Prince lyrics:

> *Lemme tell ya somethin'*
> *If you didn't come to party*
> *Don't bother knockin' on my door*
> *I got a lion in my pocket*
> *And baby he's y to roar*

11:58 P.M.

J.J. was dancing her heart out, and laughing it up. What a time it was, indeed. The tight little musical group played. Everybody bounced to the beat. The room itself seemed to bounce. The people, the band, the servers, all shared one thought—a happy New Year/New Millennium moment was near.

But, she suspected still that something was not quite right. J.J. wondered why Nick kept reaching out to move her position on the dance floor, steering her shoulders one way, then another.

I think he's spotted Stuart, oh God, don't let him see him, she thought, never dropping her smile.

In their tuxes, Nick, and Nate, with J.J. and Betsy in their best party dresses, jumped with the rhythm of the tune, and kept exchanging glances and laughing. Nick and J.J. sang along with Charlie and the band:

> *They say two thousand zero zero party over*
> *Oops out of time ...*

She looked at Nick on the word 'oops' hoping he'd join her in a lip sync duo for fun. But instead, Nick's gaze focused across the room.

She took her eyes off Nick and enjoyed the music for a while and the freedom of dancing intoxicated.

But then, he moved her shoulders again. He looked stunned like something was going on by the elevator entrance to the Rumba Room. J.J. tried to see, *Oh no, Nick looks like he's seen a ghost. I heard him say the word 'impossible.'*

J.J. shouted, "What's impossible Nick?"

She saw Nick's eyes bulge open wide and his jaw drop.

"Nick, what's wrong?" she called out. He didn't hear.

Yet, the music was loud; the scene confusing.

He moved her again.

"Nick! Nick, what is it, Nick?"

She stopped dancing and again tried to see what he saw.

Chapter 34: Nick's Midnight Thoughts

While J.J. enjoyed the Prince song "1999," the song worried Nick as he danced with her.

Absent-mindedly, he picked up the first lyrics and listened analytically, too analytically:

> *I was dreamin' when I wrote this*
> *Forgive me if it goes astray*
> *But when I woke up this mornin'*
> *Could of sworn it was judgment day*

"Me too pal," Nick muttered to himself.

Then, three hours into his much-anticipated New Year's outing at the Belvedere Hotel, three hours of tolerating the required socializing, Nick was comfortable again to see things in his own inimitable way: a little pondering, a little fantasizing, a little visiting.

However, there are positive visits and those not so positive.

When big Charlie Dupree began belting out the perfect song for the millennium party, "1999," Nick became claustrophobic with all the dancers squeezing into the dance floor. Nearly all 150 party guests in black tie and evening dresses were jumping around and singing, clapping and laughing while bumping and shoving into him and J.J.

As in Prince's lyrics, Nick was getting dreamy. He decided to focus on the words to maybe keep in touch with reality. He sang along:

> *Yeah, they say two thousand zero zero party over*
> *Oops out of time*
> *So tonight I'm gonna party like it's 1999 ...*

The excited crowd noise filled the festive room across the entire fourteenth floor. With the lights dimmed, the glass-enclosed millennium party hovered over a blanket of sparkling city lights.

Nick watched his beautiful wife, twirling and hopping with him, flaunting her happiness. People stepped back to give her room as she strutted her stuff. It worried Nick.

He liked hearing J.J. shout over the loud music, "Nicky, this is way better than I expected. Thank you!"

She looked stunning. J.J.'s radiant beauty drew the attention of everyone, especially the men. It seemed so to Nick, at least. Her long auburn curls danced over her bare shoulders. J.J. was simply glowing—her laughing chestnut eyes, her still-perfect complexion at thirty-nine, and her glamorous smile, full lips lifting a little higher to the right side, that sexy nuance that Nick loved so much.

Mindful of his wife's allure, her irresistible beauty, Nick spun J.J. around to a different perspective as they danced, as if he wanted to control what she saw or who saw her.

Nick wondered if sensible J.J. was sincerely happy to be there, or was performing to please him. He feared his mind might drift. He picked up and lip-synched more lyrics:

We could all die any day
But before I'll let that happen
I'll dance my life away

He recalled J.J. saying just days ago that Nick's party idea "to live a moment in history" was pretty stupid. He allowed a dreamy, self-gratified grin to show for just a second. She had finally given in, put away her fears of the city on that night, and decided to go along. Now it was on. He heard her yell over the music, "This is my time, Nick. Looks like a 1979 disco!"

Sassy Betsy Bowen and big dependable Nate Bowen moved closer to J.J. and Nick on the parquet dance floor. They too were enjoying the delightful sight of J.J. dancing joyfully, freely, and were happy for her. Betsy knew all too well it hadn't been easy for J.J. to put up with Nick that year, his sour moods and despondent attitude.

Nick heard J.J. say, "Oh, why not," she shouted to Nate and Betsy. "It's time to party! Boogie on down, you guys—not to worry!"

"Do we know this girl?" Nate hollered to Betsy, with a hearty laugh and a wink to Nick. They both looked at the band and gave thumbs-up.

Nick smiled cautiously and swung his lanky body around to face the singer, the one and only Charlie "Fireman" Dupree.

Charlie slung his big, polished saxophone across his tall and bulky frame from side to side. Although a part-time musician, Dupree was born for these moments. His broad smile lit up the room. A local legend in North Baltimore, Dupree made his bread at nighttime gigs, and then hung with his fireman buddies during the day at the historic Engine 21 Firehouse on Roland Avenue.

Nick looked at J.J. and nodded toward Dupree's jolly face. They laughed and sang along. Anyone who had been at that party on that night would vividly remember big Charlie Dupree's round, cheeky face laughing with the guests at midnight.

At 11:58 P.M., Nick saw Nate watching him and held up two fingers of victory to Nate to cover his shifting mood. Nick was feeling light-headed. He again listened closely to the Prince lyrics to stay in the moment:

> *Yeah, everybody's got a bomb*
> *We could all die any day ...*

Nick was afraid that everything swirling around his mind—the silly party idea, anticipating the chime of midnight magically cleansing him of his troubles, the crowd of strangers all going absolutely nuts for an artificial celebration. He tried listening to the next lyrics, but barely heard them:

> *They say two thousand zero zero party*
> *... zero party, party ...*

> *We're runnin' outta time, time, time, time ...*
> *So tonight, we gonna, we gonna party like it's 1999*

Nick became alarmed.

He noticed a commotion at the hotel elevator. He felt nauseous because J.J. saw him grimace.

He then saw men pushing and shoving.

Nick hid his face from J.J. and gently put his hands on her bare shoulders. She mouthed, "I love you" but he didn't see her pantomime. The men at the elevator were becoming violent.

Oh no. It is a fight. Damn. Nothing like that should ruin her night, he thought.

Nick saw two large men dressed in hotel staff uniforms tussling about. They looked angry. Nick's gut tightened and his heart sank as he realized J.J.'s beautiful evening could be lost just as the celebration was reaching midnight, when he'd hoped more than anything for it to bring a more agreeable year. Again, he wondered what drew him there.

He avoided her glances.

She wore a worried expression.

Nick saw a little man among the big hotel men. The little man was much older and was wearing a brown trench coat.

J.J. was straining now to locate what Nick saw. He moved her about by the shoulders and kept moving in a pseudo dancing step.

He saw the little man struggling fiercely with the bigger men, trying to get into the party, Nick thought. The men were forcing the little man back toward the elevator doors.

Nick glanced at the band. Dupree and the players hadn't noticed any disruption as they continued to drive the revelry. No one stopped dancing.

More Prince words leaked into Nick's head:

> *Lemme tell ya somethin'*
> *If you didn't come to party*
> *Don't bother knockin' on my door*

I got a lion in my pocket
And baby he's y to roar

Only Nick apparently saw the fight going on at the old elevator. Everyone was continuing to dance, laugh and shout with each other.

This is too strange, he thought.

J.J. stopped dancing and stared at Nick.

Nick froze. He looked back toward the elevator. Over the heads of J.J. and others, Nick saw a young blonde girl at the elevator encircled by the men. The little man seemed to shove her to the floor. *It's that pretty Nazi girl. No, maybe not. I don't know.*

"This is just awful!" Nick blurted.

"What?" J.J. mouthed.

Nick ignored her question.

He thought he heard a gunshot.

Goddamn it, the band's too loud! I better stop them. He finally shouted to the band, "Hey, why isn't anyone helping that poor girl?"

But, no one except J.J. heard him shout.

"Nick, what's wrong?" she called out.

Nick lost all sense of being there. He stopped moving, stood on his tiptoes, and watched in horror as the little man infuriated the beefy hotel men. They grabbed him and whirled him around.

"Nick! Nick, what is it, Nick?" screamed J.J.

He didn't hear her. He saw the little man's coat separate for a second. There was a gun on his hip. The fire arm looked like an Esposito family relic, a familiar pearl-handled .38-caliber pistol. Such a rare, antique model once belonged to Nick's great-grandfather, Baltimore's famous police inspector Michael Esposito. *It can't be the same,* Nick thought. *That pistol is locked up at Pop's.*

In a feverishly quick survey of the dance floor, he realized that no one else was watching the melee. The party kept going like nothing was wrong.

"Impossible," he said out loud.

Nick thought that he was the only person at the party to spot the little man and his apparent pistol or something resembling one because of his superior height.

J.J. stood frozen on the dance floor, staring at Nick's tortured face. She shouted back, "What's impossible?"

Nick was too distracted to notice that J.J. stopped dancing. He watched the hotel men spin the little man, kick him, and throw him down and the little man began running. Nick's jaw dropped. "My God, where is he? I can't see him."

J.J. turned again to see what was distressing Nick, but she was too short to see over people. But even in heels, she wouldn't have seen past the others on the dance floor.

Nick was crying. He held his head in his hands and blocked out J.J.'s gaze. *Her night will be ruined,* he thought.

J.J. reached out and embraced her Nick.

He saw her mouth open to question him. He recognized her puzzled expression as 'I'll get you through this one my love.'

But it was too late for questions.

11:59:50 P.M.

The music stopped. Charlie Dupree put down his sax and pulled in a microphone, "Okay folks, here we go!" Charlie let the gang of revelers shout out the countdown from ten, nine, eight to . . .

"Happy New Year, folks!"

Chapter 35: Why Did Those Days Ever Have to Go?

No one stopped the fight at the elevator or even noticed it. Even as everyone yelled 'Happy New Year' and cheered, Nick was thinking *What is happening to me? I know what I saw.*

For the sake of J.J., Nick shrugged and dismissed his vision. He gave her a quick hug and absent-mindedly looked toward the south window to escape his paranoia, as she had closed her eyes and leaned toward him with lips puckered.

'Mr. romance' missed her move. Instead, still looking at the south windows, he yelled, "Come on, Nate; come on J.J., honey, hurry. Come on, Betsy," without noticing his friends embracing in a passionate kiss or seeing J.J. leaning in for her New Year's kiss.

Nate looked up from kissing his wife to see Nick running and remembered why. He took off after Nick.

Betsy shrugged her shoulders, rolled her eyes, and laughed affectionately at crazy Nick hightailing it to the south windows, Nate in pursuit. The women followed the men back to their table. Nick was eager to see the grand fireworks display at the Inner Harbor. That would save the evening for sure.

They all peered intently out the big windows toward the harbor.

Nothing.

They looked left and right.

Nothing.

"So, where's the big show, Nick?" J.J. snickered, still wondering when she'd get that kiss.

Betsy added, "Yeah, Nick."

The two women kept up the good-natured ribbing.

Meanwhile, just a half minute into 2000, Charlie Dupree led the band into Stevie Wonder's 1976 hit, "I Wish," re-released in 1999 on his four-disc "At the Close of the Century":

> *Looking back on when I*
> *Was a little nappy headed boy*
> *Then my only worry*
> *Was for Christmas what would be my toy*
> *Even though we sometimes*
> *Would not get a thing*
> *We were happy with the*
> *Joy the day would bring*
> *Sneaking out the back door*
> *To hang out with those hoodlum friends of mine*
> *Greeted at the back door*
> *With boy thought I told you not to go outside*
> *Tryin' your best to bring the*
> *Water to your eyes*
> *Thinking' it might stop her*
> *From woopin' your behind*

It was, of course, another perfect millennium song, fit for the moment.

J.J. and Betsy were jumping and clapping.

Nick and Nate peered through the big window over the city. Dupree sang with great excitement. It was all good. The entire roomful, including Nate and Nick's wives, joined the chorus:

> *I wish those days could come back once more*
> *Why did those days ever have to go*
> *I wish those days could come back once more*
> *Why did those days ever have to go?*
> *'Cause I love them so*

Convinced there weren't going to be any fireworks, Betsy yelled back to Nate, "Nate . . . hey Nate, let's dance some more."

"Ah . . . I don't want . . . Oh Nick, I see them!" said Nate. "There they are Nick, the tiniest fireworks ever!"

Nick said, "Where, where? I don't see—"

"Way over there, see?" Nate was holding back his laughter as he spotted tiny blips of multicolored lights appearing just off the ground, way past the Inner Harbor a couple of miles off. They were, maybe as tall in their view as a thumbnail held at arm's length.

The women and Nate couldn't look at Nick while hiding their laughter.

Nick was embarrassed and tried to sit at the dinner table, but a crowd of people standing around him prevented it.

With the entire room of people still chanting the Stevie Wonder refrain:

I wish those days could come back once more
Why did those days ever have to go?

He cringed hearing Betsy say, "That's it? That's your best in Baltimore history pie-row-tech-nics, Nick?" She started laughing uncontrollably.

Nate and J.J. also burst out in hilarity, pointing at Nick. They really thought Nick, after all the fun, would be okay with their mocking. It was beyond ludicrous and surely Nick would get it.

He didn't.

Nick was just too smashed drunk to be his forgiving self. He shook his head and looked down, embarrassed, and smiled a little. The joke was on him.

"Hey buddy, don't take it so hard. It's fireworks, just like you've been saying . . . somewhere . . . way down in Virginia, or someplace!" Nate said, hugging Nick around the shoulders.

Nick twisted off his hug.

Betsy and J.J. kept right on laughing.

Nick didn't expect being such a goat and resented it. It was something he had harped on and they simply were laughing at him. *That damn song, I wish those words would stop,* he thought. *Days not coming back again. I'll say.*

But the chant went on and on for ten minutes and more. Two young guys started blowing their party kazoos in Nick's face to the rhythm of the Stevie Wonder anthem, all in fun they sang in his face:

> *I wish those could come back once more*
> *Why did those days ever have to go?*

Nick nearly screamed at the kazoo boys, but managed to hold his tongue. He could only smile at their joyful faces, despite his sour disposition. He patted one of them on the back and simply walked away toward the bar for another double Old Grand-Dad. He faintly heard Nate say, "Aw, Nick'll be alright."

But he wasn't 'alright.' At that stage of Nick's evening, a man adverse to seeking attention, past and present events, objects and people had begun to twist and circle in and out, up and down and around his mind's eye. He was not yet showing outward signs of his wavering consciousness—between drunken spells of despair over his lost identity—as he wondered to himself, "why was I brought here anyway?" No longer 'why am I here;' it became 'why was I *brought* here?'

He looked out onto the streets. There he surrendered more and more to the comfort of his 'gift,' those glimpses into the hotel's past—ladies in long dresses and fancy hats climbing from horse drawn sedans down on the street, mustached men in suspenders, undershirts and gloves working the furnaces and mechanical elevator workings in the basement, those Italian stone masons on scaffolds outside of the party windows.

More fantasy, more disruption of his plan. He knew he was lost but could not control himself.

While returning to the Rumba Room bar, Nick spotted in the corner of his eye a familiar figure approaching him rapidly from across the room. It was that little man he'd seen in the fight at the elevator just before midnight. The little man wore an oversized poor boy cap and an old-fashioned brown trench coat. His figure came running across the room, approaching Nick from the side. Nick caught a good look at him. The little man bumped hard into him, sending them both down to the floor. Dazed, Nick looked up at the little man who had hit him, got up and ran off in a great hurry.

As the little man took the sharp turn around the bar and toward the kitchen, he glanced back at Nick with fear in his eyes. He seemed to recognize Nick. The little man's brown coat parted slightly to again reveal the pearl-handled pistol.

Yes, now Nick was sure: The gun resembled the .38-caliber Colt double-action revolver that Pop kept locked in the tavern display cabinet just below his prized antique liqueurs. Long ago, that revolver was confiscated by Pop's policeman father, Mike Esposito, as he arrested a thug in Baltimore, as Pop told the story many times.

The vision of Pop's prized pistol flashed through Nick's mind. It was a very vivid image because earlier that very day Nick had seen that revolver in Pop's display cabinet.

Maybe the man came out of the masquerade ball, Nick thought. Still, Nick was in a panic. *There's a gun at the party—J.J.'s party—damn it!*

He got to his feet, stumbled back down to the floor, then up again, to get a better look at the man in the coat. Nick reached the bar, looked behind it, and saw the man disappear into the kitchen, knocking down stacked dishes on the stainless-steel prep table. He disappeared without any voices or screams from the kitchen workers. *Didn't anybody in there see that guy? I'm clearly nuts. Need to go home.*

He glanced at Penny the bartender. She was wiping the bar, not disturbed at all. She looked casually across the room, enjoying the band and the people still chanting the Stevie Wonder song together.

Nick ran to a little window in the swinging kitchen doors.

Things were surprisingly calm. The chefs were focused on the prep tables, meticulously preparing after party treats. He whiffed a strong aroma of chocolate cake icing. There was no sign of the little man in the coat or any damage that he surely would have caused a moment ago.

"Hey Nick, you okay?" Penny hollered.

Perplexed, Nick moved around the bar and reached over to hold on to Penny's shoulder. He needed reality. He was about to ask her if she had seen the man run into the kitchen. She was pouring him another double Old Grand-Dad. But, also at the bar was Vice Principal Walter Bunker—a far worse vision than the ghostly little man. Nick gulped his bourbon when he saw Bunker leaning on the bar, close to him.

Bunker was doing the same, ordering a strong drink. He turned to see Nick. He was obviously there by himself. "Hey Nick, you didn't say where you're working."

Nick lost it. "Goddamn it, Bunker—nowhere, okay? Is that what you want to hear? I'm working nowhere. I'm not teaching anymore, I'm tending bar for my grandfather, as if you didn't know." He imagined a lesser man being driven to pounding Bunker's head against the bar. Nick moved away a few steps and sat on a stool some distance from Bunker. "Hey Penny, switch me to beer from now on, okay?" Penny set up a cold Heineken, his favorite.

He took a gulp to quiet his temper. He looked at Penny for any sign she might have seen him blow up at Bunker. He was embarrassed. She hadn't changed her expression at all. He felt great remorse and walked over to Bunker, who had moved back to a little round table further into the darkness between the big, full-rectangular bar and the kitchen doors. He was sitting by himself, looking down at the table.

"Listen Walter, I'm sorry, okay? I'm trying to keep my wife on the up and up on this party. This was my big idea and things were goin' okay for a while and now I don't know. So, I'm a bit touchy about all this Y2K shit, getting fired at the high school, or anything bad at all. I didn't mean to bite your head off. Can I buy you a beer?" He managed a half smile as Bunker saw the real Nick Esposito resurface on Nick's face again, the one he used to know.

"Sure, Nick, sure. You can buy me two since they're free," he said with a forced laugh. "Hey, great party, huh? And, honest, I didn't know you were out of work. I'm not at Glen Burnie High anymore, either. I retired in June and my wife died in September. So I . . ."

"Oh God, Walter, your Audrey died? I'm so, so sorry. I had not heard," said Nick with some clarity and great compassion suddenly for the man who let the system end Nick's career.

"Cancer of the pancreas, it was over for her in a few months after she got diagnosed," Bunker said. "She died in September. Did I say that? I'm just here to get cheered up for the millennium, Nick. It's a good tonic. "I always thought this old hotel must be full of romance and intrigue. So, I bought a ticket."

Nick nodded. He thought better of asking *Gee, wonder if Bunker met old lady Krantz too?*

"I figured I might not actually go," Walter continued, "but would give the ticket to somebody at the last minute if I got asked someplace else. But, as you can see, here I am. I didn't get asked out by anybody." He chuckled sadly.

"You're here by yourself, Walter? Come on over and say hi to J.J. She'd like to see you. But please, please don't mention Y2K. She believed in that bullshit. Okay?"

Nick was stumbling drunk, but still ashamed for yelling at Bunker. He guzzled his beer and grabbed another for the trip across the room and put his hand on Bunker's shoulder while they walked.

"By the way, Walter, how 'bout that guy who ran by us into the kitchen. What the hell was that all about?"

"What guy?"

"You must've seen him. Knocked me down; didn't you see that?"

"I saw you fall, Nick. Are you alright? I forgot to ask."

Nick nodded.

"No," Bunker continued, "I didn't see any guy running. I just thought you tripped. I've seen that before. Oops—I'm sorry I said that, Nick."

When they found J.J., she, Nate, and Betsy were hanging out near the band to speak to Dupree.

Nick said loud enough in a slurry voice for J.J., the others, even Dupree to hear, "I thought that Stevie song would never end. But it's all good, huh?" He shouted into J.J.'s ear, "Say hello to Wa ... wa ...Water Blunker. Remember Walto?" He caught J.J.'s eyes, which could have said, 'God, he's losing his senses.'

J.J. looked puzzled, glanced toward Penny—why has this happened?—and then Betsy, who shrugged.

J.J. knew that Bunker was one of the officers at one of Nick's schools.

"It's okay. Walter is not the one who wa, ... I mean, who ah, that is, fired me at Glen Burnie High," said Nick with the best positive face he could manage. Nick's mind wrestled with mixed emotions—too much merriment all around—he had been drinking too much—Bunker might mention Y2K—J.J. was looking too apprehensive, he thought. All the thoughts had come at once and none clear to him at all. Nick then spun around as if ready to faint and blurted, "Maybe time to leave, honey?" he said.

Despite being drunk, Nick was compassionate and saw the hurt on Bunker's face, a look of vulnerability that Nick had never seen before, though the two had worked under the same roof for several years.

J.J. saw Walter's expression, too. Her nursing instincts demanded that she should try to cheer him up. A party was no place to be solemn. She took a chance. "Hi Walter, you want to join us at the table? We've got a great view of the fireworks, eh, Nick?"

Nick shrugged again, chuckled this time, and led them away from the band.

As they walked to their table, Nick leaned in close to J.J.'s ear. He told her Walter had just lost his wife to cancer, it happened quickly, and that he was now retired. "And Walter is alone at this party, J.J., this party, mi-magine that?"

J.J. motioned to Betsy and Nate to come over to the table to join them.

Nick was still nice, yes, but a bit leery about dumping sad-sack Bunker into her lap and putting a downer on the evening. The more he thought about it, the sorrier he was about bringing Bunker and his wife together.

He reviewed; more analysis. "Well so far," he muttered to himself, dragging back to the bar. "Yeah, this party might just be what we need—J.J. seems happy with it. But this Bunker thing could ruin it. *God, I can't stand to watch. What the hell were you thinking, Nick? Stupid, stupid. Oh man, do I need a drink!*

For the better part of the year, Nick told people at the tavern he was a recovering alcoholic and was dry. But Nick Esposito was not at all the kind of guy who was about to face a whole room of Nicks at an AA meeting. No, not him. He thought he was smart enough to deal with his love of drinking. He was sure he could cope at the party too.

Chapter 36: Wellborne

Nick got to the bar and leaned on it with one elbow again, as he'd been doing every day at the Ellwood Avenue tavern. He looked over to the table where J.J., Nate, and Betsy were talking to Bunker.

He tried to think it out the best he could, *Oh well, I tried and we are here. What's wrong with me that I can't just relax like most people? This is what I wanted . . . I think. I don't know what I want. No matter, J.J. can always drive me home; I'm okay . . . I guess . . .* "Hey, who the hell is that?" he said out loud.

"I don't know Nick, but he knows you and J.J.," Penny remarked.

He'd spotted Stuart Wellborne, the handsome young physician from Hopkins, who had slinked himself over to J.J. at their table.

Nick watched.

Wellborne leaned down and kissed J.J. on the cheek. He left his hand on her bare left shoulder.

It infuriated Nick. It looked to Nick like she was introducing everyone to Stuart Wellborne. Nick made out 'Stuuu' on her lips. Maybe she had lost sight of Nick, but Nick hadn't lost sight of her. His eyes flared and his face tightened in anger. "Wellborne!" Nick screamed.

"Who? What, Nick?" Penny asked. She reached for his hand, which he pulled back instantly.

"She invited Wellborne. It's him, damn it, anyway."

"Who's him?"

"Give me that damn bottle, Penny. I'm going to hit him over the head and end their affair right now right here. Call the police; get me arrested. I'll get off. My Pop will get me off; you'll see."

He was enraged. Nonviolent Nick Esposito reached for the Old Grand-Dad one-liter bourbon bottle and missed it. Penny jerked it away. She was shocked by the sudden change in him.

Nick stalked quickly to the table. Penny scrambled out of the bar and went after him.

Wellborne was then sitting close to J.J., both with their backs to approaching Nick. They never saw him coming.

"You!" Nick screamed.

Wellborne turned and began to say hello, but didn't get the chance. He likely knew it was Nick.

Nick screamed again, "You. It's you! What are you doing here in my party? You! Get off her. Hey!"

Not satisfied with his incoherence, Nick grabbed the back of Wellborne's chair and flung him to the floor. He was standing over the dazed man.

Penny grabbed Nick's arms from behind and locked them together with considerable strength.

Nick started kicking the man on the floor.

Nate jumped up and wrestled his best friend to the floor, along with Penny.

Nate shook Nick, "Hey my man, calm down. It is not like that. It's a coincidence that he's here, Nicky. Please listen to me, brother."

Nick's blood cooled with the sound of Nate's voice. It was the word 'brother,' the reminder of the affectionately silly hip greetings between the two pals, which brought Nick's eyes into Nate's compassionate gaze.

Finally, Nick uttered, "I'm sorry. I really am." Embarrassed and miserable, Nick turned away from Nate and looked for J.J. in shame.

"It's okay, Nick," she said. "I understand."

Wellborne, rubbing his head, got up and let an anxious security guard escort him away from the table, telling him, "It was all his fault, not me." The brash Stuart Wellborne collected his coat and his girlish little date and left the Rumba Room entirely.

Chapter 37: Extra-Pour Penny

It appeared to everyone, as J.J. sat next to Nick at their dinner table, stroking his head and back, that he seemed to be fine. He had acted a bit drunk but seemed composed and was friendly again. Only J.J. knew how good an actor he could be when he needed shelter.

He wasn't really composed on the inside. Nick felt defeated; couldn't look at her. After her petting, Nick grabbed his overcoat from her chair, putting it on as he whimpered, "Guess we'd better go, hon."

"Don't be silly, Nick. Really, I mean it. It's okay, please take that off and sit down with us," J.J. said in her most nurturing tone.

Nick glanced around. Bunker, Nate, and Betsy, even strangers at the adjacent table, were waiting for his response. He couldn't handle their stares. *What a disaster I made of this,* Nick thought, as he scanned the faces. He turned and walked away with his coat still on. With his ears always keen to Nate's voice, he heard his friend say something like, "He'll be back, J.J., don't worry yourself."

* * *

Nick washed his face and hands in the restroom. He saw himself in the basin mirror. He'd forgotten to take off the coat. He patted the coat pockets like it was a tender pet. He felt the hard object he was fishing for inside the top buttoned pocket.

Nick returned to the bar, not the table, mulling over the hard metal object in his pocket. Yes, it was still there. His secret flask.

(Earlier that day at Pop's Tavern, Nick unlocked Pop's display case of antique liqueur bottles. He then uncapped Pop's prized hundred-year-old absinthe. He figured that at Pop's age, he would never know. Nick carefully poured about six shot glasses of the 170-proof liquid into the "slim boy" flask. This was Nick's 'secret' flask he kept in his garage for whiskey at football games, which J.J. knew about anyway. And then, before driving to the Belvedere with J.J. that night, he deliberately left the party tickets in the house when they got into their car so he could return for the flask. If things went badly he may need an extra strength kick of the absinthe, he reasoned foolishly.)

At the back, dark side of the Rumba Room Nick pondered his absinthe. He knew the complete history of the wicked liqueur. History was his friend. How could he go wrong with a little nip? Since 1912, it had been illegal to import absinthe into the United States because of a reputation of hallucinogenic potential of the chemical ingredient thujone from wormwood. In nineteenth-century France, doctors thought the wormwood chemical used to make absinthe was like the active chemical THC in Cannabis sativa, or marijuana—it was psychoactive, could cause psychedelic effects, and at times insanity.

Nick knew these were myths. He knew that absinthe was said to be mainly dangerous only if consumed in massive quantity.

Still, his inner, rebellious streak, the desperation side to know who he was, commanded him side to pack some of the "green fairy" tonic in his coat pocket flask for the party. He felt justified.

Sitting in the shadows, he 'visited' some of his imaginary friends, who told him it was a good idea: Absinthe was once favored by crazed painter Vincent van Gogh, anti-establishment playwright Oscar Wilde, and French symbolist poet Paul-Marie Verlaine, all of whom Nick could easily see sipping absinthe in an Owl Bar–type bistro in a beaux art, neoclassical hotel in nineteenth-century France, like Baltimore's Belvedere. He smiled with some satisfaction.

He didn't consider how the 100-year old liqueur at the late stages of a drunken party in the 100-year-old building might affect Nick's weakened reasoning powers. He was already hammered. His thoughts were reduced to just simple notions, little private dilemmas that seemed eminently important.

Well now, he thought, *if I must, who might I share this delight with?*

He heard the chefs getting busy in the kitchen again. He looked in through the small windows to the kitchen out of childlike curiosity. *Maybe it's early breakfast.*

The party package included a breakfast at 1:30 a.m. that was still a half hour off.

Instead of dwelling on his sweet tooth then, he looked elsewhere for someone to share the absinthe.

At his dinner table, he saw J.J., Betsy and Nate still well engaged with Bunker. He surmised that Nate would be especially helpful to the lonely, retired educator. *Nate's like a mother hen at this damn thing, talking kindheartedly to everyone.* Nick felt a bit envious.

Nick then saw J.J. point at him. He imagined her saying to the others, 'He's over there at the bar. Don't worry about him,' in her soothing nursing tones. He watched Nate seem to nod in agreement. Nick thought, *I bet if Nate knew I brought absinthe in, he would not be so concerned over Walter Bunkhead, He'd give me that hard-love shit, flush the vile stuff down a toilet or toss it out a window.*

At any other time, his guests at the dinner table might have expected Nick was feeling isolated and perhaps nauseous in the crowded club. There could indeed be something seriously wrong with Nick, yet still, his guests over at the table with his ex-vice principal, of all people, took him for granted because they loved him.

Nick forced himself to drift closer to the discussion at his table. It was more of a move of instinct than reason. Soon, he could hear strangers at an adjacent next table telling Bunker about Nick's amazing "lecture" on Baltimore history during dinner. One fellow sounded like a university professor, who was raving about Nick's knowledge and ability to tell his stories.

Whoops, this is not for me. Been there, done that, thought Nick. He strolled off again toward the bar to avoid having to repeat the same history stories for Bunker and strangers. *My God, not that again. They didn't appreciate it the first time. I need a drink.* But who could he share his potent European liqueur with? Maybe Bunker. He wobbled closer to the table again, hiding behind some big men. *Yes, I'll get him up. No, bad idea.* At that moment, Bunker appeared to Nick as a man playing a pathetic, lonely, starving orphan child talking with Nate and the ladies, something Walter Bunker desperately needed.

He heard Nate's voice, "Walter, come to service Sunday. Our church is not far from your house. I can pick you up." Nick thought how grateful he was to be Nate's friend.

He thought stupidly again that Bunker would be a great candidate to share the absinthe. Bunker, ironically, had been well known as a rum pot himself when he was high school vice principal, which might explain why he did not get involved in the dismissal of Mr. Esposito, the alleged drunken history teacher.

Bunker had always secretly admired Nick's style, though didn't defend him to the supers, being afraid he would be blamed for problems Nick created for the system. Bunker told the gathered listeners with J.J. that Mr. Esposito was "actually very popular with the kids" and would take students to at least a dozen actual sites of historic events, instead of just making them read about them, several times for all day trips to the nation's capital. He told the group that Nick did no pre-paperwork for the school for permission, no notice to parents at first, none of the preliminaries required by the county school system until forced to. "If it was a good day, the American history class would simply just take off somewhere in their own cars, in a cue behind their eccentric leader," he said.

Thanks for that, Bunk brain. Now tell my friends I'm nuts ... and a drunk like you are, fool. Nick thought, fighting himself to stay out of it.

Although "Mr. Esposito's kids," Bunker confessed, "consistently pulled the best grades, the county office hated the history teacher," said Bunker, "as if Nick was some evil Marvel Comics villain. He was not seen as a real educator, but a performer in the classroom, which was completely the opposite of

Nick's nature. I know that; I'm sure you do to. The man simply blossomed before the kids," said his former boss.

J.J. began to resent the cowardly Bunker because she had taught Nick how to perform well in the classroom.

Nate and Betsy too were outraged by Bunker's knowledge of Nick's brilliance and indifference to the system's punishing their best teacher.

The underlying trouble with Bunker's astounding and wonderful story about Nick was that while getting emotionally distracted with contemptible thoughts of Bunker, J.J. and Nick's friends Betsy and Nate temporarily forgot about Nick.

He looked on. From where he stood, their apparent ambivalence deepened Nick's desperate state of isolation at the party he once so coveted. He gave up sharing the green liquid with Bunker and resumed his trek toward the dark side of the bar near the kitchen.

Chapter 38: The Spell

Betsy's pre-party dress repair sprung open on the dance floor showing her slip at the waist. She ducked into the ladies' room shielded by Nate, who then returned to talk with J.J. at the table and wait for Betsy. In a few minutes, Betsy returned to their table and asked Nate to call it a night. She was too embarrassed to stay any longer, she said.

He asked her to try to fix it. "I'd like to stay if we can. I promised Nick," he said.

"No! It cannot be done. Oh, I'm sorry. Please, Nate, before it gets ruined. I love this dress. J.J., we've got to go, honey. I'm sorry."

Nate reluctantly agreed. He said to J.J. then standing nearby, "I'm sorry. Can you explain to Nick? Can you drive him home? Tell him I'll see him in a day or two?

J.J. heard little of it. She was en route to the ladies' room herself. "Okay, be right back." But, Bunker told Nate he'd look after J.J. and Nick.

And, just like that, Nick's watchdog Nate was gone.

Meanwhile, Nick was left to confide in his new best friend, the flask in his pocket. He was considering introducing himself to the six band members; maybe they'd like to share. They were on a break. As he stared at the musicians resting and smoking on stools behind their instrument stands, Nick again thought Charlie Dupree looked very familiar. *Hmm, it's got to be more than Dupree's face looking at me on the party flyer every single day at Pop's. Or maybe that's just it,* he dismissed.

Nick drifted over to strike up a conversation.

Too late. Dupree struck up the band. They broke into medley of heavy funk tunes from George Clinton. About twenty people rushed to the dance floor, nearly trampling unsteady Nick. Talking to the band was out.

Nick then had a brain storm or very stupid idea (he didn't know which, probably thought both), *How about Thomas Edison, the guy dressed like Edison? Perfect.* In his drunken state, Nick rationalized that he already knew the Edison impersonator. The guy was playing Edison after all, one of Nick's favorite imaginary friends come to life.

Nick thought, *Maybe he's a wacky actor, this Edison look-alike. Actors like absinthe; even Pop's favorite, Frank Sinatra, tried it. Why yes . . . Sinatra won an Oscar.* Muttering then, he said, "Maybe my Edison friend would like to take a sip or two, with champagne—yeah, like Hemingway's Death in the Afternoon cocktail at Key West. Just somebody to share the buzz."

He needed a plan to slip into the ballroom downstairs again. Mumbling through some ideas while anchored on that dark side of the bar with his back to the light of the kitchen, he plotted.

"Who are you talking to, Nick?" Penny asked.

"Hey Penny, can you help me here?"

"Sure Nick, anything you like. Where's your darling wife? She is so cute in that strapless. You're lucky. Bet she's yummy in a bikini."

"What? Oh. Yeah, that's right. Hey, she's found my old boss over there. He once fired me, now he's acting like my best friend. Well . . . he didn't 'zacly fire me, but he didn't say stop it, neither. Or is it either, no, neither. Oh, she's them over there with, see them there, see?"

"Interesting," said Penny. "What's the deal with him and J.J.? Then that doctor guy? You guys havin' trouble?"

"Kinda. But she's just giving guy .. the guy a pep talkie. She's not real happy with me anymore, though . . . so, hey, you got a glass and a little very cold champagne just for me?"

In the shadow under the bar, he poured some of his green wormwood liqueur into the glass and quickly added champagne. The green absinthe clouded and Nick sipped and sipped. Then he chugged it. Penny studied him.

"Hemingway's drink, eh Nick? You like good books?" Penny asked. "He wrote some pretty sad stories."

"He wrote my story, yes, 'deed. I do think so," Nick slurred. He mixed the drink again and tasted the sweet absinthe, different this time. He flared his eyes open. It was powerful.

It was not Nick's first taste of absinthe, but this was clearly different than the few times before and more potent. This was a real strong European potion from two decades before World War I. He liked bonding with that time. Nick closed his eyes and there was Teddy Roosevelt delivering one of his famous whistle stop speeches from the back of a locomotive, for just a second or two.

He was proud of himself for achieving such a warm enjoyable feeling all over to cap off the crappiest year of his entire life.

"Yeah, that's right," he said in response to nothing. "Dare ta, ah mean care to join me, Penny, just for fun's sake?"

Penny thought better of it. Absinthe in 1999 was still illegal. Although Nick's little green drink was nearly in the dark, she said she wanted to keep her job going at least until January 2. She chuckled to herself and drifted off to serve others with an eye on J.J., still the brightest gemstone in a room of bright, cheerful folks lingering about tables and on bar stools; some in front of the band, drinks in hand.

Nick looked across the room following Penny's image. The party was thinning out, as some people were leaving, waiting at the elevator to rumble down to the lobby.

Thoroughly intoxicated, Nick decided to make one last try to find his 'friend' Thomas Edison. He had one, maybe two absinthe shots left. *Hey, why not share with my buddy Tom?* Nick could no longer differentiate between his knowledge of the real Thomas Edison that he knew and occasionally spoke with in history books and the man dressed like the inventor at the masquerade party.

He walked sideways at times along the north-facing wall, around the bar, and took the long way toward the elevator, out of sight of J.J., to make an escape to the twelfth-floor masquerade party again. He kept his head down and turned slightly away from where J.J. was sitting and still listening with several others to Bunker's confession.

J.J. had just glanced a minute ago to assure herself that Nick was there, near her ally Penny the bartender. She should have looked closer. He was staggering badly.

Nick was surprised to see the gorgeous blonde sentry by the elevator staring directly at him before he was within twenty feet of her, as if she had been watching him during his clandestine drinking in the shadows. He found her eyes enchanting. He glided toward her. Nothing else in the club seemed to be moving except the beautiful girl finger-waving him on to her.

Oh, crap. The Nazi guard is onto me again, he thought.

But closer in, the gorgeous young girl-woman was not displaying her previously stern expression. She was fully occupied with staring right at Nick as he approached the elevator entrance for one last try to find his 'friend' Edison.

He wanted to walk right past her to the elevator door. But the girl's gaze was roping him toward her. As he brushed by and glanced her way, she broke into a slight smile, still staring at him. Chalk it up to the eternal power of a pretty girl to hypnotize middle-aged men, but Nick was in danger of asking her to share a drink with him, maybe the remainder of the flask. Did the girl's trance cause him to forget about his wife J.J. momentarily? Maybe so.

There must be something about the girl… she's just a kid, though, he remembered. She had a strange power over him.

Emboldened, wanting to break free of her spell, Nick introduced himself and asked her for her name.

"Marie Krantz, Mr. Nick," she said.

He was stunned, not so much by her sudden warm disposition. That was weird enough. But she also claimed the same last name as old lady Krantz and spoke in the same sort of familiar manner to say, "Mr. Nick," as old Miss Krantz had imprinted onto his mind thirty-two days ago downstairs in the Owl Bar.

He was thinking, *She shouldn't know my name, should she? Maybe Nate told her. Wait a minute, where is Nate?* He didn't see his friend at the table with J.J.

He shivered. Nick wondered if the lovely Marie Krantz wanted him to share a drink. *What guy wouldn't ask her? No, they'd see this girl is under-aged, and here I am being dumb,* he thought. He felt suddenly familiar with the girl and liked her, liked being with her as a friend, a big brother or something, not as a lusty middle-aged guy. Despite her beauty, she was first and foremost still a minor. Nick didn't let himself forget.

"I don't want drink, even free drink," she said, perhaps recalling his joke. "Now, you want to go to masquerade party again, Mr. Nick? But why? I still cannot help you if you live such a confused life, even now you are uncertain." This new, fresher Miss Krantz, this Marie Krantz, had apparently read his mind. Her sky-blue eyes were full of compassion, and no longer harsh and intimidating like before.

Her spooky, unpredictable manner reminded him again of old Miss Ellen Krantz, offering odd bits of wisdom that pierced and stuck into Nick's brain like cactus thorns on unsuspecting creatures brushing too close. He sensed, in his confusion, this Miss Krantz too had a purpose in mind for him.

She said softly, closing in on him, and clearly, "Listen, there are no living legends for you to find here at this party, Mr. Nick. These people will die, not be remembered. Don't spoil za evening with them and die with them slowly as you are now, in present and as you have been. Steal life's light from za shadows of your past. Turn it around for the best in your future. You deserve it, Mr. Nick."

"My God . . . what the hell!" Nick muttered. He was captivated by her every word.

Quickly, she continued, "You've been muttering and brooding all year long. You've heard yourself talk and talk. Parties are not za answer. You will soon be all filled up with regrets and excuses and you won't enjoy parties, my dear Mr. Nick. You're not really enjoying this one."

She paused and looked deep into his bloodshot eyes. "Try to shine the light back into your heart, back onto your own legends and heroes, of your choices, or die a fool."

Nick was shaken, yet awestruck by her words. He was confused by their meaning, but somehow was reassured that she, the suddenly nice and caring late-teenage girl, meant well for him. Her words hit home, but he didn't know why. He sensed truth in them.

He looked for J.J., his rock. His dinner table and J.J. with friends were at that moment just a blur.

When Marie Krantz stopped speaking, she continued to peer right through his eyes. His mind was racing. *Why did this girl suddenly lose her Nazi attitude and became spiritual friend or maybe a siren?*

The girl had taken firm control of him, and then became matronly and oddly familiar with Nick's life. And, he didn't mind that at all. He was truly surprised to feel like a child himself. He needed comfort.

He confessed to her, "I'm so glad I'm here. Don't know why." He thought, *Did I really ask this sweet person to have a drink? No, I guess I didn't . . . to share my stupid adolescent absinthe? She is amazing. I like being with her. My friend. Who is she?*

"I told you, I'm Marie Krantz, Nicky." She formed a wide, affectionate smile and put both of her hands on his shoulders, looked deep into his eyes, and pulled him toward her.

Just when Nick thought she was going to kiss him, hug him, or maybe slap him silly, she swiveled him around firmly like a mother sending her child out the door to grade school.

"Go to the kitchen," she commanded. "There you will find za supply elevator to take you down there in secret, where you want to go. Where you need to. Go, please go." She gave him a firm, but loving push while pointing to a beaming shaft of light coming from the kitchen all the way across the Rumba Room.

He fixed his eyes on the light beam. Nothing else was in focus left or right.

Without daring to look back, afraid not to obey, Nick slowly walked, and suddenly steadily, toward the glowing, bluish light of the kitchen. Halfway there, he picked up the aroma of the after-party sweets, fruit tarts and individual German chocolate cupcakes that waiters were carrying out of the kitchen on oversized trays. The sweetness wafted off in waves into the happy crowd of eager, joyful guests. Even with his sweet tooth, Nick was not distracted from his goal to reach the double swinging doors to the blue kitchen light in front of him like a pinhead of daylight way off through a dark railroad tunnel. A sweet temptation averted. He was oblivious to the party, oblivious to the sweet aromas.

On the dark side of the bar near the kitchen, Nick swung open the right side of the kitchen's double swinging doors, into the bright fluorescent lights. His eyes didn't adjust well; he couldn't open them at all.

With eyes shut, Nick heard yet another disturbing and familiar voice. It was Miss Krantz, not the young and pretty one, but the old, shriveled lady, Miss Ellen Krantz herself.

"So, Mr. Nick, is everything as we planned so far? Is it good for you? No? Yes?" she asked in a manner of presenting him with a puzzle he'd be expecting.

He managed to barely squint open his eyes. He was astounded to see her in front of him.

She was wearing a white apron and a crumpled-up, yellowing-white cloth baker's hat. Old Miss Krantz was also wearing a big smile, just like the smile he just saw on young Ms. Krantz' smooth face. There was a strong resemblance in the two faces.

Nick thought, *God, creepy as always, here she is.*

"You surprised?"

"Well, I, that is . . . I . . . What doing here, Miss Krantz?" he slurred. "Oh yeah, let me be here guessin'. You always here are, right?"

There she was, glaring directly into his eyes, just like she did a month ago in the Owl Bar, with a knowing, confident glaring, yet with a proud upright posture this time.

Nick thought, *Of course! Who else could it be? This is just too weird. Nate will never believe . . . oh well, maybe I will go to church service, too, with Nate . . . with Bunker. I know I'm crazy now. And lost; I must be lost in this old tomb.*

Chapter 39: Promise Me, Mr. Nick

Nick acknowledged the madness and managed to chuckle at Miss Ellen Krantz's crumpled chef's hat. It blended well with her wrinkled face.

She said, "I know the way to the other party, Mr. Nick. Are you still muttering nonsense? I'll show you how to get in, only if you promise me something when you are there." She didn't wait for an answer but just gave him a smile. It was a lovely kind of smile he hadn't seen from her before—no, more like a devoted smile, a dutiful smile that said, 'You are mine now.' or perhaps 'I am yours now.'.

He felt possessed by her and was compelled to listen closely.

The old lady said, "Promise me this: Do not seek madness with drink down there. You know that is not really who you are, my boy. It's a crutch. Maybe from now on you'll see the path in front of you. Okay, Mr. Nick?"

"Sure, whatever you say is okay by me. What else can happen that already hasn't?" Nick said in resignation. His words saddened him. He felt new respect for her and hadn't meant to be flippant.

He had to ask, "That girl, the one back there who sent me here, who is she? Is she family?"

"You could say so."

"No, seriously, who is she? Why do you both seem to care about me?"

Miss Krantz responded with impatience, shaking her head at the floor, like she didn't want to answer, and waving her hand for him to follow her. "Come back here with me," she said. "Yes, yes, come back. You and I shall then see the way forward."

They walked through the messy kitchen, bright with blue light, and between and past the men and women working there, dressed in food-stained white clothing, some busy hustling off the party sweets while others were busy with pots and pans, cleaning up.

No one looked at them.

Nick and the old lady both moved forward in a sort of sliding sideways manner to get behind some stainless-steel shelving in the very back of the kitchen. They came to an open space by a dark blue curtain against the back wall.

Miss Krantz pulled the curtain aside without looking at it, while staring up at Nick instead, with a wry, knowing smile this time. It was the rusty door to a sort of small elevator. She said, "It has not bin used for some time, Mr. Nick, but I know this well and it will still get you into the good party."

"Ah . . . I don't know Mszz . . . but—"

"Go on. You want to speak to Mr. Edison or not? Yer za history man, ya?" She laughed forcefully, yet in a motherly, protective way. "The girl and I know each other well. You are right. Remember to help us as we will now help you, ya?"

He was afraid. *Oh my God. Too weird now. I'm not going in that th ...* he thought.

"Please, Mr. Nick, please remember me, oh restless heart, we need you too," she looked quite sad and nudged him forward. She stepped in first.

Nick was touched. He reflected on her promise of meeting up with Edison. He ducked his head and stepped aboard the little lift, tapping perhaps into his crazy adventurous side. He sensed there was something to learn. He was all in and started to say so when the door closed behind him. The little elevator was even older and dingier than the one he'd ridden with her that fateful day in November. It was tiny, in fact. Among the cobwebs across the top of the lift, there were no electronic buttons or switches, though. An iron gate screening pulled over with the clank of a prison cell door by itself and he figured they were in tight.

Nick again felt uncertain about being in the old contraption and, trying to think of anything to say. He wanted to ask Miss Krantz if she had seen that little man in the brown trench coat running into the kitchen carrying a gun like Pop's.

Before he could utter a word, Miss Krantz volunteered her own bit of a clue to help him with his puzzlement. "I am part of that girl. She part of me, you see." Her voice was more than sad, kind of despondent, Nick thought. Her voice had also faded.

She then pulled a lever and Nick felt the tiny elevator move down very fast. He seemed to catch his heart in his throat.

Chapter 40: First Night at the Belvedere

As the doors opened to another floor below, Nick wondered whether he had been asleep; he was groggy for a moment. And then, his head was clear. *I'll bet this is the missing thirteenth floor,* he thought.

He stood still in wonder, looking out from the little elevator. The room before him was another kitchen, yet lit dimmer than the one at the Rumba Room above. There was no harsh bluish lighting. This kitchen gave off a warm yellow glow. Three-quarters high, swinging doors at the other side of this kitchen were open at top and bottom by a foot or two, like on a saloon in the old West.

Over the doors, Nick could see the high ceiling of a ballroom. The many crystal chandeliers cast a moderate yellow/orange light, like the room was lit on dimmers.

All the waiters were African-Americans in formal outfits, walking deliberately with trays of sweet pastries. They pushed through the swinging doors and came back with empty wooden trays, he noticed. He had not seen them before.

His attention was drawn to the buzz of crowd in the ballroom. There was a hint of music, but not pop tunes. The melody was gentle. Straining to hear, Nick recognized it as Cesar Franck's "Piano Quintet in F minor" and dismissed it as just another of his fantasies. *Ah, spooky music, but I do love that piece,* he thought.

When he stepped off the little elevator, he discovered he was part of a very odd kitchen scene. For a working kitchen, again, there didn't seem to be enough light. The cooks, all male, wore tall white hats and were busy preparing the after-dinner tarts and small cakes. Others cleaned up the dinner pots, pans, and dishes that were piled in large, steamy tubs, all items were in white enamel.

Nick wondered, were the things he was seeing not real, not of the present? Such was his curse in life. He deliberately blinked several times. Nothing changed. The kitchen didn't have much mechanized equipment and no electric appliances or electronics—no dish washing machines, for instance, and, indeed—*My God,* he thought, *the entire room is lit by gas lanterns. Am I visiting back somewhere? No, Nick, of course it is a party, a décor for a period party, dummy.*

He reasoned that the wall lanterns and overhanging lamps from the ceiling each were controlled with sort of brass dimmer switches below them. Then he saw two bulky metallic electric lights hung from the low ceiling in the kitchen, flickering, though. *Yeah, the gas lights are fakes. Just as I suspected. I've never seen gas lights like them in photos or movies.*

Nick looked back into the little elevator to share his thoughts, "Miss Krantz, somebody went to a lot of trouble to make this party true to your old Belvedere. Miss Krantz, are you there? Miss Krantz?"

He was certain she had entered the little elevator with him upstairs, but now she was no longer there. Nick stood puzzled one step into the kitchen for only a minute.

Then he crossed the kitchen and eased cautiously into the ballroom, trying to be inconspicuous. He mumbled to himself, "Remember, I'm not supposed to be here. Or, am I? She seemed to think so. Oops, she asked me not to mumble. Why am I so obedient?" He shook his head from side to side.

The ballroom was packed with humanity, odd looking humanity. No one spoke to him and no one looked his way. Pleasant orchestral music. Polite conversations. Refined people, perhaps 200 or so, men and women, mostly men by far.

He felt strange and out of place. A bum in a millionaires' culture club came to mind.

And a couple of more steps into the ballroom he thought that maybe the setting wasn't the strangest thing affecting him. The strangest effect was how Nick felt physically—alert and sober. He was thinking very clearly. He had never sobered up in an instant like he was feeling then.

As the swinging doors closed behind him, he didn't step forward, but to the side and into shadows to take in the entire ballroom. Nick was astonished by fabulous costumes milling around widely spaced dinner tables and chairs widely spaced throughout the immense masquerade ballroom. The clothing worn by the guests was entirely, uniquely well-tailored, fabulously coordinated, as if they had all been to the same clothier, the same dress or wardrobe department.

Gone was the eclectic and bizarre assortment of outfits in the previous masquerade ball. Before him the costumes were all in a consistent theme, all sort of sedate and proper. It was a historical period party for sure, and he liked it.

A small orchestra of bearded men in tuxedos with long tails was arranged on a stage. A string quartet was left playing for the moment while the remaining orchestra members sat watching.

So, this maybe is where the Edison costumed guy disappeared to, Nick mused. He recalled that old Miss Krantz, maybe young Miss Krantz too, had put the idea in Nick's head that he'd find Edison. *I bet he is a student or professor who studied the great inventor,* Nick thought.

The entire ballroom atmosphere was intriguing to Nick. More than the fascinating costumes: the people themselves seemed to be playing clever roles in depicting the period, Nick noticed. People were all dressed in antique suits and long evening dresses, each stirring about with elegant and proud bearing. The guests were aristocratic in their mannerisms, not goofy and juvenile as the earlier masqueraders. Their costumes all seemed to be of natural cloth material—cottons, wool, linen, and maybe some silk. He decided that the entire room was full of people in costumes from the late 1800s. *I like this. Yes, I really do, he thought.* He made a mental note to get J.J. to this party as soon as he'd finish looking around.

He moved side to side to see all the people and then slowly toward an open center space free of tables and chairs arranged along the walls. He saw no costumes, as he had expected, depicting twentieth-century people—no rock stars, no modern soldiers, no aviators, no flappers, no short skirts, no cowboys in Levi's. There were no Frankenstein monsters, nor Dracula, nor Casper the Friendly Ghost. There were no costumes of movie or TV characters at all.

Yeah, this is a special history theme, he thought, wearing a satirical grin, which might have appeared to say, 'Even I could figure that out.'

He looked around, studying.

Spinning backward every few steps for a quick glance, he walked forward tentatively. On all sides, he saw the same sort of costumes, sort of 1890s urban fashion of the best kind, all buttoned down and formal. Women wore gowns nearly to the floor with a closely fitting bodice, narrow at the waist. The men wore suits or tuxedos, Nick couldn't tell which was which, they were so formal all. A few even wore a knee-length tail on their coats of a post–Civil War style, white shirts with stand-up collar and either a white or black bow tie around the neck.

As he continued to look around, awestruck by the party conversion that someone has undertaken, Nick accidentally bumped into one of the men. *Oops, at least he is really there; whew.*

He had backed into and disrupted a conversation between two middle-aged gentlemen in nineteenth-century costume suits typical of the apparent dress code. They were dressed as bankers or politicians, he guessed. Nick had bumped into the bigger of the two without budging him an inch or even getting much notice from the men.

"Excuse me, sir. I'm so sorry," Nick said. But the men, deeply engaged in a discussion, only gave him quick glances and courteous nods.

Nick reflected, *Well, this can't be one of my 'episodes,' as J.J. calls them. They see me here.*

The larger man, the one Nick bumped into, was doing all the listening. He was rotund and almost as tall as Nick. He wore a pinstriped suit with a vest and gold watch chain. His tie was tight to the chin with most of it showing around the neck.

The other man was short and thin, with beady eyes and a thin mustache, quite unpleasant-looking, Nick thought. His gray suit was loose and ill-fitted, as if he had dressed hurriedly.

The little man said to the big man, "I arrived here two days ago, Tom. We came into Penn Station, my new bride with me here, for a bit of an adventure. And she loves the air of luxury in the tall homes around that Washington Monument park."

Nick surmised that the little guy was playing a man who was not from Baltimore. If so, he would have said correctly, Mount Vernon Place with Baltimore's Washington Monument.

The little man seemed to be intermittently conscious of a very young woman cowering behind him, still with her evening coat and a cape on, though the room was comfortably warm. She was not listening to their conversation, keeping her head down, glancing at the feet of the small man occasionally. Her blonde hair was adorned with precious-stone jewelry and was mostly pinned up in a bun high on the back of her head, and with large curls on the side and forehead. In fact, Nick could not see her face. Her overcoat had a high collar turned up, as if she was ready to leave at a moment's notice.

As the smaller man talked to the rotund man, he gestured toward the young woman. It was obvious to Nick that he was referring to her as his wife, but he continued talking to the big man without bringing her into the conversation.

"She hoped I'd be willing to purchase a house here in Baltimore, of course, when the company transfers me down here closer to Washington," the thin man continued. "Your honor, I am, of course, in favor of moving closer to the nation's capital where I have built considerable influence in the government, even while I have been working out of New York, you see."

The heavy man nodded, but seemed bored.

The thin man went on, despite no encouragement from the big man, "Why would anyone want to move to the squalor, the dirty, unkempt slums of South Baltimore we saw last month arriving at Camden Station, when you can arrive at the clean streets at Penn Station? And she certainly agreed." The heavy man frowned and raised his finger to object, but the thin one kept talking. "But she's quite right, when she saw this north part of your city, Tom, which she had never seen . . . well, this northern side is another world better."

Nick was fascinated with the grave, almost desperate tone of the thin man and the patronizing look from the big, heavy one. It seemed to Nick that the thin man sensed that he was failing to make his pitch to the big man, but plowed on.

"Whenever I arrived here previously in Baltimore, I would be riding on the B&O coach from Washington to Camden Station. And all I saw were those dreary, ramshackle parts in South Baltimore with filthy piles of shabby little houses. But yesterday, your honor, what a pleasant surprise to see this side of Baltimore.

"This time arriving from New York, I took the wife along . . . you see her there. We rode in on the Penn Line this time, to your Pennsylvania Station. Lovely neighborhoods up here. Yes, what a difference. I could love this Baltimore, Tom."

Okay, that's enough, Nick thought, getting upset. *Squalor? Ramshackle Camden? What's the joke?* It was too much then to stay silent. Masquerade party or not, this was not good P.R. for his city. He jumped in, "Excuse me, sir. What do you mean by shabby ramshackle parts? Who or what are you supposed to be playing, if I might ask, please?"

The little man turned to Nick with a scowl and replied, "You know, of course, sir, if you are from this city, you would know that I refer to near and around that little pond you call a harbor here in Baltimore. In that part of town, it's mostly Negroes there. If you are not a native and from out of town then, sir, perhaps from New York? You are wearing most unusual attire. Interesting jacket? A new Paris style? A new import?" He was obviously nervous.

"No, it's not. I'm a Baltimorean. And you mean blacks, don't you? And, by the way, where are you from?"

"Yes, blacks, of course they are black. Negroes, colored, darkies, whatever. Never you mind, sir, where I'm from. It's not our kind of surroundings. I'm sorry Tom, but this man is—"

Nick countered, "But the entire city is mostly blacks, African-Americans, and not all of them live in poverty, if that's what you mean."

"The whole city of them? No? I didn't see any of them at all when we came in to Penn Station, or even when I, I mean we, taxied into the hotel here. African-Americans?"

Nick figured that the smaller man was trying to goof on the conditions in the streets of Baltimore in the nineteenth century. Even before the Civil War, Baltimore had one of the largest concentrations of free African-Americans among U.S. cities and in fact by 1900 they were almost one-fifth of the city's population.

What an ass, Nick thought. *This little guy is making a pretty clumsy attempt at humor.* He then glanced around the ballroom and noticed, *There are no blacks here, oh, except that waiter. Wow. These folks are playing this thing very well, indeed.*

Rigorous notes of a trumpet cut through the chatter and the room seemed to stop in a sort of freeze frame. People turned to listen. Nick recognized the rousing Telemann's "Trumpet Concerto in D." He loved that piece.

As the first section of the musical piece gave way to the gentler ritornello of strings, the thin man who came from New York smiled at Nick, then offered, "I'm sorry, sir, if I offended you. Have you met our new mayor, the honorable Thomas Hayes?"

The big man, the so-called mayor, spoke. "A pleasure to meet you, sir. Are you from out of town?"

He must not have been listening, thought Nick. "No, as I said, I'm a Baltimorean, raised near Patterson Park, now live in Glen Burnie."

The fellow playing the mayor said, "Well, sir, you'll have to forgive Mr. Jenkins. He's come down here from his firm in

New York to try to purchase a shipping company or merge with one. Isn't that right, Jenkins?"

The thin man nodded, ducked his head into his shoulders a bit, and looked around presumably to see if people were listening.

"He is not familiar with our Negroes," the man playing Hayes continued, turning his attention again to Mr. Jenkins. "You should remember, Bo, they vote here in Baltimore and there are a lot of them, though they want to vote Republican, unfortunately." He flashed an exuberant smile to the other man.

The "mayor" finally introduced the thin man to Nick as businessman Bogart Jenkins of New York's bustling shipyards. The mayor proceeded, "And you, Mr. . . . ?"

"Esposito, my name is Nick Esposito, Mr. Mayor."

"Italian? Good people. The new St. Peter's Catholic Church fulfilled a great need for our burgeoning Italian population and was a magnificent design by one of our great Baltimore architects E. Francis Baldwin in the heart of our Italian village east of the Jones Falls spillway for you folks. Been to Mass there?"

"No, actually. Well sir, my father was Italian; I'm just American, we don't have many ties to Italy, really. My family embraced America with full intention to work, play and be Americans."

"That explains living so far in the country, Mr. Esposito. Say, that little spot, Glen Burnie, is it? On the Annapolis Road? It's fine I'm sure for farmers, but perhaps you should move to the city, considering our recent annexation of county lands. With my influence with the state legislature in Annapolis, we are going to do some mighty big things in Baltimore Town, as we used to call it, or maybe even in Jonestown if we can clean up the Gay Street market." Hayes shared a hearty laugh with Jenkins.

Nick flipped his mind back: The Gay Street region was originally part of what was then called Jonestown, to the east of downtown Baltimore and across the trans-waterway, Jones Falls. Jonestown was often distinguished from Baltimore Town before the nineteenth century. He concluded, *This guy really knows his history. It's uncanny.*

Hayes continued, "As I said, you should forgive our friend Jenkins, Mr. Esposito. We love our Negroes in Baltimore. There are more than a half million people in this fair city and I guess more than fifteen percent are Negroes. The new Mutual United Brotherhood of Liberty works very hard for them, and Mr. Booker T. Washington has been out in rallies here trying to stir them up to start their own enterprises. But we do think the times call for separating their race in public, segregating schools for their own good safety around their fine churches, I think."

Nick bit his lip and kept silent. He just stared at the man playing the role of Mayor Thomas Hayes. *What audacity,* he thought. *Just let it go Nick, enjoy this show as long as you can stay down here, then go up to get J.J.,* he lectured himself.

He again flipped through the history pages in his memory: Jim Crow laws, in fact, had been introduced to Baltimore in 1900, under then-Mayor Hayes. Nick recalled that the same kinds of Jim Crow laws would negatively affect African-Americans for more than a half century in Baltimore, and indeed across the nation. In Baltimore, African-Americans by 1900 went on to build their own separate economic base along the Pennsylvania Avenue corridor and beyond, he remembered teaching his class.

He couldn't help thinking, *This character is aware of Mayor Hayes's fear of losing elections because of the black vote. In character, he is ridiculing himself. Well done, mister ... I guess.*

Nick thought he might have some fun with 'Mayor Hayes.' He would try bringing the gentlemen out of character, find out who he really was. *Maybe these people are local actors, Center Stage, maybe Catholic University drama graduates who might know J.J. It will be fun telling her.*

"Tell me, Mr. Mayor, what period are you representing? You do a clever impression."

"Period? Impression? I'm a politician, my good man. I'm always making impressions. I must impress, you know; clever, yes, of course, and I might say after the election, a mighty good politician, clever enough to throw out the Republicans. They didn't last long, did they, Jenkins?" the Hayes character asked the smaller fellow.

To further test him, Nick asked, "So this, sir, would be 1899?"

(The election of Thomas Hayes in 1899 was just two years after Republican Mayor Malster organized votes of tens of thousands of blacks voting for the first time and Republican, Lincoln's party.)

"Certainly, Mr. Esposito. It's December 31, 1899, and just an hour or so from the grand new year of 1900, the last year of the century. But you knew that. Do you feel alright, Mr. Esposito? You look like you need a drink." He signaled with an aristocratic wave of his hand to a black man playing a servant nearby. "Hey Jackson. Bring this man a drink. What will it be, sir? We have nothing but the finest whiskey, rum, gin. We have imported beer, brought in kindly by Mr. Jenkins' people yesterday working for a shipyard deal. What'll it be?"

"No sir, thanks. I don't drink," said Nick. The words coming out of his mouth shocked Nick. "What did I just say?"

"You said you don't drink. A fine gentleman, for sure," said the Hayes character.

Nick recovered and pressed his luck, "If you will, sir, a small favor, please? Because you are so kind, for an autograph, sir . . . I have this sort of invitation I'd like you t—" Nick reached into his pocket to retrieve the Belvedere party brochure that he had picked up five weeks ago in the Owl Bar. "Here, could you autograph this little . . ." The paper didn't feel right in his pocket. He pulled out a piece of white crumpled paper.

"Let me see that," said Jenkins, grabbing the paper from Nick's hand. "Yeah, that's what I thought; it's just a piece of plain paper. You must have misplaced your invitation," he said, mocking Nick. "Was he invited, Tom?"

Before Hayes answered, Jenkins seemed to regret asking. He quickly added, "Oh, what am I saying. Here, have this one,

Mr. Esposito, my invitation. My wife there has another." His young woman again quickly turned to ignore Jenkins and moved away from Nick before he could see her face. "You should get the new mayor to autograph it. Mayor Tom Hayes will soon be making history. He is certain to see Baltimore remade, especially Locust Point, right, Tom?" said Jenkins, "There is a booming shipping business and merchandising trade in Baltimore."

Nick wondered if the man playing Jenkins was acting out a premonition of the 1904 fire that would destroy most of downtown and set back all the progress in mercantile Baltimore.

"Mr. Jenkins is right. Here, I'll sign it if you want; here, let me have that please, sir," said Hayes. He took the party invitation from Jenkins and said, "But Mr. Esposito, perhaps you are worn down tired and misplaced your invitation. You say you work in Baltimore and ride all that way into the city just to gain employment, do you?"

Nick was finding Hayes to be more and more genuine with each moment. He put the autographed paper into his pocket. "Well . . . yes, sort of employment, if you can call it that. I run my grandfather's tavern, a family business I now handle since my father died. It's near Patterson Park. I keep watch on the old tavern while my grandfather tries to follow renovations that are supposed to be happening at his new tavern, the one downtown.

"He is very old, retired. Pop hired a construction company working on the new tavern to replace the old one because there is not enough business these days in East Baltimore. And the tavern my grandfather bought in '91 downtown, though, is going to be doing great." *Why am I telling these guys all this?* he thought.

Nick redirected his conversation to Jenkins in a terse, sarcastic voice. "The new tavern is in that squalor of the Camden Yards area, which you may know." He added a wink for emphasis, not his usual conversation style at all, but he'd started to feel comfortable crashing the remarkably authentic period party without the slightest hint of any explanation from the hosts. It was rude of them, he knew, but Nick believed he had a rare social advantage.

324

In fact, conversation became rather easy for Nick, as if he were his dad or his Pop.

The orchestra began again quietly with the sweet sounds from George Frederic Handel's "Water Music," which J.J. often played at home on the stereo.

Nice, he thought, then wondered, *Could I be channeling my inner Esposito perhaps, like Dad always wanted. I sure miss him. I'll be more like Dad in the new year, yes, that's it. This is really helping me, this party theme.*

The two men, Hayes and Jenkins, gave Nick patronizing smiles and shook their heads.

The man playing Mayor Hayes continued, "I think the new cable lines brought in before my predecessor, Mayor Malster, are a good piece of progress and I plan to extend them to the suburbs past North Avenue and past Walbrook to the Ridgewood amusement park. You have been there?"

"Sure. You mean Gwynn Oak, don't you—or maybe you don't?" Nick said, chuckling a little over his new found loquacious self. It was fun.

He tried again to shock the men into revealing their true identities. "I didn't know we're having new cable TV lines installed."

Hayes continued, maybe ignoring the TV reference, or not, "Yes, that's right, Gwynn Oak. And Roland Park is already serviced, of course. The overheads are a bit of a problem, particularly for my fire chiefs. But they don't seem to keep them from containing fires quickly. Our firemen have a great record since the '80s. I don't think we have to worry about them. Besides, my friend here is working a deal for New York and Philadelphia bankers to invest more into the city's electrification."

Nick was unconsciously nodding while thinking, *Well, of course, all this is true to historical records. This guy is good. The great fire hadn't yet happened in 1900. He's being sarcastic in costume over the fire dilemma. Well done again, guy.*

He smiled in appreciation and glanced across the room and, *There! It's that Thomas Edison guy just over Jenkins' left shoulder.* Just as quickly, he was gone. Nick moved his head to see if he could find Edison behind other figures in the distance, but couldn't.

"Well, ah, 'Mayor,' I guess you don't want the city burning down again, eh?" he said, still trying to shock the Hayes guy out of character. Nick laughed at his own joke but abruptly stopped when the "mayor" looked puzzled. *Guess he didn't study the city well, after all,* Nick thought.

Hayes said, "Jim McLane's BTC has worked quite well, starting with tracks on Gilmore Street and Druid Hill Avenue, but we can't support expansion, no matter how many nickels are being dropped into those cars."

"Oh God, this is great—BTC, Baltimore Transit Company, you're talking about street cars," muttered Nick. "Excuse me for interrupting, Mr. Mayor. I'm sure you have a lot to discuss about cable and new cars and stuff with this gentleman from New York, but I must ask you a question about this party. Have either one of you seen a fellow dressed in all black with a watch chain and mussed-up gray hair?"

"Sure, that sounds like most of my university friends; lots of them are here, too." Hayes and Jenkins laughed. "Just look around. They all look like that!"

Nick added, "How about a short man in a brown raincoat with a scar across his cheek and looking rather dangerous?"

"What?! No, can't say that I have," said Hayes flashing a new expression of fear. He was clearly worried by Nick's question. Hayes gathered himself and continued, "Speaking of dangerous, we are also going to do something real soon about all that clutter on Gay Street. I guess you maneuver through all that mess when you come into town, eh? This year, Mr. Esposito, the new Baltimore Municipal Art Society will begin to oversee further development of the city neighborhoods and parks, you know."

Nick remembered this exactly in his history studies: In Baltimore, by the turn of the twentieth century, open-air markets along Gay Street in the northeast of downtown central, were so congested that the morning and evening traffic was completely clogged and a harbinger of rush-hour congestion to come, except back then it was with mostly draft animals pulling wagons and horse-drawn buggies and carriages.

Yet Nick responded with, "What clutter?" again testing the man to stay in character.

"Well, you are a gentleman, indeed," said Hayes. "You fight your way through the market for sure coming to your tavern, yes? But I guess if you take a horse trolley early morning, the clutter of cabs and lorries are not so bad yet, eh? Anyway, the problem is just a remnant, a leftover, of the '93 Depression. We've certainly moved past those times and the financial shock of 1897, eh, Jenkins? We lost the city elections because of that. But now we're back. This city is the fastest-growing one in the nation, third-best city in America in shipping, Mr. Esposito. Did you know that, sir?"

Oh please. Did I know that? Nick thought. *Boy, this guy is whacked right out of his mind and right back into the nineteenth century, all right! Maybe he studied with me; doesn't look like anyone in my grad classes. But who else but me would know that stuff—'saved the city from financial ruin in '97'—but me?*

"Mr. Esposito? ... sir? Are you with us?" the Hayes man asked Nick, who was still lost in time, staring blankly.

"Me? Oh, yes sir. I'm fine. Just thinking." Nick reflected again on his history studies: Baltimore did become the most rapidly growing industrial city in the country. By the mid-1890s, Baltimore led the world in oyster sales and was among the world leaders in canned fruits and vegetables. Fresh produce poured into the city canneries and groceries from Southern Maryland and especially from the Deep South. It was a city full of high-production canneries. The more than a hundred canneries also fed Baltimore's thriving international shipping industry. Baltimore even led the country in making and distributing farm

327

fertilizer from guano, the bird droppings shipped in all the way from South America and the Pacific islands.

Nick stepped away from the gentlemen and pondered their look, stature, attitudes. Nick remembered studying about Mayor Hayes good fortune: In 1900, the newly elected Hayes was also the political benefactor of a city which was booming in the manufacture of chrome and copper as well as textiles, clothing, and even umbrellas, all industries supported by a steady flow of European immigrants.

Scanning the big room of people dressed as dignitaries, Nick was astonished by the imagery. He was imagining the party to be a collected assembly of the very entrepreneurs and manufacturers who built Baltimore's industrial base. He was especially taken by the man playing Mayor Thomas Hayes, a well-known local politician one hundred years ago, in post-1880 Baltimore—when the last of the men who fought in the Civil War and their contemporaries pretty much ceased causing discord in the war-torn city. Nick was astounded, *He is playing him to perfection. He is right on point, all of his points!*

Chapter 41: Time Trap

Nick drifted off into the crowd to think what Hayes said earlier, 'It's December 31, 1899, and just an hour or so from the grand new year of 1900, the last year of the century.' Nick realized, *He clearly said 'the last year of the century. 1900, and to him, it meant the last, not the first. Hmm.*

Nick had walked into the old-time masquerade ball believing the theme was celebrating New Year's Eve of the new twentieth century, the year 1900. But the Hayes character was not anticipating the turn of a new century at all, just the last year of the old one. *I don't think this fellow playing Hayes would have known the difference, unless he is actually in the year 1899, and is actually Hayes,* Nick thought, scratching above his right temple. Nick was well aware that scholars in prior centuries considered a new century beginning on the '01 year, such as New Year's Day 1901 or 1801, not on the round year, such as the year 2000 as it was being celebrated upstairs at the old Belvedere that night upstairs.

Still, New Year's Eve, 1899 would be an opportune time for the business community reception to celebrate the next big business addition soon: the exciting and luxurious Belvedere Hotel up on the north side.

Nick walked back to Hayes and Jenkins filled with considerable doubt as to where he really was. He built courage to ask Jenkins about his business in Baltimore. Nick listened with intense curiosity as the little creepy man from New York explained to Nick that the chamber of commerce had invited him to this New Year's Eve reception to talk to "important" businessmen before the official opening of the Belvedere, the finest hotel the city ever had offered.

"It is a prime opportunity for my company to make connections in Baltimore," Jenkins told Nick. Many of the city's prominent leaders were attending with their wives on this New Year's Eve, Jenkins said. "Great people here, great food and music, I think."

As Nick listened with some skepticism to the self-serving Mr. Jenkins character, his gaze drifted about the ballroom, again hoping to spot Edison. Instead, Nick saw a strangely familiar figure of a man walking with a determined gait approaching. He thought, *Ah, here comes somebody I definitely know, maybe someone who can explain this perfect reenactment of 1899. But who is he?* Nick chastised himself for not placing such a familiar figure. He was a very large, mustached gentleman about his own age, but with a balding head, round face and a serious air.

The big man was clearly not sharing in the fun of the party. He had other things on his mind, Nick thought.

Nick moved closer and noticed the big man's dark, woeful eyes that seem to bear the weight of the world. "Holy cow. It's Charles Bonaparte!" Nick said loud enough for Hayes to hear and dismiss Nick's ignorance. Hayes shot a look at Nick that said "Of course, it is Mr. Bonaparte."

He looks exactly like Charles Bonaparte, Nick realized from historic photographs. The man presented a perfect image of the great reformer Charles J. Bonaparte, down to the cleft chin and strong brow. He was taller than anyone in the ballroom except for Nick. He had a massive head with jet-black hair. He wore a dark gray suit of the era with tight lapels to the upper chest and a black tie between the collar points of his starched white shirt.

The Bonaparte character seemed to be prepared to speak directly to Mayor Hayes, but first stared at Hayes intently for a moment, as if to read the mayor's facial expression.

Meanwhile, Nick noticed that Jenkins had crept away.

"Mr. Mayor," the Bonaparte man said at last. "I just want to congratulate you on your victory and hope that if you do wish to continue Mayor Malster's reforming program in the city, I would very much be pleased to be at your service. I am not wedded to only Republican reforming in city government, sir, but desire to have a popular government, one built on good care of its citizens. And if I may say, as I did often to Mayor Malster, when a community gets afflicted with misgovernment, we can safely and fairly believe that it does not deserve a better fate than to fail."

Wow! Nick thought. *Those are the kind of words you'd hear from Charles Bonaparte a century ago.* Nick knew Bonaparte's life story well, had role-played him in his history classrooms many times--one of his heroes.

Hayes glad-handed the Bonaparte man with a hearty greeting and firm grip. "Nice to have you aboard, Charles. I know that you are not so much political as you are a patron of clean government."

Nick was overwhelmed by what he was witnessing, directly from his history lessons. He momentarily withdrew into his old pensive self. He felt quite humbled. At that moment, Nick's extensive knowledge of the history of the city he loved enveloped him, became him. He feared he had finally become permanently trapped in one of his whacky visits. The experience at the Belvedere 100 years earlier was far too detailed and too real. He was scared stiff.

This indeed topped all the weirdness he'd experienced so far at the Belvedere Hotel. Nick Esposito at this point realized he had been transported somehow, someway back in time. His mind screamed at him, *IT REALLY IS 1899. THESE PEOPLE ARE REAL!*

Would he ever see J.J. again? His friends? And Pop?

Was he the only one from the future there, privileged to crash a party that happened a hundred years ago? Nick asked himself the question as he considered if and how he'd been lured to the Belvedere seemingly against his will and contrary to his shy nature. He was faint. *Okay, Nick,* he leveled with himself, *my nutty brain plays tricks, okay? Has seeing the past finally gone too far? This is not a game now. It's no longer fun, I think.*

He was trapped in the past. His mind raced, *Maybe it was that creaky kitchen elevator. Maybe this is the doings of weird old Miss Krantz. She took me here deliberately, her and that girl also named Krantz. Why?*

He had arrived to witness an upper-crust Baltimore party in the city's heyday, which happened to be Nick's favorite period of Baltimore history. Characters, politics, events, even the music among his favorites from the period. How weird? yet how logical?

He reflected, *The Krantz's have been messing with my head for weeks now, I bet. Oh, God. The brochures, the handwritten note, the luring to the hotel in November, not realizing I parked at a fire hydrant. I was duped.*

He shook his head to dispel the madness. Nick stepped back several paces from Mayor Hayes and his guests and nearly fell to his knees.

Someone caught him and straightened him to his feet again.

Nick accepted his fate: He was insane. Yet, he still had his wits about him.

The old Nick kicked in with a bit of his own brand of biofeedback, which he'd perfected during his life. It calmed his nerves. As long as he was there, he'd keep listening, he rationalized. Maybe there was a way out if he truly accepted what has evidently happened. As always, Nick Esposito would count on his superior intelligence to get out of this vivid visit, he believed, just like he always gets back from his visits.

Mayor Hayes spoke something incomprehensible, bringing Nick's mind back into the room.

"I'm fine mayor, just a little faint, but fine now."

Reassured about Mr. Esposito, Mayor Thomas Hayes then asked Bonaparte, "Did you and Mrs. Bonaparte have a pleasant carriage ride down from your home at Mount Vista, Charles? I hope the hotel stables are satisfactory for that beautiful, white four-horse team of yours."

Nick remembered that Bonaparte did have such a team. He also knew that Bonaparte and his wife, Ellen Channing Day Bonaparte, attended social events near their townhome in the city.

Bonaparte nodded his approval of Hayes pleasantries. He smiled guardedly as Hayes turned on his charm, "Charles, maybe

332

it's time you abandon your daily carriage rides into town and join modern Baltimore. We'd like to see more of you." The city in the 1890s had replaced most of its horse cars with the electric streetcars, a boon to suburban development, though they had not yet reached north to the Bonaparte estate in the county.

Bonaparte spoke in measured rich tones that impressed Nick, who imagined how his voice would have conveyed when the reformer waged his personal campaign for honest government.

Almost comforted, certainly proud that he had seemed to become a captive of his favorite time in history and not Gettysburg, or worse, the slave trade or some other dark chapter of America's past, Nick became less frightened by his entrapment. *There has to be a way out of this eventually,* he figured.

Hayes was engrossed talking with the great reformer.

Not wanting to interrupt, Nick took a seat at a nearby table to watch the two men. He took comfort in reflecting on a lesson he used to teach his students in which he'd pack his clothes to bulk up and play Bonaparte, one of his students' favorite character portrayals. As Nick watched Hayes and Bonaparte talk, he recalled how he would connect the kids to the famous/infamous Bonaparte in his classroom: *Listen up, class! I am a grandson of Jérôme Bonaparte, Emperor Napoleon Bonaparte's youngest brother. You know about Napoleon.*

I, Charles, though, was a native Baltimorean, born in the city in 1851. Betsy Patterson of Baltimore had married Napoleon's younger brother Jérôme in 1803. When their marriage ended, Jérôme stayed in Europe when Betsy returned to Baltimore. And, you know about Patterson Park, named for Betsy's father who donated the land to the city.

And class, Betsy Patterson later took charge of her two grandsons' education, sending me—Charles remember—to private schools and providing tutors. She taught me not to push myself through life on royal blood, though, such royal blood was questionable. She wanted me to be instead a prominent part of the community and one of the people.

After graduating from Harvard Law School in 1874, I got back to Baltimore where I established a successful private law practice. I drove a coach pulled by four draft horses fifteen miles south every day from our Mount Vista Mansion in the northern county to practice in the city.

Nick was proud to know that at the time of that first Belvedere New Year's Eve party, Charles Bonaparte—that very man standing with the mayor—cofounded the Civil Service Reform League. Along with Catholic Cardinal James Gibbons, Baptist Minister Henry Wharton, Reverend Hiram Vrooman of the New Jerusalem Church, and others, the goal was to reform the election process in Baltimore. *No wonder he is dominating the mayor's time,* Nick thought. By that year of 1899, as Hayes returned the mayor's office to the Maryland Democratic machine, the league had significantly reduced the level of voting fraud and helped elect politicians not necessarily tied to the machine. *Whew! Democratic machine. How things have changed, NOT!* Nick chuckled.

Crime of the period was also on Nick's mind as he watched the reformer and the former Baltimore mayor while reflecting on his classroom lessons. Older members of the Esposito family—Pop, uncles and aunts—told stories about their elder, the police inspector Mike investigating over-blown Baltimore industry leaders who tied into organized crime in New York City. Pop always said the crime bosses were unhappy with the reforms going on in Baltimore, which they had targeted for expansion. The mobsters correctly measured the booming, yet largely unbridled, city of Baltimore as prime territory for organized crime, especially in shipping.

Nick was well steeped in such history and didn't want to miss a word between Hayes and Bonaparte. The Espositos had passed down from Officer Mike that the ground was fertile for infiltration by organized crime. Political corruption in state and federal governments was already rampant.

334

Nick soon felt revived. He stood up and walked closer to where Bonaparte was working the mayor over. He thought, *Who else would know this stuff!*

In Nick's former classroom, he taught that President Theodore Roosevelt, also a Harvard man and friend of Bonaparte, later made Bonaparte Attorney General of the United States.

Nick contemplated, *Oh yes, this man not only wanted to clean up his native Baltimore, but also wanted to reform on the U.S. political stage. I think I will have some fun and ask him ....* *No.* "That's enough," Nick said out loud. "Enough of the history lesson, Mr. Esposito. This time you will be fired from real history if you meddle. You will seize to exist in the future."

Still, he wondered if it would not be so dangerous just to listen to confirm or dismiss facts he'd read in history books, which he always considered slanted by various historians' perspectives. At least he would know the truth, he rationalized.

He watched the eyes of Bonaparte. The big man at that time knew all the politicians. And the heavy industry and government leaders knew all about him. They wished they saw less of him. Maybe, he pondered, they wanted the big man to disappear for good and let them alone with their bribery and schemes.

However, the talking revealed no new perspective or juicy nuggets to the 20th century high school history teacher from Glen Burnie, in the mayor's talk with Bonaparte to change the history records.

* * *

Nick stopped dreaming of his better days, his teaching days, and refocused on looking for a way out of the first night at the Belvedere and back to the future to J.J.'s night at the Belvedere.

The small orchestra struck up Ludwig van Beethoven's "Piano Sonata no. 8 in C Minor," the "Sonata Pathétique," one of Nick's favorites. He listened to the music for a minute and then looked over at Hayes, studied him again, and was completely convinced once again that he had been taken back in time.

This was indeed Mayor Thomas Hayes next to him.

He noticed that Hayes' expression had changed from the arrogance of power to a look of intimidation while facing the impassioned eyes of Charles Bonaparte. It fit, according to Nick. Hayes said, "Charles, we certainly got Mr. Hopkins's railroad back into the black this year, too. I expect the B&O to reach Lake Erie soon. We already use it to rail goods to Chicago and St. Louis. Things are looking up."

Bonaparte was unimpressed but managed a polite smile.

Nick conjured up enough courage to finally address Charles Bonaparte. "Sir, it is a great pleasure to meet you. My name is Nick."

Hayes seemed to welcome Nick's return and said, "Ah, sir. You are back. So, you know Mr. Bonaparte?"

"Not personally mayor. I've followed your career Mr. Bonaparte. If I may say so, reform is indeed needed nationally and in other cities, cases like Tammany Hall in New York City and that Mayor Curley gang in Boston."

"I don't have federal authority or powers, sir, but have worked through the National Civil Service Reform League, which I founded almost twenty years ago," he said. Bonaparte would in just a few years start the Federal Bureau of Investigation by hiring the first G-men in Washington under Teddy Roosevelt.

Nick could not resist pushing his luck. "Well . . . what about Roosevelt, sir?" Nick swallowed hard.

Bonaparte, puzzled, started to walk away. Then he said, turning politely so as not to slight the stranger, "Mr. Roosevelt is a fine man, for a politician."

Nick watched his reaction and was pleased. Bonaparte had indeed met Roosevelt in 1892 in Baltimore and that meeting started a long association between the two, most of which Nick knew. Nick thought that in 1899, Bonaparte would not have known.

Hayes rescued the confused stranger in the peculiar tuxedo. "Charles, this fellow addressing you is Mr. Nick Esposito, an upstanding citizen who runs a tavern near the Italian neighborhood, although I must say he doesn't seem to claim much of his rich heritage."

Bonaparte raised his eyebrows and tilted his giant head toward Nick, studying him with a sustained stare, and then excused himself. He walked off and was soon engaged in a heated conversation with a man who, even in the antique clothes, looked to Nick like a policeman. They were joined by two well-groomed, erect men at a distant corner of the ballroom, where they sat in an alcove of easy chairs.

Those two are cops too, for sure, Nick thought. He could almost read their lips, and certainly their gestures, which were contained and minimal.

(Pop once told Nicky that the New York police department had been cooperating with efforts in Baltimore led by Inspector Michael Esposito to deport key figures of organized crime back to their native Italy. The gangsters had worked their way into the city's burgeoning shipping and transportation industries. Members of the forerunner of New York's mafia, the Black Hand, had slipped into Baltimore shipping circles unnoticed by authorities, Pop had said. Nick remembered that his library research supported Pop's story.)

My God, yes, the cops were sniffing into activities of the American Century Shipping Company of New York in the autumn of 1899. Jenkins!

Nick knew that the ACSC was negotiating to transfer most of its business from New York City to the Locust Point docks in Baltimore to escape increasing expenses and regulations at the New York docks. *Wow, Jenkins is, was, this skinny guy right here tonight!! Where is he?* He saw Jenkins again. This time about 30 feet from Hayes and Bonaparte pretending to engage other men, but still with a woeful eye on Bonaparte.

Nick once read that shipping companies like ACSC paid Black Hand protection money at the New York docks. *Of course,* Nick figured. *That's why Charles Bonaparte is here.*

By watching Bonaparte's body language and eye movements closely, Nick concluded that Bonaparte had calculated his comments to Mayor Hayes to get a measure of Jenkins. In his excitement to unravel a mystery, Nick nearly forgot his desire to escape the old party and rejoin J.J. He reveled in knowing he was the only person in the ballroom who knew everything, what each player wanted, why each player was here. *Man, oh man, I hope I can work their body language into my class lesson one day. Oops, I'd probably get fired once again.*

The classroom lesson played out instantly in Nick's fertile mind. He'd teach, 'The price of freedom and wealth in Baltimore in that period was in part paid in the corruption. While reformers worked to clean up voting fraud by politicians, class, the long-arm of organized crime was also gaining a foothold in the transportation and mercantile industries'.

The ballroom Beethoven piece faded and Mozart's "Piano Concerto #40" began, Nick's favorite Mozart concerto because of the exciting and vital first movement. Nick was puzzled by seeing a much larger orchestra on the stage. *Well, it's a little overdramatic,* he thought, *but yes, it is almost like they are playing for me.* He then felt a little foolish for such a stupid idea.

Bonaparte drifted back to whisper something to Hayes while keeping an eye on Jenkins. Nick saw Jenkins slip farther away from Bonaparte's piercing gaze. Jenkins was talking with some attractive ladies, got them laughing and responding, while his young wife trailed along, still in her evening coat.

Taking notice of Jenkins' absence, Bonaparte excused himself from the mayor and walked back to the alcove. It was better lit than the ballroom. Two electric lamps on high tables were casting even light over the men, while the entire ballroom was evidently not yet electrified.

Meanwhile, with no one to talk with, and one eye to the alcove, Nick wandered to the ballroom stage, where he thought the Edison figure had been. If the Edison impersonator was there too, he might know how to escape. *Maybe that guy was the real Edison. After all this nonsense going on, J.J. is going to think I'm nuts. Scratch that—she already does.* He hung his head. *That is, if I ever see her again.*

Nick again searched through his mental history archives, hoping there was some project that brought Mr. Edison to Baltimore in 1899: *I know something bad happened to him in 1899. What was it? Did Mary Edison die that year? Was he fighting in court over George Westinghouse's patent infringements? AC or DC—yeah, that's it. He fought Westinghouse's alternating current. AC was too dangerous. Nah, wrong year. What was it, then?*

Nick slouched with a puzzled expression. He was unable to focus on historic facts he should know. Something was wrong with his brain. The imagery in the ballroom began to fade. Had he lost his third eye to the past?

He sat on a hard-back chair in the shadows for a minute to remember his history books: *Okay, let see. Mary Edison died fifteen years before 1899 but still that was not a good year for Edison,* he remembered correctly. He recalled that Edison that year had been determined to promote his iron ore separating invention to the level of success he enjoyed for electric lighting. After spending millions of dollars on a seven-year operation in New Jersey's Musconetcong Mountain, he closed it down in 1899 and returned to his new labs at West Orange. *Oh, that's it! He had to get away for a time, to Baltimore. No, that's not it. John D. Rockefeller had outflanked him with rail lines and ships to transport iron ore from his operation in Minnesota to the Great Lakes and beyond. Edison was busy recovering, not relaxing.*

Then he remembered, *Well, in 1899 Edison was still rich, distinguished in business and the public for lighting up parts of cities and towns across the country. He was looking for new projects. Maybe he did come through Baltimore,* Nick surmised.

As he stood, Nick spotted young William Jennings Bryan near him in the ballroom as well as Andrew Carnegie. *This is amazing! Maybe Edison, as well as Bryan and Carnegie, are here to honor Carnegie's friend, Enoch Pratt. The hardware industrialist turned philanthropist Pratt had died 'recently' in 1896. Correct again!* Nick was rolling again. Feeling it.

Nick approached Hayes again. "Mr. Mayor, could you tell me if there are other distinguished guests at this occasion?" Nick asked.

Hayes was taken back a bit to see Nick again. He seemed preoccupied. He gulped his drink and blurted, "I'd say so, Mr. Esposito. Of course. Where have you been, in the restroom or something? Look all around. The room is full of people I consider distinguished. For this night? To be here? At this time in history?"

Did he have to say that?

"I wouldn't have it any other way," the mayor continued. "As I said, Jenkins over there is here to make business connections in Baltimore, just as those others there, though he says he is on vacation with his girlfrie ... his wife there. Those four fellows over there are creditors. They're lusting over former Mayor Malster's old company. Before running for mayor, poor man, he was president of the now-failed Columbian Iron Works and Dry Dock Company, you know."

Nick did know. Malster was not all that illustrious for business strategies in the 1890s. But Nick didn't say anything.

Hayes continued, "But now we are greatly concerned. The Navy is upset over the company's dire financial condition while the Navy's torpedo boats and the submarine 'Plunger' are still on order and half constructed here in Baltimore."

Nick knew that, too, and sighed, *I could not have invented all this by myself, some of my favorite stories come to life?*

Mayor Hayes pointed, "And there, Mr. Esposito, those men in the light of the ballroom chandelier are talking to Henry Parr, the smaller man—you must get to know him. They are bankers from Philadelphia and New York. They met in my office and decided to keep Parr as the sole receiver of the Navy work and the company until it can be reorganized."

Nick didn't think he knew that, and felt better for not knowing something.

"Poor Mr. Malster—he's not even here tonight," Hayes went on. "He wasted his time as mayor, I suppose, and his former company went adrift in rough currents, you might say. Republicans should stick with business and not try to buck our Democratic connections."

Yeah, the Demo machine, say you, thought Nick, recalling the stronghold of the Democratic machine on city politics he'd learned from his studies.

Hayes still seemed troubled to Nick. He was turning about, surveying the big room. He then smiled back at Nick and continued, "But our military is just one of many contractors for Baltimore's thirteen steamship companies. Six of them go to foreign ports all over the world. We are just beginning to flex our muscle, Mr. Esposito. Why sir, we now have the Baltimore–Bremen Line with regular runs between Baltimore and Germany. And that gentleman over there by the fireplace is our own Baltimore native Samuel Shoemaker, who got the Adams Express Company going. Ask him and he'll say, 'We can deliver anything, anywhere, anytime.' Just the beginning, sir."

In his melancholy state of mind, Nick ticked off each of the points Hayes made and all were right out of the American history lessons he'd taught at Glen Burnie High School, although not part of the official curriculum. He reflected, *This is a video Nate should take. I'd shove it right in front of Principal Palumbo.* He replied to Hayes, "It has been a remarkable growth of a city, sir, since the War between the States. Baltimore just seemed to be in the right location for trade coming from both the North and South."

"Yes, we are very proud," said Hayes, looking about, with a distinct air of still being distracted.

Nick felt an urge to confide in Hayes about the upcoming twentieth century. Then he remembered that, except for the brief World War II period, Baltimore would never see such a rate of industrial growth again. He somehow felt sorry for Hayes and didn't want to burst his bravado.

Hayes, impressed, said, "Well, if you're interested in trade, sir, you might be interested that another business tycoon is in the room—that fellow over by the north windows. None other than Harry Skinner, owner of our most successful company yet on the Baltimore docks. His father, William Henry Skinner, headed a great shipbuilding tradition."

Nick added, "Baltimore from colonial days on was a leader in shipbuilding, led by the Skinner family. I know that, sir."

"Very good, Esposito. But it is NOW, now, not was. Harry also has his eye on Mayor Malster's old company," quipped the mayor. "But Mr. Jenkins' dry dock firm from New York could trump them all, I say. There's lots of money coming here from New York if chips fall as I expect, that is, if some undesirable elements don't move into town with Jenkins. The New York docks are filled with criminal activities, sir. But Mr. Bonaparte is keeping his people on top of it." Hayes's voice quivered.

Wow. Nick wondered why the mayor would tell him such a thing. He didn't believe the mayor would confide in a total stranger. "Why me?" he mumbled under his breath. He caught himself as Hayes looked quizzically at Nick looking at him crossways.

Nick felt a shiver, *I'd better respect his pre-1900 comments as truth. I can't change history. Too dangerous. But, why again am I here? I miss J.J. so much.*

Nick felt self-conscious as Hayes continued to stare at him. Nick covered his silence with, "Well, I sure hope the Jenkins deal goes down, sir."

"What? Why's that? It will NOT go down, sir! We must have that deal," Hayes said. He was very disturbed.

"It's just an expression, sir. I mean, I hope it is consummated very soon, goes down on paper."

Hayes laughed. "Oh, you certainly have a unique way of expressing yourself, Mr. Esposito. Well sir, anyway, you won't get any of these business men to admit they came to this party to make those kinds of connections. But I know they are here for precisely that reason. They see our celebration as an opportunity to make points with me. Part of my new little job, you see, ha ha ha!"

Hayes could afford to express some humility, Nick figured. He was a seasoned politician with experience as a Maryland legislator, and a U.S. Attorney for Baltimore in 1886.

Hayes continued, "But this evening is also planned for many distinguished guests to celebrate this wonderful new hotel that we are building," he said. "When it opens, it will be the finest in the East. There, over there, is Enoch Pratt's great friend Andrew Carnegie. He's talking with—"

Nick loved this. He interrupted, "Pratt was the hardware guy on Charles Street downtown, right sir? Carnegie was inspired by Pratt to start his own libraries, you know."

"Yes," said Hayes, not to be outdone by the stranger, "I did know that. But Pratt's wholesale hardware was hardly downtown. It was just south of here. Oh, and you should meet Joseph E. Seagram, the old Canadian distiller of 83 Canadian Whiskey himself."

"Where?"

"Right over there. He bought out his partners. It is said they make five thousand barrels every year. Mr. Seagram is probably looking for people just like you, people in the restaurant business, Mr. Esposito."

Chapter 42: Black Hand Killer?

Hayes stopped rambling.

Nick observed that the mayor was increasingly troubled and Nick didn't have a clue why his demeanor had become testy, no, perhaps just less sure of himself. Nick thought he was also becoming suspicious of Nick's presence.

Hayes frowned, looked at Nick's face, and leaned closer to his ear. "Oh say, that reminds me. Do you know . . . oh, I probably should not say this . . . but if you will keep this confidential . . ."

"Sure, my lips are sealed," quipped Nick.

"Oh, that's clever, Mr. Esposito. But what I was saying is . . . well, you must know Inspector Esposito? He is one of our finest law enforcement officers."

Nick, aghast, responded as his voice cracked in a high-pitched tone, "You . . . you mean Michael Esposito, the cop?"

"You do know him. Wonderful! But he's more than just a cop."

"Well, . . . ah, I just know of him," Nick said quickly.

Hayes said, "I don't think he is here yet, but he will be soon. There was some police business downtown he's involved with tonight, as I understand it. People get out of hand on New Year's Eve."

Oh, do tell, so, that's it, Nick thought in Hayes's pause.

The mayor then said, "But that kind of thing will not delay the inspector here because of new call boxes I had installed for the police. There's one on Chase Street just outside. I expect he'll be in here soon and leave a patrolman at the call box if there's trouble."

"What kind of trouble? *Oops, don't meddle, Nick.*

Ignoring Nick's question, Mayor Hayes continued, "But sir, now you must promise me. Don't go talking much about

344

Inspector Michael Esposito at this reception sir, please. Michael tries to maintain a certain level of anonymity. I am not at liberty to say why. But he is one hell of an investigator for the city. Lost his wife, you know, to the fever and now he's literally married to his police beat."

"Yeah, I know—er . . . I've heard . . . I mean, that's too bad, Mayor."

"Are you related to Mike, Mr. Esposito? You must be."

"Me? Oh, ah . . . no, no, not related."

"Say, I do wish the inspector would arrive. Love to introduce you. I'll bet you are indeed related and you don't even know it. Haven't you read about him in the papers? How many Espositos could there be in town, anyway? There is a resemblance in your face, even I can see."

Nick wanted to disappear, completely vanish. If there was ever a good time to get back to J.J., that would be it, he figured. *That is quite enough of this. I'd better scram, take the kitchen elevator. I want to see J.J.*

First, he wanted to at least duck the mayor before he would be confronted with his own, dead yet very alive great-grandfather in the prime of Michael Esposito's life. *How weird is this? What could I say to my great granddad? Hi, I'm Nick, the weird Esposito, your worst nightmare from the future?*

Nick was excited and frightened at the same time. He lectured himself, *Do not speak to great-grandfather Mike if you see him at the reception. This is just too freaky. I don't have any idea how I got here. I don't believe in ghosts, for God's sake. I do see dead people doing famous things sometimes, but here I am with these folks. Whew!* Nick let out a giant exhale and felt his heart racing like never before.

He also thought it odd that he didn't want a drink after getting so super stressed out. He pondered that thought, liked it, and his heart slowed.

Nick looked about the room, from face to face, trying to find an excuse to walk away from Mayor Hayes. He saw William Jennings Bryan again; this time Nick recognized him talking with

Maine banker Arthur Sewall, who ran as the vice-presidential candidate in 1896 on the ticket with Bryan. Nick thought of asking Bryan about his chances in 1900, knowing full well that the great orator lost to William McKinley. He was afraid of saying something dumb, however, like McKinley didn't survive an assassin's bullet.

Nick then spotted Henry Walters, no doubt just back from Paris, Nick surmised, with new paintings for his nearby Walters Art Gallery. Nick saw Walters talking with the first president of Johns Hopkins University, Daniel Coit Gilman, one of Nick's favorite imaginary friends. He got closer.

Nick heard Gilman say he was so happy with the medical school now going into its seventh year. Gilman was gushing on over how he was completing the wishes of Johns Hopkins for a medical school, a companion institute to Johns Hopkins University twenty years after Hopkins's death. Nick was pleased to hear Gilman brag that women were being admitted on the same terms as men. *I'll tell J.J.*

Nick was fascinated, but he just had to get away from the mayor, who was still nearby.

Nick glanced out the south windows of the ballroom and saw a pretty flicker of hundreds of orange lights, the city as it used to look lit with gas and early installations of electric lighting. But the rural view from north windows was black as coal.

He then saw that Hayes had lost interest in him.

He saw an aide to the mayor stepped forward and give his honor a note. The mayor grimaced and looked around after reading the note perhaps to see if people were watching him.

Because Nick was no longer on Hayes' radar, he returned to listen. Hayes composed himself and recovered his good humor as he saw Nick staring at the note in his hand.

"It's from your non-relative, Inspector Mike," Hayes said reluctantly to Nick, with an uncomfortable chuckle.

"Oh, I wasn't going to pry."

Hayes said, "If you will pardon me saying, it was a real pleasure to meet someone who is clearly an individual among individuals. I have never met someone with your perspective, Mr. Esposito. May I drop in at your tavern sometime for a beer?"

A chill ran down Nick's body. "Sure." *But it's not even there yet for another three decades or so,* he thought, unable to find a better answer.

He thought Hayes was shaken by the contents of the note. After another glance at it, Hayes face turned pale and his eyes were withdrawn and pensive. He turned to huddle with his aides. He failed to stuff the slip of paper into his tight, tiny vest pocket and the note dropped to the floor, at Nick's feet.

Nick quickly bent down to grab it, a second before the mayor's aide reached for it. Nick made out the writing to say: *Two suspects, likely Black Hand, entering building. Officers secured ballroom. Pls. Alert Mayor, Bonaparte that . . .*

The mayor's aide ripped the note from Nick's hand, but not before Nick saw that it was on official police notepaper, with a familiar signature. He had seen that signature many times on Pop's old legal papers: *M. Esposito, B.C.P.D.*

Black Hand is here. Oh my God! Nick was desperate to avoid further eye contact with the mayor or his aide. He turned away to remember details from his studies. He recalled that members of the criminal group formed one of the most notorious mafia arms in New York. His great-grandfather was responsible for deporting several leading Black Hand hit men to Italy. The Black Hand, or La Mano Negra, was an extortion organization set up in Italian-American communities in several major port cities by immigrants from southern Italy. The group often sent letters to a community leader, printed in black ink, threatening violence, even murder or kidnapping, if they were not paid protection money.

Nick was clear on one thing for sure, *Bonaparte is their target. Has to be.*

Nick had to get away from the mayor. He could, at any minute now, see or even bump into his great-grandfather Mike, the great Esposito elder so revered by Pop and the family. Nick reasoned with himself, *At this time, Pop isn't yet born. Interfere in what's going down here and there might not be any Pop, no me.*

Nick felt a rise of tension in the room, which was more than just from his own fear. The mood across the big room was somber. Chatter was quieted. People stood more upright and alert.

As he assessed the change in the room, Nick noticed another intriguing man from his history studies, but could not yet place him. The man wore a close-fitted double-breasted dark-brown suit buttoned in the style of the day to within eight to ten inches of his chin and a black bow tie. He was clearly an academic. Nick thought it was strange for an educated man to be standing alone, not talking with anyone. *Professors never stop talking. And why is this man worried sick?* Nick wondered.

He walked over to face the man directly, "Hello, are you here by any chance as a guest of Dr. Gilman of the Johns Hopkins University?"

"Why, yes. I am Dr. Frederick Jackson Turner from the University of Wisconsin, indeed here at the invitation of Dr. Gilman."

"I know, I know, I know!" blurted Nick, excited to meet another of his favorite historical figures. He felt himself rise onto his toes feeling intellectual Turner's energy. Nick couldn't believe he was talking with perhaps the first scholar—and one trained at Hopkins—to capture the true soul of twentieth-century America.

"Dr. Turner, I know your theory that the pervasiveness of our frontier ideology molded us as a distinct American culture. It was right on, sir. Certainly, right on. The idea has taken root and proven to be exactly what you predicted, the character of our people that shaped our institutions, and—" Nick caught himself. He was out of control, referencing the future. A no no.

Turner, puzzled, said, "But how could it be known to you? I just wrote that paper a few years ago. Aren't you getting ahead of yourself, Mr. . . . ."

"Esposito, Nick Esposito. I teach your theory in my classrooms, at least I used to . . . er. . . I should say I wish I could teach it in my classroom. Could I? I mean, if I had a classroom."

Nick needed to slow down. His heart was racing. "Oh, I'm sorry for being so forward. Yes, I read your paper three times, 'The Significance of the Frontier in American History.' It was from the journal of the American Historical Association, the one you presented at the Chicago World's Fair."

Turner corrected, "You mean the World's Columbian Exhibition in Chicago six years ago, don't you? That speech was not received well at all. Colleagues laughed at me—those who stay enamored by our ties to English and European cultures. Even my parents did not like it. They didn't even attend the speech, thought I shouldn't have presented it."

"I know, I know . . . er . . . I mean, I know it was not well accepted. I wasn't there, but I read it with great recognition of its truth. Dr. Turner, you have no idea how much twentieth-century America will prove you right. Or, well, I can just feel it will happen. The pioneer spirit, the traits of those who pushed the frontier from east to west in the nineteenth century, created the self-awareness of our individualism, nationalism, mobility, egalitarianism—not the previous European values. I loved to follow your theory through history. It was right on."

As he had hoped, Nick got Turner's undivided attention. Turner looked at Nick as if he had encountered an insane man, maybe a dangerous man. He stopped scanning the room, and asked, "What on earth do you mean by that? And what do you mean by 'right on'? You said it again."

Nick quickly responded, "The painful transition, Dr. Turner. The painful transition of America's consciousness from endless boundaries to accepting our own unique character, that is. . ."

"No, not that. How you talk! What part of the country are you from, sir?" Turner was bewildered by Nick's twentieth-century phrasings. "But six years is hardly history, Mr. . . .what did you say your name is?"

349

"Esposito."

"Thank you, Mr. Esposito, for your enthusiastic endorsement of my theory. But, really, it does seem that no one else agrees with you."

"They will. Just wait and see." Nick tried not to laugh at the absurdity of what he was doing, talking with the great sociologist, even before sociology was recognized as a field of study.

Turner said with finality, "I do think the United States is evolving into a completely unique society. So, let's let that be our agreement, then." He looked around, perhaps to distance himself from the crazy man in the funny tuxedo.

However, Nick's name Esposito had caught Turner's ear and he asked Nick, "Are you here as a guest of Inspector Esposito? I thought you might be, as you asked me if I were a guest of Dr. Gilman. The inspector, too, is curious about the people around him, like you are, sir. He briefed us this afternoon about the need for security."

"No, I'm not related to the inspector at all," said Nick, uncomfortable that the topic of his famous great grandfather had come up again.

So that was it; Nick knew then that security was a concern that night at the new hotel building.

Turner continued, "You obviously share that curiosity trait, though, Mr. Esposito."

"Oh." Nick said flatly.

Turner cupped his right hand over his mouth and moved closer to Nick. "Dr. Gilman told me that Inspector Esposito has received information that a dangerous man might have infiltrated our celebration."

So, it's true. Something is happening here, Nick deduced.

Turner continued, "Dr. Gilman told me further that Mr. Bonaparte asked us to separate. He wants Dr. Gilman and I, as well as Mr. Wilson and Dr. Osler and Dr. Pierce over there, to spread through the room, and help the authorities know if anyone unusual should not belong."

"How odd."

"Yes. Can you imagine being desperate enough to count on intellectuals as spies? I'm not sure why Mr. Bonaparte asked us to help. Maybe, as we are academics, he thinks we can observe from a broader realm. Or maybe we are the only ones here he can trust—lots of slippery characters about, you know." Turner gave a peculiar little shrug and a grin, revealing some discomfort.

Nick suggested, "You do have a broader realm than some other folks I've met here so far. Oh, my goodness, Dr. Turner, look. There is President Wilson. Nick had spotted the future U.S. President Woodrow Wilson, a Hopkins alum, also standing alone and watching the crowd.

"President Wilson? How did you know? Woodrow is being considered the next president of Princeton, yes. Are you a Princeton man, then, Mr. Esposito?'

Nick shrugged. "No."

"Well, you are remarkably astute. Woodrow is a progressive and is here with Mr. Bonaparte—reformers both, you know."

Oops—got to be more careful, Nick thought. *Strange to meet these historic giants right off my bookshelves and out of my head! This can't be real, but I've physically touched people here. They ARE real. They are here,* he reminded himself.

He replied. "Ah, is that right. I didn't know that." He then saw the famous physician William Osler, whom Turner had mentioned. Osler was behaving in the same odd way as the other professors—standing, watching, worrying. It was apparent that the party, which had been a picture of thoughtful, yet affable celebration, was not all that jolly anymore.

Nick was doubtful that he'd get out of there any time soon.

The little man who crashed into him upstairs at J.J.'s party running into the kitchen came to mind, then also spooky old Miss Krantz and the visions he'd had in the Owl Bar and changeable lobby décor, the trouble upstairs with Bunker and then Wellborne, the mysterious Belvedere brochures popping up at

Pop's, his senseless opening and stealing Pop's prized amaranth with no shame, Pop's warning about the old hotel. All those and more distressing forewarnings or, at best, queer goings on in his life since the darkening days toward winter added up in Nick's thinking to nothing good coming from his visit to 1899. *Why now? Why here? A premonition?*

He could think of nothing else to do or resolve his entrapment than to join in on the "spying" with Dr. Turner, whom he would like to think he could trust, maybe. They each kept looking around intently. But, Nick was now looking specifically for that little man in the long coat. He glanced quickly from face to face and studied the body movements around the room, while Turner did the same for anyone moving or acting suspiciously.

Should be easy to spot in a brown trench coat, Nick thought. *I need to share that. Damn it anyway, I can't. But, this might be the man they fear. I alone saw him upstairs. Was he there or a spirit back in time, an illusion up there only I could see? God, help me; I am so nuts.*

"Dr. Turner? Did Dr. Gilman say what this man might look like? Why is he considered dangerous?"

"I'm not sure, Gilly said it has something to do with the activities of Charles Bonaparte, who received a scribbled letter threatening his life a couple of days ago."

Nick asked, "Was that before Mr. Jenkins arrived in town. Jenkins is a shipping executive from New York, you likely know. He is over there, near that electric light hanging so precariously in the alcove."

Turner replied, "Oh, those intriguing things, electric yes. Mr. Esposito, I probably shouldn't have told you, but you look like an honest man. I do know that Bonaparte showed his letter to the inspector, the city people said. They said the man they are looking for is short, balding, and disturbed."

"Kinda creepy paranoid like?"

"What? Well anyway, that is the description we are looking for. Why do you ask such a question? Are you alright?"

Nick just nodded, opening his hands out from his chest and tilting his head as Pop would, to give a reluctant 'yes.'

Turner continued, "I did hear he is from New York. I don't know if this is all connected, but I wouldn't want anything to happen to dear Mr. Bonaparte. He is the one fellow who may be molding the character of this country all by himself, by exposing government corruption. None of that corruption is in this room, of course." Turner laughed sarcastically under his breath, touching his lips with his palm briefly. "My gosh, this certainly is not what I was expecting tonight. But I am pleased to help any way I can."

Nick wondered if Turner's second-hand description was the little man with the gun he alone saw upstairs. He considered a possible coincidence, *I came here by a small elevator in the kitchen. After the creepy little guy bumped into me, he disappeared into that same kitchen. Did he find his way down to the reception in the same elevator?* He felt a throbbing pain in his head as he wondered, *Was he there ... or here in time?*

Nick tried to reassure Turner, "Bonaparte, over there in that alcove, is with some policemen, I think. He's maybe safe then, away from the crowded ballroom. Maybe they are trying to stay clear of any danger. Oh my. Look, sir." As Nick pointed toward Bonaparte's group in the corner alcove, he spotted the man impersonating Thomas Edison, also standing in the alcove. The Edison character was reaching his hands out to touch one of two iron lamp fixtures jutting out from the high tables against the walls of the alcove.

"Could that be Edison, actually Thomas Edison himself?" he asked Turner.

Turner responded, "Yes, Edison is indeed here just by chance. The hotel construction underway included some experimentation with a few applications of innovative electricity. Edison's company is in charge. The mayor's business administrator, in fact, contacted him and invited him to the business reception tonight. Yes, that's him. Want to meet him? He knows me."

Nick's heart nearly stopped. He forgot worrying about any dangerous little man with a gun or his grandfather Mike or even getting back to the future.

As he walked with Turner toward the crowded alcove, Nick thought that Edison wouldn't be at the Belvedere reception to deal with bankers and businessmen. However, maybe he was helping engineer the electrification of the Belvedere, as Turner had guessed. The hotel when new would have been considerably north of the electric grid downtown. *Yes, he could have been—is—in Baltimore tonight!*

Turner touched Nick on the arm and said, "We can continue looking for our dangerous character later, if there really is one. Mr. Edison is not talking with the others there, see? Just studying those new light fixture things, I think."

Nick said with some trepidation, "Of course. That would be fine." But, he was still worried; being in a corner near Bonaparte might not be the best thing at that moment in time.

He quickly changed his mind, *Well Daaah! What moment in time would that be exactly, Nick?* He put worries aside, eyes fixed on Thomas Edison, THE Thomas Edison of Menlo Park!

When Nick and Turner got within listening distance, it was evident that Bonaparte and the plainclothes police officers in the corner were grilling Jenkins there. They evidently had summoned him over. Scrawny Jenkins was looking hassled, standing against the back wall of the alcove with his bundled-up young woman in tow, slightly behind him but looking down, still hiding her face.

Remarkably, Bonaparte's group was ignoring the great Edison nearby. He was incidental to these men, who had more pressing things to do than entertain conversation with an inventor. *Maybe he isn't that much of a star yet,* Nick thought, as he and Turner got within a few feet of the alcove. *Oh stupid, what am I thinking. Of course, he is.*

But Edison was certainly the main attraction to Nick. He'd already had a conversation with the noble Charles

Bonaparte. Who would be next? On the top of his list of historic heroes, there was Edison right in front of him.

Turner whispered to Nick, "I met Thomas several times in Chicago. Come on, Mr. Esposito, you go in first. I'll follow." He followed Nick right up to and behind Edison's back and said, "Hello Thomas, nice to see you again."

Edison turned to see who was there. He seemed annoyed at being distracted from his analysis of the hanging lamps. But, then, with Nick smiling broadly, proudly, the great inventor spoke, "Yes . . . oh yes, it's you, Dr. Turner. How are you? I saw you over there earlier. Meant to greet you. I really didn't expect to see you here tonight, though I did anticipate Dr. Gilman's presence. Who is your stylish friend here?"

Nick felt faint. He feared collapsing again, but regained strength and managed to begin speaking then was distracted, "Hello Mr. Ediso—"

But, as Nick reached out to shake the great inventor's outstretched hand, he missed grabbing it because he averted his gaze to catch sight of a fast-moving figure over and beyond the group, coming from the open ballroom floor.

It was the face of none other than Inspector Michael Esposito approaching quickly. It was that face, the very image Nick had seen a million times on a faded, fuzzy portrait that greeted every patron entering Pop's Tavern on Ellwood Avenue in East Baltimore.

It took just a second for Inspector Mike to reach the group of men in the alcove as everyone scattered. He was in a great hurry to reach Charles Bonaparte, pushing people right and left. He looked desperate.

Nick's fear of meeting his great-grandfather ended abruptly though, as the inspector screamed at the top of his lungs at Mr. Bonaparte, "Look out behind you, sir!"

Nick's eyes were glued to his elder's face, while everyone else—Turner, Jenkins, Edison, the undercover cops, and Jenkins' cowering wife—all turned toward Bonaparte.

Only then could Nick see the object of Inspector Mike's terrified eyes and movements: It was the little man in the brown trench coat again, standing in front of Bonaparte with that same pearl handle pistol, drawn and pointing directly at Bonaparte's face.

"Ya damn no-good Napoleon bona-bastard!" he shouted. "Go back to where ye come! Hell's the place for you!"

"Oh God—it's him!" Nick cried out. He rushed the little man, "Oh no, you don't!" Nick screamed. Nick instinctively moved in to protect his hero Bonaparte. Nick tackled the little man around the waist belt of his loose brown coat, knocking him down from behind. The two fell together. Their fall mirrored the exact body movements of the fall they'd had together upstairs near the rectangular bar.

This time, though, the firearm discharged with two very loud explosions in rapid order, with a burst of flame each time from the barrel of the gun.

* * *

Because of Nick's quick reactions, the shots were diverted.

They missed Charles Bonaparte.

The first bullet hit Jenkins directly in the temple and killed him instantly. The second shot went past Bonaparte and Jenkins, but hit Jenkins' young 'wife' in the chest. She doubled over, and then fell backward into a stuffed armchair. She said to no one in particular, "Why diz man shoots at me? Oh! Oh, why dat . . ."

She was critically wounded.

Two plainclothes cops smothered the shooter and possibly Nick.

Despite Nick's heroics in evidently saving the life of one of his greatest heroes of Baltimore history, he didn't see what happened next.

The little man squirmed free of the cops for a moment and started running toward the kitchen. Nick was semi-conscious. Before he passed out, he barely made out the limp body of young Mrs. Jenkins being carried out by Dr. Gilman and Bonaparte,

356

along with Bonaparte's wife, en route to the new Johns Hopkins Hospital.

The incident also meant that Nick missed chatting with Thomas Edison, because Nick, while tackling the assailant, had smashed his head violently against one of the cast iron electric lamps Edison had been studying.

Nick was out cold.

Chapter 43: Where's My Nick?

Rumba Room, Belvedere Hotel 14th floor

Before Nick disappeared into the kitchen shortly after midnight, J.J. was enjoying a welcomed relief from her daily life. She had not gotten out much lately while raising the twins and working part time. For a little while, she was the center of conversation at her table at the south side windows.

Walter Bunker was still with her as she comforted him over the loss of his wife. When that ran its course, J.J. felt a little guilty about it. She missed Nick. He hadn't sat with them after he deposited his old vice principal. She asked Bunker, "Hey, where's Nick? He was with you, Walter. Did he say what he was doing; he didn't stay with us."

"He's over there, J.J., by the kitchen. I saw him go toward the kitchen a few minutes ago for some of the after-dessert sweets, I guess. I expected him to sit with us also," Bunker said.

"Nick's probably still way on the dark side of the bar talking with Penny. She is my designated Nick keeper," J.J. quipped.

That was the last time they would think to look for Nick for a while. They accepted that Penny was watching over him.

Perhaps J.J. felt strange being left with Nick's former vice principal. She asked, "Walter, we all know Nick is a fabulous student of history. Is there a chance he could get his old job back at Glen Burnie High School?"

"I suppose you didn't know. I'm retired. I certainly would take Nick back. But that would be up to someone else now."

Several other people nearby had begun listening in on their conversation. One especially good listener was a heavyset man with a neatly trimmed beard and mustache, gold-rimmed spectacles, and wearing a stylish maroon sweater over a blue shirt and festive tie. As he had during dinner, this man showed interest in J.J. He asked her, "Was that man who was with you your husband, you say?"

"Nick Esposito. I'm his wife."

"Well Mrs. Esposito. It is a great pleasure to meet you. I'm Matthew Hastings," said the man. "I couldn't help hearing your husband Nick—dashing through the history of Baltimore legends, all during this terrific dinner. Is he a historian or a—"

J.J. stopped him. "I'm really sorry about Nick, Mr. Hastings. Was he ruining your meal?"

"No, not at all. Well, maybe at first, we thought it a bit distracting, yes. But that was not our overall impression of his lecture. I mean, it was very interesting, yes. Is he the official historian for the city or something like that?"

No, he's a bartender, J.J. thought of saying, turning her head to keep from laughing in the face of the man. She thought better and said, "No, just a student of history, you might say."

A young woman with her date stood over their table. She said, "I think what Dr. Hastings is saying is that your husband was wonderfully entertaining. My boyfriend and I were sitting having dinner just over there, two tables over. I also thought your husband was a scholar and Bradley (her boyfriend standing beside her) thought he was paid by the hotel for this party."

Bradley nodded, and added, "Yes, we listened to the whole thing. It was great stuff."

J.J. said, "Well, he is very well read, that's for sure."

Next to Hastings was his wife, a stylish middle-aged woman with graying auburn hair. She was clearly there to be seen, wearing a dark-purple dress and lavender scarf, earrings and necklace of gold and diamonds. Mrs. Hastings was also eager to compliment Nick's performance. She put her hand on Hastings' arm as if to hush him and said to J.J. in a matronly way, "My dear, I have lived in this city all my life and I didn't know those things about those famous names—you know, Pratt, Peabody, Gilman, and of course Johns Hopkins. My gosh, no."

J.J. beamed with pride, while Bunker slouched listening to the glamorous lady.

"Oh, let me introduce myself. I'm Gladys Hastings, Matthew's wife." She shook J.J.'s hand. And, while keeping her eyes fixed on the beautiful Mrs. Esposito, she continued, as if to cut off her husband's gazing, "This is just the kind of party I asked Matthew to find, a party like this for New Year's. I'm so glad we came, mostly because of your husband Nick."

J.J. laughed and said she was glad they were there, too.

Gladys Hastings then looked around the room, still holding J.J.'s hand and asked, "Where has Nick gotten to? I've got some questions I'd very much like to ask him about Hopkins." She turned to her husband. "Wouldn't you like to talk with him some, dear?"

Hastings replied, "I certainly would. I am, or was completely captivated."

* * *

Charlie Dupree's party band finished playing. The conversation became more intimate. A discussion that had begun with consoling Walter Bunker gained clarity and inspiration with unanimous praise of Nick's dinnertime lecture from the Hastings, the young couple and other supporters standing near the table. Even Bunker said, "I'm sorry I missed all that."

The band was finished. The hotel piped in pop songs at low volume, leaving the Rumba Room's ambience better suited to after dinner talk

As the band packed its instruments, big Charlie Dupree approached the microphone that previously was in front of his sax. With a characteristic wide grin, he thanked the crowd once again, raising a loud, appreciative, if somewhat drunken round of cheers and applause. Dupree followed with reading a short list of the band's next gigs. No one seemed to listen. He then announced that breakfast would be served promptly at 1:15 a.m. Everyone cheered again.

Charlie and the band filed into the kitchen for their complimentary breakfasts, the well-deserved first served.

The group at J.J.'s table continued to praise Nick, the amateur historian.

Hastings asked Bunker why Nick was no longer teaching.

Bunker defended Nick, "He was too good. I was his vice principal at Glen Burnie High School and supported his unorthodox methods because the kids loved him and they seem to get very good grades in his classes."

J.J. was memorizing each and every word to tell her husband later.

Bunker continued, "I can say now that he was brilliant with his impromptu stories, and he took the kids on trips constantly—to Fort McHenry, the old Shot Tower, Edgar Allan Poe's grave in downtown Baltimore, the Naval Academy in Annapolis—all over, really. Once he took them to Winterthur, the former home of Henry Francis du Pont, the antiques collector and horticulturist in the Brandywine Valley, Delaware. The kids got home at 9:00 p.m. I'm sorry the way things worked out J.J."

After a pause waiting for response from J.J., which didn't happen, Bunker added, "The man's classes never seemed to be in the school building. But Nick made no effort to kiss up to the school system and did not follow or complete the curriculum, ever. He was a risk—a big one—for the hard-ass superintendent. She hated Nick."

"That's really too bad," said Hastings sincerely.

Bunker's out-of-sorts comments were not helping J.J. feel better about Nick's lost career.

She tuned out and let her eye's drift around to locate Nick. She grew more and more worried over his disappearance, though she was trying to justify it quietly. She whispered to herself. "It's just like Nick to disappear, just at the wrong times."

She didn't see him at the bar.

Penny was gone, too.

When the Rumba Room lights came halfway up and the waiters began to bring out trays of breakfast platters at 1:13 a.m., she had worked herself up into the kind of internal panic she only felt twice before, the kind of panic that reminds a human being she is terribly alone in this world. It was the panic she'd felt when Nick had disappeared without a word at the medical clinic in Lagos, Nigeria—leaving her delirious with malaria while he took off with bribe money to dash officials for airline tickets to Paris. And it was the same kind of panic she'd felt as a child when her drunken father had abandoned his family.

This was the third time she felt such panic. She became every bit as desperate. Her mind was racing.

She spoke to each face at the table with rambling words, "I just can't understand why I can't see Nick. Where do you think he …? He's lost or … has passed out someplace. Does the room look so much smaller. I can see all of it easily. No Nick. Oh, my, he's probably out of control. And what bad timing. No Nate, now. They're gone. Where's Betsy when I need her? God, this is awful. I feel sick. Nick should be taking a cue from the breakfast announcement. He could use some food, too. The party is ending and, if I know Nick, he'll come out of hiding to eat. He's not even in the room. Where? Where?

"I'm at a loss, Walter. I so wish Nate was still here. Did he say anything to you about Nick before he took Betsy home?" Her voice was now tight and despairing.

"I don't think so," said Bunker.

J.J., grasping at straws, said, "I bet he's gone to try to talk with that Edison guy he was set on seeing at the masquerade party. Oh, my Lord, I see that Frau Blondie is gone too."

Hastings picked up on that, "That's the blonde girl they were flirting with, I guess. Just honest fun, Mrs. Esposito. I saw her too. Remarkable beauty, that girl, yes," he said dreamily.

She said in a rage, "So, they were flirting!"

"Oh, I'm just kidding, Mrs. Esposito. I heard them talking about her. 'Quite a looker,' they said."

"Well, who the hell cares? Okay, where's Nick, damn it!" Desperate for support, J.J. said to Bunker. "You don't think Nick went with her somewhere, do you? If he did, I'll—"

In the next instant, J.J.'s heart nearly stopped when a woman screamed.

It was a loud, screeching ear-splitting scream from the kitchen. Waiters crashed trays to the floor, splattering eggs, toast, coffee, Danish, and dishes everywhere. The Rumba Room house lights came up full. Dozens of people rushed into the kitchen at once, filling the room instantly with commotion.

"Oh no, I knew it!" cried J.J. as she and the others jumped to their feet. As they left their table, J.J. grabbed Gladys Hastings around the shoulders and clung to her. J.J. was in a furious panic and felt a heavy pressure on her heart. "Something's wrong, Gladys. It's Nick, I know it is." Her eyes begged Gladys and Matthew to give her a logical answer.

They just shook their heads.

As they raced toward the kitchen, J.J. added, in almost a whisper, "I knew this was a bad idea. Betsy was right."

Security guards seemed to appear out of thin air, rushing past people to the back of the kitchen. They pushed away prep tables, portable steel shelves and cabinets crashed to the tile floor.

And there was the woman who screamed on her knees and hands on her head at the very back of the kitchen. She was facing and pointing at a dark, rectangular opening, about six feet square, which was framed on the back-kitchen wall with drapes pulled back on either side. In the opening were dull glimmers of light reflected off silver-gray pulleys and cables running down the center of the opening with no floor.

The first person to arrive after the scream had been Charlie Dupree, who just finished his breakfast about 20 feet away when the woman, a kitchen employee, screamed after peering down the mysterious dark opening in the wall. The woman then told Dupree, "There, there. I hear moans and scratching down there, mister. There, there."

Dupree was a frequent visitor to the hotel and knew about the opening in the back of the kitchen. It was the door to the shaft between kitchens above and below.

Charlie yelled back to the security guards, "It's that big ol' secret dumbwaiter thing for the old penthouse parties. Somebody's pried it open." Charlie dropped his head into the shaft to block the kitchen light. He said, "Somebody's down there. He's hurt!"

J.J. screamed and cried. She knew without looking.

That somebody was her husband, Nick Esposito, who lay motionless.

A security guard tried to push Dupree aside but could not budge the bandleader's bulky body an inch. He handed Charlie a big flashlight instead.

Now, Nick's body could be seen. He was unconscious on top of the dumbwaiter car, just inches next to rusted, jagged cable boxes. He was about fifteen feet down.

"Sir, I don't think you should go down there," a guard called to Dupree. "Let us—"

The guard reached out to grab Charlie and got a handful of the musician's shiny dinner jacket. Charlie grabbed hold of cables with some kitchen rags to protect his hands. He was going to lower himself to Nick's limp body.

The guard's hand slipped from Dupree's jacket and Dupree, oh so carefully, let himself down, holding on to the cable with one hand and the side of the shaft with the other.

After a pause that J.J. seemed was forever, Dupree shouted up the shaft, loud enough that most of the gathering people in the kitchen heard, "It's okay—I'm trained in CPR at my firehouse and a medevac technician for Shock Trauma."

J.J. said, "Oh my!" and buried her face into Gladys's shoulder.

Charlie continued to slide down the cable. He discovered that Nick had a nasty wound to the front of his head. Nick's face was full of blood. His limbs were twisting in unnatural ways. He was breathing, slowly.

Charlie Dupree, shouted up the shaft, "He is alive, but hurt badly."

A few people peered down the shaft to watch Dupree with the wounded man. They heard him ask Nick softly, "Can you hear me? Can you hear me, mister?"

Cradled in Dupree's big hands, Nick opened his eyes just a slit and looked directly into Dupree's face. He asked the musician, "Are you okay now, Mr. Bonaparte?" Then he moaned and fell unconscious again.

It so happened that Charlie Dupree's face was a near double for the face of the late Charles Joseph Bonaparte, minus Bonaparte's mustache. Same round face, cleft chin, dark hair, with deep-set serious, intense eyes.

Soon a medevac crew arrived. They lowered a stretcher and Dupree carefully lifted Nick's limp body onto it.

Chapter 44: I Must Have Been Nuts

Charlie Dupree rode in the medevac ambulance with critically injured Nick Esposito to the University of Maryland's Shock Trauma Center entrance on Pine Street at the university's hospital, some twenty blocks south of the Belvedere Hotel.

J.J. sat at Nick's side in the ambulance

A few times during the ride, Nick looked up at Dupree's face to mumble something about Bonaparte as he went in and out of consciousness.

For the next five days, he was in the intensive care unit.

Only J.J. and the twins were allowed to visit him in the hospital intensive care unit, and after the first time, only J.J. The precocious twins ran the hospital halls disturbing the staff and patients on their daily walking therapy.

It was on that first hospital visit, though, that J.J. brought into Nick's bedside a beautifully framed photograph that captured perfectly, she said, one of their happy moments from their night at the Belvedere. She and Pop thought the picture might cheer Nick up. It was the portrait of their party foursome in the lobby—Nick with his arm around J.J., and Nate and Betsy Bowen on either side of the Espositos. A caption in old-fashion script read, *Night at the Belvedere, 8:26 p.m., Dec. 31, 1999* and was signed neatly *by Lenny Stein, photographer*.

Stein had captured J.J. at that the moment with a delightful smile. It was one of those moments that night when she looked ready to give Nick the benefit of her many doubts about the outing. Nate and Betsy in that moment made pooh-pooh faces at Nick, all in good fun. And, Nick had rolled his eyes up, revealing his impatience with them stepping out of line to the elevator.

"Nick, your expression in this picture is precious," J.J. said.

As he was stretched out in the hospital bed writhing in pain, Nick hid his chilly reaction to the photograph. He had looked deeper into the picture to find the scrawny, ugly face of the "hat-check boy," Mr. Bojay, whom only Nick had seen that night reflected in the gold-mirrored doors of the elevators. The disturbing image was missing in the shot.

"This is great, hon. But something isn't right about the photograph. It's been doctored, I think," Nick said. "Mr. Bojay should have been in that shot, but he's not."

Instead of Bojay in the photo, there was a young man in a Belvedere uniform. The younger man appeared to be taking hats and coats, and not Mr. Bojay.

"Who is Mr. Bojay, Nick?"

Oh God, the creepy guy's not in the picture. I must have already been visiting the dead in the Belvedere lobby that night. Don't tell her, Nick thought. He was frightened. All he could say was, "Oh, nobody really. Hey look, J.J., that boy back there got his face into our picture."

"Yeah, that was that nice hat-check boy, remember? You told him no because you asked us to keep our coats with us to the party room. I wondered why," she replied.

"I guess I don't remember why I said that. J.J., my head hurts." He reached up and touched extensive head bandages. Nick grew tired and stopped talking.

J.J. soon left to let him rest but not before saying, "I love this picture, Nick. I'll leave it here by your bedside." But he was already sleeping and J.J. spent the next half hour tracking down her misbehaving daughters Hilary and Heather.

* * *

When the swelling of Nick's head injury contracted without any life-threatening complications, he was moved to a private room where he could receive more visitors.

And plenty came, in droves.

Nick didn't know he had so many friends. There were constant visits from concerned friends and family, Glen Burnie neighbors, former teaching colleagues, former students—some from across the country—and delivery men from liquor and beer distributors, and regulars from Pop's Tavern. Pop and Minnie came with J.J. once. She had done her due diligence, so to speak, to put the word out: "Please visit Nick. Help Nick recover."

The guests even included the one and only, cleaned-up and sort of sober, Buddy Burkhart. The good ol' last-out-of-the-tavern Buddy caught a bus by himself to University Hospital so he could give ailing Nick the latest gossip from his soaps, "General Hospital" and "All My Children." It's what they had shared.

Still, the most surprising visitor, in Nick's opinion, was Dr. Matthew Hastings from the millennium party. Nick didn't remember him from the night at the Belvedere. He looked more like one of the professors at the 1899 reception with his full beard and academic demeanor. That too frightened Nick at first. He had not actually met Hastings at the party, because Nick had drifted off, perhaps destined to his 1899 'visit' after depositing Walter Bunker with J.J.

He wondered why the stranger Hastings came to see him at all.

Hastings came because he knew Nick from listening to the dinner table talk. "I just have to meet him," he told J.J. He looked her up at Johns Hopkins Medical Center. She was delighted and invited him to see Nick with her and Betsy one afternoon.

It wasn't until Hastings and wife Gladys visited the hospital with J.J. and Betsy that Hastings revealed his full identity. He was the provost and senior vice president for academic affairs at Johns Hopkins University in East Baltimore.

It was no coincidence that Hastings and his wife were intrigued by Nick's stories at the Belvedere. Hastings was originally from Buffalo. But Gladys, his second wife, was a native Baltimorean whose interest in the city's history was aroused by Nick Esposito's ramblings at the millennium party dinner table.

For their New Year's outing, Gladys wanted to celebrate with "real Baltimoreans." The Hastings had turned down invitations to attend parties at the homes of several senior Hopkins faculty members. J.J. was endeared to Gladys ever since the stylish lady said that night at the Belvedere, "I just couldn't stand another evening with those codfish aristocrats on that faculty."

Gladys Hastings' request to her husband for New Year's landed them at the swinging Rumba Room at the Belvedere and, serendipitously, seated at the table right next to Nick Esposito's 'performance.'

Dr. Matthew Hastings was the more eager of the two to meet Nick. His first marriage had failed partly because of his unwavering devotion to his work at the University of Buffalo and, as a result, his lack of devotion to his spouse.

After Hastings was blessed with a second love of his life, his Gladys in Baltimore, he wasn't about to make the same mistake. Gladys was his full partner this time, he determined. It was only natural that Gladys Hastings' interest in Nick's Baltimore led to Matthew Hastings desire to cultivate a friendship with Nick Esposito, the American history teacher. Hastings knew little of the city's rich history of philanthropists and industry. He saw a chance in Nick to enrich his marriage and get to know his adopted city better.

He also saw in Nick a chance to enrich his own position on the Hopkins faculty. Hastings was a scientist who had risen to prominence in the field of optics and photonics, the science of light. He would also discover in Nick an amazing coincidence. Hastings shared Nick's hero worship of Thomas Alva Edison of Menlo Park, the great American inventor. Hastings already knew Edison's life story well. But he was thrilled to soon learn that Nick knew more than he did about the inventor.

They indeed hit it off. Hastings visited Nick in the hospital frequently. His enthusiastic interest in Nick's knowledge of history grew into a fond friendship. Nick also took a liking to Hastings and, before he thought better of it—perhaps his head injury still affected his judgment—Nick risked telling Matthew

Hastings about Nick's vision of the ghostly party below the party back in time at the then new Belvedere Hotel.

Rather than dismissing Nick as a kook, the professor was all the more intrigued. He told a colleague about an anonymous man who talks with ghosts, "So, what if the man is a little eccentric, I just won't tell Gladys how crazy he might be."

As the two men enjoyed interesting discussions during Nick's two-week stay in his single-bed hospital room, Hastings also enjoyed reporting home to Gladys what he had learned about Johns Hopkins, Enoch Pratt, George Peabody, and other Baltimore legends, while holding back any reference to Nick's claim to periodically get lost in past events, especially Nick's ghostly visit to 1899.

They became such good friends that Nick trusted Matthew Hastings, and only he, by sharing those historically accurate details of what he'd seen, heard, and experienced at the "other" party—Nick's code for his 1899 VIP ballroom reception visit. Hastings told Nick his story would lead Gladys to sentence Nick Esposito permanently to a category of first-class nut case. "Let's keep it to ourselves, Nick."

Hastings continued to listen and acted like he believed Nick's every word.

Chapter 45: Reconciliation

Nick had never met someone like Matt Hastings, someone who believed so much in his paranormal ability.

Hastings had not shared with Nick any of the skepticism he felt about the bizarre tale.

Nick asked Matt if the two men could join forces to find the truth about the other party at the Belvedere that only Nick knew about, or thought he did. They would research actual, documented events of December 31, 1899 and January 1, 1900, in Baltimore.

Hastings didn't really think Edison had been in Baltimore at that time and he didn't really believe Nick's explanation. He held privately that Nick's so-called "vivid visit" to the 1899 party left dozens of unanswered questions, not the least of which was whether there actually were murders that night at the Belvedere that remained cold cases, as far as he could determine.

On the other hand, Hastings was worried about the mental health of his new friend. He could not say no to Nick's proposed partnering. He agreed and stayed committed to go along, to help investigate the 100-year-old events with Nick Esposito, together, as he grew very fond of Nick.

For Nick's part, the partnership was simpler. He was gratified to find a research partner who shared common interests in light, history and Thomas Edison. He was focused and energized.

* * *

Meanwhile, Nick's hospital stay might have been a blessing, perhaps just what he needed to find his roots, to shed his eccentricities and settle down. Such was the loving hope circulating among the Espositos. Would then the mixed-up son of the late Carlo Esposito finally gain a secure hold in life, perhaps answer his true calling--be a true Esposito?

The women—Grandma Minnie, aunts and nieces, sister Katrina who traveled across the Pacific to see him, even J.J.—smothered Nick in the hospital with words they felt he should to live by when he got out.

He had nowhere to run to escape their incessant advice and mothering. He just smiled, listening to them say things like:

"Oh Nicky, you really did it this time. Better be more careful, hear?"

"Nick, you gonna settle down now; act normal? You got kids to raise."

"I hope this taught you something, Nicky boy. All your history fantasies are crazy stuff." You should teach again; least then, you put your dreaming to good use."

"Use your head Nick."

"Nick, you been going to church, my son? You need to get out more; have a normal life around people."

Minnie reported Nick's progress to her hardheaded husband back at Quiet Oaks, who concluded after an arduous trip to Nick's hospital bed that one visit was enough. He was now too weak to travel, but not too weak to go to bat for his special grandson.

"Phooey," Pop snapped at the idea of the women counseling Nicky. "I'm just happy he is doing well. He's my boy Nicky. Leave him alone."

Nick was privately amused. He'd never be a social, out-going Esposito and he knew the family knew it too by now. The family visits recharged Nick's love for his family, nevertheless, as he watched and listened to their concerns for him. It was indeed settling.

A hospital patient, of course, has too much time to think in isolation, to keep to his own thoughts when there are no visitors. Nick's time spent there mostly allowed him to reflect on just what he saw that night at the Belvedere Hotel. He wondered and analyzed how any of it or perhaps all of it fit into his well-read history lessons, which were firmly imprinted into his brain.

He considered any possible explanation of how the people at the 1899 New Year's Eve reception could have been fabulous impersonators of favorite historic figures. Or were they the people at all? When and how did he get his injuries in the dumbwaiter, going to the 1899 room? or coming out of it? What were his dreams going to the hospital? Dreams? A vivid 'episode' to the past? A real-time trip? A visit, indeed?

Nick needed to know. He needed to think it through. Whenever nurses offered to dial up television or radio in his hospital room, he refused. He didn't speak to hospital staff. He answered with a simple 'yes' or 'no' to doctors' inquiries. He was too preoccupied.

Day and night, he looked for the answers on the white walls and plastic curtains of his single patient room. He remembered many images, the strongest and most persistent were:

- Charlie Dupree's uncanny resemblance to Charles Bonaparte;
- His great-grandfather Mike's pearl-handled revolver had indeed still been locked in Pop's display case at the tavern the afternoon of December 31; and it was there in January, Mr. Triandos said, when Nick called the tavern from the hospital.
- The irresistible attraction to the Belvedere, which he could not ignore day after day.

None of it made sense. He'd experienced hundreds of his visits into the past. None of them were so detailed, so apparently purposeful. Did it all mean something? Had he been hand-picked by the hotel's ghosts to be there at that moment, at that incident 100 years ago? Maybe. He was brought to the scene of a murder attempt. Or, was he? And most troubling was whether he had just read about all of it sometime?

And, there was Pop's odd warning about the curse of the Belvedere, which Nick had rationalized as a sign of senility, even though he knew Pop's mind to be clear and still functioning well, perhaps too well? Why would he disrespect Pop's wishes to stay away from the Belvedere? That alone, made no sense to Nick. He never disrespected his idol, Pop.

373

Nick thought over the "Dead Man's Party" song. The flash-back Stevie Wonder song. The Edison costume. The quick visit to the real masquerade party—a deliberate teaser to focus on Edison?

Nick analyzed his own psyche and concluded that everything in this trip to 1899 might fit historically accurate facts. "Okay, so I made it happen," he muttered. And then he proposed to his ego, "Well, if so, I am very impressed. Enjoy the experience, Nick." He was far too sober to figure it any other way.

He eventually decided to turn to Hastings for help. He needed evidence of any of the historically facts he saw and heard during the visit.

* * *

Meanwhile, Nick displayed a headstrong confidence during his recovery.

Due to his stoic attitude in the hospital, Betsy Bowen suggested to J.J. that she allow a friend, one of the University of Maryland School of Social Work professors, right on campus near the hospital, to intervene.

Nick was not Nick, she said. "He just lays there smiling like a damn fool. I think she (the social worker) could interview Nick while he was too helpless to object," plotted Betsy. She had heard from Nate that Nick mentioned in a weak moment that he had been to a party 100 years ago that night at the Belvedere. Betsy then believed, without telling J.J., that Nick had finally gone over the deep end, that he was clearly cracking up.

Nick pegged the social work professor's motives to Betsy immediately and vowed not to tell Nate any more about his experience. *Must have been a forgiveable slip up by my buddy Nate*, he reasoned.

The women's plot to examine Nick while he was incapacitated next included a University of Maryland psychiatrist they recruited at University Hospital to join Nick's team of physicians. The shrink did not reveal his specialty of psychiatry to the clever patient. He prescribed lithium, a traditional medication at the time for bipolar symptoms along with the painkillers and antibiotics from his other docs.

Nick rarely swallowed any of the medications. His mind was too busy, and quite settled, thank you, to be medicated. (A month after his accident at the Belvedere party, he admitted to J.J. he had stopped swallowing the lithium pills. He tossed out repeated prescription refills she got for him under her Hopkins prescription drug plan.)

Betsy's efforts, though well intended, were a joke to Nick. Just to be alive and recovering at the hospital after experiencing the bizarre ghost party with all its historic texture and details, was more than enough therapy. It also offered Nick a giant dose of appreciation for his own being, his unique identity, a bit of needed self-actualization he'd been missing for more than 30 years.

He could not remember the exact words of young Marie Krantz and old Ellen Krantz that night, only that he knew at the time they framed and delivered to him some of the most profound and highly personal advice of his life. He tried and tried to write down their words, but could not. He was not sure, but the entire evening could have been a painful affirmation of his place in this world, his remarkable teaching skills, his great knowledge of the lessons of history, his compassion for others. He felt far better mentally for it, though the considerable physical pain remained for a long time.

He returned repeatedly to the notion that he had been receiving some sort of awakening given him by those shadowy Krantz women. He thought, *Was it a gift? Yes, I do believe they put me at that 1899 New Year's party.* But, why? Was he helping them in return some way? Maybe they beckoned Nick to the Belvedere in the first place.

"Oh, crap! I'm completely nuts," he unfortunately said out loud one evening as his nurse just then entered his room.

"No, you are not dear. Drink your apple juice with your pill."

The explanation of having received a gift would be convenient to end his speculating. *Yes, that's it.* He thought. *I'll use it to cement a new outlook. That will please the family. Oh no, it won't. It will please me.*

After Nick's release from the hospital, Nick turned to the task at hand, as far as he and his sanity were concerned. He and Matthew Hastings vowed to find out what, if anything, might have happened on December 31, 1899 and January 1, 1900 at the yet to be opened Belvedere Hotel north of downtown Baltimore.

* * *

Nick returned and reopened Pop's Tavern on Ellwood Avenue to regular hours delighting Buddy Burkhart and the few regulars.

The new millennium hadn't brought on any practical change in Nick's life, but he was in better spirits about his reluctant bartending profession. He installed a big-screen TV with cable, feeling that was the least he could do for the loyalty shown to him by Buddy and friends who supported him in recovery.

The tavern would again be his regular job, just the same as before that extraordinary night at the Belvedere.

But now Nick also had another routine. Each morning from 7:00 to 9:30 before opening and some evenings, when he got a bartender to stand in for him, Nick met Hastings at the Baltimore Sunpapers building on Calvert Street.

They searched the paper's morgue files for any events of the late 1890s. Their browsing freedom was a courtesy from a reporter who owed Hastings a favor for tips on Hopkins stories. Nick and Matt Hastings didn't come up with anything about a reception or party at the Belvedere on New Year's Eve 1899.

As they left the Sun basement late one night, Nick offered an explanation. "Matt, maybe the Baltimore Sun reporters were assigned other stories that night. It was New Year's Eve and they may have been spread thin. In fact, I think Mayor Hayes said, if he did say, that the Belvedere reception was not a New Year's celebration as much as a reception to honor the creation of the hotel. It would not be open to the public for many more months. I think it was not finished yet. In fact, I know it wasn't. It may not have been covered at all by the press."

"If all those dignitaries were there, there must be some record somewhere," said Hastings, scratching his head. "I'd at least like to know who opened the Belvedere to the public when it did open. I know Gladys would like to know, too."

"Okay, let's keep at it. There were two prominent newspapers in Baltimore at the time, the conservative Sun and the liberal Baltimore American," said Nick.

The two met the next evening at the main Enoch Pratt Free Library on Franklin Street. It was one of the oldest free libraries in the United States, first opened in 1886. Nick and Matt found microfiche newspaper clippings galore about events on December 31, 1899. The Pratt Library also had records of stories from the Baltimore Weekly Sun, Morning Herald, Baltimore American, Baltimore Telegraph, and Baltimore News. Yet they found nothing about the Belvedere Hotel reception, if there had been one.

Nick asked his favorite Pratt librarian for help. She suggested that a business meeting would be reported perhaps in the old Baltimore Journal of Commerce, which, she said, was the business bible for Maryland back in the day.

They cranked the microfiche viewer to the BJC for December 31, 1899, then to January 1, 1900, then to January 2, 1900.

Nick was delighted to finally see:

Alleged Shooting at New Hotel Site; Officials Hushed

An unidentified man was killed and a woman seriously wounded at Mayor Thomas Hayes's VIP reception held on New Year's Eve at the fourteenth floor of the deluxe Belvedere Hotel under construction in northern Baltimore, according to eyewitnesses.

Police Inspector Michael Esposito confirmed that shots were fired accidentally from a pistol in the hand of a police officer, as he fell from the ballroom stage. According to medical reports, the shooting victim was the alleged Bogart T. Jenkins, businessman visiting from New York City. The wounded woman, believed to be Jenkins' wife or girlfriend, was taken in critical condition to the new medical center at Johns Hopkins University at Homestead. She was believed to be underage and intoxicated. Inspector Esposito said there were no charges filed against the clumsy patrolman, who had lost his footing and fallen off the stage into several people. He did not confirm the victims.

There are no further details of the mayor's reception, which was believed to be held in confidence of selected invitees, to meet and promote new business opportunities for the city's manufacturing and shipping companies, in anticipation of convention and hospitality resources for the new hotel.

Witnesses on Chase Street outside the hotel site said they saw several prominent citizens enter the building that night, including Charles J. Bonaparte and Daniel Coit Gilman, president of Johns Hopkins University.

No persons interviewed at the scene had any knowledge either of Mr. Jenkins or of his business intentions in Baltimore.

Hastings was speechless. With his eyes bulging, he turned his head slowly toward Nick's devilish smiling face with an expression of disbelief. "Holy cow, Nick. It happened!"

Nick took on a whimsical grin and waited for Hastings to compose himself. He then said, "I told you, Matt—it all fit, my visit fit the actual history, I mean."

After some thought, he also explained, "But that is not what happened. I don't think it was that way. And 'alleged'? No. The victims were Bogart and his young wife. I think she was the one in the coat with the tall collar the whole time."

"Yeah, you said that," Hastings replied. He bit his lower lip and twisted his head to the side looking worried. The staid, buttoned-down professor would admit years later that, at this point of their research, the game he was playing with his nutty friend took on a frightening twist.

Nick was thirsty for more with no fear of finding the truth. He cranked the microfiche viewer and on the same page of the business newspaper was a photograph of Bogart Jenkins of New York City.

"Matt, it's Mr. Bojay."

"Who's Mr. Bojay?"

"You wouldn't know. When we got to the Belvedere that night, this old man was checking coats near the elevator. At least I thought he was; he didn't show up in our photograph from the lobby as he should have. I saw him, though. He was a creepy little, ugly old man with a thin mustache. He is that man seen here in this picture, who was reported killed—but much older, very much older. The old coat checker Bojay is Jenkins!"

Nick's hands shook with excitement. He clasped them together. He was alarmed by the very powers he'd always possessed, and usually enjoyed, of seeing the past. After several weeks of pondering at the hospital and Pop's tavern about the legitimacy of his visit, he was looking at actual evidence that he may have been transported one hundred years back to 1899 in a flash.

"Nick, have you ever seen this clip before?"

"No, Matt."

"Are you sure?"

"Not absolutely, but I don't think I would have ever looked at these clippings. I've spent tons of time here, though, doing research. [He paused to think.] … It is possible, I guess."

* * *

There was no more information reported in other stories in the Journal about that night a century ago. And no follow-ups from those first January days in 1900.

The two left the library more perplexed than a punch-drunk Buddy Burkhart forgetting the way home. Hastings departed for Hopkins muttering to himself. Nick drove back to close up Pop's Tavern. He was convinced of his theory that the vision into the past was a gift, which might improve his view on life. He felt warmed by some of the words of comfort he then remembered from Ellen and Marie Krantz. *They were family, I'm sure now. Maybe Marie was Ellen's daughter, both spirits trapped there. They knew me. Why?*

He needed more evidence.

* * *

The next day was Sunday.

Nick declined to take J.J. and the twins with him on their usual visit for Sunday breakfast at the Quiet Oaks retirement center with Pop and Grandma Minnie. Instead, he got up early and slipped over by himself to see Pop.

"Pop, I don't want to bring up a sour subject, but…"

"Go on Nicky boy," Pop said, straightening up in the chair in his apartment. He turned off the TV. "If I can help with anything, I will, as always."

Nick swallowed hard and said, "Do you remember if great-grandfather Mike, our famous police inspector, ever said anything about a shooting at the Belvedere before the hotel's official opening about a hundred years ago?"

Pop asked, "Why do you want to know about that, Nicky?" with obvious fear on his face.

Nick's idea to go see Pop was solid. He didn't go there to share the visit to 1899 with the old man. That very idea petrified Nick. Pop might die believing his favorite grandson was loony.

Instead, Nick's idea was that Pop, like his father Mike, had great natural instincts for snooping. Nick eased into his case as, "It's just a story I heard at the bar Pop, that's all. Maybe I'll write about it."

Pop told Nick quickly that he couldn't remember Inspector Mike telling him such a story. "If there was, Papa might never tell nobody and I weren't born yet," Pop explained. "Remember what I said about him. After losing my Mama to the fever, Papa Mike spent little time with me anyway when I was a kid," Pop said. He took his eyes off Nick and looked at his folded hands.

After a pause, he looked lovingly at his 45-year-old Nicky boy, "I tell you what, my Niccola Augusta." Pop patted Nick's check with his right hand affectionately. "I'll call my old friends what I got trainee jobs years ago at the precinct. They run things now down there. They will get you into police records for the years 1899 and 1900, if that's what might help with your story tellin.' They owe me for makin' them good cops on their East Balmer beats. If you don't get full access, you call me. I can get them fired." Pop laughed at himself and pulled Nick's head toward him for a kiss on his head, then mussed up Nick's ratty hair. "Oh, too, here take this." He reached into his pants and pulled out his dry-rotted billfold.

From the billfold, Pop handed Nicky his yellowed honorary Baltimore police ID and a hundred-dollar bill. "Any trouble, use one of these, Nicky," and he laughed again. "This was what they gave me long time ago for all my help. It'll work; always did. They won't take the dough, though. So, you gonna publish that story?"

"I don't know yet, but thanks Pop, I knew you'd find a way to help," he said, a little too enthusiastically. Nick's excitement seemed to worry the old man. Pop watched Nick leave. Maybe for the last time.

When he was sure Nick had left the senior center, Pop joined his poker buddies and confessed, "I just can't think of why that boy is so excited about that hunnerd-year-old shootin' at that old gypsy hotel."

Chapter 46: Pop Comes Through Again

First thing Monday morning, Nick called the number for police records and learned that Pop had already cleared the way for him.

He met Hastings there at 7:00 a.m. Tuesday and easily uncovered the story of what had really happened on December 31, 1899 at the unfinished Belvedere Hotel.

According to the handwritten report by one Chief Inspector Michael Esposito, BCPD, dated 5:45 a.m., January 1, 1900:

A pair of suspected members of the Black Hand mob were seen by detectives entering and disappearing into the unfinished basement of the new Belvedere Hotel on Chase St. late in the evening of December 31.

Approximately one hour later, one of the suspects wearing a dark-brown overcoat appeared in the kitchen of the main ballroom, surprising the chefs. They asked the building supervisor to get word to the mayor, who was holding a business reception for company executives including one Bogart Jenkins, wealthy shipping company magnate visiting from New York, and other business entrepreneurs and university professors. Jenkins has a record of corruption with city officials and racketeering in New York.

Mayor Hayes and his guests were informed of possible trouble when officers discovered the evidence that the intruders had also entered the basement carriage stalls, still unfinished and not secured properly.

In the ballroom later, one Fritzy McShay, a dock worker from the Locust Point neighborhood, was seen rushing toward Charles Bonaparte, one of the mayor's guests, then fired two shots while threatening Mr. Bonaparte.

McShay stumbled while firing. Shots missed Mr. Bonaparte and struck Mr. Jenkins and a seventeen-year-old female German immigrant.

382

Jenkins died instantly. Several guests at the mayor's reception said they had seen the girl earlier this week staying with Jenkins in a downtown boarding house.

McShay is in custody at the North Baltimore Precinct, as is his companion, a mentally retarded man who called himself Freddie, who was apprehended trying to escape by the ballroom kitchen dumbwaiter.

The girl, Marie Krantz, was rushed to the medical center at Homestead, accompanied by Mrs. Bonaparte and her attendants. Miss Krantz was pronounced dead at the emergency room but doctors could induce the birth of her baby girl. She will be turned over to the Catholic orphanage and settlement house after six months care at the medical center, according to attending nurses.

The report ended there, leaving Nick and Hastings with more questions than answers.

They dug further and found several follow-up reports on the incident, filed January 5, 9, and 21, 1900. According to those police reports, Fritzy McShay and his slow-witted companion Freddie were not with the Black Hand as the good inspector had first wrote. Both had extensive criminal records in New York and Cleveland and had been sharing a room at a rooming house near the Locust Point shipping and rail lines in Baltimore.

Interviews with fellow dock workers revealed that the labor union leaders were vocal in wanting Bogart Jenkins' considerable shipping business to Baltimore. Meanwhile, union bosses were voicing a lot of public complaints that Charles Bonaparte and his reformers were interfering. He was possibly making it difficult for the Jenkins deal because of Jenkins' alleged payoffs to city officials, according to numerous newspaper articles.

Friends of McShay from the docks deposed at the precinct that McShay displayed a fiery temper at labor meetings and had threatened to kill Bonaparte as a foreign intruder from "Napoleon's clan" sent to America to stir up trouble.

Nick said, "No one apparently bothered to tell the thug that Bonaparte had been born and raised in their town, in their country, not in Napoleon Bonaparte's France."

He and Hastings read further that police thought McShay might have been noticed by mobsters infiltrating labor meetings. There were rumors from dock workers that McShay had been paid handsomely by "some gentlemen in expensive suits who were here to kill Bonaparte."

* * *

After reading the reports, Hastings spoke first. "I just can't believe all this is really here, Nick. It fits your story. Come on, now. You must have read about all this before, huh?"

"I did not. Even Pop would never have taken his nutty grandson to the police precinct to read official records for fun," Nick said without looking away from scanning the reports.

He then nearly shouted, "Hey, just take a look at this January 21 report from interviews of the social workers. It's simply amazing. I thought Marie was Ellen's daughter, but it was the other way around."

Matt and Nick read the next police report in stunned silence.

The report stated that teenage Marie was the daughter of German immigrant Hans Krantz of East Lombard Street, a textile mill worker. Mr. Krantz sometimes brought his young daughter into work to give him some free help in the mill. The police investigations revealed that clothing manufacturing executives visiting the mill where her father worked evidently induced the girl at age 15 to model clothing in store windows.

Employees at a Fayette Street store reported that Mr. Bogart Jenkins, on one of his frequent trips through Baltimore, spotted the girl in a store window.

The police report also stated that Jenkins picked up the girl and seduced her with drink, according to witnesses. He showered the girl with money and fashionable clothes, first to be photographed for his company advertisements, then to be his lover. It was rumored that Jenkin's got the girl pregnant and promised to marry her.

Her family found out about the affair when her mother, Hans's wife, discovered hundreds of dollars in Marie's purse while cleaning her bedroom. Her father blew up. He said he refused to raise a prostitute under his roof and threw her out of their home to save the family from further embarrassment.

Jenkins and the girl attended a pre-opening party at the Belvedere Hotel site where Marie Krantz lost her life to a bullet fired at but missed Charles Bonaparte, a guest. But her baby was saved at the hospital. The police report said that doctors named the baby Ellen in honor of Ellen Bonaparte, Charles Bonaparte's wife. The surgeons realized Mrs. Bonaparte had unwittingly saved the child's life by helping to rush her wounded mother, pregnant Marie, to a horse-drawn ambulance stationed at the hotel that night. Arrangements were made to turn baby Ellen Krantz over to the Catholic orphanage and settlement house in North Baltimore, the police report concluded, confirming Inspector Esposito's first report on Jan. 1.

"It is not MY theory anymore," Nick was in a state of roaring fright and elation all at once. "Except that Ellen Krantz was not Marie's mother, but her daughter. I had it backward!"

Matt was confused, and mumbled, "So?

"Don't you get it, Matt? The old lady was baby Ellen. You remember? The old lady I saw at the Belvedere in November. She was the younger girl Marie Krantz's daughter, baby Ellen. Marie was Ellen's mother.

"Back in November, Ellen Krantz, her ghost I guess, lured me into buying the Rumba Room tickets. Then after Marie--the beautiful teenage girl checking our tickets at the Rumba Room—the ghost of Marie, I guess—sent me to the kitchen and the old dumbwaiter. I never saw them together because they were not of the same time period.

"Ellen—ghost of the grown and aged baby Ellen, I guess—lured me into a hundred-year-ago party. She was there, though, Matt. I swear. I touched her, I think, maybe shook hands.

I don't know. This is just astounding? And, look. See the picture?"

Nick put his index finger on a photograph in the report of the blonde-haired seventeen-year-old beauty in the report. It was indeed Marie Krantz.

Matt Hastings was shaken to the core and sweating. He at least needed clarity, and asked, "According to your theory, the girl in the picture who was killed was the mother? She would be a ghost at the age when she died. And old Miss Ellen Krantz, who lived, was her daughter? Logically, then, what you are hinting at is that her spirit still haunted the place. It seems too crazy to believe," Hastings admitted.

Another police report from two years later read: *"In unconfirmed statements, Baby Ellen Krantz was believed to be adopted by a couple who are neighbors of Mayor Thomas Hayes of Peabody Heights. Her whereabouts, with her adopted name, is unknown, according to the report.*

Hastings said, "Wow Nick, so you think you met the young mother Marie and her daughter Ellen, who had aged to be the old lady at the hotel? Yet no one there has ever seen or heard of her now, right? It's an unsolved case until you uncovered it?"

"Well, yeah, I guess no one has heard of her. I hadn't of course. Not the bartender who gave me the tickets and not the cleanup man on the 14th floor. I think I asked others too. And, no one knew her."

Hastings wished he could tell Gladys Hastings, but, again, she'd conclude they were both total wackos.

* * *

Nick and Hastings visited the Baltimore Catholic Diocese days later, where an administrator priest found the adoption papers for baby Ellen. The diocese also showed them notes on orphan histories. Those loose records placed Ellen working at the Belvedere Hotel café near her adopted parents' home sometime in the 1920s.

"Nick, do you see what this means?" said Matt, knowing full well Nick did see the connection. Matt said, "The old lady wanted you to see and know what happened. She wanted her identity back. You, the history scholar, were her best shot!" Whether Matt he truly believed Nick now or was playing along to make Nick happy, he sounded convinced.

"Maybe it was a trade," Nick shrugged, at loss for further words. "Could they use my gift? You don't believe I can visit the past, but I do. I visit the past, almost at will sometimes. Maybe I crossed by their spirits once on a visit. They knew me then, huh?" He didn't expect an answer.

"I am simply amazed at this," said a befuddled Hastings, but still you could have read all this before, right?"

"No, no, no ... absolutely no!" Nick noted that Matt didn't buy into his 'spirits crossing paths' theory. Nick didn't care.

* * *

Nick kept digging the next day on his own. He found another report at Baltimore police headquarters, one from January 25, 1900, on McShay. He immediately called Matt at his office at Johns Hopkins. The police report stated that indeed, McShay was no crafty Black Hand gangster, but a local thug who was capable of lunacy. He was a convicted killer who had escaped custody near Philadelphia while being transferred by train to prison in Virginia.

Nick suggested, "You know Matt, he could have been paid anonymously by the Black Hand to stop Bonaparte."

"Why?"

"To keep Bonaparte from exposing their influence in city circles while he was busy uncovering some scandal in the Jenkins deal."

Hastings responded, "Well, it's more likely that McShay was just a crazed lunatic who in his sick mind didn't want Bonaparte to ruin the comfy gig he had as a convicted convict, hiding and working at the shipyards of humble Baltimore, out of sight of the feds."

Nick told Matt that the reports revealed that McShay had been at Locust Point working as a laborer. He rode in produce trucks into town. He had built up a fanatical hatred for Charles Bonaparte.

"Sounds like Bonaparte was a man who was everything McShay wasn't and couldn't be," said Hastings.

"Right," said Nick. "I also found a police report on the shipyard rumors. It says officers were being tipped by Bonaparte's group to block suspect shipping contracts from New York companies. McShay was vocally upset about such rumors, according to his fellow dock workers." Nick scratched his head and speculated, "I know that Bonaparte, who wrote prolifically against public and private crime in popular as well as scholarly magazines had openly opposed opening Baltimore shipping companies' business to New York firms. He wrote that the yards here were possibly infiltrated with 'unseemly and dangerous elements,' as he said."

"As who said, Nick?"

"Bonaparte said . . . in a letter to the editor, I think," Nick replied.

"You are incredible, my friend. I still think it is possible you already knew all this. Hey, listen, this is a bad time. I have a lecture to give in three minutes."

"Please stop saying I knew this stuff previously. I didn't, Matt." Nick ignored him and continued: "I'd say McShay, the dimwit, was a perfect stooge, soaking up the hatred for Bonaparte building up at the docks. Seeing his chance to be a hero, McShay plotted to kill Bonaparte. Workers were growing restless following the depressed economy and slow work at the docks.

"You know, Matt, a month before the shootings reported here at the precinct and in the Journal, Bonaparte published an exposé in Baltimore newspapers of questionable dealings of East Coast shipping companies and officials of city governments from New York to Miami. It was an excellent piece of journalism. He listed the current state and federal court cases and concluded that organized crime was set to gradually follow New York shipping firms to Baltimore, and he aimed to stop the corrupt deals."

Matt had heard enough, "See, you are well versed in the period. I've got to go, my friend."

However, Nick was then convinced that he had helped save Bonaparte's life, or somebody did that night in 1899 to make McShay stumble, and maybe he filled in for that person. Nick lived to tell about it for the first time.

He said, "If Bonaparte had been killed, Matt, there would have been no FBI, Baltimore shipping would have become further corrupted, and President Teddy Roosevelt would have been denied his best attorney general."

Nick Esposito, always insecure, nervous, and often desperate, really believed the Krantz's summoned him to witness somebody committing murder that night and coincidently saving the life of his hero Charles Bonaparte and doing the nation a huge favor. It felt good, even though he knew full well the reformer did not die that night but continued his brilliant career. *It is all whacky*, he thought, *but what else could be expected from me.*

He said, "Go do your class, Matt. Thanks for listening. I've got to get off the phone now."

He felt a chill run through his entire body to the bones. Still Nick sat in the humid warm attic of the police precinct file room for several minutes pondering. He promised himself firmly and out loud, "Nick Esposito, don't you dare ever, and I mean ever, tell anyone about the ghosts I met that night at the Belvedere."

"You alright up there, Nick," someone shouted up the stairs.

"Especially these cops," he mumbled. "I've got to get out of here before I embarrass myself and Pop. ... I'm fine, officer. Just finishing up. Thanks."

Chapter 47: Matt's Touch

Matthew Hastings was most impressed by Nick's logic, how the historical revelations they unearthed fit Nick's vision nicely, yet perhaps too nicely to be true. He was still not convinced that Nick didn't, perhaps unconsciously, know or read the story of his 'visit' to 1899 sometime in his studies. Nick's mental capacities were off the chart for sure.

However, Matt Hastings WAS positively convinced that Mr. Nick Esposito belonged in the classroom. Nick was just crazy-intelligent enough to get back into teaching history again. Dr. Matthew Hastings, senior vice president and provost of Johns Hopkins University, a man of considerable influence, set out to do something about it.

He asked Nick if he would be at Pop's Tavern on Ellwood Avenue that evening. "Nick, I just want to have a talk over a beer. That's all."

* * *

Hastings didn't think through why he had to go to the tavern to meet with Nick and not somewhere else. It seemed right. It was where Nick was most at ease outside of his home.

He would level with Nick: When Nick's so-called visit was verified by actual documents in newspapers and police records, Hastings was concerned for his new friend's sanity. This extraordinary intellect had struggled in an ill-advised career and lost it in cruel and unusual circumstances. He believed that Nick was a kind and good soul floating continually in and out of extreme insecurities without always knowing why.

Hastings, also an educator, believed that if Nick shared this thing about the Belvedere ghosts to anyone, it would surely ruin any future chances to rejuvenate a career.

Certainly, the good professor had never encountered anyone like Nick before. Hastings concerned for Nick was genuine. But Matthew Hastings wasn't "built" for social work, for psychology, for saving people from crisis. He was a scientist. Hastings' sensitivity failures in his first marriage were evidence enough that he was not the sensitive type, he realized.

Nick's situation, called for someone to try to help, and Matt Hastings just happened to have been given a very close look inside the hopes and fears of the recalcitrant Nick Esposito. Only Hastings, or perhaps J.J. who was in denial most times about Nick's craziness, knew that Nick's head was still mixed-up about his eerie night at the Belvedere.

For Hastings, guilt played a part too. He wanted to talk with Nick also because he felt partly responsible for encouraging Nick to find the evidence of an 'imaginary' killing at the Belvedere one hundred years ago. It had been innocent fun for Dr. Hastings, the Baltimore history compatriot. Learning more Baltimore history did him a lot of good at home with Gladys, big time husband points, and maybe points with his new career at Hopkins.

His guilt was tangible. After they'd found actual evidence of real events matching Nick's vision, it wasn't fun anymore. Yet he had kept with Nick on the crazy venture.

It was more than worrisome that Nick was unstable. After arranging the meeting, he said to himself, "What the hell might he do now, tend bar forever, surrounded by booze? I have to try."

* * *

That evening sitting across a table at the tavern over a draft of Natty Boh for Hastings and a Coke for Nick, Hastings opened with, "Nick, you are so talented, so well educated and well read. Don't you think you could have another go at teaching if the conditions were better this time?" Being an academic all his life, Hastings had decided this was the only path he could safely walk Nick down with any hope of finding a way to help his new friend. He wanted Nick to come to his senses about what he 'thought he saw' at the millennium party.

Nick exhaled. "Is that what you wanted to talk about, Matt? My God, I thought I had done something wrong, maybe you had gotten yourself fired when they found out how much time you've taken from Hopkins for our silly research project," he said, looking relieved. "I was worried about you all day."

Hastings looked around to see if others in the tavern were listening. "Yeah, that's pretty much it, Nick. And ..." He paused to look around again.

"Well ... and also what?" asked Nick.

"It's that vision, that dream, or whatever it was, Nick. ..."

"Visit? I call it a visit," Nick laughed.

"What do you really make of it?" Hastings asked, looking intently into Nick's eyes.

"Well, I drink too much. Or at least I did before this. I walk around wondering why I'm such a wimp and nothing like the real men in my family. I see glimpses into the past. Who knows why. I liked it most of the time. It has not happened since that night.

"Me? What do I make of it? Nothing really. I worry over virtually nothing at all sometimes, and constantly lack direction, even though my wife and kids depend on me. They love me, I them. And I know now that I was stupid to get depressed last year. So, I still escape in books. I read. I've been that way since I was little, since I felt I wasn't anything at all like the outgoing folks my parents were, my grandparents were. I was imprinted by them that their way is the good way. They know I'm flawed and I know it too. So be it."

He stopped to make sure Matt Hastings was interested. Nick sipped his Coke and continued, "So at that party where I saw Bonaparte, Mayor Hayes, our mutual friend Edison, Jenkins and his teenage girlfriend, and all that detail . . . man . . . I just don't know how . . . it could have been something I pieced together from history reading." Nick just shook his head, and dropped his gaze into his beer mug of Coke, as if he didn't believe what he said.

"Nick," said Hastings, cautiously, "I don't know anything about psychology. I'm a scientist. I deal with facts and formulas. But I do know highly qualified people you can see, if you ever want to talk this over."

"You mean a shrink?" Nick's face scrunched with disappointment and disbelief that Hastings would make such a suggestion.

"Nick, don't get me wrong. As I said, I do not know anything about how the mind works, just how to use it in my field and in teaching. That's why I came here today; I do know teaching. And you are good. Everyone says. I say if there is anything I can do to help you teach again, I'd do it because I believe in you after all this. I believe you are a great teacher whose talent is hidden away. If that means seeing a psychiatrist just to talk over what your visions, excuse me, visits, mean, I'd set that up completely in confidence. Gladys wouldn't ever have to know. You know how much she adores you. No one would know."

"Look, Matt, I appreciate those are very kind words from a very kind person. But teaching is about more than learning—it's about learning about life, learning from a teacher who sets a good example. I don't think I am a good example for young kids and probably never will be. You've seen how nuts I can act. I've come to grips with that fate.

"Besides, I don't need a shrink. Do you know what that experience would do to further erode my confidence? I'm actually feeling pretty good these days. That could set me way back, my friend. It'll be like 'Tell me more … How was your relationship with your father, Nick… What kind of dreams ….' Well, you know."

"You're not drinking now?" Hastings asked.

"Right."

Hastings saw an opening. He took a risk, "Maybe that's why you are feeling better about yourself. But what happens if you start drinking again? You might. Lord knows you are around it all the time. No Nick, you're not flawed. That's ridiculous and you know that."

He was losing Nick, who was now checking out people who entered the tavern.

Hastings took a wild shot, to use Nick's visit, "It sounds like that's what old Miss Ellen Krantz saw in you, an opportunity for the ghosts, because you are so knowledgeable and so diligent about understanding historic records accurately. Consider that she was there to get you to acknowledge those qualities. Consider that she is also a smart woman, or was one, who realized she could help you help yourself. You said she knew about you being a history buff?"

"Well ... I guess. Keep your voice down; we are talking about ghosts." Nick tried to divert his friend.

They shared a brief laugh.

Hastings said, "No guessing. Tell me. Is that connection perfectly clear to you? Admit it."

Nick blurted through his laughter, "Of course it's not clear."

Hastings enjoyed laughing at his own sort of twisted pretzel logic and his psychological inadequacy. He plowed ahead, "Consider if that old Krantz woman in your mind's eye, at least, saw something in you when you entered the Belvedere in November. Now I see it in you. Everybody does. Open your eyes, Nick."

Nick had enough and chose to come clean, "Okay Matt, I think those people existed. They were all real long ago. Yes. Ellen Krantz was the daughter of a beautiful girl named Marie who was cast out by her stern father Hans Krantz and then abused by a man named Jenkins, a traveling charmer who wooed and abused the child. She got killed. They saved baby Ellen. Ellen's spirit 100 years later had had it with the secrecy over her mother's murder. Found me. Wanted my help, Matt. In her own way, she asked me to bring the tragedy of her mother's ice-cold murder case to light.

"I also believe now that Ellen, old Ellen Krantz, has been trapped in that hotel for one hundred years. Don't shake your head. Yes, I believe it. So, I'm nuts, but I saw it all and then I read about it in records a century later with you. It is all true and, believe me when I say emphatically, I'm not tellin' noooo...body, ever! For one, I think it would hurt my Pop." Nick continued to laugh at himself.

Undeterred, Matt cut to the chase, "If I may say, as a professional, I think you need to change direction, get into a new challenge. If so, we can talk. I'm here for you." He got up quickly, patted and squeezed Nick's shoulder, and left before Nick could utter another word.

Chapter 48: Professor Esposito

On April 2, 2000, the long and colorful life of Stephen "Pop" Esposito ended peacefully.

It was also opening day for Pop's beloved Baltimore Orioles at Oriole Park at Camden Yards, which was only three blocks from the painfully slow renovations still under way at Pop's II tavern on Pratt Street. He would never see the restaurant side of the bar open.

On that last day of his life Pop spent the afternoon in the recreation room at Quiet Oaks retirement home with his card-playing buddies. They each pitched their cards with one eye on the Oriole game on a big screen nearby. The five old men watched the Orioles lose to the Cleveland Indians 4 to 1.

Pop ate sparingly at dinner that evening. He complained of indigestion, and retired early.

Pop died in his sleep. His jovial, generous heart simply stopped ticking.

After decades watching and worrying over his favorite grandson's abnormal behavior, he did live long enough to finally witness a sea change in his Nicky boy.

Yes, Pop was still cognizant that his favorite person on Earth, besides his Minnie, no longer desired to drink, not since Nick's New Year's scare. Pop knew when he died that Nick was in fine spirits every day, happy to be alive, and sharp as a tack, like all the Esposito men before him.

However, Pop didn't live long enough to know what Nick did with his new attitude; that during the next two years he would work hard to earn a Ph.D. in American history studies at Johns Hopkins University, encouraged every day by his new friend and mentor Dr. Matthew Hastings.

* * *

"Encroaching Nationalism in American Sports" was Nick's dissertation. He chose the topic as a tribute to his Pop.

The dedication read: *My heartfelt gratitude to my inspiration in life, Stephen Michael Esposito, ex–juvenile delinquent, early twentieth-century Baltimore sports legend, youthful business entrepreneur, and son of legendary Chief Police Inspector Michael J. Esposito, who still lives in my dreams.*

Six months after publishing his PhD dissertation Nick dedicated his first novel to his mother Miriam and "With appreciation of Charles Joseph Bonaparte, in life, death and beyond." To the dismay of his Johns Hopkins University Press editors, Nick's agent, his friend Hastings, insisted that they keep Nick's title:

Ghosts of the Belvedere Hotel
Baby Ellen Krantz's Cold Murder Case Revealed

Epilogue

Friday, September 27, 2002, Gilman Hall, Johns Hopkins University

He was at it again.

Dr. Nick Esposito wanted to dress as a baseball umpire for this special day. He could only find an umpire's cap, but he substituted his old tuxedo and a black shirt and tie for a more complete umpire look.

"Listen up class. You might hear this more than once this semester: My grandfather Stephen "Pop" Esposito, a juvenile delinquent at the time just like you folks, taught Babe Ruth how to throw a curveball."

The two dozen college students broke out in raucous laughter.

"As you will see, class, an important lesson today, as we begin your history course, is the following 'So goes the nation, so goes baseball'," said Professor Esposito with a devilish smile.

Some students laughed again, not as much.

"It's Friday. So, as I said yesterday, we are going to adjourn to the ballpark to learn our history."

He was all set to introduce his first, typically Nick, wacky field trip as a college professor.

"That's right, you doubters. First, you are all invited to my place, Pop's II—actually, it was my grandfather's place before he passed two years ago. Pop's II Camden Tavern is on Pratt Street. We'll meet there for a bite before the game with the hated, first-place New York Yankees."

Two male students in the back led a loud cheer.

One yelled, "You buyin', professor?"

"No. And, by the way, no beer drinking on this trip. I will pick up your tab for sandwiches if you agree. It's an official class lesson," said the new Hopkins professor, just three weeks into his first semester and already risking his success on a lark. He had rehearsed at home with an audience of one, J.J. And, for once, got permission from his employer, through Dr. Hastings, for the field trip.

He continued, "My best friend and minority owner of Pop's II, Dr. Nathaniel Brown over there in the corner, is my new night manager. He's a professor himself, at Morgan, right, Nate? Stand up and wave to my baseball-is-history fans."

Nate, laughing continuously with his best pal, stood and waved. He was in uniform, an off-white collared shirt with a large 'B' sewn over the heart, wide black belt, and baseball pants with stirrup black socks to the knees and a black hat.

Nick said, "You see Nate? He is wearing the uniform of the 1897 baseball champion Baltimore Orioles. Nate wears it to church."

More laughter.

Nate sat down quickly, saying "I'm just glad it's not an original WOOL uni."

"If you have any questions on the revitalized Camden Yards, it's Professor Brown you want, professor of urban development. And, he is tough. He will be watching you people, so don't get all silly before the game like he does."

Nate Bowen didn't lose his beaming smile, happy for making Pop's II his first financial investment in city property and happy for the teaching rebirth of his best friend Nick. A year earlier when Nick told Nate he could not afford to buy out his sister's and Uncle Al's inherited shares of the new tavern, Nate bought in as minority owner. After all, Nick and Nate were both great baseball fans and this was essentially a neighborhood upgrade as well as a baseball tavern.

Nick chose to bring his students to Gilman Hall to start his inaugural class trip, just this once, for a pre-game pep-talk lecture because of the historic significance of the famous Hopkins centerpiece. It was not his normal classroom. Gilman Hall was symbolic to Nick. It was the first major academic building on the Johns Hopkins Homewood campus, in 1915, and named for Daniel Coit Gilman. It was fitting, he thought, to launch his class's first field trip there. "The kids will remember it better from Gilman," he told J.J.

Professor Nick, the new Nick at the ad hoc classroom at Hopkins, was up to his old tricks, surprising his students with one of his extra-dramatic field trips. But this time was different. There was no grade school superintendent scowling and disapproving. There were no worrying parents. These students were adults. And, this time, Hopkins' senior vice president Hastings, no less, was the "super." He was also in the room. He planned to attend the game as well.

Not only was Dr. Hastings very supportive of Nick's unusual Johns Hopkins University field trip for a history class, he was holding the baseball tickets, sitting by the exit in an Oriole cap. Hastings was waiting to hand them out to the students.

Now it was Hastings who needed Nick. He needed to make sure his new, eccentric teaching project stayed the course, and kept demonstrating to the university Nick's superior knowledge and elegant skills. He was Nick's watchdog. Already, Nick's college students in just a few classes, knew his wit and, just like his high schoolers, were hard pressed to know if Prof. Esposito was joking or not at times. Matt Hastings knew though.

Nick told his class, "Now remember, on Monday there will be a quiz. It won't be a piece of cake. There are history lessons to be learned on this trip, class. Oh, you chuckle, eh? Well there will be, and they are tough brain busters too." His lips betrayed him with the hint of a smile.

Nick put his hands on his hips. "Okay, here is a preview of the quiz: You will be asked what happens to pro sports in America when the economy is down, like it is now, or when the country's mood is depressed or angry, like it has been since 9/11."

A tomboyish female student at the front of the classroom blurted out the answer, "You can tell the economy is down because sports will spawn more scandals and there is more-blatant cheating by the teams."

Nick put his index finger to his lips, but it was too late.

She continued with an endearing bit of laughing at her prof, "And when the country has trouble, the government uses sports to boost nationalism whenever it can."

Nick nodded and responded, "Well, guess that's off the quiz now!" But he seized the moment. He asked the class to report to him on Monday of any signs of nationalism at the Oriole-Yankee game that their parents of the 1980's or so might not have witnessed.

"Keep in mind that for Americans, people who have always valued individualism and democratic society, embracing baseball as their favorite sport is natural. I want you to tell me Monday how you think sports are manipulated to measure patriotism. And you will analyze whether it has gone too far, and threatening the integrity of the game, never mind the state of the country. The country is safe from sports; it can take care of itself. We're resilient. I should know, not being the most gifted player in my schoolyards, mind you."

Some of the students snickered.

The wiry, egghead professor standing before them in the goofy umpire attire was most likely a real klutz at sports.

Just for fun, Professor Nick changed direction and hit them with his lesson for the day: "Any tough economic time in our history has within it a parallel story in the history of baseball. Let me take you back to where the Orioles of old played. That was in Union Park at 25th and Barclay Streets. That's where Baltimore's old professional team, the original Orioles, played in four consecutive Temple Cup Series, the early version of today's World Series, beginning in 1893.

"By the way, that is the same year our Hopkins patriarch, Daniel Gilman, fulfilled the dream of his friend, the then-deceased Johns Hopkins, to open a first-class medical school here. But I drift.

The Baltimore Orioles were the best team of the 1890s. The times were tough for baseball as well as for the country. The economic panic of 1893 led to the most serious Depression up to that time in our country, as far as we know, with unemployment reaching fifteen percent by 1897.

"Railroads had been overbuilt and speculation led to shaky financing, then bank failures. Entering the 1890s, Baltimore City was a high-speed growth engine with a great shipping and trading port at Locust Point and a strong infrastructure for the B&O Railroad, which incidentally was once rescued financially by your own Johns Hopkins himself.

"Baltimore was a prominent trading route to Midwestern cities by rail and to Europe by ship.

"Meanwhile what was happening in baseball? At the depths of the 1890's Depression, baseball was also nothing short of a nasty, dark industry. Greedy owners colluded to hold down players' salaries, usually to only one or two hundred dollars a game."

Some students snickered, and then looked side to side to see that others did not.

Nick continued, "That's right. There were no million-dollar players then. You were lucky to be paid at all for just playing a boy's game, ah, a child's game. Sorry ladies.

"Self-serving players mixed with gamblers and deliberately threw games for payoff. Betting on games was universal. Pete Rose would have loved playing then. Please don't ask me who Pete Rose is. Too complicated; another day perhaps.

"And, the business interests were brutal. Owners would wrench teams from their cities and start over in another city for no rhyme or reason other than some shady, under-the-table deal, kept secret from their vulnerable players, who had no choice but to go with the team.

"The Baltimore Orioles were not only the best team, but the roughest group of thugs in the game. It was an era of dirty baseball, and the Orioles were the dirtiest by far.

"In the 1895 Temple Cup Series, they were playing the Cleveland Spiders, who finished second to the Orioles—there was only one league, and the top two teams in the standings played for the Cup.

"The Spiders' star pitcher was Cy Young. Yes, that Cy Young, who won 511 games and whose name is now on the annual trophy for the major leagues' best pitchers.

"The Spiders and Young had already won the first three games of the series in Cleveland. They booked into a Baltimore hotel for the fourth game. As they left their hotel in Baltimore to go to Union Park in a horse-drawn omnibus, hundreds of Oriole fans greeted them with a shower of rotten eggs and vegetables.

"Do you think that many people would have been out in the street unemployed and angry that morning throwing eggs if economic times were good?" Nick raised his arms and waved his hands inward.

"Nooooo," rang out a chorus of laughing students.

"Of course, . . . not."

More laughter.

"But that was nothing compared with the behavior of the players. Here is a lineup page for the Orioles right out of the Temple Cup Series program for that game, sponsored by Von der Horst's Purest Extra Pale Standard beer. You'll find this framed at Pop's this afternoon, by the way."

He held up a tattered newspaper clipping.

"The Orioles were also the greatest hitting lineup in baseball. The entire team hit better than .300. For those non-baseball fans, that batting average would immortalize any player today into the Baseball Hall of Fame. But did they rest just on their hitting talents?" Again, he signaled with his hands for response.

"Nooooo," rang out the students, even louder.

"Here are some of the 'plays,' so called, which were performed by our old Baltimore Orioles. Listen carefully. As part of your assignment, look for these plays at the game tonight against the Yanks and write them into your reports for Monday.

"First, Wee Willie Keeler had the great Cy Young in his pocket. That is, he always hit well against Young because Willie's teammates or the batboy would use a mirror to reflect the sun into Young's eyes at the very instant he released his pitch.

403

Wee Willie would walk on four pitches or be able to 'hit 'em where they ain't'—his trademark phrase.

"Keeler on first base would invariably try to steal second base after signaling the Orioles' next batter, who would club the Spiders' catcher on the back of his head with his bat on an 'accidental backswing.'" Nick made the quote/unquote sign with his hands.

"Then, the catcher missed the next ball from Young—I wonder why?—and Keeler would go to third base. Watch for that trick in the game tonight." Nick was smiling broadly at his friend Nate Bowen who was losing it in the back and had to slip into the hall to hide his big laugh.

"Then there was their pugnacious third baseman John McGraw, who had a face that one writer of the day said looked like a clenched fist. McGraw hit .369 that year. But did he always just rely on his natural talents, did he class?" He just held up one finger and pointed to the students.

"Nooooo."

"Let's say McGraw was called out on a third strike with two outs and Keeler still on third. McGraw would likely turn to the umpire with filthy obscenities and drive the metal spikes of his baseball shoes right through the umpire's shoes to bloody the ump's feet. Let me know if you see that tonight."

Uproarious laughter.

"That's right. McGraw said if he couldn't curse, he would quit the game. In fact, the Orioles' cursing toward the umpires was so vile it drove some of the umpires to quit umpiring. It was competition in a tough time—tough economy, too. McGraw was such a fierce competitor as the team's third baseman that he would trip runners passing by his base or grab their belt and hold them up from scoring. See if Cal Ripkin tries that tonight, will ya? Cal's a sneaky one. Look closely."

More laughter.

"We also have to keep an eye on cheating by the outfielders tonight. The old Orioles fielders would hide baseballs in the deep outfield grass. When the other team hit a ball that was too far to chase, they would retrieve a ball they had hidden closer in and have a better chance of throwing out the runner at second.

"Also, the catcher, Wilbert Robinson—no relation to Frank or Brooks—would hold his big mitt in the umpire's face so he wouldn't see the Oriole shortstop, spunky Hughie Jennings, tackle or spike a base runner.

"Now here's what I want you to do. If anyone sees any of those plays in the game tonight, please find a designated driver immediately."

The classroom filled with uproarious laughter again.

Dr. Esposito was on a roll, but not without touching on his goal to teach them a memorable American history lesson. "McGraw once started a fight with players at the Boston Beaneaters' ballpark in 1894, a year when the Boston and Baltimore teams were the best two teams. That's right, the Beaneaters. That team stunk."

More laughter.

"That is until 1894. Anyway, when the fight broke out both teams joined in the mayhem that followed. Fans joined in too, rushing the field and beating up ball players and each other. Those not on the field, fought in the stands. Someone started a fire in the stands. The ballpark burned down along with nearly two hundred buildings in the old Boston neighborhood. That, my friends, shows the passion in this country for baseball and baseball at its purest.

"More than any other sport, baseball shapes our national character. The baseball field is a green oasis in our great cities like Baltimore that transports Americans, urban Americans especially, back to our roots, to the farms and forests that spawned America's greatness.

"Baseball honors the individual but celebrates the team. America gets things done with strong individuals working as a team. So, does baseball.

"Out of all that passionate competitive verve, the old Orioles, dirty players that they were, still pulled together as a greatly talented team. That legacy is in innovations they created that still in the game today, especially because that team literally reinvented, reengineered the game into a science.

"Under manager Ned Hanlon, a former outfielder, the Orioles innovated the sacrifice bunt, the hit and run, the squeeze play, and the Baltimore chop, where the hitter deliberately hits a pitched ball straight down, not out, onto the rubber home plate, sending it sky high. It allowed the batter to beat out a hit to first base.

"That team won three straight pennants from 1894 to 1896 and played the game with great hustle and gusto.

"So, I ask you . . . in all sincerity . . ." He paused and pumped his palms upward. "Who wants baseball tickets for tonight's game at Oriole Park at Camden Yards?"

The class cheered and rose to their feet, many of the young men pumping their arms into the air, mimicking Prof. Esposito who started a chant, "Let's go O's, let's go O's ..."

"Dr. Hastings? I believe you will do the honors of handing out the tickets at the door?"

Hastings nodded and waved the tickets over his head.

Nick added, "Class, we meet at the Babe Ruth Museum promptly at 5:00 next to the tavern for a pre-arranged, quick tour of baseball history, then reassemble for dinner at Pop's II Tavern on Pratt Street, then the game. Right, Dr. Brown?"

Nate Bowen, in his back-row seat with a big smile, nodded and tipped his cap.

"Class, all fun aside, I do expect an essay from each of you on politics, nationalism, and sports on Monday," said Professor Nick Esposito.

* * *

Twenty minutes later, after some chatter with lingering students, Nick watched with pride as his rookie historians filed out of the classroom, one-by-one taking a baseball ticket from Dr. Hastings' outstretched hands.

Nick was a changed man. He could enjoy little celebrations as well as big ones, faces of the present as well as the past, just like Ellen Krantz wished for "Mr. Nick." In dreams, drifting off with a clear head, he often recalled her words of advice. Her part of their deal, he believed, was to help Nick be his own man and stop his doubting and fussing.

When the students left the ad hoc classroom, he spotted J.J. beyond the door waiting for him, waving and laughing. Her reaction to his lecture would be the litmus test. If his lecture clicked with J.J., his bizarre history lesson that day had worked.

It evidently did. She said, "Wonderful, professor." And he was pleased.

J.J. didn't say she was also laughing at him because of his rumpled tuxedo. He didn't wear it out of the house that morning but carried it in a gym bag. Although sober, he was still absent minded and oblivious to his appearance. J.J. hadn't seen him in his old tux since the notorious night at the Belvedere.

She let it go; didn't mention the tux and just smiled with, "Come on, Nick, I got the twins out of school early today. Are your classes done for the day? We have stuff for a nice family lunch at home."

Nick hugged her and said, "I promised Matt lunch. He gave out the tickets. The thing is that he told me the university paid for them, but he lied. Matt bought them out of his own pocket."

Hastings heard. "That's okay, Nick—you go ahead. We can catch up tonight at the game. You can buy me a hot dog, alright?"

"Thanks Matt. See you tonight."

They reached the garage. Nick said, "I'll drive. I just feel great, J.J."

Their new car was a 2003 BMW M5, a gift from Nick to J.J. He bought it with money from the sale of Pop's Elwood Avenue tavern. He has also sold the old rust-bucket Toyota Tercel, the glorious chariot to the ball, to a student for $100 who renovated old cars.

When they bought J.J.'s new car, Nick insisted on jet black, like the Tercel, in honor of their one-way trip to the

Belvedere Hotel on the millennium eve, which ended with their ambulance ride.

"You'd better take that jacket off first, Nick. Don't want to wrinkle up that tuxedo, dear," she said with loving sarcasm. "After all, you'll need it in, say, another two years or so." J.J. stood still admiring him and laughed again at his look.

Nick instinctively reached into the jacket pocket for the car keys. He then remembered that J.J. had the keys. His hand instead felt paper in the pocket where he had expected keys. As he walked around the car to the driver's door, he peeked at the paper quickly and then just as fast shoved it into his pants pocket. The paper was a yellowing, folded invitation:

One Admission
Baltimore City's Exclusive Pre-Opening Reception
Belvedere Hotel
December 31, 1899

"My God," Nick mumbled to himself. "There's the autograph."

Lightly scribbled but legible on one corner was:

To my new friend Mr. Esposito, Mayor Thomas G. Hayes.

"Do you have the car keys, J.J.?" he asked softly, with a quivering voice.

She didn't answer immediately. She might have caught a glimpse of a piece of paper Nick stuffed into his pants pocket and hid from her. "Yea, here are the keys." She tossed them to him. "What was that you are looking at, Nick?"

"Oh, it's nothing. Just some scribbling to remind me of something I have to do." Regrettably, he saw that old look of dread on her face, like he'd been lying, or drinking, or worse, 'visiting.' But he remained silent.

* * *

The following Monday evening, Nick left Nate in charge of Pop's II and drove east on Pratt Street from the tavern, up Charles Street to the timeless Belvedere Hotel on the hill.

Inside, he re-discovered the refurbished lobby he and his guests saw on December 31. "Hmm, a new era begins," he mumbled, but this time there was no one to hear him, no ghostly old woman popping up from behind him. The delirium he experienced in 1999 when he first viewed a hotel lobby morphing gaudy, rundown, back to stylish, back to rundown and back, had left him. It was a beautiful lobby in truth and to his new eyes—the tiered framed ceiling mirror was polished, a cast-iron table with marble top was adorned with a spectacular burst of red roses and, of course, there was no hotel desk or long-dead movies stars checking in.

He found the shadowy Owl Bar. People chattered, watched TV as the ceiling fans, back again, whirred quietly.

The cloakroom boy said he had never heard or seen an old lady named Ellen Krantz. Nick was not surprised.

He peaked into the main dining room and smiled at a cute young lady helping other employees, he assumed, to set elegant tables for an immense banquet, perhaps with two hundred settings. She resembled one of the flirty Bavarian dressed girls working for Miss Krantz at her ghostly version of the Owl Bar in November of 1999. No flirting this time. The girl and the others were putting the final touches to the lovely, tall room of varying shades of white.

Then, feeling full of emotional relief, he tried the main ballroom. He rode a new elevator to the 12th floor and found a magnificent scene. A young couple was shifting into a position face to face in front of a large round-top window being directed by a priest in traditional black. Relatives, undoubtedly, all stood by for instructions. They had chosen the ball room for their wedding and this was the rehearsal. It resembled the ballroom, which Nick believed was hosted by Mayor Hayes, more than a century ago. This ballroom was a much gayer, cheerful setting with gilded 3-foot arched ceiling, two sparkling crystal chandeliers and much to Nick's surprise, he knew the style of the chairs set out—Chievari mahogany—in lieu of pews.

Nick felt very proud. He had overcome his ordeal and was clear thinking and sober for his reminiscing.

The elevator then took him to the fourteenth floor to the Rumba Room, still there, still a nightclub, but too early to be crowded.

Nick ordered a beer and sat on the dark side of the bar on a stool, the same stool where he had talked with former vice principal Walter Bunker and where he had sipped absinthe under Penny's watchful eye.

He just played with the beer glass until the small Latino man tending bar walked off, leaving Nick alone.

He made sure no one was looking.

Nick slipped into the kitchen. He walked to the back wall and pulled back the curtain behind the same stainless-steel shelves, which he distinctly remembered being there after midnight on New Year's Eve.

The large dumbwaiter, which he once mistook for a tiny elevator, was indeed still there. But it was locked tight with a heavy padlock.

He looked down at an open seam between the floor and the dumbwaiter door, a half-inch gap of blackness. Nick bent down slowly. Again, he made sure no one was looking his way. He felt icy cold air from the elevator shaft blowing onto his face. He shivered.

"Thank you, Miss Krantz," he whispered. "You knew I could find my way. Sorry I gave you a hard time."

He paused and reached into his pocket. "Here. This is not supposed to be with me in my time. It belongs to history."

He slipped Mayor Hayes's autographed invitation through the slot to the shaft below, where it disappeared into the shadows of New Years past.

Boo!

Author's note

The Belvedere Hotel was a real place in Baltimore, Maryland. It was constructed in 1902-3. Today, the Belvedere is a building consisting of delightful apartments and condominiums and remains to this writing a stylish extravagance of décor of a bygone era, a favorite party and wedding venue.

"Night at the Belvedere" is a work of fiction. The novel's hotel is fictional as are the characters, some of whom may resemble actual people in some ways. Descriptions of the fictional Belvedere Hotel and its contents, dates, history and description are entirely created from the vivid imagination of the protagonist Nick Esposito and not from the real place, which served as a model for this story.

To my knowledge, an Owl Bar is still there, both at the real Belvedere and the one in Nick's mind.

Special appreciation for editing and critiquing by
Cathy Irwin
Steve Monroe
Carolyn Haley
Pamela Armstrong
Maryland Writers' Association

Selected Reviews

"Nutty Professor or Ghost Whisperer: Set in Baltimore, Maryland, during the Y2K bug scare, Nick Esposito is having a difficult time convincing his wife and friends to party like it's 1999. Before we can get to New Year's Eve, Nick's failure's as a child and then as an adult are thoroughly examined. Try as he might he doesn't have the Esposito social butterfly gene." *SHReviews*

"An epic tale revolving around a man who has not fully achieved validity in his own mind. He appears to go into 'trance-like states' with flashbacks, hearing and seeing things others don't see. He perceives characters in his family tree as 'larger than life' and his own individuality was not fleshed out partly because of the power of their personalities, their stories, their social standing and style. The family thinks magically and mythically." *Dr. Pamela Armstrong, Maryland psychologist*

"Nicky Esposito is the brooding, day-dreaming, sharp protagonist whose penchant for history takes him on some strange, paranormal journeys back in time. He can vividly view historic events, such as the tragic 1904 fire that destroyed much of downtown Baltimore, a slave auction, and the transmission of the first telegraph signals to Baltimore's B&O Railroad Station." *Kevin James Shay, author of "Death of a Rising Sun: A Search for Truth in the John F. Kennedy Assassination"*

"An enjoyable read. A highly entertaining, imaginative novel with memorable characters and packed with interesting Baltimore history." *H.S. Parker, author of the bio-thriller "Containment."*